A STORY
LIKE OURS

ALSO BY ROBIN HUBER

A Love Like Yours

A STORY LIKE OURS

ROBIN HUBER

FOREVER
YOURS

New York Boston

Forever Yours
Hachette Book Group
1290 Avenue of the Americas, New York, NY 10104
read-forever.com
twitter.com/readforeverpub

First published as an ebook and as a print on demand: June 2019

Forever Yours is an imprint of Grand Central Publishing. The Forever Yours name and logo are trademarks of Hachette Book Group, Inc.

The publisher is not responsible for websites (or their content) that are not owned by the publisher.

The Hachette Speakers Bureau provides a wide range of authors for speaking events. To find out more, go to www.hachettespeakersbureau.com or call (866) 376-6591.

ISBNs: 978-1-5387-3288-5 (ebook), 978-1-5387-3287-8 (print on demand)

For my mom, Kathie.

She could not make sense of the things that were meant for her, but she was drawn to it all, and when she was alone, she felt like the moon: terrified of the sky, but completely in love with the way it held the stars.

—R. M. Drake

CHAPTER 1

LUCY

Joe!" I shout from Sam's dressing room, praying that he isn't far.

"Lucy? What's the matter?" Joe asks, rushing into the room, but before I can answer, he sees me on the floor with Sam and runs over to us. "Sam," he calls, patting Sam's cheek, but he doesn't respond.

"What's going on?" Miles asks from the doorway.

"We need a doctor!" I say to him, keeping my eyes on Sam.

Seconds later, I hear Miles yelling down the hall outside the room.

"What's wrong with him?" I ask Joe, feeling the edges of panic seep across my skin.

"I don't know," he says calmly, but I can hear the underlying panic in his voice too. "Maybe a concussion. He took a lot of hits from Ackerman tonight."

"Okay, everybody, back up," the doctor says, following Miles into the room.

The doctor kneels down beside us, but I can't move.

"Come on, Lucy, let him work," Joe says, pulling me back by my elbow, but I stay on the floor and watch the doctor inspect Sam's eyes and ears, feeling each one of my heartbeats thump inside my tight chest as he examines Sam.

"Lucy," Miles says, but I ignore him.

"Lucy."

I look up and see Sebastian leaning over me. He reaches for my hand and I let him pull me up into a hug.

"He's going to be okay. Just let the doctor work on him."

"What if he's not, Bas? What if..." I bury my face and cry quietly inside his arms.

"Shhh..."

"I just got him back, Bas."

"I know."

"Sam, can you hear me?" the doctor asks him, and I quickly kneel down beside Sam again.

Sam opens and closes his eyes a few times, and I feel my breath catch. Finally, he nods and rasps, "Yeah." He tries to sit up, but the doctor holds his shoulders down.

"Don't move, Sam, we need to get you onto a stretcher."

I hold my hand to my mouth and try to push down the fear that's gripping me.

"Lucy," Sam mumbles, and I reach for his hand.

"I'm right here," I say, hovering over his battered face.

"Don't leave," he says quietly.

I shake my head softly and blink back tears. "I'm not going to leave you." I give Sebastian a knowing look and he gives me a subtle nod. We're going to be in Quebec longer than we planned. I look at Sam and say again, "I'm not going anywhere."

* * *

"How you feeling, champ?" Miles asks from across Sam's hospital room.

"Fine. Just ready to get hell out of this place."

"Sam, you need to rest," I urge, squeezing his hand. "You have a serious concussion and two broken ribs."

"She's right," his doctor says, entering the room.

Joe follows him in, and Sebastian lingers by the door.

"You need to rest, Sam," the doctor says to him. "You have a grade three concussion. Your brain needs time to heal. And so do your ribs."

"What's he need to do, doc?" Joe asks.

"Take a break. Rest. That's the only way to get better."

Joe nods firmly. "You got it."

"How long does he need?" Miles asks.

"At least three weeks."

"Three weeks?" Sam chides. "In this place?"

"No." The doctor smiles. "But somewhere you can relax and lie low for a while. Somewhere that *doesn't* have a gym."

"So, nothing then?" Miles says. "No conditioning? No running?"

"Well, maybe a slow jog in about a week, but other than that, no. No conditioning. Definitely no boxing."

Miles smirks at Sam. "Tristan's sure gonna have his work cut out for him when you get better."

"Tristan has enough on his plate right now," Joe says. "He could use the break too."

"Where is Tristan?" I ask, wondering why he didn't come to Quebec.

"He's back home in Atlanta," Sam answers. "He had to have the battery replaced in his pacemaker."

"Oh." I try to hide the alarm in my voice. He had heart surgery when we were kids, but I assumed he was better now. "Is he okay?"

"It's a minor procedure," Joe says casually, but I see the worry in his eyes.

Sam squeezes my hand and assures me, "He's okay."

"So the question is, where are you going on vacation?" Miles asks, lightening the conversation.

"Vacation?" Sam looks at him and laughs softly. "I just want to go home."

"Sam, there's literally a gym inside your apartment," Joe says. "No way you'll stay out of it for three weeks." He crosses his arms and shrugs. "I think a vacation might be good for you."

"It's not be a bad idea," the doctor says. "As long as it's somewhere you can relax."

"I've got the perfect place," Miles says, scrolling on his phone.

Sam looks up at him. "Yeah, where?"

Miles turns the screen around and shows him a picturesque scene with blue water and palm trees. "Exuma."

"What's Exuma?" I ask curiously.

Miles looks at me with wide eyes. "What's Exuma? Only home to some of the bluest water in the entire world, white sand beaches, and sunshine," he says exuberantly.

"It's in the Bahamas," Sam says to me.

"Oh." I frown softly at the thought of him being gone for three weeks.

Sam looks at me with smiling eyes and dimples that he can't

hide. "What do you say? Want to disappear with me for a while?"

"What?" I laugh and shake my head. "Sam, I can't go on vacation with you. Not right now anyway. And especially not to the Bahamas. There'd be people everywhere." I think we've caused enough media frenzy for the time being.

"Not on a private island," Miles says, dropping his phone into his pocket.

"Private island?" The foreign thought clouds my head.

Sam smiles and pulls me down onto the bed next to him. "You're telling me you wouldn't want to spend three weeks on a tropical island...alone?"

I smile over the inviting thought. "Of course I would. But I can't." I shrug and say quietly to him, "I have to go home. I have to get the rest of my things from Drew's house. And I still have figure out what's going to happen with my studio."

"No you don't," Sebastian chimes in, inching his way into the room. "I can handle it for you while you're gone."

"See, that's why you have Sebastian," Sam says, rubbing his thumb over the back of my hand. "He can handle it for you."

"I don't have any clothes. And neither do you. We'd have to go home anyway."

"I can help with that too," Sebastian offers, giving me an enthusiastic grin.

"Go," Joe encourages, giving me an approving smile. "It'd be good for both of you."

I drop my head to my hands and laugh softly. "A private island?" I peek up at Sam between my hands.

"Come on, Lamb. Come away with me." He reaches for my face and says softly, "Let's go to paradise and leave everything else behind for a while. Catch up on the last ten years." He gives me a grin, and irresistible dimples.

I bite my lip and laugh again. "Three weeks?"

"Just you and me."

I smile wide and for the first time in my life, throw caution to the wind. "Okay...let's go."

CHAPTER 2

LUCY

I squeeze Sam's hand and close my eyes as our small seaplane skips and skids across the surface of the turquoise ocean, spraying the windows with saltwater. I feel Sam's warm breath against my cheek as his smooth, deep voice settles softly on my ears. "Open your eyes, Lamb."

I cautiously peek up at him with one eye, keeping the other closed. "When you said private island, I assumed it had a runway."

He chuckles quietly under his breath. "It's not that big."

"There's only one island in Exuma with a landing strip," our pilot says in a thick Bahamian accent, "and that island doesn't look like this."

Intrigued, I open both eyes and take in the view through the small window, unsure what is more breathtaking—the white sand beach and lush green that surrounds it or the contemporary mansion just beyond its shallow dunes.

"Wow," I say softly.

As we flew south over the Exuma Cays, the islands looked

like tiny emeralds scattered across a canvas of blue, strung together by shifting sandbars and crystal clear water. It was one of the most beautiful things I've ever seen, but I couldn't have imagined *this*.

I look at Sam. "This is incredible."

He smiles and it crinkles his bruised eye. "It's been a rough few weeks. I think we deserve it."

I smile softly, recalling the tense weeks leading up to my impromptu trip to Quebec. And the following three days I spent in the hospital with Sam, while they monitored his concussion. I'm grateful that his injuries weren't worse, but I haven't been able to shake the unsettling feeling that it won't be the last time he gets hurt. I reach for his cheek and say, "I think maybe we both need a break."

The pilot gets out to unload our bags from the back of the plane, but Sam keeps his eyes on me. "It wasn't all bad, was it?"

"No." I smile and pull his face to mine. "In fact, I'd say there were some pretty incredible moments."

"Yeah?" He gives me a sexy grin. "Like what?"

"Well, there was the match in New York, when I saw you standing in the ring for the first time. I was so proud of you that night," I say softly, and he drops his forehead to mine. "And when you walked into my studio and turned my whole world upside down. I'll never forget that day."

"Neither will I," he says, making me smile again.

"And when you kissed me and you reminded me of everything we were and everything we could be again."

He reaches for my face and says quietly, "When we made love." His eyes burn into me with desire and anticipation.

"Yes," I whisper, because it's all I can manage through the

fire he ignites that burns slowly across my skin. I press my eager lips to his and kiss him firmly.

The pilot clears his throat and I glance up at him from our kiss. He's standing on the dock smiling at us, waiting for us to exit the plane.

I give him an apologetic smile and reach for his extended hand, and he pulls me out of the plane into the thick island air that wraps around me. After nearly freezing to death in Quebec, this might take some time to get used to, but three weeks should be enough time to acclimate.

Three weeks in paradise with Sam.

The thought puts a smile on my face that I'm pretty sure will stay put until we're back in Atlanta. I try not to think about the clouded reality that awaits our return. Especially when I'm standing in front of the most magnificent house I've ever seen, on the most incredible beach, under a piercing blue sky that's filled with sunshine. The only thing I want to worry about right now is Sam.

As much as I'd like to use this impromptu vacation to make up for lost time, Sam's going to have to take it easy and get as much rest as possible. I take a contented breath of the warm island air and think, *That sounds perfect.*

Our pilot escorts us up the travertine steps to the white stucco house and I see an infinity pool that overlooks the ocean. It's surrounded by large canopy beds and oversized planters that are spilling over with tropical plants. He sets our bags down and tips his straw fedora. "Mr. Cole, Miss Bennett. I hope you enjoy paradise. I'll see you in three weeks."

"Thank you," I say, gazing into the house through the giant

glass doors. I see Sam tip him and shake his hand in the reflection, then he makes his way back down the steps.

"Ready?" Sam asks, pulling a key from his pocket.

I nod eagerly and watch him open the front door.

"After you," he says, pushing it open, and I'm greeted by a rush of cool air that escapes the house.

Air conditioning. *Thank goodness*.

I walk inside before him and take in the beautiful coastal space. "Wow," I whisper, walking through the foyer and into the living room, which, much like the living room in Sam's apartment, is surrounded by glass. Except that this view is a little different. Instead of the tall mirrored buildings that surround Sam's widows, all I see is blue, in every direction. I spin around in Sam's arms, which are suddenly wrapped around me. "Sam, this is beautiful. I couldn't have dreamt up a place like this."

He gazes into my eyes and says, "This is just the beginning, Lamb."

I smile over the nagging thought of how much it costs to rent a home like this for three weeks, on a private island no less. Or how much everything in Sam's life must cost.

It's a strange concept, Sam having so much money, one I haven't quite wrapped my head around yet.

"You know, you don't have to take me to places like this to make me happy, Sam."

His eyes narrow slightly.

"Don't get me wrong, I may never want to leave." I rest my chin on his chest. "I just mean, I'm yours, free of charge."

"I want to take you to places like this. It makes *me* happy." He rubs my bare arms and says thoughtfully, "I want to take you everywhere. I want to show you everything I've seen. And everything I haven't. I want to see the whole world with you, Lamb."

My heart stands at attention with a suitcase in each hand. "I hear it's pretty big. It might take a while."

"Hopefully the rest of our lives."

I press my smiling lips together and nod. "I like the sound of that."

He glances over my shoulder with a glint of excitement in his eyes. "For now, I'd like to show you the kitchen."

"The kitchen?"

He lowers his hands to my waist and picks me up, and my sandals fall to the floor.

"Sam, put me down!" I scold as he carries me to the kitchen. "You're not supposed to be lifting anything heavy!"

"You're not heavy."

He deposits me on the white marble island in the middle of the open kitchen and tugs my hips forward so that I'm sitting on the edge of it with my legs slung over his hips. He rocks up against me and pushes my long skirt up my thighs.

"Sam, this isn't resting. You're supposed to be taking it easy."

He reaches for my face and pulls it to his. "I can't think of a better way to relax." He presses his lips to mine and kisses me slowly, stroking my tongue with his until I've completely melted in his arms. I'm at his mercy. He moves, I move. He pushes, I pull. The call to nurse him back to health is suddenly silenced by the overwhelming need to extinguish the fire that's consuming us. He tugs his shirt off, wincing when he raises his arms above his head, and the caretaker in me returns.

"Sam, stop, we shouldn't—"

He silences me once more with another passionate kiss and tugs my crop top down, exposing my bare breasts.

"Oh, my goodness, I'm so sorry," a delicate British accent says, and I shriek.

Sam curses under his breath and I scramble inside his arms to pull my top back up.

"I'll just be in the foyer," she says, spinning around quickly.

"Who was that?" I ask with wide eyes as I adjust my top and try to compose myself.

Sam pulls his shirt back on and shakes his head. "I don't know." He takes my hand and leads me into the foyer, where we're greeted by a graceful smile.

"Hello." The woman stretches her small manicured hand out to shake Sam's. "I'm Jacinda. I work for Paradise Properties." She smooths a few stray hairs that have worked their way out of her tight top knot and straightens her crisp white skirt. "I take it no one mentioned that I'd be here to familiarize you with the home and ensure you have everything you need for your stay with us." She gives an apologetic smile and I see the blush in her olive-colored cheeks.

"No," Sam says to her.

"I'm so sorry, I didn't hear you come in."

"That's okay," Sam says, unfazed by the interruption.

"Not to worry, though. This won't take long." She winks and the blood burns in my heated cheeks. "Shall we begin?"

I swallow the awkward lump in my throat. "Sure."

Sam gives me a sly grin and follows her into the living room, where she begins to run through a list of instructions for the amenities. Then she takes us on a tour of each room.

By the time we make our way back to the kitchen, I feel like I probably should have been taking notes.

"Per your request, the kitchen has been fully stocked," she says dutifully. "But your chef will arrive at these times to restock and prepare any meals you'd like." She hands Sam a printed schedule. "Your cleaning services will take place during these times," she taps the paper with her shiny fingernail.

I shoot Sam a worried look. "They'll be here with us?"

"Not to worry, Lucy," she says gently. "Your privacy is our utmost concern. You can relax here, I assure you."

"So, you won't say anything, then…about earlier?"

She gives me a warm smile and says softly, "Of course not."

"Thank you."

"Now, if you need anything at all, my number's here. You're my top priority for the next three weeks, so please don't hesitate to call. My job is to make sure you leave here happy, well rested, and ready for your next big match." She winks at Sam.

He smiles and nods. "You spoke to Miles."

"Yes. He's gone to considerable lengths to ensure you're well taken care of here."

I smile at Sam and wrap my arm around his waist.

"You, as well, Lucy."

"Oh." I bob my head and smile graciously.

We follow her to the front door.

"Thanks for showing us around," Sam says to her. "I think we're going to settle in just fine," he adds, giving me a wink.

"My pleasure. Talk soon."

Sam closes the door behind her and flashes his unique eyes at me, and his dimples almost make me forget the embarrassment of being topless in front of our welcoming committee...almost.

I purse my lips over a smile. "I take it Miles forgot to tell you she'd be here to greet us?"

He pulls me into his arms. "Well, either that or I've taken one too many hits to the head."

"Sam, that's not funny. And since when does Miles care so much about my well-being?"

"Since your well-being is directly tied to my well-being. If you're not happy, neither am I."

I look up at him and exhale the worry I've been holding in for the last few days. "I'm really happy."

He drops his hands to my waist and lifts me up again.

"Sam, don't!"

He ignores me, wraps my legs around him, and hugs me tight. "I'm happy too," he says against my lips, before enveloping them in his.

"Let's go the bedroom," I mumble against his mouth.

"Lucy, there's no one here."

"You might have convinced me of that before Jacinda saw me topless. But I'm not likely to forget it anytime soon."

He puts me down. "Come on. Follow me." He takes my hand and leads me through the house, pushing the giant glass doors open and pulling me through them until we're standing outside next to the infinity pool that seems to disappear into the turquoise horizon. He stands behind me and puts his hands on my shoulders. "What do you see?"

I gaze out at the crystal blue ocean, searching for signs of life, but the only thing I see is the fading wake of a boat that must have been Jacinda's transport off the island.

I turn around in Sam's arms and say, "Okay, you've made your point. We're alone." I reach for his hand and spin around to go back inside, but he plants his feet and pulls me back to him, his lips landing on mine again.

He reaches for my skirt, gathering it around my waist, and groans against my neck. "I want you," he grumbles between his eager lips, which leave blazing trails on my heated skin. "It's been days. I can't wait any longer."

Sweat sheens my forehead and beads down the back of my neck, dampening the strands of hair sticking to it. It's so hot, I might melt before he has his way with me. "It's so hot out here."

"Mm-hmm," he murmurs, his sticky wet lips finding their way back to mine, and the way that his dewy skin rubs against me makes me forget that I care. I want to melt, if it means melting with him.

I reach behind him and run my hands under his shirt and over the thick muscles in his back until I've carefully removed his shirt over his head and pulled it down his tattooed arms. It falls to the travertine tiles at our feet. I run my hands over his round shoulders and across his broad chest, reflecting on the words tattooed beneath his collarbone: *Pain Is Fleeting.*

I smile softly and look up at him. "It really is, isn't it?"

His hungry eyes soften and he shows me his dimples, which are accentuated by the flush of the Caribbean heat in his rosy cheeks. "It's relative, but for the most part, yes."

"I guess it depends on the source of the pain."

He furrows his brow and drops his forehead to mine. "I've had broken ribs, countless black eyes, a broken hand and hundreds of cuts and bruises. I've been hit by some of the strongest men in the world. I've spent hours having my skin tattooed with a needle, repeatedly..." He lets out a soft breath that blows against my heated cheek. "But none of that compares to the pain of losing you."

"Sam." I close my eyes and swallow down the echo of the pain that used to hide in the far corners of my heart, hidden away from Drew and Janice and even Sebastian, but mostly from me. "You don't have to feel that way anymore. You never have to feel that pain again."

He gazes at me with his beautiful, strange eyes, the blue brightened by the reflection of the sky and the brown lit by the warm sun that reflects the shimmering layers of gold and amber, like the sand meeting the sea. "I'll never let myself forget what it was like to lose you. To pine for you. To see you with someone else. And to want you so badly I could hardly breathe." He reaches under my chin and vows, "I will never take you for granted."

I wrap my fingers around his wrist and promise, "I won't take you for granted, either."

The fire returns to his eyes and his lips return to mine.

His hands tangle in my skirt again, the gauzy material clinging to my legs as he fights to get it up around my waist, and I stumble backward onto a dark wicker canopy bed that's covered with a sheer mosquito net. He shoves it to the side and pushes me back against the creamy white pillows that line the circular bed, kissing my thighs as he moves my skirt out of the way.

I pull my long hair up and lay it over the pillows, giving my neck reprieve from the infringing heat, and relish the shaded cushions that cool me slightly.

Sam shrugs out of his shorts and closes the mosquito net around us, and it billows in the breeze, dappled with shadows that dance in the filtered sunlight.

"Stop." I hold my hand up and sit up a little on my elbow.

"What?"

"Don't move."

"Lucy, if there's a fucking spider on me, you better get it right now!"

I crinkle my eyes and laugh softly, remembering his fear of the little eight-legged creatures. "There's no spider, Mr. World Class Champion."

"What is it then?"

I sit up all the way and pull my bottom lip between my teeth. "You. This place. Right now. I just want to remember this moment. Forever."

He smiles and his dimples light up the darkest parts of me, sending a cool rush through my veins, which beg to be heated again. He crawls over me and kisses me passionately, pushing me back against the pillows as he tugs my lips between his teeth, the way that I love, the way that leaves them tingling and begging for more. He yanks my crop top down, leaving it around my waist while he takes turns cupping my breasts and rubbing his thumb gently over my warmed nipples.

I push his boxer briefs down over his hips while he tugs my panties down, and I wriggle my legs against his until at least one of mine is free and he's lying on top of me naked, rocking his hips against me, though I'm still partially skirted and somewhat crop-topped.

With both articles of clothing corralled around my stomach, he pushes into me with an audible groan that resonates deep in my soul. I wind my arms around his back, careful of his injured ribs, which I know must be aching, though he'll never admit it, and savor the feeling of him sinking into me, filling me the way only he can, the way only he ever has.

I drop my head back and breathe in the warm island air that only he and I are sharing, overcome by the freedom of being miles away from another human being. It's just me and Sam. *No one else.* And with that, every ounce of worry, every extraneous thought that has overshadowed our reconciliation disappears.

"Sam…" I breathe against his mouth, my body absorbing every ounce of him. I put my hand on his face, and he smiles when he sees the smile on mine.

He reaches for my hands and holds them above my head, lacing his fingers with mine as he looks down on me with every slow, intentional thrust.

"I love you," I whisper, gazing up at his handsome face.

"I love you," he whispers back and the flames licking my thighs ignite in an explosion that's fueled by all the oxygen in my body.

I cry out as he continues with slow, strong thrusts, holding my hands and watching me writhe beneath him. I rock my hips up to bring him closer, but he just gazes down at me, holding my hands above my head, keeping his slow, steady rhythm that fans the glowing embers still burning just below the surface of my skin. .

"What are you doing?" I whisper.

"I want to remember this moment. You. Like this. Forever."

I lie beneath him with a satiated smile, watching him watch me as we make love in the shaded heat of the Caribbean, pink cheeked, sweat beading, eyes seeing places inside each other that no one else has ever seen. *He's mine.* I bite my tingling lip and sigh with pleasure that resonates through my body and soul. *And I'm his.*

Finally.

CHAPTER 3

LUCY

I bend over and wrap my freshly washed hair in a towel, twisting it on top of my head as I stand back up. Sam follows me out of the bathroom, dripping water all over the floor.

"Do you ever use a towel to dry off?" I ask, laughing and steeling a glance of his naked, wet body. His week-long Bahamian tan is beginning to turn the color of honey.

"Not when it's eighty degrees out," he says, opening the balcony doors and walking outside *naked*. The sheer white curtains billow into the room with a warm breeze, and thunder rolls in the distance. The sun is still shining, but it won't be long before an afternoon thunderstorm moves through.

I unwrap the towel from around my body and drop it on the floor at my feet while I search through my half-empty suitcase for a pair of panties.

"In there," Sam says, pointing to the dresser next to the hand-carved four-poster bed, which is draped in white sheers.

I give him a curious look.

"I washed everything last night while you were snoring, I mean sleeping, on the couch."

"What? I do not snore!"

He laughs softly. "Only when you're really tired. I think you were worn out from our hike across the island yesterday."

I shake my head, but I don't refute him.

"I put all your clothes away in those drawers," he says, gesturing to the dresser again. "I figured it was time you stopped living out of your suitcase." He smirks. His suitcases were promptly unpacked and tucked away in the back of the closet the day we arrived.

I narrow my eyes and pull one of the drawers open to find all my bras and panties neatly folded in little stacks.

Sam wraps his arms around me and presses his sun-warmed body to mine. "I wouldn't protest if you skipped putting on clothes altogether, you know." He kisses my neck beneath my ear, knocking the towel off my head, which tugs my long hair.

"Ow," I say, leaning over to unwrap the towel from my hair—it falls to the floor. I stand up and rub my scalp, and run my fingers through my damp hair to separate the strands.

"You okay?" Sam asks, picking the towel up off the floor.

"Yes. And I'm still not going to start running around outside naked with you, okay?"

He laughs and picks my other towel up off the floor, taking them both back to the bathroom while I get dressed.

Without warning, the sun disappears and it begins to rain sideways into the room.

"Ahh," I squeal, running over to the doors to close them. I fight with the wet sheers that wrap around my arms when I try to move them out of the way. "Sam," I call as thunder crashes loudly and a flash of lightning lights up the darkened sky, making me jump.

He steps beside me, dressed in shorts now, and manages to the get doors closed with the curtains on the inside. "It's really coming down."

"Yeah." I wipe my wet arms and head to the bathroom for another towel. "Guess that's why they call it the tropics." I dry my arms and face, inspecting my reflection in the mirror. I'm definitely not as tan as Sam—I've been bathing in SPF 70 all week because my skin is fair—but I like the sun-kissed glow on my cheeks.

I reach for my brush and run it through my hair, then I flip my head upside down couple of times to tousle the long pieces.

"What are you doing?"

"Flipping my hair."

"Why?"

"I don't know. I always do it. It helps it dry, I think."

He gives me an amused look. "You're weird. Cute, but weird."

"I'm weird? You're the one running around naked all the time. This isn't *The Blue Lagoon*, okay?"

"You have a problem with me being naked?"

I fight hard against a smile that turns the corners of my mouth up. "No." I wrap my arms around his waist. "I most definitely do not have a problem with it. It's just a little unconventional."

"That's what's so great about this place, Luc. There are no rules to follow. Now, I know how hard that is for you"—he narrows his eyes—"but before we leave, I want to see you throw caution to the wind."

"You want me to get naked with you?" I say, sighing with inevitable defeat.

"Well, that's easy." He grins. "What I want is for you to get naked with me and go swimming, or jump in the ocean, or maybe even roll around in the sand," he says, arching an eyebrow. "Like in *The Blue Lagoon*."

"I was pretty sure I heard *you* snoring the other night when we watched it."

He smirks. "I was awake for the good parts."

"Okay." I laugh. "I'll consider it. But I might need a little liquid ambition before I go stripping my clothes off outside."

He holds his chin back and says, "I think we can manage that." He takes my hand and pulls me through the house, until we're in the kitchen.

I follow him around the corner to the butler's pantry, which must hold every kind of liquor there is.

Sam opens the cabinets and stands next to the wine fridge. "Pick your poison," he says with smiling eyes.

I glance over my shoulder at the darkened windows, which are still being pelted with rain. *Why not?* I sigh and say, "Dealer's choice."

Three hurricanes and one Fireball shot later, I'm sprawled across Sam's legs on the couch, asking, "What's the coolest thing you did while we were apart? After, you know…"

"Prison?"

"I was going to say after you got famous."

"Oh. Well, let's see…I got to meet Rocky."

I sit up straight, bumping into his hand and sloshing his drink over the side of his glass a little. "You met Rocky?" I ask, ignoring the spill. "Like, *the* Rocky? Sylvester Stallone?"

"Yeah. I've met Sly a couple of times."

"Shut up!" I say, shoving his shoulder. "You call him Sly?"

"Yeah"—he laughs—"that's his name."

"Oh my, God, that is so cool. Did you tell him that you've loved him since you were a kid? That you wanted to *be* Rocky when you grew up?" I ask dramatically.

"Yeah, I mean, maybe not so enthusiastically, but I let him know he was important to me."

I slouch against the back of the couch and whisper, "Wow." I watch the rain coming down and sip my drink. *He's so out of my league.*

"What about you? What's the coolest thing you did while we were apart?"

"Nothing like that," I say softly. "For me, just going to New York City for the first time was pretty incredible. Being exposed to all the culture, the diversity, the food." I shrug. "I really love New York."

"I've been a few times, but only for work. I haven't really seen much of the city."

"Okay," I say, sitting up again, "we have to go together. I have to take you to the Met. If I end up going to the Aurelia Snow exhibit this summer, you are coming with me."

"Who's Aurelia Snow?"

"Only one of the most successful, talented modern artists in the industry. Her gallery is hosting an exhibit this summer that's featuring emerging artists like me. It's the one I told you about. The one I hoped my exhibit would land me an invitation to. Not so sure about that now."

"So, we'll go to New York anyway. I'd love to see the... whatever it's called."

I smile. "The Met?"

"Yeah."

I finish my drink and stand up. "Come on," I say, reaching for his hands.

He puts his drink down and stands up. "You want another drink?" he asks uncertainly.

I shake my fuzzy head. I've had enough. "No. I want to go swimming."

"Luc, it's still raining."

"So what? The thunder and lightning stopped a while ago. I want to go swimming with you." I arch an eyebrow and shimmy my shorts down my legs.

He watches me and laughs. "So just like that…all I had to do was get you drunk?"

"Yep." I giggle and push the glass doors open, stepping out onto the cooled travertine tiles in my T-shirt and panties. "You coming or what?" I ask, leaving the covered patio and stepping out into the rain. I close my eyes and hold my arms out, and spin around.

After a few seconds, Sam catches my wrist and pulls me against his warm chest, which I can feel through the cool rain, and a soft melody begins to play through the outside speakers.

"You put on music?" I ask, smiling up at him.

"Yeah."

The delicate plucking of guitar strings is the perfect accompaniment to the rain bouncing off the tiles at our feet. Sam holds me close and sways me back and forth to the soft male voice that croons the lyrics, *You were mine, at one point in time…*

My breath catches in my throat and I grip his arms tightly as we begin to slow dance in the rain under a gray-blue sky.

"Sam," I whisper, squeezing my eyes shut. "I love you," I say quietly.

He presses his hand to my back and grips my wet shirt in his hand, twisting it up in his fist as he brings his mouth to mine and kisses me slowly.

I kiss him back with everything I am, feeling the buzz of alcohol tingle on my tongue against his. My heart pounds inside my chest as the beautiful lyrics remind me of the pain we both felt without each other. *What do I gotta do, to erase every piece of you?*

We dance for a few more seconds, then he drops his forehead to mine and sings softly, "I don't want you to go, so I'll just keep on talking slow."

"Sam." I blink back tears that mix with the rain falling on my cheeks.

He wipes my face and says, "I used to listen to this when you were gone. It always made me think of you." He rubs his thumb over my cheek and gazes at me through the rain that's dripping from my hair and T-shirt. "You're so beautiful like this." He smiles and brings my chin up to his. "I love you." He kisses me softly.

"You know, for somebody who beats people up for a living, you're pretty sweet. And sensitive."

"Shhh…don't tell anyone."

I smile and reach for the bottom of my T-shirt, and pull it off over my head.

Sam watches me take off my bra and panties with a satisfied smile on his face.

I throw them on the ground and wrap my arms around his neck, pressing my naked, wet body to his. I kiss him again and savor the feeling of his wide hands on my back and bottom. I drop down off my tiptoes and put my hands on my hips. "Well, come on, champ, it's your turn."

He grins and tugs his wet T-shirt off, then he pushes his shorts down while I watch. He stands beside me facing the pool and reaches for my hand. "Come on," he says excitedly, and we jump into the warm water and sink beneath the quiet surface.

"Okay," I say when we resurface, catching my breath. "There might be something to this." I kiss him and we sink back down into the quiet water below, where there's only us, tangled together. No noise, no worry...just peace.

I may never resurface again.

* * *

I lie back in one of the open cabana beds by the pool, gazing up at the twinkling stars that are shining in the dark, indigo sky—one of my favorite things to do here at night.

Sam joins me with a bottle of white wine, two long-stemmed glasses, and a smile. "Thought we should celebrate our last night here." He sits down beside me and pours me a glass.

"How is it possible that three weeks have gone by already?" I ask, taking the glass from him. I sip the cool, crisp wine and a soft breeze raises goose bumps on my arms. "I've finally acclimated to the humidity and now we have to leave," I pout, rubbing my arms.

"If we could stay here like this forever, I would." He holds his glass up to mine and says, "Here's to the most incredible three weeks of my life."

"Mine too," I say, clinking my glass with his.

He takes a sip and presses his wine-soaked lips to mine, and I try to etch the moment to memory—the warm, breezy air, the twinkling stars, the glow of the house, the rustling of the palm trees blowing against the night sky, the waves crashing on the salty shore in the distance, and Sam's full, sweet lips pressed against mine.

He leans back against the pillows beside me and looks up at the sky I've been memorizing for the last twenty nights. "I just got off the phone with Miles."

"Is he lost without you?"

He laughs and nods. "As soon as the doctor clears me, I've got to start training again."

"I figured you would."

"All this down time's got me out of shape."

I raise an eyebrow and glance at his *very* muscular arms.

"Seriously, I'm going to have to put in a lot of time with Tristan when we get back to get ready for the match in LA next month."

"LA?"

He nods and looks at me with a hint of hesitance in his eyes. "I know it's soon, but I really want you to go."

I lower my wineglass and reach for his hand. "Wild horses couldn't keep me away." Especially after what happened in Quebec. It's going to be hard to watch him fight, taking hits like he did with Beau Ackerman, but it would be agony to watch on TV, not knowing if he was okay.

He smiles and I kiss his hand, grateful that he's back to good health now.

"I'm going to be pretty busy too," I say, thinking about everything that's waiting for me back home. "Sebastian's been doing what he does best, but I still have a lot of loose ends to tie up at the studio."

"Does one of them happened to be named Drew?"

A rock lands in the middle of my stomach, and I instantly grow angry at it for interrupting my last night in paradise with Sam. I may have made mistakes, but I ended things with Drew the right way. *So why do I still feel so shitty about it?* I make a mental note to take this up with Sebastian when I get back.

I sigh. "Yes, Drew. He still owns the studio." I sip my wine and gaze up at the endless sea of stars above us. "I'm just grateful he hasn't kicked us out yet. At least not as of yesterday when I talked to Sebastian. He's been trying to get hold of Drew, but Drew hasn't returned any of his calls. And he said he's too scared to call Janice." I laugh, but the truth is, I don't blame him.

"Ah, she didn't seem very scary to me."

"Yes, well, she was quite smitten with you, but that was before you stole her future daughter-in-law."

"I'm pretty sure you left willingly."

"Even worse." I sigh and say honestly, "I care about Janice. She was like a mother to me for the last couple of years. It's weird to suddenly not have any contact with her."

"Well, maybe you should try to call her," he says, sipping his wine, and I can't tell if he really wants me to or if he's just trying to be supportive.

I look at him and admit, "I did call her, before we left Quebec."

He raises his eyebrows curiously. "What did she say?"

"She didn't answer. So I left her message to let her know where I'd be for the next few weeks. I just didn't want her to worry," I explain.

He nods, but I see the concern in his eyes. "No one is supposed to know we're here, Luc."

"She would never tell anyone. Besides, I only said we'd be in the Bahamas, I didn't say where."

"Did she ever call you back?"

"No. I've texted her a few times, but I think she's pretty upset with me. I need to go see her when we get back. Hopefully I can mend things with her in person, or at least apologize." I shrug. "What's the worst that could happen? I'm probably going to lose my studio anyway." I sigh dramatically. "What could be worse than that?"

"Lucy, I told you. I'll buy you the studio. You don't need to worry about that."

"Drew will never sell it to you," I say surely. Not that I would let Sam buy it for me anyway. I drop my head to the side to look at him and link my pinky with his. "It's okay. I knew what I was risking." I smile softly and exhale a quiet breath. "You're worth it."

He puts his wineglass down and says tenaciously, "I'll buy you a new studio, then. I'll buy you anything, Lamb. Just name it and it's yours."

I put my glass down next to his and sit up. "Sam, I don't need you to buy me things."

"But I want to."

"No. You've worked so hard for everything you have. For this." I gesture at the house and the spectacular pool we're sitting next to. "I'm so proud of you for all that you've accomplished, but I want to make something of myself too. I want to make my own way. It's important to me…I think it's what my mom would have wanted for me."

He nods softly. "I want that for you too."

"You do?"

"Yes, of course."

I smile softly at him.

"But I also want to help you. I want you to *let* me help you. The way Drew did. You can always pay me back."

I pick up my wineglass. "Sam, it's different with you."

"Why?"

"Because Drew treated it like a business deal. You would just be doing it because…you love me."

He gives me an impossible look. "What's wrong with that?"

"It's the principle of the whole thing," I say, my voice rising a few octaves.

He lets out a defeated breath and says, "Okay, then. No studio."

"Sam…" I reach for his hand and hold it in my lap. "I love that you want to help me. But I want to figure out how to do it on my own. Especially now." I shake my head and explain, "Everything's different now…I'm different."

He gives me a sincere look and asks, "How?" Before I can answer, he adds, "Besides the fact that you'll freely take your clothes off and run around the beach with me now."

I laugh. "Well, yes, there's definitely that. But, I don't know, I'm just not who I was with Drew. Being here these last few weeks, without distractions, learning new things about you and rediscovering all the things I already loved…about you, about us…" I smile and say, "I'm *me* when I'm with *you*, Sam. Who I always was, deep down. The me who isn't afraid to stand on her own two feet. I want other people to know her too."

"Then they will."

I smile and lean back against the pillows in the cabana and stare at the sparkly sky.

Sam leans back beside me. "So, besides the studio, are there other stipulations to me spending money on you that I should know about?"

"Sam, I love that you want to give me things and take me to amazing places like this. But I told you, I'm yours, free and clear. You earned your money, not me. I'm not going to let you go bankrupt spending it on me."

He pulls his eyebrows together. "Luc, I don't think you understand exactly how much money I have." He gives me a contented look, but it makes me uneasy. "I couldn't spend it all in this lifetime or the next."

"Oh." My mouth suddenly feels dry. Maybe it's the wine.

"I mean, I guess I technically could, but I never would. I'm smart with my money, and I've made good investments."

I give a tentative smile. "It's still *your* money. Not mine."

He nods thoughtfully and his face grows serious again, but then he reaches for my hand and the corners of his mouth turn up, setting his eyes alight. "Well, I guess I'll just have to do something about that then."

I laugh and shake my head. "Sam, I was literally engaged to someone else less than a month ago. We're not getting married." I smile and put my hand on his cheek. "Not yet anyway."

"Well, maybe we could get a head start by you moving in with me when we get back."

I laugh again, unable to escape the power of his dimples, or the joy that's filling my chest. "You want me to move in with you already?"

"Yes," he says certainly.

"Don't you think we should give it a little more time?"

"For what?"

"I don't know. To get to know each other again. I mean, we only just got back together. And what would people say?" Thoughts of the media and Drew and Janice bounce around my head, squandering my happiness.

He sits up and drops his elbows to his knees. "Lucy, I don't care what people say. And what do you mean? We've known each other our whole lives. Besides, we've technically been living together for the last twenty days."

"Well, as much as I hate to admit it, I *do* care what people say. People can be judgmental. I don't need rumors derailing my career right now. The last thing I want is to be known as your gold-digging girlfriend."

He laughs softly and fights a smile. "So you think moving in with me makes you a gold digger?"

"Well, maybe a freeloader."

"Okay, I'll tell you what. If you move in with me, I'll let Jean-Luc go and you can be in charge of buying all the groceries. It will actually *save* me money."

I smile softly. "Have you even considered that you might not like living with me? I'm not the tidiest person in the world."

"I've noticed," he says, cutting his eyes at me.

"Uhh." I laugh and shove his arm lightly. "We're on vacation, okay?"

He laughs and shakes his head. "You never did pick your clothes up off the floor, even when we were kids."

He really does know me. It makes me smile. "Well, you're freakishly tidy, okay. When did that start?"

"Prison. When I got out, I was a lot more careful with my belongings, because I didn't have anything for three years."

"Oh." I drop my head and fight the familiar guilt that squeezes my chest whenever he talks about his time in prison.

He pulls me over to him and wraps his arms around me. "I love that you're messy. It's part of who you are. And I want all of you, Lucy. Even the messy parts."

I nod against his chest. "I felt like I had to hide the messy parts for a really long time."

"Not with me. You never have to hide with me, Lamb. I love everything about you. No amount of time *or space* will change that. So, please, move in with me. I want the first thing I see in the morning to be your face…with your messy hair, in our messy room."

I laugh softly. "Okay."

"Okay?"

I tilt my chin up and smile at him. "Yes, I'll move in with you, Sam."

He kisses the top of my head and hugs me tight. "That makes me so happy."

"Me too," I say softly, pushing away encroaching thoughts of the media and Drew and Janice. They'll all have something to say, but nothing is more important than Sam's happiness. Or mine.

CHAPTER 4

LUCY

Sebastian!" I stand on my tiptoes and wrap my arms around his neck.

"Hello, gorgeous!" He pulls me back by my shoulders and smiles at me. "Seriously, you look amazing." He takes my hands and inspects my face and arms. "A little Sam, I mean sun, looks good on you."

I laugh and arch an eyebrow. "Maybe a little of both."

He sighs and removes his burgundy Burberry scarf from around his neck, which he reserves for the month of November. "You know I can't wait to hear all about it—I want details—but first, I have one hundred and one things to go over with you." He hands me a paper cup of coffee and takes my hand. "Come on."

I sip it as he drags me to the back of the studio, reluctantly lifting the Sam veil I've been blissfully hiding behind for the last three weeks. Paradise was wonderful, but it's back to reality.

I did miss my latte macchiato.

And Sebastian.

I smile when we reach my *very* organized office, which I've avoided since I arrived twenty minutes ago. I chose to spend the morning reacquainting myself with my paintings, especially those that technically no longer belong to me since being sold at my exhibit last month. "You've been busy," I say, eyeing my shelves.

"Okay," Sebastian says, handing me my laptop and several folders that are exploding with papers. "Follow me."

"What is all of this?"

"Purchase orders mostly. All awaiting your signature. And a contract," he says casually as he plops down onto one of the giant throw pillows on the floor. He pats the rug beside him and pulls another pillow over. "Sit." He purses his lips over a smile he's barely containing.

I narrow my eyes and coerce my heart to maintain a slow, steady, unexcited rhythm as I swallow down the butterflies I refuse to acknowledge and sit on the floor beside him. "So what's the contract for?" I ask coolly.

"Oh, just this gallery in Chelsea that's hosting an exhibit for up-and-coming contemporary realist artists next summer."

I sit up straight, no longer able to restrain my excited heart. "Shut up."

"Aurelia Snow or something." He pulls his mouth to the side and shakes his head. "Something like that."

"Bas, are you joking?"

He smiles wide. "Nope."

"Shut up!" I squeal and jump to my feet, blinking back tears. "Oh, my God!"

Sebastian jumps up with me. "I know!"

"Aurelia Snow wants to showcase me? Really?"

"I wanted to tell you so badly, but I decided to wait until you got back so I could do it in person. I'm so glad I did, because the look on your face is priceless."

"Oh, my God!" I shout and grab his arms.

We proceed to jump up and down together.

"Sebastian?" I stop and look at him, then I wrap myself around him and begin to cry softly.

"Lucy. Don't cry." He laughs and rubs my back.

I wipe my eyes. "You were right."

"Of course I was," he says, wiping the lenses of his round tortoiseshell glasses. He pushes them back on. "What was I right about?"

"The exhibit. Waiting to break off things with Drew until after it was over. Even though I did actually try to do it sooner." I shake my head. "Sebastian, without the exhibit, there's no way this would have happened."

He smiles and says, "Thank God. I was kind of going out on a limb with that advice. But it just felt like the right thing to do."

I sigh and fall back into a sitting position on the floor, feeling like I can finally exhale the breath I've been holding since I decided to host the exhibit. "Aurelia Snow wants to display my work in her studio for all of New York to see." I reach for the contract and start scanning the paragraphs. "What piece does she want?"

"Sam."

I give him a confused look. "What?"

"She wants *Lionheart*," he says, sitting on the floor beside me.

"My painting of Sam?" I put the contract down. "Uh—" I huff, but Bas stops me.

"I know how you feel about the painting, Luc. You can always say no. But…" He squints his eyes and shrugs his square shoulders. "It's not like she wants to buy it. It'll just be on loan."

"What if someone at the exhibit wants to buy it?"

"We'll just have the contract amended to state that it's not for sale, so it'll be a nonissue."

"I don't know."

"What don't you know? This is your dream, Lucy."

"It's Sam, Sebastian. It feels wrong to put him on display for my benefit."

He grabs my hand and pulls me to my feet again.

"What are you doing?"

"Follow me." He drags me across the studio and stops in front of my painting of the Atlanta skyline that I originally painted with dime-store paints when I was seventeen. "Tell me about this painting."

"You already know."

"I forgot. Tell me again."

I give him a funny look, but entertain him anyway. He's obviously trying to make a point. I stare at the painting, thinking of how the colors make me feel, even now. The way the two halves of the canvas are divided by the shadowy outline of the Atlanta skyline that cuts across the crisp cobalt blue sky and drips carefully into the sultry magenta below.

"I was seventeen. Sam bought me some cheap paints and plastic brushes." I smile thinking of the sweet gesture. "We climbed up on the roof of an old abandoned building in Brighton Park, and this is what we saw in the distance. *Possi-*

bility." I exhale a quiet breath. "The original was a little more rudimentary, but the colors were similar. I used red to represent love, because it was the only thing we had, and well, I was seventeen…it seemed like a romantic notion." I laugh softly and point to the bottom of the painting. "We were way down here, stuck in that broken place, dreaming about a better life. And this"—I touch the top of the canvas thoughtfully—"this represented our future. Wide open, just like the sky that day." I glance up at Bas, who's studying the painting carefully. "What did I know?" I shrug.

"This is her second choice," he says, keeping his gaze fixed on the painting.

"What?"

"I sent her a copy of every painting in your portfolio and *this* was her second choice." He turns to me and lowers his chin, keeping his dark eyes on mine. "Sam is in all of your best work. Don't you see that? You can't take him out of it because *he* is what makes you so damn good."

I release a small breath and nod in silent agreement.

"Sam is part of you, Lucy. Not just now because you're together, but way back before anyone even knew who either of you were. He was one of the first people to see you for the amazing, talented artist you are. Isn't it only *right* for him to be part of this?"

I nod and blink back tears of gratitude, for Sam, for everything we went through, for this incredible opportunity, and for Sebastian, who always helps me to see the truth through my uncertainty. "Yes."

"First choice it is then."

I swallow down my hesitation and agree, "First choice."

Bas claps excitedly. "Okay, there's more." He hands me another document that looks a lot like the Aurelia Snow contract. "This is from a gallery in Dallas. It's a little uppity, but they want to showcase you in an exhibit too!"

"Seriously? How did they even hear about me?"

He shrugs. "Your paintings made quite the impression after the exhibit got so much press. I've been fielding calls and sifting through emails since you and Sam left for Exuma. You've been invited to participate in seven exhibits, Lucy."

"What? Really?"

"None of the others are quite Aurelia Snow, but they'll showcase your talent none the less." He smiles wide. "You did it, Luc."

"I don't believe it." I smile back. "Thank you so much for handling all this while I was gone. I don't know—"

"What you'd do without me. I know."

"Seriously. I feel like such a slacker. I spent the last three weeks lying on a remote island with Sam, while you were here doing all this for me. I don't deserve you."

"Don't forget you pay me. Quite well." He raises his eyebrows and smirks. "Speaking of lying on a remote island with Sam. Tell me everything!"

I sigh and slouch against his arm. "It was uh-mazing. I want to go back," I whine. "It was like time stopped and the rest of the world just slipped away. We had no agenda, no alarm clock, no interruptions."

"Sounds incredible."

"It was. The days and nights just sort of blended together. But we spent a lot of the time swimming, because it was hotter than the surface of the sun."

"Something tells me you did other things too." He bites the end of his pen and widens his eyes playfully.

"Maybe." I raise a suggestive eyebrow. "Maybe we did *other* things all over the island. On the beach. In the ocean. In every room of the magnificent house. Want me to keep going?"

"I get it." He laughs. "You were making up for lost time."

"Something like that."

"Must have been nice to have a private island all to yourself," he says wistfully.

"It was. I mean, it took a little coaxing from Sam to embrace the idea of being able to do whatever we wanted, *wherever* we wanted, but it was pretty freeing once I did."

"I bet."

"We did other things too, you know."

"Like?"

"We just hung out together. We watched movies, listened to music, talked. We talked a lot. It was nice to be able to get to know each other again without any outside distractions. A lot has happened in our lives over the last ten years. It gave us a chance to fill in the gaps. And at the end of the day we just want to be together." I smile. "He asked me to move in with him."

I can see the hesitation in Bas's eyes when he asks, "Are you going to?"

"Yes," I say confidently. "I've given it a lot of thought and it's what I want."

"Good," he says without judgment. "I'm happy for you, sweetie." He gives my hand a squeeze, but I see a flicker of sadness in his eyes when he releases it.

"Hey, what's wrong?"

He sighs. "It's just Paul. He and I have been fighting lately."

"What? Why?"

"Because he's decided that we should be parents now."

I nearly choke on my coffee. "Oh."

"That was my reaction too."

"Sorry, I'm just surprised."

"You and me both. I mean, we've talked about having a family one day, but not anytime soon. I'm twenty-nine—I thought I'd have at least another decade before bringing a baby into the mix."

"Paul's ready now?"

He shrugs a shoulder. "He's thirty-five, which according to him, is when he always planned to start a family—something he probably should have mentioned to me *before* we got married."

"Would it have changed your mind?"

"No," he says with an exasperated huff.

"Well, what are you going to do?"

"I don't know. He's been researching options, and it's a pretty long process. It could take years, whether we decide to adopt or go with a surrogate. And don't even get me started on the cost."

"I'm sorry. That sounds really stressful."

"Well, Paul thinks that if we don't start the process now, it could be five years or more by the time we actually have a baby."

I press my lips together over a smile I can't hide.

"What?"

"It's just, the thought of you with a baby is kind of awesome. You'd make a great dad. So would Paul."

"Okay, please don't tell me you're teaming up with Paul on this."

"No." I laugh softly. "I'm team Sebastian all the way. I'll support you any way that I can. And provide babysitting services as needed."

"Lucy."

"Aunt Lucy."

"Oh, my God. Stop."

"Okay, but seriously, how am I ever going to take care of kids of my own if I don't start practicing? This could be good for me. I don't know anything about babies."

"Me neither!"

"Well, sounds like you're going to find out before I do."

He narrows his eyes. "I missed you. But only a little."

I shove his arm. "Mean."

He laughs, and it chases the worry away from his face. "I really did miss you. A lot."

"I missed you too. It was a wonderful, unexpected break from reality, but part of me felt off-kilter without you for so long. Especially when I needed some Sebastian-brand therapy."

He pulls his dark eyebrows together over the rim of his glasses. "What for?"

"Oh, you know, just normal stuff, like realizing my boyfriend has more money than I'll make in my lifetime. Worrying that I'm going to end up on the cover of *In Touch* magazine. And wondering what my jilted ex-fiancé plans to do with my beloved studio. Nothing quite as life-altering as having a child, but problems, nonetheless."

He puts his hand under his chin thoughtfully and holds

a curved finger over his mouth. "Well, you knew Sam had money. Why the sudden concern about it? Most people consider that a good thing."

"I know. It's definitely a very good thing, for *Sam*. But I'm not really comfortable with him spending it on me so freely. I mean, he wouldn't hesitate to buy me a new studio altogether, if I let him. Which I won't."

"Funny, you didn't have a problem letting Drew buy this one."

"That was different. Drew bought it as an investment that we could eventually benefit from, jointly. It was meant to be a source of income for both of us. Sam's motivation is just…me."

"Just you?"

I shrug. "He knows how much my career means to me. He just wants to help."

Bas sips his coffee and narrows his eyes at me. "So now that we've got that worked out."

"No, Bas. I won't let him buy me a studio. It's going to be bad enough when people realize I don't have my own money. Not the kind Sam has, anyway. I can just see the headlines now. *Lucy Bennett… Gold Digger.* It's inevitable."

Bas laughs and puts his coffee down. "That's what you're worried about?"

"Yes. You know that's what everyone's going to think. *Where was she before he got famous? She's only back with him because he's got money now.*" I close my eyes and try to drown out the imminent rumors before they consume me.

"Listen to me. You're no longer just Lucy Bennett. You're Lucy Bennett, up-and-coming contemporary realist artist *and* Sam Cole's girlfriend. You don't get the luxury of filtered thoughts and polite smiles anymore. You're going to be judged *loudly*, and you'll be criticized loudly. But you'll also be loved loudly. Everyone who loves Sam will love you too, because they'll see how much he loves you and how happy he is with you. Sure there are going to be people who call you a gold digger. But screw those people! You think Sam has only ever had nice things written about him? No. But there's so much more good than bad. So, starting this very moment, I want you to make a vow to ignore any and all negative things written about you and focus on only the good things instead. Okay?"

I sigh. "Okay."

"Say it. Out loud."

"What? Bas."

He grabs my hand and holds my open palm up in between us. "Repeat after me." He clears his throat. "I, Lucy Bennett."

"I, Lucy Bennett."

"Promise to ignore all the negative, hateful things people might say or write about me."

I pull my eyebrows together and repeat, "Promise to ignore all the negative, hateful things people might say or write about me."

"You can put your hand down."

I drop my hand and give him a small smile.

"Okay, that's two issues resolved. What's left?"

"Drew."

"Well, we've established that Sam will *not* buy you a new studio." He sighs. "So first order of business is buying this one from Drew."

"Even if I can come up with the money, who's to say he'll sell it to me? Honestly, how can I even ask him to, after everything I put him through? I broke his heart. It would just be salt in his wounds."

"He might be more forgiving than you think."

"What do you mean?"

"He finally reached out to me."

"He did? When?"

"Yesterday. Apparently Janice told him where you were. He knew you were on your way back."

"Great."

"He wasn't upset. In fact, I thought he was going to ask me to close the doors to the studio, but he didn't. He just wanted me to tell you that he was working on the building contract with his lawyer and that we should hear from him in a few weeks. He said in the meantime to keep running business as usual."

"Really?"

"He also asked if I'd tell you something else."

"What?" I ask, eager for more clues about the fate of my studio.

"That he misses you. And that it's not too late."

My shoulders slump. "Yes…it is." I close my eyes and sigh. "I have to go talk to him. I need to get the rest of my things from his house anyway. Maybe then I can talk to him about buying the studio."

"You want me to go with you?"

"No, I should go alone. I'll go tomorrow morning."

My phone rings, echoing across the studio, and I jump to my feet to answer it. I follow the strumming ringtone to the front of the studio and find it vibrating on the front desk. I'm startled to see a small sea of people standing outside on the sidewalk, staring at me through the glass windows. Several of them are holding professional cameras and others are holding up their cell phones, shouting at me.

Lucy, Lucy!…Where's Sam?…How was your vacation?

I suck in a sharp breath and feel the room start to spin around me. I'm only vaguely aware that my phone is still strumming away and buzzing on the desk when it vibrates off the edge and lands on the floor with a loud smack.

"What's taking so long?" Sebastian asks, walking out of the back of the studio. "Oh, my God," he gasps, and grabs my arm. "Lucy, go to the back. Now."

"My phone." I bend down to pick it up off the floor with shaking fingers and follow him to my office. My phone rings again and I answer it when I see who's calling. "Sam?"

"Lucy, where are you?"

"I'm at my studio. Sam, there are people outside. They're taking pictures."

"Is Sebastian with you?"

"Yes. What's going on?"

"Just stay with Sebastian. I'm two minutes away."

"Okay." I end the call and look at Sebastian. "Google Sam."

"What?"

"Google Sam," I repeat.

"Why?"

"One of them asked about our vacation. That no one was supposed to know about. Just Google him. Please. I can't do it."

He unlocks his phone and starts scrolling. "Lucy, you're jumping to conclu—" His face falls and his eyes bounce around his screen. He looks up at me hesitantly. "There are pictures."

The breath leaves my lungs in a dizzying rush. "Pictures of what?" I fumble for his phone, successfully snatching it out of his hand. "Oh, my, God," I gasp when I see a picture of me and Sam on our private beach in Exuma. He's carrying me into the water, kissing me, and I'm wrapped around him, practically naked in my bikini. "How?" I exhale a shocked breath and blink back tears. "How could they get this picture? How did they even know we were there?" I look at Sebastian with disbelief, feeling myself shrink under a cloud of violation.

"Lucy?!" Sam calls from the front of the studio.

"Back off," I hear Miles shout, closing the door behind them. "Fucking vultures."

Sam makes a beeline toward me, still wearing the sweats he was training in this morning. "Hey. Are you okay?"

"Yeah." I give Sebastian his phone back and let Sam envelop me in his arms, as if he can somehow hide me from the prying eyes of the entire world.

"I'm so sorry."

"It's okay," I say, fortified by his presence. "There could have been worse shots."

He lets go of me and gives me a troubled look. "You saw the pictures," he says cautiously, but it sounds like a question.

"I saw *a* picture."

Bas holds his phone up and shows Sam the picture, but I can tell by the look on Sam's face, it's not what he's talking about.

"That ain't the one that's got everybody so excited," Miles

says over my shoulder, and Sam shoots him an exasperated look.

He turns his attention back to me. "Lucy, there are other pictures."

I look at Bas, whose thumbs are dutifully scouring the internet for more pictures. It doesn't take him long, before he scrunches up his face and gasps, "Oh, my God."

I swallow down the bile rising in my throat. I don't even want to know what he's looking at. I look at Sam, whose worried face does little to comfort me. "I'm not looking," I say to him. "Just tell me what it is."

"It's you," Sebastian says, appalled. "Topless on the beach."

A quiet breath escapes between my lips, but I keep my eyes on Sam, afraid that if I look at anyone or anything else, I might disintegrate.

"It's my fault," Sam says quietly to me. "I'm so sorry. I convinced you that we were secluded there. I thought we were. I was so stupid."

"Yeah, you were," Miles says. "You know these parasites find a way."

"How did they even know we were there?" I push thoughts of Janice out of my mind. *She wouldn't tell anyone.*

"My guess is, they didn't," Miles says. "They just got lucky."

I give Miles an incredulous look that's met with one of sympathy.

"Lots of celebrities stay there, sweetheart. They probably cruise the island a few times a week, hoping to spot one." He points to the tattoos on Sam's arm. "You're not exactly Mr. Inconspicuous. With a telephoto lens, it probably didn't take them long to figure out who you were."

"Why didn't Jacinda tell us that?"

"Not to run around outside naked?" Miles smirks.

"I wasn't…we weren't…" I sit down on my old leather sofa and drop my face to my hands. "This is my punishment."

Sam sits beside me and gently pulls my hands away from my face. "Punishment? For what?"

"For you!" I look at him and his face falls. "For what I did."

Sebastian quickly chimes in. "What Lucy's trying to say is that she knew there would be consequences for leaving her old *boring* life behind, but that you're totally worth it." He cuts his eyes at me and raises his dark eyebrows. "Right, Lucy?"

"Of course," I say to Sam. "Of course you are."

"Are you sure?" Sam asks, raising an eyebrow with worried amusement. "Because you seem pretty upset."

"I am upset. I'm *very* upset. I'm humiliated."

Sam's face softens again. "I know." He drops his chin and I see the guilt on his face.

"It's not your fault, Sam."

"Guys, look, I'm doing everything I can to get it taken down, at least from some of the smaller sites."

"It doesn't matter. It's out there now. For the whole world to see." I groan.

"Lucy, it's going to be fine," Bas says calmly. "There are literally topless pictures of Kate Middleton on the internet. And the whole world still loves her."

"Last I checked, I'm not royalty."

"You're *my* queen," Sam says, trying to lighten the mood, and I flash him a fleeting smile.

"Have you checked your email lately, Bas?"

"Not in the last hour. Why?"

"Oh, just waiting for Aurelia Snow to rescind my invite to her show." I throw my hands up. "There goes my career."

"The exhibit in New York? You got an invite?" Sam asks eagerly.

I give him a small smile and bob my head. "Yeah. I did. And I got invites to six other exhibits too."

"Lucy, that's incredible." He pulls me into a hug. "I knew everyone would want your paintings once they saw how talented you are." He releases me and says, "I'm so proud of you."

"We'll see how many still want them now."

"Lucy, this will die down in a couple of days," Miles says. "If you want, we can put a statement out, address the violation of privacy. That can go a long way sometimes."

"It can also bring more attention to it," Sam argues.

"No, no statement," I say, shaking my head. "Sam's right. I don't want to bring any more attention to it." I sigh and stand up. "I should have known better."

"*I* should have known better," Sam says. He looks at me like there's no one else in the room. "I'm so sorry, Lamb."

"It's okay." I smile softly and try to convince myself that my art will speak louder than these junk sites that posted my picture. But only time will tell.

CHAPTER 5

SAM

I watch the orange glow of the rising sun peek through the high-rise buildings outside the bedroom window, careful not to wake Lucy, who's sleeping peacefully on my chest. I brush the blond hair off her forehead and stare at her beautiful face, trying to memorize the shape of her nose and the curve of her lips. I run my hand over her shoulder—tan from spending the better part of a month in Exuma—and pray that I get to spend every day of the rest of my life waking up like this.

She sighs and wraps her arm around me. "Good morning," she mumbles.

"Morning."

She opens her sleepy eyes. "What time is it?"

"Seven."

"Is there a reason you're awake?"

"I wanted to watch the sunrise."

"Now that you've seen it, can we go back to sleep?"

"Not that sun."

She smiles wide and closes her eyes. "I love you."

"I'm still waiting."

She laughs and opens her eyes, flashing their brilliant blue that rivals the color of the sky outside.

I tilt her chin up and kiss her, and she moans softly, waking up any parts of me that were still asleep. I sit up and pull her on top of me and gaze into her sleepy eyes, which fill with desire I know all too well now. "Hi."

She parts her lips and inhales a slow breath, drawing my mouth to hers like a moth to a flame. "Hi," she says against my lips.

Sam, Fifteen Years Old

"Stop it!" Lucy warns, peering at me over the roof of the car she's hiding behind in the grocery store parking lot.

I smile as I creep around another car parked a few spots away. "Or what?" I challenge, dropping my backpack and leaping over the hood.

She runs between another row of cars, giggling as I get closer. "Sam, stop!" she squeals, pulling her arm out of my grip. "Get away!" She laughs, running a little farther, until she's off the pavement and on the sparse grass that covers a path to the adjacent park. As soon as she's on soft ground, she takes off like a bolt of lightning, backpack and all.

I go pick up my backpack and run even faster.

I catch up to her quickly, chasing her onto the empty playground, but she hides behind a rusty old merry-go-round. She wraps her small hands around the peeling red handlebars and crouches down in the dust as I make my way over to her. She watches me with excited eyes as I step up onto the merry-go-round, which creaks under my weight.

"Ahh," she squeals, giving it a pull and sending me for short ride, before I leap off it and chase her over to the swings.

She holds one of the rubber swing seats in her hands, and the chains clink together as she backs away from me. "I'm going to let go," she warns, but I step closer to her anyway. She lets go and the swing flies through the air at me, but I dodge it and chase her over to the slide.

She runs up the metal and I wait by the steps, but when she peers down and sees me, she turns around and runs back down the slide, her sneakers squeaking on the slippery metal. When she's about halfway down, she sits and slides the rest of the way.

I make it around to the end of the slide just in time to catch her. "Hi," I say, leaning over, gripping the cold metal lip on either side of her.

She laughs and looks up at me. "Hi." She starts to sit up, but I don't move, so she lies down against the slide and smiles up at me.

"You can try to run from me, but I'll always catch you."

She laughs and wriggles her legs between mine, but I don't move. Her chest rises and falls inside her jacket as she gazes up at me and her creamy white skin flushes pink. "Promise?"

I stare at her pale blue eyes, nearly colorless from the bright sun shining down on us. I watch her parted lips move when she draws in a breath, wanting so badly to know what they taste like, and my heart races inside my chest, even faster than when I was chasing her. I lean in closer, unable to resist the pull drawing my mouth to hers.

She closes her eyes and I press my lips firmly to hers. And everything falls away—the slide, the cars in the distance, the smell of the rusty playground. I reach for her face and hold it in my hand as my lips move over hers, pushing and pulling for several long seconds. I exhale a heavy breath, ignoring the way my body is screaming for more, and drop my forehead to hers.

She smiles up at me.

"I may never stop wanting to do that," I admit.

She winds her hands in my hair and pulls my mouth back to hers. "Good."

* * *

"Sam…Lucy," Miles shouts from the living room. "If you're naked, put some clothes on. I'm coming in."

I grumble against Lucy's neck—her smooth, warm, perfect neck—and kiss it softly, tasting her skin on my tongue for a brief second, before she climbs off me.

"Stop, enough people have seen me naked this week," she says with wide eyes, giving me a salacious smile as she quickly gets to her feet. She fumbles through a large mound of clothes on the floor and pulls out a T-shirt and a pair of her sweat-pants.

I get up and pull on a pair of joggers and head to the living room with a very sexy, messy-haired blonde on my heels. "Miles, you can't just barge in here anymore," I say when I see him.

"Don't look at me." He glances over his shoulder at Tristan, who has an annoyed look on his face.

"I called you like ten times," Tristan says, dropping his gym bag on the couch. "Hey, Luc," he says to her with an unapologetic smile. "How you doing?"

"Hey, Tristan," she says tentatively.

He looks at me and throws his hands up. "You want to beat Antoine Phillips or not? Because we've got to be on a plane to LA in a few weeks, and by the looks of you, you're not ready for him."

"Yeah, I want to fucking beat him. What kind of question is that?"

"Then get dressed and meet me in the gym. We were supposed to start a half hour ago." He picks up his bag and crosses my apartment. "See you later, Lucy. Sorry to wake you up."

"My phone was in the other room," I call after him. "I forgot you were coming at six thirty today."

He ignores me and disappears down the hall.

Lucy looks at me at me and sings quietly, "Somebody's in trouble."

I roll my eyes. "He had to wait thirty minutes. He'll survive."

"Well, while you two are working out your differences in the gym, I think I'm going to go get the rest of my things from Drew's house."

His name smacks me in the middle of my chest and my shoulders tense reflexively. "Okay, well…I can go with you. We can go this afternoon."

She presses her lips together and shakes her head. "You two are like oil and water. I think it's probably best if I go alone."

"Okay," I say reluctantly, ignoring every overprotective bone in my body.

"Why don't you let me come with you, sweetheart?" Miles offers, giving me a knowing glance. "After everything with the media this week, it's probably better to have somebody with you. Safer."

"He's right," I urge.

"Don't you have better things to do than be my bodyguard, Miles?"

"Yeah, actually, I do. But none that are more important. And I can spot a telephoto lens from a mile away."

Lucy smiles softly. "Okay, fine. But you're following in your own car." She points at him. "And you're not getting out."

Miles looks at me and I shrug. "You heard her."

She stands on her tiptoes and kisses my cheek. "Don't let Tris work you too hard."

* * *

"You're not focused," Tristan shouts at me over the music blaring through the gym speakers.

"What do you mean?" I hit the punching mitt on his right hand a little harder.

He circles the ring, leading me around the mat. "Since the Sanchez fight at the Garden, your head hasn't been in it. It's even worse since Ackerman. I don't know if it's because of the concussion or—" He stops himself, but I know what he was about to say.

"You weren't even at that fight," I grunt, smacking the other mitt. "So what do you know about it?"

"I know that if I was, you wouldn't have gotten a concussion first place. And you damn sure wouldn't have needed to take a three-week break on some remote island."

"Is that was this is about? You're pissed because I took a vacation?"

"I'm pissed because you're letting your personal life affect how you fight."

I hit his mitt and challenge, "Want to elaborate on that?"

"Okay. You got the shit beat out of you in Quebec and nearly lost the fight because you weren't focused on Ackerman. You were thinking about Lucy."

"Lucy," I shout, "is the only reason I won that fight."

"Yeah, well, like you said…I wasn't there, so what do I know?" He lowers his mitts and climbs out of the ring. "The new battery in my pacemaker is working great, by the way."

I drop my gloves and look at him, letting go of my anger. "I'm sorry, okay?"

He turns down the music and grabs a bottle of water. "I don't need your pity."

I cross my arms over the top rope. "It's not pity. It's just an apology."

"Well I don't need an apology."

"Fine, then I'm not sorry. I'm fucking pissed."

"Why?"

"Because you're twenty-seven and you have the heart of an old man."

He sits down and chugs his water. "Yeah, well, you don't need to worry about me."

"Okay, so then why don't you tell me why the hell you're so worried about *me*? I know you like to win, but—"

"Lucy." He gives me a frustrated look. "The way you are with her. It's ten times worse than when we were kids."

I feel my blood pulse as he crosses a dangerous line.

"Don't get me wrong. I like Lucy. She's was too good for you then, and she's too good for you now. She's a great girl, but—"

"She's *the* girl."

"Okay, then. If she is, you have your whole lives together. So just give me the next couple of years, because that may be all I've got."

I climb down out of the ring. "Come on, don't say that." I tug my laces with my teeth. "You know I don't like to hear you talk like that."

"It's a fact, Sam. The pacemaker's just buying me time."

"Says who? Your doctor?" I look up at him. "We'll find another doctor."

"All the doctors. There's no opinion here. My heart isn't going to last longer than a few years. If I'm lucky."

"What about a transplant? You're on the list."

"Someone gets added to the transplant waiting list every ten minutes. And about twenty people on that list die each day waiting on a new heart."

"Then I'll call somebody. I'll…get you moved up."

"You can't buy your way up the list, Sam. Your money can't save me."

A wave of anger rushes through me, leaving through my fist, which I pull back and slam into the nearest punching bag.

"What the hell are you doing?" he asks, jumping to his feet. He lifts up my glove and inspects the loose laces.

"That's fucking bullshit."

"Look, I care about winning, because this—you, Joe, the

ring—it's all I have. This is it for me." He tightens my laces back up. "I just want to see you win a few more belts. The right way."

"Okay."

"And it wouldn't hurt if you knocked out Antoine Phillips." He looks up at me and laughs. "I hate that cocky mother-fucker."

"That's the plan," I say over the tight feeling in my chest.

"You know…I do envy what you have with Lucy. I'm never going to have *the* girl."

"You don't know that."

"Find the girl of my dreams and then kick the bucket?" He laughs grimly. "I would never do that to someone." He shrugs. "It's just not in the cards for me."

"Hey…I'm sorry, okay? And it's not pity. I'm just sorry. Because I want it for you, brother. I really do."

"Yeah, well, just because I can't have *the* girl, doesn't mean I can't still have fun. Women love a guy with a heart defect. Especially when they look like me." He grins.

I tap my gloves together. "Don't think I won't hit a pretty boy," I say, knowing good and well I'd never hit him.

He puts his mitts back on and climbs into the ring. "Come on, then. Show me what you got, champ."

CHAPTER 6

LUCY

I drive down the familiar tree-lined street to Drew's house—my old house—pausing in front of it when I see Janice's car parked in the driveway. I need to talk to them both, but I wasn't planning on doing it at the same time.

Maybe I should come back later.

Miles pulls up behind me in his Escalade and I reluctantly pull into the driveway. *Is that thing supposed to be inconspicuous?* The matte back rims and blackout windows aren't exactly subtle. I park behind Janice's car, looking for signs of Drew, but I don't see his car. Maybe it's in the garage.

Miles parks at the end of the driveway and rolls his window down.

I get out of my car and give him a small wave, hoping he'll roll his window back up, but he just nods and watches me walk to the front door. I hold my breath and press my finger to the doorbell, but the door swings open as I push it.

Janice peers over my shoulder at Miles and asks, "Is that your security detail?"

I glance over my shoulder and watch him disappear behind his tinted window. "No. He's just a friend."

"I know who he is, dear." She presses her painted lips together into a tight smile. "I know everyone in this town."

I bob my head and smile uncomfortably over the uneasy feeling she stirs inside me. I knew this was inevitable and that it would be difficult, but I didn't know I would suddenly feel like the old me—the person I was with Drew—who I realize now was far less tenacious. *Be brave.* I clear my throat and ask, "May I please come in?"

"May I?" she repeats, raising her thinly plucked eyebrows. "So proper. And here I thought all the manners we taught you had worn off already."

I pry my tongue off the roof of my dry mouth, but before I can say anything, she leans in and adds, "Maybe it was just those tacky pictures making me think that. I'm sure you can imagine Drew's reaction when he saw them."

"No, actually, I can't," I manage to say over my pounding heart. It takes everything in me not to ask if she tipped someone off that I was there. *She wouldn't.*

"You really had us fooled, didn't you?" She splays her fingers over her chest and puckers her lips. "I suppose it's a blessing what happened, really. You would have tarnished the Christiansen name eventually. One can only hide their true colors for so long."

I swallow the hurt she inflicts, briefly wondering if mothers normally talk to their daughters like this—maybe she didn't care about me as much as I thought she did. I fight the tears that prick in my eyes and stand up straight. "May I come in now? Please."

Janice steps aside and lets me in, and the familiar smell of the house comforts me in a way that makes my chest ache.

"Is Drew here?"

"No, darling, he's out of the country."

"Out of the country? Where did he go?"

"He went to Europe. He was in Barcelona yesterday, but he's probably in Paris by now."

I release a quiet breath that somehow leaves my chest painfully tight. "He's on our honeymoon," I say quietly to myself.

"It was nonrefundable. It was transferrable, however, so he moved the dates up to get away for a little while."

"He went alone?" The thought saddens me.

"Don't be silly. He has several friends abroad."

"Oh…of course."

"So, what exactly is it that you need, dear?"

"I, um…" I close my eyes and shake off thoughts of Drew country hopping in Europe without me. "I just need to get the rest of my things. It shouldn't take long."

"Of course. Follow me." She leads me to the garage and points to two plastic bins labeled *Lucy* in black marker.

"He packed my things?"

"I did, actually. At Drew's request. He said it was too painful for him. You understand."

I swallow the lump in my throat. "Yes."

"Rest assured," she points to the bins, "everything that belonged to you in this house is right there." She smooths her shiny silver hair back and spins around. "Speaking of things you don't own…"

I pick my heart up off the cold garage floor and follow her

back inside, wondering what dagger she's going to throw next.

She grabs a manila envelope off the kitchen counter and hands it to me. "Drew wanted you to have this. Though, I can't imagine why."

"What is it?"

"It's the deed to the art studio."

"What?" I ask, shocked and a little confused. "Why?"

"My thoughts exactly."

"No." I hand it back to her. "I need to talk to him." I pull my phone out of my bag, but Janice wraps her long skinny fingers around my arm and lowers it.

"No," she says firmly, placing the envelope back in my hand. "Giving you the studio was his way of letting go. Now let him do that."

"But I can't—"

"Let. Him," she says again.

I swallow hard and blink back tears that fill me eyes, but one escapes and rolls down my cheek. "I can't. I'm sorry, but I can't take it."

"Yes you can."

"No I can't. It's not right. I won't."

"Lucy Marie Bennett, you listen to me, because I'm only going to say this once." She loosens her grip on my arm and the armor falls off her shoulders. "You are one of the most talented artists I've ever had the pleasure to know. You have a gift. Don't let my feelings, or anyone else's, get in the way of the success you deserve. Take the studio." She closes her eyes and lets out a sorrowful sigh that resonates through me and tugs hard at my heart. "Please. Do it for me. And do something great with it."

I press my lips together over the emotions that are sloshing around inside me. "I'm so sorry, Janice. I never meant for any of this to happen."

She rubs her fingers over her sparkly diamond earring and leans against the kitchen counter. "I know. We never intend to hurt the people who love us."

I smile weakly over the tears that keep coming. "I'll never forget everything you've done for me. And if you never forgive me, I understand. But…" I shrug and wipe my eyes. "I'll always be grateful for you. You made me feel like a part of your family and I'll never forget that."

She smiles softly and sighs. "I really wanted you to be a part of it."

"I know." I put my hand over hers. "Drew is really lucky to have you."

"Oh, pfff…I don't think he would say so."

"He is." I give her a sincere look. "Take it from someone who didn't have a mother growing up. He hit the jackpot with you."

She smiles over the sadness in her eyes. "Thank you."

I reach into my purse and pull out my key and garage door opener, placing them on the kitchen counter. "I suppose it will be a little while before I see Drew again. Will you make sure he knows I left these here?"

"I'll make sure he gets them."

"And would you please tell him to call me when he gets back?"

"I'll tell him."

"Okay. Well, I should probably get going. I'll just go get my things from the garage."

"Wait." She pulls me into a quick hug, wrapping her long, skinny arms around me. "Take care, Lucy."

"You too, Janice."

* * *

"Lucy," someone calls across the parking garage while Miles and I are unloading my belongings from his trunk. I look over my shoulder and see a bouncing brunette walking over to us with a glossy smile on her face. "Lucy, hey!"

"Hi, Molly."

"Do you guys need some help?"

"We got it," Miles says shortly.

"Thanks, I think we've got it," I say cordially. "But maybe you could get the elevator for us?"

She smiles and bobs her head. "Absolutely."

I text Sam to let him know we're back, and then I pick up one of the heavy bins and follow Miles over to the elevator.

"So does this mean what I think it means?" she asks with curious eyes.

"It means you need to mind your own business," Miles says to her, and I shoot him an exasperated look.

"Sorry, I didn't mean to—"

"You don't have to apologize, Molly." I cut my eyes at Miles. "Yes, it does. But please don't say anything to anyone, for now."

She presses her lips together and winks at me. "My lips are sealed."

I give her a tentative smile as we wait for the elevator doors to open, and when they finally do, we step inside. Molly presses the button for the first floor and we begin our *slow* ascent to the main level of the parking garage. When the doors eventually open again, I'm surprised to see Sam and Tristan waiting on the other side of them.

"Hey," Molly and I both say to Sam at the same time.

He looks at Molly and then he looks at me. "Hey," he says, reaching for the bin in my hands.

"You didn't have to come down here," I say to him, but he ignores me and proceeds to carry my things to the building.

"Is this everything?" he asks.

"Yep."

He glances over his shoulder at me and gives me a small satisfied smile.

"Let me get that for you, Sam," Terrance says when we walk into the lobby.

Sam smirks. "Thanks, but I think I can handle it."

"Oh, I know you can, champ." He walks beside Miles. "How about you, Miles? You need any help?"

"I might be a little thick around the middle, but I can carry a plastic storage bin, okay?"

Terrance laughs and shakes his head. "I don't know, I see you struggling."

"Get outta here," Miles says, and Sam and Tristan laugh.

"I'm Tristan, by the way," he says to Molly, flashing a big, bright smile at her.

"I'm Molly."

"It's nice to meet you, Molly."

Miles turns around and looks at them over the bin in his hands. "Molly and Sam used to screw."

"Miles!" I shout at him and he walks backward into Sam,

who has stopped in front of the bank of shiny stainless steel elevators.

"Just saying." He shrugs.

"Say less."

He smiles and turns back around to stand beside Sam.

"Real classy," Sam says to him.

"Hey, Miles, why don't you let me take that from you," Tristan says, reaching for the bin in his hands.

"Nah, I got it."

"How about you let Tristan take that from you," Sam says.

Miles looks at Tris and hands it over. "I got shit to do anyway." He shoves his empty hands into his pockets and begins to make his way back across the lobby.

"Miles," I call, and he spins around. "Thanks for going with me."

His face softens and he gives me a small smile. "Anytime, sweetheart."

We take the elevator up to Sam's apartment, stopping on the sixteenth floor to let Molly out.

"I'll see you guys later," she says to us. "It was nice meeting you, Tristan." She smiles softly at him.

"I'll see you around." He winks at her over the bin in his hands before the doors close.

When we get to Sam's apartment, Tristan deposits my bin in the foyer and picks up his gym bag. "I've got to go. But we'll start the same time tomorrow. Six thirty."

Sam stacks the bins together. "Yeah, okay."

"You"—Tristan points at me—"make sure he gets up on time."

"All right. I will."

Tristan gives me a wide smile, coaxing an unabashed smile back from me. He winks and turns around for the door. "See you tomorrow."

"Bye, Tristan."

Sam closes the door behind him and narrows his eyes at me. "What was that?"

"What was what?"

He shakes his head and smirks. "You got all girly just now."

"No I didn't."

"Yes you did."

I step around him and pick up one of the bins. "I don't know what you're talking about."

"You fell for the old Tristan Kelley charm."

I carry the bin to the bedroom and put it down on the floor. "Well, even if I did, so what?" I turn around and look at him. "He's got nothing on the spell you've cast over me."

He reaches for my hand and pulls me close to him. "Is that so?"

I smile and gaze into his watercolor eyes, the brown bleeding into the blue, and willingly succumb to the power they have over me. "Yes." I drop my eyes to his mouth, which yields its own kind of control over me.

"I need a shower," he says, releasing me with a knowing grin. "I've been training all morning."

"Okay." I watch him discard his sweaty shirt and shorts.

He looks at me before he rounds the corner to the bathroom. "You coming or what?"

I bite my smiling lip and begin stripping off my clothes, even though I already showered earlier. I take off my jewelry and pull my hair up, and walk into the bathroom, which is already starting to fill with steam.

When I step around the glass wall that encloses half of the shower, I pause to drink him in. His elbows are pointed up to the ceiling as he washes his hair, and lather is dripping down his chest and stomach, following the lines of the V between his hips. He rinses the shampoo from his hair and reaches for the soap.

"You didn't waste any time, did you?" I ask, stepping into the shower with him.

"Just wanted to get it out of the way."

I laugh and walk under the water, taking the soap from him. "Mind if I help?" I rub the soap between my hands until it lathers and then I rub it over his painted chest and shoulders, kissing his skin where the water rinses it clean. I walk around him and wash his back, taking my time massaging his thick muscles. I rub his round bottom and he groans quietly, sparking a fire that slowly sears across my skin.

He turns around and pulls me against him, pressing our wet bodies together, and his mouth consumes mine. I wind my fingers in his wet hair, and he tugs my bottom lip between his teeth before picking me up and pressing me against the shower wall. He holds me there while I wrap my arms and legs around him and then he reaches between us and draws his hips back, guiding himself into me with a husky groan.

I exhale a satiated breath as he fills me up and satisfies a place deep inside me. Then he pulls his hips back and pushes into me hard, making me cry out and hold on to him tighter. He does it again, and again, pressing me against the wet marble tiles with each strong thrust, over and over, until I can't take it anymore. I bring my mouth to his and kiss him hard, and he moves faster, sending flames racing across my wet skin, searing up my legs and wrapping around me until they've completely consumed me. "Sam," I cry, squeezing him tightly.

I soften beneath the weight of his strong body pushing me against the shower wall as he shudders inside me, groaning softly against my neck and grinding his hips against mine in an effort to bring us closer, as if it were possible.

He lifts his head and his shoulders rise up and down with ragged breaths. "I love you"—he smiles—"so damn much."

I hold his flushed cheeks in my hands and kiss his wet lips. "I love you too."

He lowers me onto my wobbly legs and I hold on to him as I find my footing on the wet tiles. "First shower sex," he says with a satisfied grin.

"Um, if memory serves me, we had lots of shower sex in the Bahamas. In lots of different showers," I say, narrowing my eyes.

"Vacation sex doesn't count," he says, following me out of the shower. "This was our first shower sex at home."

I laugh into a towel, but Sam pulls it away from my face and says seriously, "In our home. In our shower."

I pull my eyebrows together at the unfamiliar thought and nod, trying to will Sam's apartment to feel like home. But first I have to rid myself of the feeling that my real home is nestled on the tree-lined street I drove down this morning for the last time.

"You okay?"

"Yeah. I just need to unpack and get settled in, that's all." I smile and wrap myself in the towel. "Now that I have the rest of my stuff, I can do that."

"Speaking of which…" He follows me into the bedroom. "How did it go?"

"Drew wasn't there, so, fine I guess."

I see the contentment on his face as he watches me gather my clothes out of the pile in the corner of the room. "So how did you get your stuff?"

"Janice was there. And to say she wasn't happy with me is the understatement of the year."

"That bad, huh?"

"Janice Christiansen can be your best friend or your worst enemy. Right now, I'm behind enemy lines."

"I knew I should have gone with you."

"It was fine. She actually softened up a little before I left." I grab the manila envelope out of the bin I put it in for safekeeping. "She gave me this."

"What is it?'

I plop down on the bed and look at him. "The deed to the studio."

He furrows his brow and sits down beside me. "He just gave it to you? Free and clear?"

I shrug. "I told you, Drew's not a bad guy. Janice said it's his way of letting go."

"It's his way of messing with your head."

"What?" I roll my eyes at the notion—even though I wasn't planning on taking the studio free and clear—and I start getting dressed. "Is it so hard to believe that he just wants to move on?"

"Okay, let's say he does. But then how do you move on?" He gets up and heads back into the bathroom.

"What do you mean?" I ask, following him.

"It'll always be the studio that he gave you. There'll always be some small piece of him in it. You think he doesn't know that?"

"It doesn't matter if he does. I'm with *you*, Sam. I think we've established that."

"I'm sorry, I'm just having a hard time understanding. So he can buy you a studio and give it to you outright, but I can't?"

"I wasn't going to take it as a gift. I was already planning on talking to him about buying it…somehow. I still plan to."

"And you really think he'll let you do that now? He's already signed the deed over to you, Lucy."

"I don't know. Yes?"

"Luc, please…will you just consider buying a new studio? One that isn't tied to the Christiansens?"

I chew the corner of my mouth, trying to ignore the turmoil that's clouding my head. I love my studio. I love that it's where I met Sebastian and where I held my first art exhibit. It's where Sam and I found each other again. But it's also where Drew and I began our first venture together as an engaged couple. We oversaw the renovations together, we opened the doors together, and we celebrated it together. Sam's right. Drew will always be a part of its history.

"Okay. I'll think about it."

CHAPTER 7

LUCY

He wants me to buy another studio," I say to Sebastian, who pauses mid-sip and lowers his soy cinnamon dolce latte.

"But Drew gave you this one, no strings attached. It was the best-case scenario." He takes another sip.

"Sam thinks there *are* strings attached." I sip my latte macchiato and sigh. "He thinks it's Drew's way of keeping me tied to him. I don't know if it is or not, but it's really bothering Sam that Drew gave it to me."

"Well that sounds like Sam's problem."

"But, what if I feel that way a little too?" I ask over the rim of my paper coffee cup.

Bas takes my hand and drags me to the middle of my brightly lit studio, gesturing at the walls that are adorned with my paintings. "*You* created this. No one gave this to you. These paintings belong to you."

"Yeah, and they're hanging on the walls that Drew paid for."

He rolls his eyes and marches across the hardwood floor

to answer the studio phone that's ringing on the front desk. "Hello?...No comment." He hangs up.

"Who was that?"

"Nobody." He unbuttons the sleeves of his fitted navy blue dress shirt and begins rolling them up on his way back over to me. "Some stupid reporter."

"What were they asking about?"

He drops his head to the side and gives me a dubious look.

"Well, obviously, but I meant specifically. What did they want to know about me this time?"

"Your due date."

I choke on my coffee, spitting a little bit of it on Bas's shirt. "Sorry!" I say, pulling my hand to my mouth.

He flares his nostrils and wipes his front buttons with the inside of his wrist. "I assume you don't have anything to tell me."

"Of course not!" I shriek and grab my phone.

I Google Sam's name.

Sam Cole expecting first child with artist girlfriend.

Sam Cole's girlfriend pregnant with ex's baby.

"Uhh!" I huff, and keep reading.

Sam Cole trapped by unexpected pregnancy with girlfriend from his past.

Sam Cole and Lucy Bennett to marry this Christmas.

I look at Bas and start laughing hysterically.

The corners of his mouth turn down as he watches me. "Are you okay?"

"Yes," I say over the giggles that are bubbling out of me like a pot boiling over. "It's so...stupid." I laugh harder.

Bas starts laughing too. "After all these years, you finally trapped him."

"It was my master plan all along."

"And now you're having Drew's baby!"

I gasp for air in between wails of laughter and wipe my eyes, but the tears keep coming, and before I know it, I'm actually crying.

"Oh, honey," Bas says, squeezing my hand. "I told you not to read that crap."

"I finally got my big break with my exhibit and now everything I've worked for could be overshadowed by a bunch of lies. They shouldn't be allowed to write that stuff. And now they're talking about Drew? It's one thing if my career is ruined, but I'd never forgive myself if this affects Drew's. He's one of the hardest-working people I know. He shouldn't be a newsflash."

"Neither should you."

I nod softly and wipe my eyes. "I'm just glad they're not hanging outside the studio anymore."

"Look, I'll make you a deal. You promise not to Google yourself or Sam, and I promise to keep you abreast of any rumors worthy of a good laugh." He sticks out his pinky. "Okay?"

"Okay." I wrap my pinky around his and he gives it a shake.

"Now, more importantly. Have you found a dress for LA yet?"

"No, but I still have a couple of weeks. I'd like to get my stuff unpacked at Sam's first."

"Sweetie, you live there now. Stop calling it Sam's. And why haven't you unpacked yet? It's been days."

"A week actually. And I don't know. It just doesn't feel like home yet. It feels like I'm sleeping over or something, at a *really* nice hotel."

Bas holds his clean-shaven chin between his thumb and forefinger. "Maybe because you're living in an episode of *Lifestyles of the Rich and Famous.*"

"I know, right? It's weird. There's too much space, and everything's so perfect."

"Well, would Sam care if you changed some things around?"

"Like what?"

"I don't know, maybe you could start with a picture frame," he says seriously, and it makes me laugh. "Surely you took some pictures in Exuma."

I raise a mischievous eyebrow. "Perhaps."

Bas rolls his eyes. "One you could display in your living room."

I grin and pull up my pictures, and start scrolling through them. "What about this one?" I show him one I took of me and Sam on the beach with the turquoise water as our backdrop.

"That one's great. Now frame it and put it in your living room."

"Okay. I will." I put my phone down and follow him to the back of the studio. "Speaking of LA, are you sure you can't come?"

"As much as I like watching the Lucy-Sam saga unfold, I have my own love life to tend to. It's our anniversary that weekend, remember?"

"Oh, that's right. Speaking of your love life, how are things on the baby front?"

"For the time being, we aren't talking about it."

"How's that working out?"

"It's basically *me* not talking about it and Paul leaving adoption pamphlets on every surface in our apartment, like breadcrumbs."

"Have you read any of them? Maybe you'll find something in one that'll make you feel better about everything."

"On principle alone, no."

"Sebastian."

"Look, I'm not ready to be a parent, okay? And I honestly don't know when or *if* I ever will be."

"Have you told Paul that?"

"And crush his dreams? No way."

"Sebastian, you have to tell him. You can't just *not* talk about it."

"I know. He's taking me on a weekend getaway for our anniversary. Maybe after some relaxation, and a few drinks, I can bring it up."

"Where's he taking you?"

"I don't know." He twists his pen back and forth between his fingers. "Hopefully not Florida."

"Why? What's wrong with Florida?"

"Paul's family. His mother, specifically."

"Oh, Sebastian, she can't be that bad."

"Let's just say she's no Janice Christiansen," he says, biting the end of his pen.

I roll my eyes. "One is enough."

"Are you sure you don't want to reconsider your choice? I'd put up with Drew if meant we got to keep Janice."

"Sebastian."

"Ugh," he groans, and plops down onto one of the floor pillows. "I'm going to miss her. I should have known she was too fabulous to be true."

"She wasn't so fabulous yesterday," I say, sitting down next to him with my laptop.

"Well, what did you expect? You broke her heart—I mean, her son's heart." He smirks and sips his coffee.

"Yeah, well, as much as I hate to admit it, I'm going to miss her too. She was the closest thing I've had to a mother since I was little. Probably the closest I'll ever get."

He puts his hand over mine and drops his chin. "What I said before was shitty. I'm sorry."

"For what?" I ask curiously.

"Paul's mom isn't that bad. She actually gives really good skincare advice."

I laugh softly and give him an adoring smile. "So do you."

He closes his eyes and shakes his head. "So what you're saying is that…I'm the new Janice?"

I laugh and narrow my eyes. "You're just as fabulous, but way cooler."

He presses his fingers to his chest and inhales a dramatic breath. "I am, aren't I?"

"And you're a lot nicer."

"Well"—he shrugs a shoulder—"I try."

* * *

After two weeks of shopping for the perfect picture frame, I place the photo of me and Sam on the beach in Exuma beneath the glass, and carefully position it on one of the shelves next to the fireplace in the living room.

I take a step back to see how Sam and I look on display. I turn the frame to the left a little and take another step back. I move it to the shelf on the other side of the fireplace and consider it there. I turn it to the right this time.

"Perfect," Sam says, walking up behind me.

I turn around and take a step back when I see what he's wearing—a charcoal suit and matching vest, a crisp blue button-down, and a skinny gray tie. His hair is combed back, and his clean-shaven face showcases the dimples in his cheeks and the matching one in his chin. I reach up to loosen his tie and breathe in his warm, clean scent. "How'd your meeting with the endorsement people go?"

"Oh, you know, same as always. Miles talks, I nod, we all sign." He narrows his eyes. "Exciting stuff."

I smile at his indifference, because I know how much his endorsements really mean to him. "I didn't hear you come in."

"You looked deep in thought," he says, wrapping me in his arms.

"I wasn't sure about the frame. It took me a while to decide on one. Do you like it?"

"Yeah, I do."

"Are you sure? I know you don't really like a lot of knick-knacks."

He frowns softly. "When did I say that?"

"Well, you don't have any other pictures in your living room."

"Because I didn't have any pictures worth framing in my living room, until now."

I rest my chin on his chest and grin. "Maybe we could give it a friend?"

He laughs and rubs my arms. "Buy all the frames you want. You'll never have enough for all the memories we're going to make."

I smile wide and look over my shoulder at the picture again. "It feels homier already."

He gives me a curious look. "Homier?" He looks around the clean, contemporary space. "Is that what you want?"

I shrug. "It could use a little warming up in here."

"Why didn't you say something sooner?"

"Because I didn't want to move into your home and start asking you to change everything around. I've seen *How to Lose a Guy in 10 Days*."

"Lamb…" He smiles softly, showing me his dimples. "This is *our* home now. At least until we find something more permanent. I want you to make it yours. Change every room. Paint every wall. Put knickknacks on every shelf, if you want. I don't care. I asked you to move in because I want to share *our* home together."

"Really?"

"Yes." He puts his hand under my chin and says softly, "Just don't ask me to take care of a love fern, okay? I don't do plants."

I laugh. "No love ferns, got it."

He kisses me softly and I melt into his strong arms.

I move my hands to his waist inside his suit jacket. "I can't believe you've seen that movie."

"Yeah, well, it wasn't by choice."

"Molly?"

"Yup."

My phone whistles on the coffee table. I pick it up and read the text from a number I don't know.

Hey it's Molly. Just wanted to see if you've given any more thought to working together. Let me know!

"Speak of the she-devil," I say, turning my screen around so he can see the text. "How did Molly get my number?"

"I gave it to her," he says, shrugging out of his jacket. "I figured she could stop bothering me and go straight to the source."

I pull my eyebrows together and lay my phone back down on the table. "I don't know how I feel about working with her, Sam. Even though it *would* be a great way to get my name out there and showcase my work online. It's just...too weird, to be quite honest. I mean, you two slept together. A lot."

"It was casual."

"Is that supposed to make me feel better about it?"

"You should give her a chance. Her company has designed websites and created graphics for some pretty big names. A lot of clothing brands."

"Really?"

"Yeah. You should talk to her about it. See what opportunities she can offer you. She can be a pretty good friend too."

"Okay," I say, nodding softly. "I'll think about it. But, are you sure it wouldn't be weird for you?"

"Not weird. Molly has far better things to do in her free time than think about me. Like Tristan," he says nonchalantly.

"Molly and Tristan?"

"Yeah. They've been *talking*." He fights an amused smile.

"You're funny." I purse my lips at him. "So it really doesn't bother you that they *talk* now?"

"No. Molly's my friend. That's all she ever was," he reiterates. "If Tristan makes her happy, then that makes me happy."

"But Tristan's kind of a player, isn't he?" I ask, smirking.

"If Tristan could settle down with someone, he would, but he can't." He heads to the kitchen and grabs a bottle of beer out of the fridge. "You want one?"

"No, but I'll take a glass of wine," I say, hopping up onto the counter. I reach behind me and get a wineglass down out of the cabinet while Sam gets a bottle from the wine fridge.

He uncorks it and fills my glass.

"What do you mean, he *can't* settle down?" I ask.

He leans against the counter beside me and sips his beer. "Tristan doesn't think he'll live long enough to share a life with someone." He exhales a rough breath through his nostrils and takes another sip of his beer.

"What?" I ask over the shock that's suddenly squeezing my chest.

"His heart is too weak. Even with the pacemaker."

I climb down off the counter and stand next to him. "How long does he have?"

"A few years, maybe more if he's lucky."

I suck in horrified breath and blink back tears. "Isn't there something we can do? What about a transplant?"

"He's on the waiting list, but he has to wait his turn like everybody else. It could take years."

I sip my cold wine and swallow it down over the lump in my throat. "I'm sorry."

"Me too." He takes another sip of his beer. "Tris won't ever get to experience what we have."

"So then, Tris playing the field is really just Tris trying to live as much as he can before he..."

"Something like that."

"Does Molly know?"

"That's for them to work out." He shrugs.

I take another sip of my wine and exhale a breath that's laced with sadness I can't hide.

"Don't be sad, Lamb. Tris isn't. And he wouldn't want either of us to pity him."

"Tris isn't here."

He wraps me in his arms and kisses my forehead. "No, he isn't."

"It's going to be okay. Miracles happen."

He lets go of me and says softly, "Just look at us."

I give him a gentle smile. "Yeah."

"If Tristan were here, he'd tell us to stop moping and go pack for LA." He nods toward the bedroom. "Want to get started?"

"Can I bring my wine?"

"It's your house."

I smile and lead the way to the bedroom. "I wonder what LA is like in December? They must have the best Christmas lights with all the rich celebrities that live here," I say wistfully.

"I've never been in December, but I imagine the Christmas lights are pretty good."

"Maybe when we get home, we can put some up here... outside on the balcony? And...I was thinking it might be fun to put up a Christmas tree and celebrate our first Christmas to-gether."

"Okay." He smiles. "I'd like that."

I grab my notepad off the nightstand and scribble down *xmas tree* and *lights*.

"What else is on your list?" He looks over my shoulder and reads aloud, "Tampons."

"Sexy, I know. But it's reality. And I should be starting any day now, so this little honeymoon of ours is going to have to go on hiatus. Just in time for your pre-fight celibacy rule to take effect."

"Well, you see, that's not until tomorrow. Tonight, I'm all yours."

I fight a smile and shrug casually. "Good to know."

CHAPTER 8

LUCY

"Y ou ready?" Miles asks me as we pull up to the Staples Center in LA.

Although we've arrived at a back entrance of the arena, the SUV is surrounded before the driver even puts it in park. There were paparazzi at the hotel too, but only a few. Not like this.

"No."

"Okay, we can wait a minute, we have time."

"They're everywhere," I say, glancing up at the tinted windows.

"Look, Grady's gonna get out of the front seat first. He'll open your door and keep them all back while we walk in."

"I won't let anybody touch you, Lucy," Grady says in a gravelly voice that resonates from somewhere deep inside his barrel chest.

"Okay." I tug on the hem of my lacy long-sleeved cocktail dress where it hugs my thighs. Sebastian chose the merlot color for the holiday season. I wish he was here. *Note to self:*

Add "Must attend all boxing matches with Lucy" to his job description. Not sure how Paul will feel about that amendment.

"You look beautiful, Lucy. Just breathe," Miles says calmly.

I inhale a deep breath through my mouth and blow it out slowly.

"They're going to fire questions at you about Sam. Don't answer any of them. Just smile and walk to the door. Okay?"

I bob my head, but I don't move. I can't.

"We have to get out now."

"What if I trip? I'm nervous. I shouldn't have worn these shoes," I say, glancing down at the shimmery gold stilettos on my feet.

"I'll be right behind you. I won't let you trip." Miles says.

"Lucy, I'm going to get out now and open your door. Okay?"

"Okay."

Grady gets out and opens my door, and I'm flooded with unfamiliar faces and flashing lights.

Lucy, how's the baby?… Did you set a date for the wedding?… Over here!

I smile and focus on putting one high heel in front of the other, until I'm on the other side of the arena door, which Grady quickly closes behind us.

Miles looks at me and smiles. "See. You did it."

I nod and blow out a breath.

"You're not gonna throw up are you? You look a little pale."

"No." I roll my eyes. "I don't think so. I actually do feel a little queasy. I may *have* to resort to watching Sam's matches on TV. I don't think I'll ever get used to that."

He laughs. "Come on, Sam's around the corner."

A wave of relief washes over me, reminding me that Sam is worth the media mayhem.

I follow Miles down a long cinder-block hallway that's peppered with arena staff who are far too busy to pay any attention to me. He takes me into a dressing room that's filled with faces I recognize from the Quebec fight. Sam is sitting in a chair in the middle of them all, bobbing his head to the beat of whatever rap song is blaring through his headphones. I'm not sure who they all are or what exactly each of them do, but one of them is wrapping Sam's hands in white gauze and tape while another suited man is marking them up with a black marker. Sam seems oblivious.

I watch intently as they pull his gloves on and lace them up under the watchful eyes of the man I assume is the commissioner. He turns Sam's gloves over and inspects them, before giving his nod of approval and shaking Joe's hand.

I stand against the wall across the room, waiting for the commissioner to leave, but Sam notices me and stands up. He pushes his headphones off his ears and walks over to me. "Give us a minute," he says to his team, and they migrate to an adjoining room.

The determined look of a warrior slides off his face and his dimples make an appearance as he drops his eyes over me. "You look incredible," he says, wrapping his arms around my waist.

"Do they always do what you tell them to?"

"When it comes to you."

I run my hands over his shoulders. "Good to know."

"How was the ride in?"

"Fine. Did you know that I'm pregnant?"

"Is that so?"

"Mm-hmm. The paparazzi outside told me."

"Is it a boy or a girl?"

"Probably an alien."

"Well, as long as it's healthy."

"We're getting married too. Soon, I think."

"So you said yes then?"

I smile and put my hand on his scruffy cheek. "It's never even been a question."

"Luc, I know you didn't ask for all this, but I'm so proud to show you to the world. Thanks for being here tonight."

"There's no place on earth I'd rather be."

"Sam, we've got to go," Joe says, leading the rest of his team back into the room. He smiles at me and opens his arms. "Hey, Luc. You look great."

"Hey, Joe." I wrap my arms around him and give him a quick hug. "Thanks."

"Okay, quick introductions." He points to each person in the room and recites their names, "Leon, Mikey, Jordon, Will, and you know Tristan."

Tris winks at me and I smile at him over the tugging I feel in my heart.

"Fellas, this is Lucy."

They all smile and say hello over each other.

"Hey guys. It's nice to meet you all, officially."

"Lucy, come with me," Miles says. "We'll go take our seats while they finish up."

"Okay. Bye, champ." I smile at Sam, whose face hardens as soon as his eyes leave me.

I follow Miles out of the room, and Grady follows me as

we head back down the cinder-block hallway to a set of double doors that rumble to the beat of the music blaring on the other side. I should be used to this by now, but a wave of excitement and trepidation washes over me, making me feel light-headed.

I take a deep breath as Miles pushes one of the doors open, and then I'm enveloped by the energy of the excited arena. I follow closely behind Miles, sandwiched between him and Grady, as we walk in between two sections of screaming fans, whose faces are only occasionally lit by the bouncing blue lights that dance around the arena. Staff members with glowing red batons line the walkway and guide us to the brightly lit ring in the center of the crowded floor.

I quickly take my seat beside Miles, who leans in and shouts, "You hear that?"

I notice the sudden spike in applause and shout back, "Yeah. Is Sam coming?"

"No, look up. They're cheering for you."

I glance up at the giant monitors over the ring and see my face in ultra HD for the entire arena, and people watching on TV, to see. I smile shyly and lean into Miles again. "What do I do?" I ask, smiling over the mortification that's showing in my blushing cheeks.

"Just act normal."

"Right, just pretend my face isn't plastered across the monitors for everyone to see."

"You want to be with Sam? This is Sam's world. You gotta get over it, Lucy."

I nod and pull out my phone, which keeps buzzing inside my clutch.

Sebastian: OMG you're famous!

Sebastian: You look gorgeous!

Sebastian: I'm so jealous!

Sebastian: I'm coming w you next time!

Me: Good bc I'm making it a requirement of your job. FYI

Sebastian: Best job ever! Best boss ever

Me: I wish you were here. I'm freaking out

Sebastian: Doesn't show. You're doing great

I look up, relieved when they begin to showcase Antoine Phillips and flash pictures of him on the monitors as the announcers highlight his career achievements. I don't know much about him, other than what Sam has told me. He comes from a wealthy family and has had the best trainers money can buy. There's a steady roar of applause as the blue and white spotlights bounce around the arena, but when the showcase turns to Sam, the applause turns into thunder, like always, as the crowd cheers and screams and stomps their feet.

I gaze up at Sam in high definition, recalling the first time I saw his highlight reel at Madison Square Garden, and it still overwhelms me. I'll never get used to the sound of twenty thousand people screaming for him. No longer concerned with who's watching me, I beam with the same pride I felt that night, thinking about where he started. Where we *both* started. We were just a couple of kids from Brighton Park. And now look at us. He has everything he ever wanted. *And so do I.*

I know Antoine is making his way toward the ring because everyone's attention turns to the far corner of the arena as an entourage of people and flashing lights move through the crowd. My heart flutters with nervous excitement, because in just a few more minutes, Sam will be standing in the ring with him. I push down the worry that always accompanies Sam's matches and smile as the cheers and applause turn to thunder again. Everyone's attention turns to the opposite corner of the arena as Sam makes his way to the ring.

My heart stands at attention when he looks at me and I no longer notice the blaring music or thundering cheers. I only see him, climbing effortlessly between the ropes and taking the ring like the champion he is. He entices the crowd, jumping up onto the ropes and pumping his gloves in the air, and everyone goes crazy. But I no longer see the warrior they see. When I look at his strong body, I see his painted armor differently. All of his thick muscles that protect him in the ring are the same ones that hold me at night, that protect *me*. I have a feeling it's only going to get harder and harder to watch him take hits inside the ring. Especially after what happened in Quebec. Memories of him lying unconscious on the floor of the dressing room fill me with fear that I try to ignore.

I look at the tattoos that cover his chest and wrap around his arm, following the details of the ones that are spelled out, thinking of the day I painted them in my studio. A day that changed the trajectory of our lives. When he raises his gloves up and I see *Lamb* scrolled across his rib cage, I beam with pride and gratitude for the quiet gesture he made, long before our fate was sealed.

The fight begins and the familiar dance commences, leading the thundering roar of the crowd as Sam and Antoine begin to throw punches at each other. Sam takes the first hit, like he always does, and air hisses through my teeth, like it always does.

Sam Cole taking the first hit of the night… To give Phillips a false sense of advantage… That's right, Cole said recently that he likes to do a little reverse psychology, let his opponent think he's got the upper hand. The commentators laugh, but I don't find the humor in letting a heavy hitter punch you in the face on purpose. Isn't the idea to block the punches so your brain doesn't turn to mush? I personally like Sam's brain very much and would like it to remain fully functional.

Joe shouts from beside the ring, "Throw the jab, Sam, throw it!"

Antoine hits him again.

Another hit to the head for Cole and he loses his footing.

"Keep those hands up, Sam!" Miles shouts.

Sam stiffens his shoulders and throws an uppercut that leaves Antoine disoriented. Then he takes the opportunity to throw several punches at Antoine's ribs and face, pushing him across the ring into the ropes. But Antoine has a sudden burst of energy and explodes off the ropes, returning several punches to Sam's ribs, which had only just healed from the Quebec fight.

"Jesus." I gasp and grab Miles's arm.

"He's all right. He's not hurt."

"You always say that."

"He's not. He's on his feet. He's fine."

I watch the skin that covers Sam's ribs begin to pinken as the blood penetrates it just beneath the surface. *He's not fine.*

By the seventh round, it's clear that he has a broken rib. *Again.* The blood is pooling in a spot beneath his arm, and he's keeping his elbow drawn down to protect the area from another blow. He's in pain, whether or not anyone else can see it.

I glance at Miles, who's cheering Sam on excitedly. *Or is willing to see it.*

By the tenth round, Sam isn't the only one who looks like hell. He bloodied Antoine's nose in a hard blow to the face that knocked him to the mat. But it didn't keep him down long. He was back on his feet before the ten count and ready for more.

Antoine throws a right hook, followed by an uppercut and finally a jab to Sam's bruised ribs that knocks the light out of his eyes.

Sam falls to the mat and I scream behind my hands.

The referee counts, *One…two…three…*

The arena is going crazy and everyone is on their feet.

"Get up, Sam, get up!" I shout, but he doesn't, and I know he must be ravaged by the pain radiating from his ribs. I try not to think of the damage that's been done, but it's holding me prisoner to my seat, where I sit with my face in my hands.

"He'll get up," Miles says to me. "He won't stay down for the whole count."

But by *five*, when he's still not back on his feet, I begin to feel sick.

Screw the title. What's wrong with him? "Can't you see he's hurt?!" I scream at Miles, who doesn't argue with me.

"Come on, Sam! Come on, baby," Miles shouts at the ring. "You're the fucking champ. Get on your feet!"

This could be it for Sam Cole tonight…I'll tell you, after breaking his ribs in Quebec, a fight he nearly lost to Beau Ackerman, this might be enough to keep him down…He's definitely in a lot of pain.

Seven…

Sam pulls himself up on the bottom rope and drags his knee under him, and the crowd erupts again.

Eight…

"That's it, Sam. Get up!" Joe shouts from beside the ring.

Sam pulls his feet under him and stands up.

The referee stops counting and my heart begins to beat again. He grabs Sam's gloves and pushes down on them, and Sam nods to his question. He looks terrible, but he gives me a wink and I can't help but smile back, even if it's fleeting.

I don't believe it, he did it again…Sam Cole might just be the new comeback kid…Using the term kid *loosely, right?…I still think he's got a few good years left in him…I don't know, there's been a lot of talk about his retirement.*

"Retirement?" I say to Miles.

"Ahh, don't listen to them. Sam's not going anywhere. Not yet."

Sam takes his stance in front of Antoine, who immediately throws a punch at his face, but misses. *Thank God.* Sam screws up his battered face and lets out a ferocious roar that somehow settles the fear inside me. He begins throwing punches at Antoine faster than I can count, eventually knocking him off his feet and onto his back in the middle of the mat. The referee starts counting again, this time for Antoine.

One…two…three…four…five…

He isn't getting up, and the crowd grows louder with each passing second.

Six…seven…eight…nine…ten.

"Yes," I say quietly, closing my eyes with relief as the crowd erupts. When I open them again, all the guys are climbing up into the ring with Sam.

"You did it, baby!" Joe screams.

Once again, Sam Cole has defended his title as the undisputed light-heavyweight champion of the world!

Miles puts his hand on my back, and I begin to walk toward Grady, but he redirects me to the ring instead. He shows me a small set of steps and points up to the ring where Sam is hanging over the top rope waiting for me. Grady stands behind me as I carefully climb up the steps and I lean into Sam's heavy arms. "You scared me," I say to him, wiping his sweaty face.

"I'm sorry." He smiles and the people in the ring swarm him, but he kisses me before they pull him away. "I love you."

"I love you."

"Come on, Lucy, I'll take you back." Grady reaches for my hand and helps me down the steps, and I follow him to the dressing room, sandwiched between him and Miles, ignoring the voices shouting at us from the encroaching crowd.

When we reach the dressing room, I'm grateful for the silence. But it's fleeting. As soon as Sam and his rambunctious team enter the room, it's anything but quiet. A win for Sam is a win for all of them, but for crying out loud, he's hurt. Badly.

"He needs a doctor, Miles. Not a party."

"Okay, fellas, settle down." Miles says, and Sam falls stiffly into a chair.

"You did good tonight, champ, but you're hurt," Joe says, standing beside me and Miles. He kneels in front of Sam and lifts his arm off his bruised ribs, making him groan. The blood pooled under his skin is turning purple.

I pull my hand over my mouth, because what I want to say will have to wait until we're alone.

"You're not going to be able fight for a while. Not after this."

Miles rubs his hand over his chin. "He's under contract, Joe."

Joe gives him a hard look. "Is that all you care about? How he's going to make you your next million?"

"I care about his legal obligations. I care about *his* financial well-being. He signed a three-fight contract that begins in January."

"Oh, fuck the contract, Miles. Don't act like it can't be renegotiated. Start it in April. March, even. He needs time to heal properly. We'll get a physician to attest to it."

"And how do you think that's going to look with these retirement rumors swirling?"

"Knock it off," Sam says weakly, the adrenaline leaving his body.

"Sam, look—"

"Shut up, Miles."

"All right, we don't have to make any decisions tonight," Joe says. "Let's just get you looked at. You ready for the doc to come in?"

"Yeah."

"I'll go get him. Come on, everybody in the other room, you know the drill."

I begin to follow the group, but Sam calls my name, "Lucy."

I stop and walk over to him.

"Not you. Stay here. Please."

I glance up at Miles, who nods and says, "Doc's gonna come in and check him out. He'll tell us what the damage is."

"Okay."

"After you get a shower, we'll do the press conference," he says to Sam.

Sam looks up at me. "I want you to come with us."

"You want *me* to go to your press conference?"

He gives me a crooked smile. "Yes."

"Why? What do you want me to do?"

"Sit on the panel. Answer some questions."

"Sam…I'm not qualified."

"You're as qualified as the other bozos that sit up there with him," Miles says, giving me an encouraging smile. "Might be a good chance to set the record straight. Put some of these crazy rumors to rest."

"Okay." I nod thoughtfully. "I'll do it."

Sam smiles softly and mouths, *thank you.*

* * *

Sam wraps his arm around me despite his broken ribs and leads me to the media room for the panel interview. We stop outside the door and he smiles down at me. "You ready?"

"No."

He laughs and takes my hand as we follow Miles into the crowded room, which is much smaller than I thought it would be. He shows me where to sit and then takes the seat beside me behind a table fixed with stationary microphones. Joe and Miles take the other two seats next to Sam, and Tristan stands behind us with the rest of his team.

"Everybody calm down," Miles says to the buzzing room. "I know you're all excited about my new suit. I'll give you the name of my tailor after the interview is over. Okay?"

The intimate crowd laughs, and it helps ease my nerves, especially when Sam looks over at me with a beaming smile and accompanying dimples.

"In all seriousness, though, we have a new member of the team we want to introduce you to tonight. This is Lucy Bennett," he says, gesturing across the table to me. "One of the most exceptional artists and kind human beings you'll ever have the pleasure to meet. I expect you to treat her with the same level of respect she gets from all of us. And if you don't…well…" He laughs. "That's at your own risk, because Sam is very protective of his girlfriend."

My cheeks blush against my will, which is working desperately to keep them creamy white. I look up at Sam, who smiles and gives me a wink.

Miles points at one of the female reporters. "First question. And I'll bet I can guess what it is."

The crowd chuckles again and I can't help but admire the effortless way Miles took control of the room.

"As much as I'd like to prove you wrong, Miles, I have to ask"—she looks at me and raises her perfectly pointed eyebrows—"how did you land boxing's most eligible bachelor?" She holds her phone out to record my answer. "You're certainly not the first to try."

The other reporters laugh quietly behind her.

Sam leans into his microphone to answer the condescending question, but I put my hand on his shoulder to stop him. A lifetime of certainty about who Sam and I were long before any of this happened fortifies my answer. I lean into my microphone and say confidently, "Actually, I *was* the first."

"How did you meet?" another reporter asks out of turn, and Miles grumbles at him.

"In foster care," Sam answers anyway. "I've known Lucy for

most of my life. She's my day one," he says, glancing over at me, and I smile at his sweet words.

When the next reporter is prompted to ask his question, my smile wanes. "Lucy, you grew up in Brighton Park, correct?"

"Yes, I did."

"But you're trying to make it as an artist now. I understand you recently hosted an art exhibit in Atlanta."

"Is that a question?" Miles asks irritably, but I beam with pride anyway, delightfully surprised that he knows about it.

"Yes, I did. It was very successful. Thank you for mentioning it."

"So, how is it that you got into the art community?" he asks with a blank look on his face.

"I'm sorry, I'm not exactly sure what you mean."

"You grew up in poverty. You didn't exactly get exposed to the arts in Brighton Park."

Sam leans into his microphone and says, "Lucy's a born artist. The community found her. And yeah, we had a hard start in life, there's no denying that. But Brighton Park made us who we are. It's the foundation of my career, and Lucy's." He glances over at me again. "Hopefully one day, we can do something to give back."

I smile at him.

"She's a fighter like you, then."

"Absolutely."

"She must be," he says, taking his seat.

"I'm sorry, what exactly does that mean?" I ask as my nerves take a back seat to my defenses.

"Just that with such a rough background, it's got to be hard making it as a real artist."

"She is a real artist," Tristan says from the back, defending me.

"I'm sorry," Sam says, laughing without an ounce of humor in his voice. "Can you just elaborate on her rough background?"

"Just leave it alone, Sam," I say, away from the microphone.

The reporter stands back up and looks at Miles, who does little to help him. "Well, you grew up in the most impoverished suburb of Atlanta, which is known for its high crime, drug use, and poor education. That's pretty rough," he says carefully.

"You think those things pertain to her?"

"I don't see how either of you could have escaped them. Sam, you're a fighter, which that environment primed you for. But it's not one that lends itself to the arts. I imagine it casts a pretty big shadow that will be difficult for Lucy to escape, no matter how talented she is. Especially with the negative media attention she's been getting lately. Do either of you care to address any the headlines you've been making?"

"Yeah, they're all bullshit," Sam says.

"Look," Miles interrupts, "the only headlines you need to worry about are the ones that highlight Sam's win tonight."

"Is there a particular rumor you'd like to ask me about?" I ask the reporter, who insinuated that my career isn't going anywhere. If what he said is true, I don't have anything to lose anyway.

"Okay. I'll be frank."

"Oh, were you not being frank before?" I ask, and soft laughter fills the room.

"I didn't mean to offend you," he says, exasperated.

"Funny. I'm pretty sure you did." I shrug. "So, shoot. Which rumor would you like me to address? The one where I'm only with Sam because of his money? Or was it because he's famous? I can't remember." I shake my head and smirk at Sam. "I bet it's the one where I trapped you with a surprise pregnancy."

Sam crinkles his eyes and laughs.

"Oh, wait, it's not even your baby. According to that super reputable magazine that published the fake story," I say, looking at the reporter again.

"Okay, you've made your point," he says, appearing unamused as he crosses his arms and sits back down in his chair.

"I'm sorry," I say to him. "I didn't mean to offend you."

The room fills with light chuckles again.

Miles winks at me and leans into his mic. "Obviously the rumors are just that, rumors. I don't think we need to waste any more time talking about them. Next question. And make it about the fight."

CHAPTER 9

LUCY

So, how was Savannah?" I ask Sebastian, who's standing beside me in the store aisle gazing at boxes of Christmas lights stacked five shelves high. "Did you and Paul get a chance to talk about kids?"

"Yes. And it went okay, surprisingly."

"Really? That's great. What did you decide?"

"That we're going to start researching options together, so that when we're *both* ready, we'll be prepared and know where to start. But no pressure."

"Oh, Sebastian, that's great."

"You know what they say, marriage is all about compromise."

"I think that's a good compromise."

"Paul and I had a great time, but our weekend wasn't nearly as exciting as yours," he says with wide eyes. "I still can't get over how you put that asshole reporter in his place. I just wish I could have seen it in person."

"I don't know. It felt good in the moment, but I really hope

I didn't make things worse." I stand on my tiptoes and stretch for a box of white lights.

"Are you kidding? It was incredible. I mean, what decade is that guy living in? Overcoming adversity is something that deserves praise. Your story is inspiring."

"I hope so."

"Believe me. It is." He glances up and down the store aisle, which is adorned with blow-up Santas and snow globes. "You could put one of those tacky things on your balcony."

"Do you think it would fit?"

He stares at me for a long second. "No."

"Can you"—I stretch—"reach that?"

Sebastian reaches above my head and grabs the box of lights with ease.

"Thank you."

"What about a tree? I saw it on your list. You're not going to get a real one are you? The pine needles gets everywhere."

"I wanted to get one with Sam, but he's not supposed to lift anything heavy. Doctor's orders—which he *has* to follow this time."

"How's he doing?"

"They think his ribs didn't heal properly after the Quebec fight because he did too much in Exuma, so he's reluctantly taking it easy."

"Isn't that why you went to Exuma? So he could rest and get better. What the heck was he doing there?"

I raise my eyebrows and give an innocent shrug.

"Lucy! You could have at least waited until the second week to start the honeymoon."

"I tried! But he can be very persuasive. And athletic." I laugh softly and bite my bottom lip.

"Oh, my God, Lucy. That's...actually pretty hot," he says, picking up a box of lights. "But no more athletic bedroom antics until he's better, or he won't be able to keep fighting."

"Are you saying this is all my fault?"

He shakes his head, but before he can get a word out, I groan, "Ugh, it is my fault. This rift between Joe and Miles is because of me, isn't it?"

"What rift?"

"Since Sam got hurt again so soon, Joe wants him to stay out of the ring for a while. He wants him to take a real break from boxing."

"And Miles wants his paycheck."

"Well, I think it's more than that. I think Miles is thinking about the longevity of Sam's career." I look at him and ask, "Is that really what you think?"

"Well, isn't that what most sports managers want?"

I shake my head, considering it, but that's not Miles. "Miles loves Sam. He's just worried about the perception it'll give off if he's out of the ring for too long, because of the retirement rumors."

"I like these, get these," he says, handing me another box of twinkle lights. "So, are they just rumors?"

I give Bas a preposterous look. "He's not going to retire, Bas. He's twenty-seven."

"Yeah, and in the boxing world, that's practically an old man."

"What? No. That's crazy."

"Not when you've been taking hits to the head since you

were a teenager. You want him punch-drunk by the time he's forty?"

I try to ignore the worry Bas has painted all over me, but it sheens my skin in the form of dewy sweat.

He looks up from the box he's reading and stares at me for a moment. "Are you okay?"

I shake my head. "I feel like I…" I pant and swallow the saliva pouring into my mouth. "I think I—I think I'm going to be sick."

I throw the boxes of lights back on the shelf and run down the aisle, which thankfully has a *Restroom* sign hanging in the middle of it. I make it to a stall just in time to throw up.

"Hi. Pardon me. Sorry, my friend's in here," I hear Bas saying to the ladies walking out, who are mumbling under their breath. "Sweetie? Are you okay?"

I wipe my mouth and stumble over to the sink, where I proceed to wash my hands and face. I dry them with a paper towel. "I'm fine. I feel better now."

"I didn't mean to upset you. Geez. I wasn't expecting that reaction."

"I think I'm just feeling a little overwhelmed by everything right now. I wanted this, Bas, I did. I do. But it's a lot to take. Between the media constantly making up stories about me and Sam—"

"Which you dispelled during the LA interview."

"And the paparazzi splashing topless pictures of me across the internet. And Sam's ex-whatever-she-was pressuring me to work with her. And that stupid reporter insinuating I'm too uncouth to make it as a real artist." My eyes start to well up. "And Sam getting beat to a pulp for a living." The tears spill over and run down my cheeks. "Now he's going to be punch-drunk?"

"Lucy," Bas says softly, approaching me with caution.

"I just want to have a house that's mine and decorate it with Christmas lights and a stupid Christmas tree," I sob against Bas's shoulder, which is pressed firmly against my cheek now. "So much for having a nice, normal life."

He holds me and uncharacteristically lets me cry in his arms for several long seconds.

I step back and look at him with pathetic, watery eyes. "I'm sorry. I don't know what's wrong with me," I say into the rough paper towel in my hands that scratches my puffy eyes.

He pulls his dark eyebrows together and says, "Nothing's wrong with you. You've just had a lot to deal with lately. It's going to get better. The media will settle down, it's inevitable. One minute you're news, the next no one cares. Sure, there will people who make stuff up about you and presume to know things about your life, past or present, but that's true of anyone. And Sam isn't going to get punch-drunk, because you won't let him."

"Let him? Have you met Sam? When he wants something, no one can deter him."

"He wants you, Lucy. You're probably the only one who can deter him, which I know you would only do to protect him. So you have to be the voice of reason when that time comes. He'll listen to you. And only you."

I bob my head and wipe my nose. "How did you get so smart?"

He shrugs. "One of my many gifts."

I inhale a deep breath, discard the tear-soaked paper towel

in my hand, and splash some water on my face. I pat it dry and look at my pink nose and watery, pale blue eyes with matching pink rims.

Sebastian snaps a picture of me with his phone and I spin around.

"What are you doing? Delete that."

He shows me the picture. "Paint this."

"What?"

"Paint this. It's…a moment."

I pull my eyebrows together and drop my chin. "What should I call it? Bathroom Breakdown?"

"Stronger."

"Stronger?"

"Stronger," he says seriously. "Because you'll only get stronger from here."

I press my lips together and nod at his poignant interpretation of a painting I haven't even created yet. "I love you."

"I know. Now…" He glances around the bathroom with distain. "Can we please exit this public lavatory?"

"Yes."

* * *

I adjust the lights in my studio and position my paint cart next to my easel, which I lower a bit so I can reach the top of the four-foot canvas that it's holding. I gauge my blank workspace, but before I begin, my phone buzzes in my pocket.

"Hey," I answer.

"What are you doing?" Sam asks, and I smile automatically.

"Painting. I was about to anyway, before you called."

"You didn't have to answer."

"Yes, I did." I smile and tell him, "I'll always answer when you call."

"Good." He laughs softly. "It's getting late. You coming home soon?"

I look at the time on my phone. "It's six fifteen."

"It's after dark."

"I won't be too long."

"Want me to bring you dinner?"

"You'd do that?" I ask happily. I'm starving, and Sebastian left hours ago.

"Of course. What do you want?"

"Chicken biryani," I say without hesitation. I've been craving it all day.

"That's very specific. Care to tell me where I can find that?"

"It's Indian. You've never had it?"

"No. Can't say I have."

"Well, you'll love it, it's spicy. There's a really great Indian place around the corner from your—I mean, *our* apartment."

"Okay." He laughs. "I'll ask Terrance. Be there soon."

"Okay, bye."

"Lucy," he says, making me pause before I end the call.

I put the phone back up to my ear. "Yes?"

"Is the alarm on?"

"Yes. And the doors are locked."

"Good."

I push my lips together over a small smile. *Always the protector.* "Remember the code to get in?"

"Yes."

"Okay, hurry up. I'm hungry."

"Okay."

He hangs up and I slip my phone back into the pocket of my painted, tattered cutoffs and my stomach growls loudly. I grab my water bottle off my paint cart and take a sip, but it does little to assuage my hunger. My mouth begins to water, so I take another sip, but it doesn't stay down for long. I run to the bathroom and heave over the toilet.

I close my eyes as the nausea leaves me and get up to wash my face. I rinse my mouth with mouthwash and make a mental not to not skip lunch again.

I walk over to the couch on wobbly legs and sit down...*just for a minute*. I lean against the worn leather armrest and pull feet up on the cool cushion.

Lucy.

...

Lucy.

...

"Baby, wake up."

I crack my eyes open and see Sam hovering over me with small, concerned smile on his face. "Hey."

I sit up quickly and catch myself on his arm.

"You okay?" He laughs softly.

"Yeah." I pull my hand to my face and rub my eyes. "I guess I fell asleep. Sorry."

"What are you apologizing for?"

"I don't know. I just...didn't mean to fall asleep. What time is it?"

"Almost seven. You couldn't have been out long. I did get a little worried when I called a few minutes ago and you didn't answer."

I pull my phone out of my pocket and see his missed call. "I didn't feel it vibrate."

"You were out cold. You sure you're feeling okay?"

"Yeah. I feel okay. I got sick after we hung up, but—"

"You threw up?" His hand goes straight to my forehead, and it reminds of when we were kids. We always took care of each other when one of us got sick.

"Yeah, but I'm not sick. I just went too long without eating. I skipped lunch today."

"Oh." He makes a funny face. "Well, don't do that again."

"I won't, believe me." I breathe in the delicious smell of the warm, spicy chicken and rice and my mouth waters again. "Let's eat."

We sit on the couch, eating our biryani, which Sam soon discovers he loves as much as I do, and we catch up on the day. When he's full, he throws his paper bowl back in the bag and waits for mine, which I scrape clean before handing it to him.

"That was so good. Thanks for bringing it to me."

He props his elbow on the back of the couch and looks at me.

"What?"

"I don't know, there's just something about being here." He grins. "Seeing you in those shorts."

I wrinkle my nose at my ratty old cutoffs.

"Reminds me of that day we kissed, right over there." He glances at my easel.

I smile automatically, recalling how he made me drop my paintbrush. "I remember."

"Our first kiss."

"Not the first."

"The first one of the rest of our lives," he says, inching closer to me until our knees are touching. "I wanted you so badly. It took everything in me not to take you right here on this very couch."

I look in his eyes and fortify my defenses.

"I still want you just as much as I did that day." He wraps his hand behind my neck and leans in to kiss me. "Right here. Right now."

"Sam, we can't."

"Why?" he asks, caressing my neck with soft, warm kisses.

"The doctor said you have to heal, correctly this time."

He sits up and rolls his eyes.

"Don't you want to be able to fight again?"

"Not if it means I can't be with you."

I drop my head to the side. "Fighting or no fighting, you have to heal this time. I want you too, but preferably in one piece."

He gazes at me with his beautiful eyes and reaches for my hand. "I have been healing. I've been wearing the wrap every day since the fight, just like the doctor told me to."

"I'm not really in the mood," I lie, and the look on his face sends my heart plummeting.

"Oh." He pulls his hand back. "Okay." He forces a small smile.

"I've just got a lot on my mind right now." I put my hand over his. "That's all."

He flexes his fingers beneath mine and laces them together. "Like what?"

"You, my career, the fate of my studio." I glance around and sigh heavily.

"Well you can take me off that list."

"Are you kidding? You're in bold caps and highlighted in yellow."

"Why? I'm fine." He gives me a serious look. "You don't have to worry about me, Lamb. Nothing's going to happen to me."

An incredulous laugh escapes quietly between my lips. "The fact that you think that is what worries me. You're not invincible, Sam." I hold his stare until he looks away. "Look at me," I say, squeezing his hand. "You are all I have."

He looks at me and says, "I know. You're all I have too."

"Then protect yourself. For me."

"What is it that you want me to do, Lamb? Just say it and I'll do it."

I stare at him for a moment, trying to lift the weight of his words off my shoulders. "Listen to Joe. He loves you like I do, and he knows what's best for you. Take a break from boxing."

He inhales a slow, deep breath through his nostrils and stands up.

"Just for a little while."

He studies me for a few seconds and then puts his hands on his hips and says, "Okay."

Okay?

I stand up and he wraps his arms around me, and I hide beneath them, afraid to face the fact that I've just become a wedge between Sam and the other love of his life—boxing. But Sebastian's words echo in my ears, and I know that it's the only way to protect him.

"You ready to go home?" he asks, releasing me.

"Yeah." I'm not really in the mood to paint anymore.

We lock up the studio and ride to the apartment together in unusual silence.

I lied when I said wasn't in the mood, because I wanted to protect him. I asked him to take a break from boxing, because I wanted to protect him. But what's the good in protecting him if I'm just hurting him in other ways?

"I'm sorry," I say, reaching for his arm.

He looks at me and then slows the car to a stop on the side of the road.

"I shouldn't have asked you to stop boxing. I did it because I'm scared, and I knew that you'd take a break if I asked you to. But it was selfish and I'm sorry. I want you to do what *you* think is right. And I'll support your decision, no matter what it is, because I love you."

"I know you do." He reaches for my face, tucking my long hair behind my ear. "You don't have to be sorry."

"And I lied."

He pulls his chin back and looks at me curiously.

"When I said I wasn't in the mood before. I lied."

He laughs softly.

"I just don't want you to hurt yourself again."

"Lucy, making love to you is not going to reinjure my ribs."

"What about last time? In Exuma."

"I wasn't careful in Exuma, because I was so freaking happy to finally have you all to myself."

I smile softly, recalling how he could barely wait to undress me in the Bahamas.

"We'll just be more careful for now, okay?"

I unbuckle my seat belt and lean across the middle console, until I'm practically in his lap. "Okay." I shove my hands in his caramel hair and kiss his full lips, finding his tongue with mine. He groans against my mouth and rocks his hips up, then slowly pushes me back by my shoulders, until our lips are no longer touching. "Maybe we should wait until we get home. I'd probably injure more than my ribs trying to do it in this car."

I laugh and fall back into my seat. "Good point."

I buckle back up and the engine purrs as he pulls back out onto the road. "I have a surprise for you," he says casually, watching the road, but the smile he's trying to hide bubbles excitement inside me.

My eyes light up with intrigue. "What kind of surprise?" I ask, like a child, and he smiles openly.

"You'll have to wait and see."

* * *

Sam blocks the door to our apartment when I try to open it.

"What are you doing?" I ask, looking up at his excited face.

"Close your eyes," he says, watching me until I do. He takes my hand and asks, "Are you ready?"

"For what?"

He opens the door and pulls me several feet into the apartment. "Okay, open your eyes."

I open my eyes and gasp when I see a beautiful Christmas tree glowing in the middle of the living room adorned with sparkling white lights and shiny glass bulbs. There's a fire crackling in the fireplace beyond it and more white lights twinkling on the balcony outside.

"Sam…how did you do all this?"

He follows me into the living room. "Sebastian, as it turns out, is *very* good at this sort of thing."

Of course. It looks like he hired a professional.

"He and I worked all afternoon while you were at the studio."

I turn around and carefully wrap my arms around him. "I love it. I love *you*. It's beautiful."

"I wasn't sure about the tree—it's not real—but Sebastian insisted. Is it like you wanted?"

"It's more than I wanted. It's perfect."

He smiles and kisses the top of my head. "I saved a few boxes of ornaments so we can finish decorating it together."

I look up at his one-of-a-kind eyes, silently scolding myself for being so selfish back at the studio. "I don't deserve you."

He pulls my face to his and kisses me softly. "I think you've got that backward."

We spend the next half hour hanging the rest of the ornaments on the tree, and it fills me with a since of normalcy that erases all of the worry and stress from earlier in the day.

I reach for Sam's hand and pull him into a hug in front of our beautiful Christmas tree, but his phone starts buzzing in his pocket, vibrating against my hip, before I can tell him how happy I am.

He pulls it out of his pocket and grumbles, "This better be important, Miles." He listens for a few seconds and then his face grows serious. "Okay, I'm on my way. Tell Joe I'm on my way."

He hangs up and my heart races inside my chest. "Sam, what is it? What's wrong?"

"It's Tristan. He's in the hospital."

"Is he okay?" I ask, knowing he must not be if he's in the hospital.

He shakes his head, but doesn't answer. "I've got to go."

I follow him across the apartment to our bedroom, but he turns down the hall and goes into the gym instead.

"Sam, what are you doing?"

He goes straight for a punching bag that's suspended from the ceiling and punches it hard.

"Sam! Stop!" I shout, and he freezes. "You can't do that."

He puts his hand on the bag and stops it from swinging, and then drops his head against it.

I stand behind him and put my hand on his back. "It's okay."

He turns around wraps his arms around me.

"Whatever it is, it's going to be okay," I say to him.

"He's not okay," he says against my shoulder.

"I know." I lift his head and look in his worried eyes. "Come on, I'll go with you."

CHAPTER 10

LUCY

"One latte macchiato," Sebastian says, handing me a cup from the coffee shop across the street.

"Thank you."

"It's the least I could do after that pompous curator in Dallas dropped you from his hoity-toity exhibit. That you didn't want to be a part of anyway," he says, rolling his eyes behind his clear-framed glasses.

"I never said I didn't want to be a part of it." I sigh and put my coffee down on my desk.

"I added that part in, but let's just go with it, okay? Besides, would you really want to work with a gallery that considers artists based on where they grew up, instead of their extraordinary, unmatched talent?"

"I just hope it's not an indication of what's to come."

"Lucy, it doesn't matter where you grew up."

"Well, it obviously does to some people," I say, swiveling my chair from side to side.

Sebastian sits on the corner of my desk and says, "Those

who mind don't matter, and those who matter don't mind."

"What?"

"You still have six other invites from galleries that think your *work* is amazing, including Aurelia Snow. That's what matters."

"I know. You're right." I sip my coffee. "Hey, can you mail this for me today?" I hand him a sealed envelope that contains a lengthy letter I wrote to Drew.

He takes it from me and eyes Drew's name scrawled on the front. "What's this?"

"A letter for Drew."

"Okay, is this nineteen eighty? Who sends a letter?"

"Well, if he would return any of my calls, I wouldn't have to."

"Maybe he's still in Europe."

"We planned a two-week honeymoon. He should be back by now. And I know Janice told him I stopped by while he was away. She promised she would tell him to call me when he got back." I shrug. "He's obviously still upset."

"Can I ask what's in the letter?"

"Everything. An apology. A thank-you. Well wishes. And my plan to sign the deed to the studio back over to him...*after* I figure out a way to buy a new one."

"Well, your sales are through the roof right now. By the end of the month, you won't have a single painting left in this studio to sell. Besides *Lionheart*," he says, tapping his fingers together.

"It's not for sale, Bas."

"Just checking to see if you changed your mind. I bet you

could get even more for it now with all the media attention on you and Sam."

"I haven't changed my mind," I assure him.

"A shame. It would pay for a new studio and a bonus for your amazing assistant."

"Noted." I laugh. "Hey, have you looked into the dates for the other exhibits that I'm *still* invited to? We probably need to start making travel arrangements."

"Yes, but they're all next winter and spring. The only one before then is Aurelia Snow in June. Which is actually kind of perfect, because if everything goes well in New York, the price tag on your paintings will soar for the other shows."

I nod pensively. "It will also give me time to focus on finding a new studio. And time to rebuild my dwindling portfolio."

"Speaking of which, how's the painting coming along?"

"I'm making progress. But it's been hard to focus since we got back from LA. Between getting my invite rescinded, everything that's going on with Tristan, and worrying about Sam, it's been hard to stay motivated. I've just been so tired lately," I say, leaning back in my chair.

"How is Tristan?"

"He's better. He's at home now, but he's not going to be able to help Sam train anytime soon."

"Train for what? I thought Sam was taking a break."

"He is, for now. They renegotiated his contract to start in March, instead of January." I give him wide eyes and shrug. "At least they pushed it back a couple of months. But he has to start training again after the new year with some new guy."

"Speaking of Sam, what did you get him for Christmas?"

"Nothing yet."

"Lucy. It's in two days!"

"I know! I just haven't really been in the mood to shop. It would help if I could shake this stomach bug."

"What stomach bug?" He stands up and makes a disgusted face. "How long have you had it?"

"Since the store incident. That was the start of it."

"Well, have you thought about going to the doctor?"

"It's not that bad. It sort of comes and goes. I just get these waves of nausea. But after I throw up, I feel better."

"That doesn't sound right. Have you been losing weight?" He drops his eyes over me.

"No, I don't think so. Probably because when I'm not puking, I'm eating everything in sight to make up for it."

Sebastian's face falls and he carefully gauges me for a few uncomfortable seconds.

"What?" I ask, shrugging a shoulder to fend off his intrusive look.

"Lucy Marie Bennett, tell me it hasn't crossed your mind at least once that you might be pregnant."

I stand up quickly. "Um, no, actually. Why is that always your go-to diagnosis?"

"Oh, I don't know, have you had sex with Sam?" he asks sarcastically.

I roll my eyes and insist, "I never miss my birth control pill, Bas. Ever."

He reaches for my hands and holds them between us. "Honey, birth control isn't one hundred percent effective one hundred percent of the time. That's like sex ed 101."

I'm thankful he's holding my hands, because I suddenly feel weak in the knees. And nauseous. "My period's late," I whisper, and he presses his lips together into a thin line. "I thought it was from all the stress I've been under." I let go of his hands and take a few wobbly steps back. "Oh, my God, I've been *so* nauseous, Bas. I'm nauseous right now." I walk aimlessly out of my office and fall onto the couch. "I've been starving and emotional." I look up at Sebastian, who's squinting his eyes as if to somehow reject the inevitable conclusion. "I think I'm pregnant."

"Oh, my God." He sits on the couch beside me. "What do we do?" He scans me from head to toe and then reaches for my feet. "Here, put your feet up," he says, pulling them up onto the couch.

"Sebastian, I need to take a pregnancy test."

"Right. Good plan. That's what my sister did. It was a first something... First Watch?"

"I don't know, but they're always right next to the tampons. Seems contradictory," I muse.

"Okay, let's go get one."

"What? No way."

Bas gives me a confused look.

"Bas, I can't go into a store and buy a pregnancy test. Someone will tell someone and before you know it there'll be another rumor swirling that I'm pregnant with Sam's baby."

"But you are pregnant with Sam's baby."

"We don't know that."

He rolls his eyes. "Okay, we'll just stick with the whole stomach bug that acts exactly like a baby theory and see what happens."

I drop my head to the side and ask, "Will you please go buy one for me?" I press my palms together in front of me. "Please?"

"Fine," he says, getting to his feet. "I'll be back in ten minutes."

"Okay." I get up and walk behind him. "What should I do while you're gone? Should I paint? Can I paint? Can you paint when you're pregnant? Shit, Sebastian, I've been painting every day."

He smiles. "Can I see the painting?"

"Focus, Bas."

"Right, okay. First Watch, on its way."

Sebastian leaves me in an ocean of anxiety with a strong undertow, but I fight against the current. *What am I going to do? What am I going to tell Sam? Will he be happy? What if he's upset?*

I fall back onto the couch and take slow, deep breaths.

How can I have a baby? I don't know anything about babies. I don't know anything about being pregnant! I thought I had a stomach bug. I'm like one of those ladies who has their baby on the toilet because they didn't know they were pregnant.

I get up and pace around the studio for the next several minutes.

Oh, God. I'm not cut out for this. I can't do this.

I pass the painting I've been working on and stop pacing when Bas's words echo in my head. *You'll only get stronger from here.* I close my eyes and inhale a deep cathartic breath, my hands moving to my stomach as if by their own will. *I'll be strong for you.*

"I'm back," Sebastian shouts from the front of the studio, and my hands fall to my sides. I turn around and see him walking toward me with a white plastic bag in his hand.

"That was fast," I say, wishing it had taken him a little longer.

"I went to the drugstore on the corner. There wasn't a line." He pulls a pink box out of the bag and hands it to me. "I'd offer to help, but..." He makes a funny face that reflects my own.

"I'm good, thanks." I take the box from him and hurry to the bathroom, closing the door behind me. I don't know what's worse, being pregnant or wondering if I'm pregnant. Or knowing that Sebastian is standing on the other side of the door, waiting for the answer.

I take a deep breath and open the box with shaking fingers. Inside, I find two paper-wrapped pregnancy tests, like little Russian fertility dolls, and tear them open. I place them on the counter while I carefully read the instructions and then follow the accompanying picture guide.

When I'm through, I wash my hands and exit the bathroom, leaving my fate to be determined on the back of the toilet.

"What did it say?" Sebastian asks, quicker than his mouth can move.

"I didn't look. The directions said it takes a few minutes to work."

"Oh." He nods and paces a few times. "Okay."

I reach for his hand and pull him over to me. "I need a hug."

"Me too," he says, wrapping his arms around me.

"What am I going to do if I'm pregnant, Bas?"

"You'll rock it, like everything else in your life."

"What are you going to do if I'm pregnant?"

"I'll support you and throw you a kick-ass baby shower."

I squeeze him tight, inhale a fortifying breath, and release him. "Okay, let's check."

He looks at me and bobs his head. "Okay, let's do it. I'm ready."

I turn around and tentatively open the bathroom door, but Sebastian crooks his neck over my shoulder and pushes me inside. I fight my self-preserving instincts telling me not to look and pick up one of the tests.

"Oh, my God," Sebastian says, looking at me.

I stare quietly at the matching pink lines in the little plastic window for several long seconds.

"I'm pregnant," I finally say over the pounding in my chest. "Sebastian"—I look up at him with disbelief—"I'm pregnant."

"Are you sure it's not wrong?" he asks, looking at the other test still laying on the back of the toilet. He presses his lips together and shakes his head. "Nope," he answers his own question. "You're pregnant."

"I'm pregnant."

His eyes widen and a tentative smile stretches across is handsome face. "You're pregnant."

"Yeah," I say, bobbing my head, and my eyes mist over.

"Oh, my God!" He wraps his arms around me. "You're going to have a baby! I'm going to be an uncle! I'm much more comfortable with this scenario." He releases me and pulls me over to the couch. "You need a doctor. And prenatal vitamins. And folic acid."

"What's folic acid?"

"I don't know. But I read about it in one of Paul's surrogacy pamphlets. You need it." He pulls his phone out of his pocket and starts tapping the screen with his thumbs.

"Bas," I say, pulling one of his hands away. "I have to tell Sam first."

"Right…of course." He stares at me expectantly.

"Not right now, Bas!"

"Why not?"

"I can't tell him this over the phone. I may never see him again."

He rolls his eyes and drops his head to the side. "You're procrastinating. And being a little dramatic."

I look at my hands in my lap and exhale. "I know. Sam's talked about having a family since we were kids. I just…I want to tell him in person, Bas."

He presses his lips together over a small smile and says, "I think you just found his Christmas present."

*   *   *

"It's like the whole city has shut down tonight," I say to Sam, stepping out onto our snow-covered balcony. I rub my bare arms and peek over the edge at the empty streets below.

"Well it's not every day we get snow in Atlanta," Sam says, wrapping me in the blanket draped over his shoulders. "Let alone on Christmas Eve."

I turn around in his arms and snuggle up against his warm body. "Remember that time it snowed like this when we were kids? You turned the garbage can lid over and pulled me down the street with a jump rope?"

"Yeah, Maxine was pissed because we put a hole in the lid. Couldn't have been more than an inch or two of snow on the ground." He laughs and rests his chin on the top of my head. "Our kids will have the best sled money can buy."

My heart jumps and races inside my chest, but before I can pry my tongue off the roof of my mouth, he pulls my lips to his and ignites a fire within me that warms me all the way to my bare feet, which I'm pretty sure have frozen solid.

"Sam," I mumble against his lips, but he pulls me back inside. "I have to tell you something," I manage in the three seconds it takes him to drop the blanket and slide the glass doors closed.

He looks at me with fire in his hungry eyes, as warm as the flames crackling in the fireplace.

"It can wait." I reach for his handsome face and his dimples cast tiny shadows on his cheeks in the glow of the Christmas tree. I wind my fingers into his wavy hair, which has grown longer in the last couple of months, and press my body to his.

He exhales a heavy breath and reaches for my waist to pick me up, but I grab his hands and push them away. "Sam, no."

He grumbles against my neck and presses me against the wall with his warm body. "It's been two weeks," he growls against my ear. "I'm better."

I shake my head and pant, "You can't pick me up. You're still healing."

"Fine." He gives me a salacious smile that makes me giggle. "Have it your way." He spins me around and holds my hands against the wall while he slowly kisses my neck. He presses his hips against my bottom and groans softly. "Don't move." He slides his hands over my waist and hooks his thumbs inside my pajama pants, tugging them down my legs. Moments later, his bare hips are pressed against me and the chill that lingers on his skin sends goose bumps down my thighs.

I exhale a slow breath that's laced with anticipation as he pushes my feet apart and snakes his arm around my stomach. But when he squeezes my tender breast through my thin cotton cami, I let out an unintentional yelp.

"I'm sorry," he says, turning me around with a worried look on his face. "I didn't mean to hurt you."

"You didn't hurt me," I say, ignoring my throbbing breast.

"Yes I did."

"Sam, I'm fine." I press my hand to his concerned face, trying to ease the worry in his eyes, and trying to wield my tongue to tell him that he's going to be a father, but it just won't cooperate.

LUCY, SEVENTEEN YEARS OLD

"You shouldn't be wearing that skirt," Sam says, squeezing my hand as we walk to school.

"Well, I thought it was going to be warmer today, but now I'm wishing I hadn't. Why? You don't like it?" I ask, looking up at him with big innocent eyes. I can tell that he does.

He pulls me into the doorway of an old abandoned building and spins me around so that I'm pressed between its cold brick exterior and his warm body. He places his hands on the crumbling wall by my shoulders and leans into me. "I like it. But so do the wolves." He takes my face in his hand and says softly, "You're so beautiful, Lamb. You don't even know it." He trails his hand down my neck, tracing my collarbone with his thumb, and pushes my jacket off my shoulder, sending a shiver through me when the cold air touches my skin. "And so pure," he says, kissing my neck below my ear. "You have no idea what they'd do to you."

I press my finger to the middle of his broad chest and drag it down his sweatshirt, feeling his muscles flex beneath it. "That's why I have you. You've always protected me. And I've never felt afraid," I say honestly.

He pulls his eyebrows together and drops his head. "What if I wasn't there?"

"You always are." I give him a reassuring smile and bring my lips up to his.

"Yeah," he says, dragging his lips to my ear. "I always will be." He brings his mouth back to mine and kisses me firmly, pressing himself against me so that I feel every line of his strong body against mine. He drops his warm hands to my cold thighs and runs them up my legs, groaning against my mouth as he squeezes my bottom under my skirt.

He picks me up and I wrap my legs around him, savoring the heat coming off him. "We can't," I say, winding my fingers in his hair, unable to stop kissing him. "We have to go to class." I try unsuccessfully to convince him, and myself. "Sam." He ignores me and kisses me harder, and I kiss him right back. "Not here," I finally say, giving in with a conflicted grin. We should really go to class, but he should really keep kissing me.

He gives me a salacious smile and puts me down. "Come on," he says, pulling me around the side of the building.

"Where are we going?" I ask, eyeing the strewn newspapers and flattened boxes that line the alley to the back of the building.

"There." He points to a ladder that leads to the roof. "Come on."

"You want me to climb up that?" I ask, dismayed as he tugs on the bottom of the ladder, checking its stability.

"Yeah, it's safe. You can go first. I'll follow, in case you slip."

I narrow my eyes at him. "Wouldn't have anything to do with the skirt, would it?"

He gives me a wicked grin. "Of course not."

I wrap my hands around the cold wrought iron and step up onto one of the rusted rungs. It wobbles a little under my weight, but feels relatively sturdy. Sam follows me as I climb up the side of the building, groaning when the wind blows my skirt up.

"Knock it off," I say, reaching for the last rung.

"Not possible."

I pause and look down at him, pursing my lips over a smile I can't hide.

"Don't stop, you're almost there." He winks at me and gives my bottom a push over the top.

"Holy crap, it's cold up here." I rub my arms through my jacket.

Sam drops his book bag and pulls me into his arms, wrapping me in his sweatshirt. When the wind isn't blowing, the sun is actually pretty warm. "Better?" he asks, rubbing my back.

"Yeah." The sky is so clear, I can see all the way to downtown Atlanta, where the tall buildings stagger across a small section of the horizon. "It's actually really beautiful up here. So quiet. Kind of makes you forget all the crap down there," I say, looking out at the low brick buildings that make up Brighton Park.

"We're going to get out of here one day, Luc."

"Promise?"

"Yeah. I promise."

I exhale a quiet breath. "How?"

"You're going to get a scholarship after you graduate next year and you're going to go to college."

I rest my chin on his chest. "No, I'm not."

"Lucy, yes you—"

"No," I exclaim, "not without you." It doesn't matter if I get a scholarship. It won't do me any good without Sam.

He nods softly and shrugs. "Joe thinks I have a real shot at boxing. Maybe that's my ticket out. If it is, I'll work night and day to be the greatest boxer this world's ever seen."

I smile wide. "Like Muhammad Ali?"

"Float like a butterfly, sting like a bee."

"And we'll live in a big house?" I ask with wide eyes.

"The biggest."

"And we'll eat pancakes every morning?" I ask, remembering how Maxine never wanted to make them for us.

"With bacon."

"And I'll be able to paint whenever I want?"

"Whenever you want."

"And we'll have a family? A *real* family?" I gaze up at his beautiful eyes shimmering in the bright sun, imagining a little boy or girl with eyes just like his.

He reaches for my face and tucks my windblown hair behind my ear. "Yeah, we'll have a family."

I carefully wrap the hope up and give it to my heart for safekeeping. "I love you, Sam. Even if none of that ever happens, I'll still love you. You're my family."

He holds my face in his hands and nods. "I love you too."

* * *

"Sam…" I gaze up at his unusual eyes, wondering if our baby will have them too. "I have something to tell you."

"What is it?" His voice is laced with unnecessary concern.

I swallow hard and force myself to confess the secret I've been holding in since yesterday. "I'm…pregnant." I pull in a deep breath with no indication of when it might be released.

"You're what?" he asks, unable to hide the shock in his voice.

"I'm pregnant." I press my trembling lips together and nod. "We're going to have a baby." I stand frozen against the wall and wait for him to respond, but when he doesn't, I begin to wonder if maybe it wasn't the right time to tell him.

After a long silent second, he takes a step toward me and reaches for my face. He looks at me with watery eyes and then kisses me hard.

I laugh softly over the tears that spill onto my cheeks. "Does this mean you're happy?"

He drops his forehead to mine and says huskily, "Yeah. I'm really happy."

"I know it wasn't supposed to happen this like this, Sam, but—"

"Yes it was…we just didn't know it."

I swallow down the emotion that's flooding me and nod. "Yeah."

He closes his eyes and shakes his head. "I'm sorry I was rough before. If I had known…"

I smile and reach for his handsome face. "I'm fine, Sam. My boobs are just a little sore, that's all." I laugh softly.

"When did you find out?"

"Yesterday. I wanted to wait until tomorrow to tell you. It was supposed to be your Christmas present."

He takes my hand and pulls me over to the couch, and we sit in the warm glow of the fire. "Lamb, you've already given me everything I've ever wanted." He gazes at me and says, "You." He puts his hand on my stomach and rubs it softly. "This baby…our baby"—he pulls his eyebrows together over his stormy eyes—"is more than I could have asked for." He looks up at me and says with awe, "We're going to be family."

"Yeah." I nod over the lump in my throat. "We're going to be a family."

He pulls me into his arms and I curl up in his lap.

"Look"—he points to the dark windows that surround the living room—"it's snowing again."

I look outside and see little white snowflakes floating gently through the night sky. "It's so beautiful."

He looks down at me and brushes my hair off my forehead. "Since you gave me my Christmas present early, I guess I can give you yours."

"You got me something?" I ask excitedly.

He pulls me to my feet and over to the Christmas tree. We

stand in front of it and I admire the beautiful ornaments glowing against the white lights.

"Lucy, you're the first person who loved me. Did you know that?"

I look up at him and smile softly.

"I'd never even heard that word spoken to me, until you said it for the first time."

I nod over the crack that shoots across my heart.

"But I knew I loved you long before that. I could feel it inside me like a force of nature." He smiles softly. "As the days and years passed, it became as necessary as oxygen. When it was gone, I couldn't breathe. I tried to, but without you..." He traces my face with his fingers and tucks my hair behind my ear. "I was half alive. I never want to feel that way again, Lamb."

I inhale a shaky breath. "You don't have to."

He looks at the Christmas tree and reaches for one of branches. "I got you this," he says, pulling a small ribbon off the tree. He holds up a diamond ring that's tied to the end of it and I suck in a stunned breath. "Marry me, Lamb. Be with me for the rest of our lives. Stay with me forever."

I nod and cry, "Yes. I'll marry you, Sam."

"Yeah?" He exhales and blinks his watery eyes.

"Yes," I cry. "Of course."

He reaches for my left hand and slides the sparkly ring onto my finger.

"I'll never leave you, Sam. I'm yours. Forever." I put his hand on my stomach and vow, "We're yours."

CHAPTER 11

LUCY, THREE MONTHS LATER

I hold Sebastian's arm so I don't topple over in my high heels as we make our way ringside behind Miles.

Miles stops and says something to one of the announcers seated in front of a laptop and a microphone.

He looks up and smiles at me as I pass him.

"What was that about?" Bas shouts in my ear over the music blaring through the arena speakers. The bass echoes off the cement floors, reverberating all the way up through my body and vibrating through my chest.

"I don't know." I shrug and follow Miles to our seats. I want to sit down, but the buzz of the crowd keeps me on my feet. Everyone is clapping and cheering with excitement, including me. I smile at Sebastian, who has a giant grin on his face.

"Okay, *these* are the best seats we've ever gotten," he says, looking up at the ring. "Paul's going to have to up his game."

"I think we might have a new in." I laugh. "Is he feeling any better?"

"What?" Bas shouts, dropping his head to mine.

"Is Paul feeling better?"

"He's fine. He's a total baby when he's sick. I still can't believe he passed this up." He smirks and turns his attention back to the ring, where two tall bikini-clad models are posing and blowing kisses to the camera.

"Haven't we moved past this as a society?" I ask, watching them strut around in their sparkly bikinis.

"Ring girls have been a part of the glitz and glam of boxing since the sixties," Bas answers. "I mean, if they didn't hold up signs indicating the next round, how else would anyone know?" He laughs and I roll my eyes.

"They've got nothing on you," I say, glancing at his burgundy slim-fit tuxedo jacket.

He straightens his black bow tie and runs his fingers down the middle of his pleated white shirt. "It does say old Hollywood, doesn't it?"

"It has Gene Kelly written all over it."

"The fact that you know who he is makes me immensely happy," he says seriously.

The girls leave the ring and the lights dim, igniting the crowd. They hoot and holler and clap even louder as red and blue spotlights move around the arena to the beat of the music. When I hear the intro to Eminem's "Phenomenal" begin to play, I know that Sam is entering the arena. Apparently so does everyone else, because the entire arena goes crazy, shouting and screaming in unison.

Sebastian gives me excited eyes. "This is crazier than Madison Square Garden!"

"Sam said when he fights in Atlanta the crowd is on another level."

"How you doing? You all right?" Miles asks, checking on me.

"Yeah."

"Sam's coming," he says, pointing up at the monitors over the ring.

"I know." I look up and watch him move through the crowd with Joe and the rest of his crew. Except for Tristan, who's in the hospital again. Thankfully Molly is there with him.

Leon and Mikey hold up two of Sam's belts, showing them off to the excited crowd, and they shine in the spotlight that's following them to the ring.

Defending titleholder Sam Cole is making his way to the ring through the excited crowd as his beautiful fiancée, Lucy, cheers him on.

Sebastian nudges me, barely containing his excitement, and I smile over the butterflies that suddenly fill my stomach. I look at Miles and he gives me a wink.

Like Sam, she, too, is a product of the foster care system here in Atlanta… You can definitely hear the excitement in this hometown crowd tonight… Joe Maloney, his longtime coach, encouraged him to take a few months off after he reinjured his ribs during the Phillips fight at the end of the year, but I'll tell you, he looks stronger than ever… He sure does. Andre Ricci has his work cut out for him tonight.

Sam climbs into the ring and my heart races on cue, like it always does when he's about to fight.

LUCY, THIRTEEN YEARS OLD

"What did you say?" Sam says to the boy who just called me a snowflake.

The boy crosses his arms over his chest and leans against the chain-link fence that surrounds the basketball court at our school. "I wasn't talking to you." He looks at me and winks, and it ties my stomach into knots.

"Sam, don't," I plead when I see his shoulders tense, but he ignores me and lunges toward the boy like an unstoppable freight train.

He grabs his shirt and pulls him off the fence, shoving him back several feet down the sidewalk. When the boy gets his footing, he charges Sam like a bull, but Sam catches him and shoves him off, throwing a right hook at his face that cuts his cheek.

"Sam, stop!" I shout, but he hits him again.

My heart pounds in my chest, but there's nothing I can do to stop him.

A crowd quickly gathers around us, and they shout with encouragement.

"Stop it!" I scream at them, but I might as well be invisible.

The crowd jumps up and down like heathens, egging them on.

The boy hits Sam in the mouth and a small cut begins to bleed, but Sam doesn't seem to notice. He hits the boy hard, knocking him to the ground, and grabs his shirt. "Don't you ever look at her again. You hear me?"

"Hey, hey, hey!" a man shouts, breaking through the crowd, and they all scatter like roaches. He grabs Sam's arm and pulls him up, but Sam yanks his arm away.

"Get the fuck off me."

"Hey!" he shouts at Sam, shoving him against the fence. "You don't know me. Don't talk to me like that."

"You don't know me!"

"Oh, I know you. You're what, fourteen, fifteen years old? You want to beat everyone up who looks at you or your girl the wrong way. I *was* you." Sam tries to move, but the man holds him against the fence. "Listen to me. You like to fight?"

"I don't like to fight. I have to fight," Sam grits through his teeth.

"Nah, that's an excuse. I know you like to fight. I can see it your eyes."

"So what if I do?"

"Then fight like man, not like some dog on the street."

"What?" Sam struggles against his hold.

"I own a gym. It's not far from here. I teach kids how to box. Kids like you, who love to fight."

Sam stares at him and relaxes a little.

"I can teach you how to fight like a man."

"Why do you give a fuck about me?"

"Watch your mouth. You want to fight like a man, you have to act like a man."

"Why do you care?"

"Because I've seen what kids like you can be. You want to

waste your life away in the Park, getting into street fights, getting into trouble, maybe even going jail…be my guest. Or you can come by my gym and let me teach you how to fight for real, show you how to earn respect for knocking people out."

Sam stares at him for a few seconds and then nods. "Yeah… okay."

The man takes a step back. "My name's Joe. Joe Maloney." He stretches his hand out in front of Sam and waits for Sam to do the same.

Sam reaches out tentatively and shakes his hand. "I'm Sam."

"Nice to meet you Sam. You got a mean left hook."

"Thanks," he says warily.

"You all right, sweetheart?" Joe asks me.

"Yeah." I inhale a shaky breath. "I'm okay."

"What's your name?"

"Lucy."

"You like seeing him fight like that, Lucy?"

"No," I say, keeping my eyes off Sam.

"I didn't think so."

I glance up at Sam, who's looking at the ground.

"Boxing isn't like that. There are rules, protective gear. You come by the gym with him, so you can see, okay?"

"Okay."

"You come by tomorrow," he says to Sam. "I open at six a.m. on Saturdays."

"Okay." Sam looks up at him.

Joe looks him up and down and nods. "Don't let me down, Sam. Don't let her down either," he says, looking at me.

Sam gives me apologetic eyes. "I won't."

* * *

I sit on the couch in Sam's dressing room with my feet in Sebastian's lap, watching a live stream of the interview Sam's doing in the next room.

"You sure you don't want to make a surprise appearance?" Sebastian asks, straightening his cufflink.

"One appearance tonight was enough," I say, folding my hands over my tight stomach. "I'll be shocked if no one noticed the newest member of Sam's team tonight."

"The dress should have thrown them off. No respectable woman in her second trimester would wear something that smoking hot." He cuts his teasing eyes at me and winks.

"Sebastian!" I smack his arm. "You picked this dress out."

"Yeah, well, your boobs look fantastic in it."

I glance down at them. "I think they've gotten bigger since last week. How is that possible?"

"You're four months pregnant, it's normal. So I hear."

I narrow my eyes at him and smirk. "You've been reading the baby books again, haven't you?"

"Well, Paul asked me to. And I need to know what's going on with you." He closes his eyes and shrugs a shoulder. "It's my job."

"So, are you and Paul any closer to crossing into baby territory?"

"Well, I'd like to say your unexpected news didn't spark the baby bug in me, but it did a little," he says, pinching his fingers together.

"Really?" I ask excitedly.

"Yeah. Now that I've gotten used to the idea, I think we might start seriously looking into adopting."

"Sebastian!" I smile. "That's great news."

"Well, it could still take a really long time."

"Sam, tonight was your twenty-sixth win, but it was another shaky match," a reporter says to him, and we both turn toward the TV. "You were on the ropes a lot."

"And he got off them," Miles says.

"You've taken a lot of hits lately, Sam. Have you given any thought to these retirement rumors?"

"They're just that…rumors," Miles interjects again. "And they're gonna stay that way. Sam's not going anywhere."

"I'm not giving my title up anytime soon." Sam smirks.

"But you do have a wedding coming up, right?" the reporter asks.

Sam leans into his microphone again. "We haven't set a date yet."

I look over at Sebastian. "Because I'm not going to be able to fit into a wedding dress in the foreseeable future."

"Which is exactly why you need to do it sooner rather than later!"

"Bas, I know you want us to have a wedding, but honestly, there's something about planning two weddings in one year that just feels, I don't know, *wrong*."

He waves his hand at me and rolls his eyes.

"Have you even thought about what that would do to Drew? Or how hard all this must be on him?"

"Um, no, not really…because you're not with Drew anymore. And for all you know, he's already got another wife lined up."

I'd say the thought hasn't crossed my mind, but when he didn't reach out to me after my letter, I couldn't help but wonder if a woman was the reason why. And I couldn't help but feel a little hurt by his silence. Still, I don't want to cause Drew any more pain than I already have.

"Seriously, Sebastian. Do you realize the baby is due a week before Drew and I were supposed to get married? That's going to be a hard enough pill to swallow, don't you think?"

"I suppose," he says, swallowing one of his own.

"What did he just say?" I ask Sebastian, after one of the reporters says something about Sam taking another break before his next match.

Bas shakes his head, but Miles chimes in again. "Champions don't take breaks. As soon as that eye heals, he'll be training for his next match."

I roll my eyes and exhale a worried breath. "Two more matches. And then this contract is up, the baby will be born, and Sam will have to take another break. I don't care what Miles says."

"Don't worry about Miles, Lucy," Joe says, joining us in the dressing room. "Sam will do what's right for his family. There's nothing more important to him than you and the baby."

I sit up and nod.

"He asked me to take you back to the hotel. He's going to be at least another hour. You ready?"

"Are you sure you don't want to stay for the rest of the interview?"

Joe gives me a knowing glance. "I just want to be his coach. I'm not interested in his PR. I leave that up to Miles."

I smile and yawn. "I am pretty tired."

Sebastian looks at his watch. "I should get going too. It's almost midnight."

"Wouldn't want you to turn into a pumpkin," I tease.

"It's a good thing the match was in Atlanta. I'll be home before the clock strikes twelve."

I laugh and give him a kiss on the cheek. "Drive safe, okay? Call me when you're home."

"Will do."

"Give Paul my love. Tell him I hope he feels better."

* * *

I yawn and slouch against the passenger door in Joe's car as he pulls out of the arena parking lot.

"How ya doing?" he asks me.

"Just tired."

"That's not what I mean." He glances over at me. "How are you, Luc? How are you handling everything?"

"Great," I say, giving him a small smile.

He laughs softly. "I've known you for over half your life. Now you're going to lie to me?"

I pull my eyebrows together and look at him. "I'm not lying."

"I've seen that look before. Not since you were a kid, but you're scared. I just can't figure out if it's because of the baby or Sam."

I nod slowly and admit, "At the moment, Sam."

He exhales a heavy breath. "Yeah, I'm worried about him too. I don't like what I saw tonight. I don't like what I've seen the last few fights."

"You have to talk to him, Joe. I can't be the only one. I've tried that before, but...I can't be the wedge between Sam and his career. Even if he won't admit it, he'll resent me. I know it."

He looks over at me and smirks. "So you want me to be the one he resents?"

"Of course not. It's just…he thinks of you like a father. He'll listen to you. He's always listened to you."

He stares at the road in front of us. "I watched that kid grow into a man. And then become a champion. I can't imagine a father more proud of his son that I am of Sam." He shakes his head and smiles softly. "Now he's going to have a kid of his own." He glances over at me. "He has a family to support now. It's not just about the fight anymore, Lucy."

I put my hand on my stomach. "What good is money going to do us if he's punch-drunk?"

"I won't let that happen." He looks over at me again. "You have my word."

I bob my head and watch the headlights of the car behind us grow closer in the side mirror. "Who is that?" I ask, looking back out of the rear window of his SUV. "I can barely see their headlights, they're so close."

We stop at a red light and another car pulls up beside us. The driver gets out with a camera.

"Joe."

"Damn paparazzi. That's who you should be afraid of."

I grip my phone and shrink in my seat, trying to ignore the man outside my tinted window.

When the light turns green Joe floors it. "I can lose them."

"Joe, you don't have to. Jimmy won't let them inside the parking garage," I say, tightening my seat belt down around my hips.

"You really want them to know where you live?"

"No."

"We'll go around the next block a couple of times. There's a one-way street I think I can lose them on."

"Just please be careful," I say, griping the door handle.

Joe turns left at the next block and speeds down the street between rows of parked cars. I call Sam, but like I expected, he doesn't answer. He's still talking to the press.

Hey, this is Sam. Leave a message.

"Hey, call me when you're done. There's stupid paparazzi following us home. Joe's trying to lose them, but at this rate, you'll get there before we do. I just wanted you to know. Love you, bye."

Joe takes a sharp right that shoves me into my door. "Joe!"

"I think I lost them," he says, glancing in his rearview mirror as we near the end of a narrow tree-lined street that's lit by a glowing green traffic light. "You okay?"

"Yeah, I'm fine. But I've never seen you drive like this." I laugh nervously.

"Yeah, well, I'm not usually being tailed." He keeps his foot on the gas. "I can make the light."

I look over at him and nod, but as we approach the intersection, I'm blinded by headlights that are glaring through his window. I barely have time squeeze my eyes shut and wrap my arms around my stomach before I'm pulled by a force unlike anything I've felt before. It shatters the windows and bends the steel in a crescendo of screeches and cracks that resonate through my elastic bones, which no longer feel a part of me, until—just as suddenly as it began—everything falls silent and still.

There's no noise. No motion. Just the putrid smell of burning rubber and the blinding pain that's radiating down my leg and wrapping around my torso.

I cry out, but when I breathe in, my lungs fight against me and my chest screams like it's on fire. I lift my heavy head and see the glowing blue lights on the dashboard flickering on and off through the powdery smoke that fills my nose and blurs my vision. "Joe," I whisper, without enough air in my lungs to speak any louder. But there's only silence.

Something buzzes on the dashboard, lighting the cracks that stretch across the windshield, and I see Sebastian's face reflected in the broken glass.

I lift my arm over the deflated airbag and reach for my phone, but my seat belt is pinning me to the seat. I try to unbuckle it, but it's locked in place. I stretch my arm out as far my seat belt will allow, and scream with frustration when I can't reach it.

I fall back against the seat and close my eyes and tears leak onto my cheeks. "Joe?" I croak, but he doesn't answer. I look over and see his head hanging. I lift my arm again and reach for his shoulder. "Joe," I cry, shaking him gently, and he groans. "Joe," I say, relieved, and cry softly. "You're okay. We're going to be okay." I pull my hand back and put it on my tight stomach. "We're okay," I whisper, trying to move my seat belt down, but it's squeezing me so tight. I wiggle my hips a little, but the pain is excruciating. "Ahh," I cry, and it takes my breath away.

"Stay…still…" Joe mumbles, and I cry harder.

My phone buzzes again and I see Sam's face reflected in the cracked windshield. "Sam," I cry, desperately trying to reach my phone, but the pain is excruciating.

"Tell him…I love him," Joe says, and the tears run in rivers down my cheeks.

"Don't say that. You're fine."

"I love you…too."

"You're fine!" I shout at him.

"Tell…Tristan."

"Joe, no…just talk to me. Just keep talking to me." I hear sirens echoing down the street. "Do you hear that? Help's coming. You're going to be fine. Joe, do you hear me? Joe?" My head pounds and my heart feels like it's going to beat through my chest. I inhale a shallow breath, but it does little to ease the dizziness inside my head. I close my eyes, but I can't fight against it.

LUCY, SIXTEEN YEARS OLD

"Do you really have to practice on your birthday?" I ask Sam, following him into the gym.

"I have a match next week, Luc. I have to be prepared. And it's training, not practice," he says, narrowing his eyes.

"Is there a difference?"

"You practice to win a game. You train to be a warrior." He winks and throws his gym bag over his shoulder.

"Okay, Maximus." I purse my lips together over a smile as we head to Joe's office in the back.

"Where is everybody?" Sam asks, looking around the empty gym, which is usually buzzing with energy and dripping with testosterone.

"I don't know," I say coyly, spotting Joe and Tristan over his shoulder.

"Happy birthday," they shout in unison, charging toward him.

I squeal and jump out of the way as they tackle him to the floor.

Joe gets to his feet and reaches for Sam's hand. "Come on, we're going out for pizza."

"Pizza? What about training?"

Tristan wraps his arm around Sam's shoulder and pats him on the chest. "You want me to kick your ass around the ring, or you want to go get some pizza?"

Sam laughs and drops his chin. "Pizza. Definitely pizza."

"That's what I thought."

"Come on. It's my treat," Joe says, grabbing his keys off his desk.

Sam looks at me and I turn my palms up and shrug innocently. "I may have mentioned that it was your birthday."

He smiles and wraps his arm around my neck, and we follow Joe and Tristan outside.

"You're closing up early?" Sam asks Joe, who's locking up behind us.

"Yeah, it's a special occasion."

"You don't have to," Sam says, shaking his head.

"I know I don't. But I want to."

Sam smiles and takes my hand, and we follow Joe to his car. "Everybody buckled?"

"I am," I say, giving Sam a disapproving look.

He reaches for his seat belt. "All right, all right."

"You should always wear your seat belt." I reach for his hand. "It could save your life one day."

"Who needs a seat belt with Joe behind the wheel?" He smirks and Tristan laughs.

"Oh, you guys think it's funny to drive safe?" Joe asks them.

"Well there's driving safe and then there's just plain driving. Are you sure your foot's even on the gas?" Tristan teases, and I can't help the smile that turns the corners of my mouth up.

"You see all these nut jobs?" Joe asks, pointing to another car rolling up to a stop sign across the street.

"The old lady who can barely see over the wheel?" Sam asks, shaking his head.

"Yeah, well that old lady might just roll right through the stop sign."

Sam and Tristan give each other an amused look and then laugh in unison.

"It's called defensive driving," Joe says, shaking his head. "If you're lucky, I'll teach you two knuckleheads when you get your own licenses."

"Which at their rate will be never," I say, looking at Sam with wide eyes.

"What's the point?" he asks, shrugging his shoulders. "It's not like I'm going to get a car anytime soon."

"Kid, you're going to have a car someday, trust me," Joe says, looking at him in the rearview mirror.

"You think so?"

"I know so."

I give Sam a small smile and squeeze his hand.

"If I ever get a car, I'm going drive right out of this shithole and never come back," Tristan says, gazing out of his window at the rundown buildings that line the street. You wouldn't know they're open for business with their torn-up signs and covered windows.

"Never say never," Joe says to Tris, watching the road in front of him.

"You know, I never understood why you came back here," Tris says to him. "I mean, you can't really care that much about helping kids. Did you lose all your boxing money in a bet or something?"

Joe smiles and shakes his head. "I wouldn't expect you guys to understand. Not for a few more years anyway."

"I've been told I'm mature for my age," Sam chimes in, and Joe smirks.

"My father raised me just a few blocks from here," he explains.

"You're father?" Sam gives him a confused look. "I thought you were raised in the system, like us."

"I was. But not until I was older, maybe sixteen."

"My age," I say, intrigued.

"What happened, did he run out on you or something? Did he go to jail?" Tris asks, but Sam and I both listen quietly from the back seat.

"No, nothing like that. He was a good man. Firm with his words and quick to set me straight when I mouthed off. He taught me to be a man. Taught me to believe in myself, and to believe in something better, something more than this," he says, glancing at the neglected houses outside. "He used to tell me about what it was like when he was growing up here. Not like it is now. It was a lot different back then."

"No drug dealers back in his day, huh?" Tristan says.

"Maybe not standing on the street corners hawking to kids, but there have always been drugs of some sort, as far back as history tells. It's the people who were different. They cared about their community and education for their kids. Houses were kept up and business was booming."

"Come on?" Tris says, dropping his head to the side.

"No, really. Brighton Park used to be one of the most popular neighborhoods in Atlanta back in the fifties."

"No kidding," I say, fascinated.

"So when did it all go to hell?" Tristan asks.

"Not until the eighties. But before that, it was a different place, far from what is now. It was safe for kids, and the streets were clean."

"I bet the men wore suits and the ladies wore hats and dresses, just like in those old black-and-white TV shows," I say, smiling.

"Yeah, like that one Maxine always used to watch," Sam says, pulling his eyebrows together. "*Leave It to Squirrels*...or something like that."

"You mean *Leave It to Beaver*?" Joe laughs. "Yeah, my dad loved that show."

"You think that's what it was really like?" I ask, captivated by the thought.

"Maybe something like that." He smiles at me in the review mirror.

I look out of my window and imagine families walking up and down the sidewalk. The mothers are lovely in their white gloves and knee-length dresses and the fathers tip their hats and shake one another's hands. Little boys and girls chase each other around their parents' feet, while their mothers tell them not to ruin their new clothes in the freshly cut grass.

"I wish I was born in the fifties," I say quietly to myself, and Sam reaches for my hand.

"Where does that leave me?" he asks softly.

I smile at him. "I think you'd look pretty cute in a white T-shirt and a leather jacket."

He laughs quietly and shakes his head.

"So what happened to your dad?" Tristan asks.

"He got cancer. Died just a few years after my mother passed."

"Joe, I'm so sorry," I say, glancing up at him in the rearview mirror. "That's terrible."

"Ahh, I was one of the lucky ones," he says, winding the steering wheel and turning into the Pizza Hut parking lot. "My parents didn't choose to leave me." He parks in the shade of the pointed red roof and looks at us over his shoulder. "There are still good people left in Brighton Park. People like my father. That's why I came back here."

Sam reaches for Joes shoulder. "You're one of those people, Joe. You're one of the good ones."

Joe smiles. "Come on, knuckleheads, let's go eat."

* * *

"Lucy, can you hear me?"

I blink at the glaring light in my eye and try to move my tongue, but my head feels like it's underwater, caught in a strong current.

"Her pupils aren't dilated, but her BP's climbing."

"We've got to get her into surgery."

The dull pain radiating down my leg suddenly stabs all over my body and I let out a scream that brings my back off the bed.

The man and woman hovering over me press their hands to my shoulders and hold me down. "Lucy, Lucy…look at me," the woman says. "I need you to be still. Okay? I know it hurts, but we're going to help you."

I feel a sharp stick in my arm.

"We're going to give you some medicine that will let you sleep for a little while, so you don't feel it anymore."

"No. No." I turn my head from side to side, searching for Sam. "I want Sam. Where's Sam?" I struggle against the fading pain and let out weak cry. "Sam."

CHAPTER 12

SAM

"You ready?" Miles asks me, and I lean back in my chair, exhausted from listening to the reporters' questions.

"Yeah, let's go."

"Okay, that's it for tonight, guys," Miles says into the microphone, getting up from his chair.

I pull my phone out of my pocket and see a missed call from Lucy. "Hold on," I say to Miles. "Lucy left a message." I hold my phone to my ear and listen to it.

Hey, call me when you're done. There's stupid paparazzi following us home. Joe's trying to lose them, but at this rate, you'll get there before we do. I just wanted you to know. Love you, bye.

"Dammit."

Miles gives me a curious look, but I ignore him and call Lucy.

Her phone just rings and rings. "Come on, Luc, answer the phone," I say through my teeth, trying to keep my worry under control.

"Sam, what's the matter?" Miles asks.

I shake my head and call Joe, but his phone goes straight to voicemail.

"Sam! Sam!" Leon shouts from the back of the room, holding his phone to his ear. He waves me over, ignoring the alarmed reporters who are staring at him with the same concerned look on their faces as I have on mine.

Miles pulls his phone out of his pocket and answers a call. "Yeah?...What?" He turns sheet white, and my heart spikes with a sudden burst of adrenaline. "Where are they?"

"What is it, Miles?"

He doesn't answer me.

"Tell me what the fuck is going on," I say, but he keeps his phone to his ear.

I run to the back of the room, shoving reporters out of the way to get to Leon. "What happened?"

He gives me a look that makes me want to throw up. "It's Lucy and Joe. They were in an accident."

"What?"

Miles shoves his way through the reporters surrounding us. "Come on, we gotta go. Come on!" he shouts, pushing the reporters back.

I run next to Miles and Leon, feeling my heart pound painfully against my ribs. "What happened?" I shout at Miles as we hurry to the car outside the arena.

"I don't know. But they're at the hospital. That's where we need to go," he says to Leon, who climbs into the driver's seat.

I get in the passenger seat and close the door, ignoring the reporters shouting questions outside. I pull my phone out as Leon tears away from the arena parking lot and I call Sebastian, who answers quickly.

"Hey, Sam. Is everything okay? I've been trying to call Lucy, but she's not answering her phone."

"You haven't talked to her?"

"No. Not since Joe took her home."

"Fuck," I whisper into the phone.

"Sam, what's going on?"

"They were in an accident. Lucy and Joe were in accident."

"An accident? Oh, my God. Are they okay?"

"I don't know, we're headed to the hospital right now."

"The hospital? Oh, God, the b—"

"Sebastian, please…I can't think about anything besides Lucy right now or I'll fucking fall apart, so please don't say that. Okay? Just…don't say it."

"Okay, yeah. Okay," he says with a trembling voice. "I'm leaving. I'm leaving right now. I'll be right there."

I hang up and look at Miles in the back seat, who's been on his phone since we left the arena.

"Let us out at the emergency room entrance," he says to Leon, and hangs up his phone. "They were T-boned, Sam. The other driver ran a red light. They were both going too fast. It's not good," he says dismally.

"No. Don't you do that. Don't you fucking look at me like that. They're fine!" I shout at him. "They're going to be fine."

"Sam—"

"You don't know shit! Okay? You don't know anything. So get that fucking look off your face."

"You're right Sam, you're right. Let's just get inside and talk to someone who can tell us what's going on."

I turn back around and close my eyes, but it does little to calm me down. The fresh cut above my eye throbs as my blood pulses through my veins and my heart aches inside my chest, which tightens around it with every tortured breath. My mind moves from thoughts of Lucy to thoughts of Joe to thoughts of my unborn baby, and I feel each one of them slipping out of my grip.

I'll never leave you, Sam. I'm yours. Forever... We're yours.

I feel the oxygen leaving my body, but I fight hard against it. *She's okay... she's okay*, I repeat over and over in my head, like a mantra.

Leon pulls up in front of the emergency room, and Miles and I jump out.

"Ignore them, Sam," Miles shouts as we make our way through a small sea of reporters who have already gathered outside the hospital. "Ignore them!" he shouts again, and it takes everything in me not to knock them out of the way.

When we get inside, I run over to the nurse behind the counter, who promptly stands up.

"Where is she?"

"Where is who?" She looks me up and down.

"Lucy Bennett," I say desperately. "Where is she?"

She puts a fisted hand on her hip and eyes the stitches over my eyebrow. "And you are?"

Miles steps in front of me. "I apologize. He's just upset. He's Sam Cole." He waits for her to react, but she just stares at him with the same unenthused look she gave me. "He's a boxer. He had a big match tonight over at the Philips arena... that's why he looks a little beat up. And it's the reason for all the reporters outside," he says, glancing over his shoulder. "Lucy Bennett is his fiancée and Joe Maloney is his coach. They were in a car accident on their way home from the match. We just need to talk to somebody to make sure they're okay." He glances up at me, giving me a reassuring look.

She pushes her lips together and reaches for a clipboard hanging on the wall. "I'll need some identification."

I grab my wallet out of my pocket and hand her my driver's license.

"Yours too," she says to Miles, who holds up his finger.

He answers his phone and speaks quietly to someone on the other end of the line briefly, before hanging up. "You might want to get that," he says to her, dropping his phone back in his jacket pocket.

She gives him a funny look, but then the phone on her desk rings and he gestures for her to answer it. She picks up the receiver and speaks quietly into it. "Yes…Okay…Okay, thank you." She hangs up the phone and looks at us. "If you'll wait here, someone will be down to escort you to the surgical waiting area in just a moment."

"Surgery? Who's in surgery?" I ask, panicked.

"I'm sorry, I don't have those details." She hands me back my driver's license and sits down behind her desk.

"Mr. Cole, Mr. Angelo." I look up and see a suited man walking over to us with his hand extended. "I'm Jason Hernandez, the hospital president."

I reach out and shake his hand. "Sam Cole."

"I'm a big fan, Sam. I'm so sorry to hear what happened tonight, but I want to assure you, your loved ones are in good hands."

"Where are they? Are they okay?"

"I only just arrived. I haven't spoken to the physicians yet. But why don't we head upstairs so you can speak to the teams taking care of Joe and Lucy. They'll be able to tell you much more than I can."

"Sam!" Sebastian calls across the waiting area. He runs over to us with Paul on his heels and puts his hand on my shoulder. "Is she okay?"

"We're about to go find out. Why don't you come with us."

He inhales a shaky breath and wipes his red-rimmed eyes. "Okay."

* * *

"Lucy's in surgery. She has a fractured hip and a few other scrapes and bruises, but she's going to be okay."

I drop my head and grab Miles's shoulder, and he wraps his arm around me. "She's okay," he says, pulling his hand to his eyes.

"What about the baby?" Sebastian asks, choking back tears, and I steel myself for the answer.

I close my eyes and recall the moment Lucy told me she was pregnant—the joy I felt, the joy I saw in her eyes, and the promise of a family we never had. *I have to be the one to tell her.* I'm going to have to look in her pale blue eyes and shatter her heart into a million pieces. I feel mine begin to splinter and break apart in my chest.

"She's fine," the nurse says, and the air rushes out of my lungs. "We're keeping a close eye on her."

"She?" I ask over the quiet cries I hear coming from Sebastian, and suddenly, without warning, I'm hit by a wall of emotion that slams into me like a tsunami, taking me to my knees.

"Mr. Cole, are you okay?" the nurse asks, reaching for my arm.

I pull one foot under me, drop my elbow to my knee, and cry into my hand.

"I'm so sorry, I thought you knew."

I look up at Miles, who's grinning at me. "I'm having a girl," I say to him, and he pulls me to my feet.

"Yeah, you are." He pulls me into a strong hug.

I look at Sebastian, whose face is partially hidden as he leans into Paul. "She's going to be so happy."

"Mr. Cole," she says, watching us.

I give her a small, grateful smile. "Just Sam."

"Sam. I need to talk to you about Joe." The look on her face pushes aside my gratitude. "His injuries are far worse than Lucy's."

"How much worse?"

"He took the brunt of the impact from the other car. He has internal injuries, and there was quite a bit of bleeding, but they're working hard to repair the damage."

"They can fix him, right?"

"They're doing everything they can. I just…want you to be prepared."

"Prepared?"

"Injuries like his are not always repairable."

"Wait, what are you saying? You're saying he's not going to make it?"

"I'm saying there's a chance he might not make it out of surgery. So if there's anyone you want to call, you should do that now."

I pull my hand to my pounding head and look at the floor,

feeling the room spin around me. "Go tell Tristan," I say to Miles. "He needs to know."

"Are you sure that's a good idea, Sam?"

I look up at Miles. "I don't really know, but Tristan deserves to know." I take a deep breath. "Is there a bathroom?" I ask the nurse, who nods and points across the hall.

I shut the bathroom door behind me and drop my head back against it. But I can't stop the sick feeling racing through me, so I hang over the toilet and give in to it.

I splash some water on my face and look in the mirror.

Joe's dying and Lucy's in surgery. *How the fuck did this happen?*

* * *

"Sam, Lucy's out of surgery," Sebastian says, rounding the corner of the snack room, where I'm getting my third cup of coffee. "The doctor wants to talk to you."

I leave the cup and rush back into the waiting area, where I'm greeted by a doctor in green scrubs.

"Mr. Cole?"

"Yes," I say over the emotional wave pool sloshing around inside me.

"Lucy's out of surgery and she's doing great. She's still a little groggy, but she's awake and she's asking for you." He smiles contently.

I exhale a relieved breath. "Is she okay?"

"She has two shiny new screws in her hip and she'll need to stay off her feet for a while, but otherwise, yes. She's doing fine."

"Can I see her now?"

"Yes, come with me."

I put my hand on Sebastian's shoulder and give it a squeeze. "I'll tell her you're here."

"Okay. I'll just be in the waiting room with Paul," he says, and I give him an appreciative nod.

"Right this way, Mr. Cole."

"You can call me Sam."

"Okay, Sam. Just around this corner."

I follow him into the room and see Lucy lying in a hospital bed connected to an IV and several monitors. One must be a fetal monitor, because I can hear the rapid swooshing of the baby's heartbeat, just like at our checkups.

She gives me a weak smile when she sees me and inhales a shallow breath. "Hi."

I drop my head and fight hard against the tears that rush to my eyes, but when I sit on the edge of the bed and reach for her small hand, I fall apart. I lean over her, hugging her through the sheets and blankets draped over her.

"Careful," she croaks, and I sit up.

I stare into her pale blue eyes, unable to ignore the scrapes on her cheek and neck. "I'm so sorry this happened."

"I'm okay," she says quietly.

I reach for her hand again, unsure if I'll ever be able to let go. "I thought—I didn't know if—"

"I know," she says, squeezing my hand weakly.

"What would I do if something happened to you?"

"I'm okay," she whispers, and smiles softly.

"Are you in a lot of pain?" I ask, scanning her.

"A little. The medicine's helping."

"Is it okay for the baby?"

She smiles and nods. "You hear that?" She looks over at one of the monitors.

"She's got a strong heart. Just like her mom," I say, squeezing her hand.

She gazes at me with a puzzled look on her face. "She?"

I smile softly and pull her hand to my mouth. "It's a girl."

"What?" She smiles and a tear falls from the corner of her eye.

"I wanted to be the one to tell you," I say, brushing her hair off her face.

"Sebastian will be so happy."

"He is."

"Sebastian's here?"

"Yeah, he's in the waiting room with Paul. Miles is here too. But he's updating Tristan right now."

Her smile disappears and worry falls over her face. "About what?"

I close my eyes and shake my head, unsure what to tell her.

"It's Joe, isn't it?" she whispers, and tears fill her eyes.

I swallow the hard lump in my throat. "It's not good. He has internal injuries. They don't know if he's going to make it out of surgery." I choke on a sob that fights its way out.

"What?" She starts to cry and her heart rate goes up on one of the monitors.

I drop my face to hers. "Shhh…shhh…" I hold her face in my hand and whisper, "It's going to be okay, Lamb. He'll be okay."

* * *

"Sam," Miles whispers, shaking my shoulder.

I look up at him from the chair I fell asleep in next to Lucy's bed. "What is it?" I whisper, trying not to wake her.

"You gotta come with me." He waves me out of the room after him. "Come on."

I get up and follow him out into the hall.

"Sam, I'm Dr. Bernard," a doctor I haven't met says, greeting me outside Lucy's room.

Miles stands next to him with his arms folded, looking down at the floor.

"Hi," I say tentatively.

"I was Joe's surgeon tonight."

"Oh." My eyes and ears perk up. "Is he okay? How is he?"

Miles looks at me with red-rimmed eyes and I try to convince myself that it's because it's so late.

"Sam, some colleagues of mine were hoping to speak to you about Joe's condition. Do you mind coming with me?" he asks, gesturing down the hall.

"Yeah, okay."

He leads us down the hall into a small windowless room, where I'm greeted by a team of doctors who promptly get up from the table they're seated around.

"What's going on?" I ask, eyeing Joe's doctor.

"Sam, I'm so sorry to tell you this, but…Joe didn't make it."

My heart pounds inside my chest and the blood pulses behind the cut over my eye. I blink at him for several seconds, vaguely aware of Miles's hand on my shoulder.

"He asked that his heart go to Tristan Kelley," one of the other doctors says, and I look up at him, confused. "He's being prepped for surgery now."

"Joe's dead?" I ask, working hard for each breath.

"I'm so sorry, Sam," Miles says, but he might as well be in another room.

"Where's Tristan?"

"He's being prepped for surgery," the doctor says again.

"Tris is gonna get Joe's heart," Miles says, unable to hide the emotion in his gravelly voice.

"Joe found out that he was a match a few years ago," one of the doctors says. "He designated himself as a donor for Tristan. It's in his medical records."

"He did that?"

The doctor gives me a small smile and nods.

"No." I shake my head. "Joe's fifty-five."

"Well he must have taken good care of himself, because he had the heart of a young man," another doctor chimes in.

"He ran six miles nearly every day." I close my eyes and say quietly, "He was running for Tristan."

"Tristan's very lucky."

"Lucky? The closest person he's ever had to a father just died. You call that lucky?"

"I'm sorry, that's not what I meant. I didn't mean to upset you."

"Upset? Why would I be upset? Joe had to die for Tristan to live. That's fair, right?"

"Sam, come on, let's take a walk." Miles says, reaching for my shoulder.

"I don't want to take a fucking walk, Miles." I blink back tears. "I want to see Tristan. Where is he?"

"I'm sorry, that's not possible. You'll have to wait until he's in recovery," one of the doctors says. "We have to act swiftly in these situations. Time is of the essence."

I sniff and nod. "How long is the surgery?"

"Around four hours. Then he'll be moved to the ICU, where he'll stay for several days."

"He's not out of the woods yet, Sam," Joe's doctor says. "He's going to need all the friends he's got."

Miles pats me on the back. "Why don't you go be with Lucy. I'll let you know when he's out of surgery."

I look at Miles, whose face is worn and weary from the night. "Yeah, okay."

He gives me a small smile that doesn't reach his eyes.

"Thanks, Miles."

"Anytime, champ."

CHAPTER 13

LUCY, THREE WEEKS LATER

I wake in the dark to Sam sitting down on the bed and jostling me a little, which causes my hip to throb. I groan, and Sam stands up.

"You okay?" he asks, walking around to my side of the bed.

I look up at his silhouette in the dark and I'm reminded of nights when he would come into my room to comfort me when we were living in foster care together. "Yeah, I'm okay." I look at the alarm clock on the night stand. It's two a.m. "What are you doing?" I ask, seeing him a little more clearly in the dim light that's coming from the bathroom. He's wearing workout clothes and his shirt is soaked with sweat.

"I was just letting off some steam in the gym."

"Sam, it's the middle of the night."

"I know."

I slowly sit up, grimacing at the dull pain that shoots down my leg when I move.

"Careful," he says, putting his hands on my back to help me. "Lucy, you should go back to sleep."

"No." I shake my head, which has been filled with worry since the accident. "Not until you tell me why you were working out in the middle of the night."

"I wasn't working out. I was just hitting the speed bag."

"Okay, well…why were you hitting the speed bag in the middle of the night?" I ask carefully, because I already know the answer.

"Lucy, come on, do we have to do this right now?"

"Joe?" I push, because he's barely spoken his name since the funeral.

His jaw clenches tight, but he doesn't say anything.

"Sam." I ignore the little voice in my head telling me to leave it alone and say, "I think you should talk to somebody."

"What, like a shrink?"

"A therapist, yes. Someone who deals in loss and grief. It's not healthy for you to keep it all pent up inside."

"I'm not keeping it pent up," he says, pulling his sweaty shirt off and throwing it in the hamper.

"Taking your emotions out on a punching bag is not the same thing as talking about it with someone."

"Lucy, I'm not going to talk to a stranger about Joe," he says firmly, "so stop pushing me on it, okay?"

I press my lips together and bob my head. "Well, then… maybe you could just talk about it with me?"

He sits down on the bed at my feet, drops his elbows to his knees, and pulls his hands to his chin. "I don't want to talk about it, Lucy. Not with anybody," he says, looking at me.

I blink back tears and swallow down the hurt. "Well, maybe you don't, but I do."

He drops his hands between his knees and huffs. "What do

you want to talk about? Huh? That I lost the closest person I had to a father? That Joe died because of the fucking paparazzi? Or that the only reason the paparazzi was even there is because of me?"

I shake my head and swallow the hard lump in my throat. "Sam? You think this was *your* fault somehow?"

He stares at me, but he doesn't say anything.

"What happened to Joe is not your fault, Sam."

He wipes his watery eyes and says, "Lucy, if it wasn't for me, none of this would have happened. Joe would still be here and you"—he drops his head to his hand and rubs his tortured face—"you wouldn't be lying in this bed with a metal pin your hip."

I want to comfort him, but I can't reach him where he's sitting. "Sam, come here."

He stares at me with a face of stone, and I see how hard he's working to fight back the tears.

"Please," I say, barely containing my own emotions, "come here." I pat the edge of the bed beside me.

After a few seconds, he gets up and kneels on the floor beside the bed, reaching for my hands, which I quickly wrap around his. He pulls them to his mouth and says, "I'm sorry." He looks up at me and a tear rolls down his cheek. "I'm so sorry."

"Sam." My heart squeezes inside my chest. "You don't have anything to be sorry for. You didn't do anything. This isn't your fault. What happened to Joe. To me. It was just an accident."

He's quiet for a few long seconds.

"It is not your fault, okay?" I say again, praying he believes it.

He lifts his head and looks at me. "I miss him, Lucy."

"I know you do. I miss him too."

"He was a good man. He should still be here."

"He was." I nod. "And he'll always be with us. In our hearts. And with Tristan. He's a part of him now. He's still with us, Sam."

He drops his forehead to my hand, and I run my fingers through his wavy hair. "It's going to be okay."

He puts his hand on my stomach and looks up at me. "I don't know how I would live if something happened to you too."

"We're okay," I whisper over the ache in my heart that won't go away. I close my eyes and exhale a quiet breath. "We're okay."

He sniffs and stands up, but I hold on to his hand.

"Sam, I know you don't want to talk to a professional, and that's okay, just promise you'll talk to me," I plead, afraid that he's going to drift further and further away from me if he doesn't. I fend off the fear of that thought and say, "I want you to tell me when you feel sad. Or angry. Or happy." I smile softly over a sob that's trying to get out. "Because you're all I have in the *entire world*," I say through clenched teeth to keep the sob inside.

He stares at me with his stone face and whispers, "I know."

"I need you right now, Sam. *We* need you. Okay?"

"Okay."

One Week Later

"Are you comfortable?" Sam asks, leaning over my wheelchair.

"Yes. But is this really necessary? I think I can stand long enough to take the elevator a few floors down to Molly's apartment."

"Better to be safe than sorry," he says, guiding me into the foyer. "I'm just glad Tristan decided to recover at her place. His apartment is all the way across town."

"I'm just glad he has Molly to take care of him."

"Me too. I don't how I would have taken care of both of you." He laughs softly, but the thought makes me sad. Sam is Tristan's only family now. That's something that we have in common.

We take the elevator down to the sixteenth floor, and Sam pushes me down the hallway to Molly's apartment.

Sam knocks on the door and she answers it quickly. "Hey," she says with a bright smile.

"Hey, Molls," Sam says, pushing me inside her apartment.

"Hi, Molly." I smile at her.

"Lucy. Oh, my gosh." She leans down to give me a hug. "How are you feeling?"

"I'm actually much better. I really don't need this wheelchair anymore," I say, glancing over my shoulder at Sam. "Can I get up now?" I ask him.

He locks the wheels in place and helps me stand up, and I ignore the dull ache in my hip.

"Well, look at you," Tristan says, greeting me with open arms and a big, beautiful smile. He looks better than I expected, just a little thinner than usual.

"Tristan." I smile at him, but as soon as he wraps his arms around me, the weight of the last month comes crashing down, knocking my emotional floodgate open. I feel Sam's hand on my back, but he doesn't say anything. Neither does Molly. They just wait while I get it out.

Tristan releases me and puts his hands on my arms. "Hey, it's okay, Luc." He inhales a deep breath and blows it out slowly. "We're all okay." He rubs my arms and hugs me again.

I nod and wipe the tears from my face. "I'm sorry, it's just…"

"A lot." He smiles softly. "I know."

I press my lips together and nod. "Yeah."

"Come on," Sam says, taking my hand. "Let's go sit down."

"Yes, please"—Tristan puts his hand on his chest—"before I pass out." He laughs and it lightens the mood a little.

We follow him and Molly into the living room and sit down on the couch.

"Molly, I love your apartment," I say, glancing around the open space that's splashed with bold pops of color, black and white pillows and curtains, and white walls that are adorned with vintage artwork.

"Thanks. It's a work in progress." She shrugs and says unapologetically, "I redecorate a lot."

"She means, she gets bored easily," Tristan teases, and she rolls her eyes playfully.

"Well, you definitely have an artistic eye." I smile at her.

"Thank you," she says, then she lightly shoves Tristan's shoulder.

"Hey. Injured over here," he says to her, and she pushes her lips into a small pout.

She drops her head and kisses his shoulder. "Sorry, pumpkin."

"Oh, my God," Sam says, getting up from the couch. "You guys are going to make me sick."

Tristan gives him a wide grin that matches Molly's, and it makes me giggle.

"Got anything to drink in the kitchen, Molly?"

She squints her eyes and shrugs. "Bottled water."

"Water's fine." He looks at me. "Want a water, Luc?"

"No, I'm okay. Thanks, pumpkin," I say before he leaves the room.

He spins around and says seriously, "No." He smiles at me and his dimples go straight to my heart—dimples I haven't seen for far too long. "Do not call me that." He laughs freely and it makes my heart swell.

I smile at him as he leaves the room. *Maybe he's starting to feel better.*

"Lucy, how's the baby?" Molly asks.

"Good. She's about the size of a banana now." I shake my head at the comparison. "That's what all the websites say anyway."

"I just can't wait to meet her," she says sweetly. "You know we'll babysit anytime." She looks at Tristan, and he shakes his head at her.

I put my hand on my small bump and laugh. "How are *you*

feeling, Tris?" I ask, surprised that he's already up and around.

"I feel pretty good, actually. Tired, but that should go away soon. Molly's been taking good care of me." He winks at her.

"I'm tired too, but because of the baby, I think. And from lying around doing nothing all day," I grumble at Sam, who returns with a bottle of water.

He sits down beside me and says, "That's literally the definition of bed rest."

"I just can't wait to get back to work and use my brain before I lose all my creativity."

"Not possible," Molly says. "I've seen your work."

"Thanks. I hope you're right. I've got a dwindling portfolio that's waiting to be filled with new artwork and several exhibits that I need to get ready for."

"Molly's right," Sam says, squeezing my hand. "You'll see, as soon as you get back at it."

"Lucy, Sam told me you're looking for a new studio," she says curiously.

"Oh, um, yes, I am." I glance over at him. *What else had he told her?*

"Any luck so far?"

"No, not yet. Everything's sort of been on hold since the accident. And I'm going to have to sell a few more paintings before I can make an offer on something."

"Well, I know you've turned me down before"—she winks—"but I might be able to help you make a little extra money." There's a glint of excitement in her eyes, and I smile over my hesitation.

"Really? How?"

"Okay, don't tell anyone, because this isn't public information yet, but I just landed an account with Rock Love Threads."

"The clothing brand?"

"The clothing *mecca* for ages eighteen to twenty-eight. They have stores in every mall in every major city in the country. And a few others."

"Molly, that's fantastic."

"What's fantastic is that they want me to do an entire graphic T-shirt line for them. If you jump on board and provide the drawings, or even digital copies of some of your paintings, we can put your artwork on T-shirts in stores across the nation."

"Wow. That would be pretty incredible."

"And the best part is, you can do it from your apartment."

"It might help pass the time until you're back on your feet," Sam says encouragingly.

"Lucy, do it," Tristan says. "Maybe then, Molly will stop talking about it."

She fights a smile and gives him a knowing look.

"Seriously," he adds, "you're crazy talented. With Molly in your corner, your career could really blow up."

I press my lips together over a hopeful smile and look at Sam.

"I think you should do it," he says surely.

"Okay." I look at Molly and nod. "I'll do it."

"Ah!" she squeals and claps her hands together. "Let's get started."

"Right now?"

"No time like the present. Also, I meet with their marketing team tomorrow. We can work out the details while these two hang out," she says, gesturing at Tristan and Sam.

"Okay." I give Sam a concerned look, which is met with a small smile.

"I'll be right back." Molly jumps up from the couch. "I'm going to go grab my laptop."

* * *

"Molly, can I ask you something?"

She looks up at me from her computer screen. "Yeah, anything."

"Has Sam talked to you about what happened?"

"You mean, the accident?"

"And Joe."

She presses her glossy lips together and leans back in her chair. "No."

I nod silently.

She leans forward, puts her elbows on the kitchen table, and rests her chin on her folded hands. "Are you worried about him?"

I shrug. "He's just been kind of distant lately."

She frowns softly. "I wish I could tell you why, but I haven't talked to Sam very much since the accident. He's been focused on taking care of you, and I've been focused on taking care of Tristan."

"I know. And he's been taking great care of me. It's just that sometimes when he's there, he's not really present, you know? Like his mind is somewhere else. But he won't tell me where."

"Yeah. Tristan gets like that every now and then too."

"He does?"

"Mm-hmm. I've tried to talk to him about it, but he's quick to remind me that I didn't know Joe like he did." She shrugs.

"Well, I did. So what's Sam's excuse?" I close my eyes and say, "I lost Joe too."

Molly reaches across the table and wraps her hand around mine. "I'm really sorry, Lucy."

I press my trembling lips together. "Thanks."

"I know it's hard right now." She squeezes my hand. "I can't imagine what you've been going through. But I know one thing. You are tough as hell." She leans in and says quietly, "Tougher than those two out there on the couch." She winks and it makes me smile. "It'll get better with time."

"You think so?"

"I do. But in meantime, if you need to talk about it, I'm only a few floors away. I'm a pretty good listener," she says, smiling lightly.

"So I've been told."

She sits back in her chair and spins her laptop around to show me the screen. "You know, I think this is going to be a really good distraction for you."

I inhale a hopeful breath. "I could sure use one."

CHAPTER 14

LUCY, ONE MONTH LATER

I sit on a wooden stool in front of my painting, staring at the brushstrokes that highlight my pink-rimmed eyes and matching pink nose. My blue tear-filled eyes reflect the sadness that's been looming over me for the past two months.

My doctors told me that when a bone is broken, it heals stronger than before the break. But they didn't make any promises about my heart. It's been two months since the accident, and I can still feel the broken pieces, like the jagged, uneven sidewalks I grew up on. Most of the cracks are for Sam, who may never get over losing Joe, some are for me, and a few are for Tristan. But the one that hurts the most, the one I can't seem to jump over no matter how hard I try, runs right down the middle of me and Sam.

"It's perfection," Sebastian says, standing behind me.

"It's sad."

"It's beautiful."

"It's broken. Just like me and Sam." I inhale a shaky breath and blink back tears that burn behind my eyes.

"You and Sam aren't broken. You're just a little cracked, that's all."

"Is there a difference?"

"Yes, there's a difference," he says, dropping his head beside mine. "Breaks don't always go back together, but cracks usually heal." He spins me around to face him. "What's the matter? I thought you were feeling better since you were cleared to start working again. Aren't you glad to be back out in the world?"

"Yes. And I was feeling better, until last night. Sam and I got into a fight." I drop my head and pull my paint-covered hands to my face. "What if things never go back to the way they were, Bas? What if losing Joe was too much for him? Joe was the only constant thing in Sam's life. He was there for him when I wasn't." I slide off the stool, and Bas grabs my hand as I stand up. "Sam made sure to remind me of that last night."

"He's just hurting. And he's probably going to be hurting for a long time." He turns me around to face my painting again and puts his hands on my shoulders. "Look. You are stronger than you were that day, Lucy. And you're stronger now than you were two months ago when that asshole ran a red light. Now *you* have to be stronger than Sam."

I turn around and look up at him. "I'm trying, but he keeps pushing me away."

"Then push harder," he says firmly. "Joe was there for him when you weren't. Now it's your turn to be there for him when Joe can't."

I nod softly.

He takes my hand. "Come on." He pulls me over to the

sink in the back of my studio. "I want to show you something. Wash up."

I turn on the water and begin scrubbing the paint off my fingers.

When I'm through, Sebastian reaches for my hands and holds them up in front of him. "Really, Luc, you've got to stop using your fingernails as painting tools," he says, appalled.

"They're the best tool I've got."

"Well you have a big day coming up and your nails are not up to the occasion. If it means no more painting until after Aurelia Snow, then so be it."

He musters a small smile out of me and I pull my hand back. "It's still six weeks away. And don't worry, I think I used the last of my energy on that one." I glance back at my self-portrait drying on the easel behind me and drop my hands to my paint-covered overalls. I pat my swollen tummy and walk over to the couch. "She's officially sucking all my energy out of me." I sit down, sprawl my arms and legs out, and drop my head back against the couch. "I don't know why everyone says the second trimester is the easiest."

"Because most women aren't healing from a hip fracture in their second trimester. Or dealing with—"

"Sam?"

"I was going to say everything you're dealing with, but if you want to narrow it down to Sam, I'll support that."

I laugh softly.

"Is that a smile I see?"

"A small one." I purse my lips. "It's hard to keep them from you."

"I'll take that as a compliment."

"It was meant as one." I inhale a deep breath and close my eyes. "Honestly, I spent the majority of the last two months on bed rest. How can I possibly be this tired?" I sit up and try to get comfortable, but there's a small basketball in my lap that's permanently affixed to my stomach.

"Maybe because you haven't had a latte in six months." He arches an eyebrow.

"Shh...don't say the *L* word."

"What about the *C* word?"

I raise a curious eyebrow.

"Coffee." He makes a funny face and shakes his head. "What about the *W* word?" he asks, slouching against the arm of the couch. "It definitely can't help matters that you have zero coping devices right now. One glass of wine and you'd probably feel a lot better."

"You know what would make me feel better? A fiancé who doesn't immerse himself in boxing to hide from the pain he won't talk about."

"Yes, well, we've established that."

"It doesn't help that he's trying to prepare for a fight without Joe *or* Tristan. He's never had to do that before."

"I'm sure they're not easily replaced."

"No. He's been really frustrated."

"Why doesn't he just wait until after the baby's born? That would give Tristan time to fully heal and then he can coach Sam."

"Because he's still under contract. Miles already had it amended once, and that was only because it was deemed medically necessary by Sam's doctor. The only thing he can do is withdraw, and he'll never do that." I roll my eyes. "Miles would never let him do that."

Bas gets up and reaches for my hands and pulls me up off the couch. "I have something that will cheer you up."

"What is it?"

"Dresses for New York. I got two for you to try on," he says, disappearing into my office. He returns with a couple of garment bags and lays them over the arm of the couch. He unzips one and pulls out a long, flowy, creamy-white dress with a delicate crocheted top. "It will be warm in New York. I thought this would be perfect with the open back and your hair swept up."

I stand up and hold it out in front of me. "It looks a little like a wedding dress, Bas."

"Pfff...not *your* wedding dress. I've got much bigger plans for that."

I shake my head. "You're not going to let it go, are you?"

"Nope. Now go." He waves his hands. "Try it on."

I carry the dress to my office and change into it, glad to find that it's fairly easy to get on by myself. I slide my arms through the thin spaghetti straps and adjust the crocheted top. I pull my long hair up into a loose bun and walk back out to show Sebastian.

"Oh, my God, it's even better on."

I turn around and show him the back.

"I love it," he gushes. "You look like an angel."

I drop my head to the side and give him an incredulous look. "A pregnant angel? When did I get kicked out of heaven?"

"Stop it, you look beautiful." He reaches for my bun and messes with my loose locks of hair. "Maybe we can add some delicate little flowers or something…give you a Mother Earth vibe." He looks at me and says, "Kind of fits your current situation, don't you think?"

"What's in the other bag?" I ask, not feeling the vibe.

He drops his hands and reaches for the other garment bag. He unzips it and pulls out another creamy-white dress, but this one is simple and elegant. He holds it up and I know without even trying it on that it's the one I want to wear to the Aurelia Snow exhibit next month.

"This one is chiffon," he says, handing it to me. "I thought the airy material would be good for warm weather."

"I love it," I say, taking it from him. I hurry to my office to try it on, and it literally slides over my body like a slip. The top dips into a soft V just above my newly developed cleavage. And the light, airy material flows over my round stomach and falls gracefully to my feet with room to grow. I turn around and look at the back. The straps are an inch or so wide on my shoulders like a tank top, and it dips down into a U just above the small of my back.

I gather the material in my hands and hurry out to show Bas. "What do you think?" I ask, smiling.

"Turn around," he says, and I follow his instruction.

After a few silent seconds I turn back around. "Hello?"

Bas pulls his fist away from his mouth and crosses his arms over his chest. "I think…you really are an angel."

"Bas."

"It's like it was made for you. You have to wear this one."

"Do you think it will still fit in six weeks?"

He tugs on the loose material that's covering my stomach. "Yes, you have plenty of room."

I pull my shoulders up excitedly and smile. "I love it. It's beautiful but, more importantly, comfortable. You did good."

He presses his lips together and nods. "Guess what the color is," he says, and then he presses his lips together again.

"Um…" I look down at it again. "Cream?"

He shakes his head, keeping his lips tightly sealed.

"I don't know." I laugh. "Ivory? Off-white? Vanilla?" I shrug. "I have no idea, Bas. Just tell me."

"Wedding cake!" he finally says, putting his hands over his mouth.

I can't help but smile at his excitement. "Tell you what, freak. You can pretend that this is my wedding dress, because it's the closest you're going to get to the real thing anytime soon."

"I'll wear you down eventually. And if I can't, I'll get Sam to." He raises his eyebrows and gathers the garment bags off the arm of the couch.

"You wouldn't dare."

He pauses and looks up at me. "Wouldn't I?"

"Not if you're not speaking to him," I say, crossing my arms.

"Slow down, killer. Who said anything about not speaking to Sam? I support you and I want him to get over his funk, because it affects you, which ultimately affects me. But that doesn't mean I'm not a fan. I'm *always* a Sam Cole fan." He narrows his eyes and whispers, "Always."

I purse my lips over a smile. "Figures."

* * *

"Something smells good," Sam says, walking into the kitchen. He grabs a bottle of water out of the fridge and chugs it down.

I smile tentatively at him over the ruminating ache in my heart left over from our fight and say, "Jambalaya."

He walks up behind me and reaches around my stomach, pressing his hand to my bump. "I'm sorry about last night," he says, kissing my neck.

"It's okay." I pull my shoulder up to my jaw. "You're sweaty."

"I know, I'm sorry." He leans against the counter and watches me sauté the diced onions and green bell peppers.

"Did you have a good workout?" I ask, glancing up at him.

"It was okay. The new guy just isn't Tristan. He's got my circuits all switched up and it's really throwing me off. I just want to get back to my old routine."

"Looks like you worked hard," I say, eyeing his sweat-soaked T-shirt.

"He's kicking my ass, just not the way I like."

"Well, maybe it's a good thing. A new challenge. Can you hand me that bowl?" I ask, pointing to the little bowl of garlic I chopped up.

He hands it to me and I add the garlic to the pot. As soon as it hits the heat, the aromatic scent fills the kitchen.

"What all goes in jambalaya?"

"Chicken, smoked sausage, onion, celery, peppers, garlic, tomatoes, spices..."

"It's making my mouth water. I'm starving."

"Good." I smile softly at him. "But it's not going to be ready for another half hour or so, so you'll have to wait. You have time for a shower," I point out.

"I think I've proven that I'm pretty good at waiting," he says, showing me his dimples, and it makes me grin.

"Yes," I say, pushing the onion and peppers around the pan, "you have."

"Luc, there's something I want to talk to you about."

I look up at him tentatively. "Okay," I say, but it sounds like a question.

"I want to buy a house. For us."

A hopeful smile spreads across my face. "You do?"

"Yeah. I think it would really help things."

Help things. As in, fill the void Joe left, not move past it.

I nod and work to keep the smile on my face. "Yeah." I tend to my pot, trying to keep my emotions corralled.

"Would you like that?"

I press my lips together and glance up at him. "Mm-hmm," I squeak, trying to appreciate the gesture, even if it's for the wrong reason.

"Good, because I talked to a realtor today."

I look up and see him smiling at me with excited eyes, and for the first time in weeks, he looks *happy.* I smile and ask, "Well, what did they say?"

"That it's not going to be easy to find a house with room for a gym and an art studio." He laughs and shakes his head. "First world problems, I know."

I shrug. "Well, just skip the studio then."

He gives me a funny look. "Where will you paint?"

"At my studio." I try to sound casual, because I know where this leads.

"You mean the studio you're giving back to Drew?"

"Until I can find a new one, yes," I say, minding the pot.

"You know, I'm starting to wonder if you're ever going to give it back him." He laughs softly, but I don't think he's amused.

"I honestly haven't given it very much thought since the accident. I've been a little preoccupied." I turn the heat down under the pot, so I can tend to our conversation instead.

"Don't do that, Luc." He closes his eyes and drops his head back.

"Do what?" My heart shudders as my hormones break through the gate and run rampant inside me. "Point out that I couldn't walk for weeks? Or that I've been worried that the baby has some kind of damage from the accident the doctors just haven't been able to see yet? Or that you've been so consumed by your next match that you've barely even noticed."

"Barely noticed?" he says, putting his hands on his head. "I know how long you couldn't walk, Lucy. Because I was the one who brought you food, who bathed you, who got up in the middle of the night to help you to the bathroom."

I close my eyes and exhale a quiet breath, corralling my hormones back inside their gate. "I know, I'm sorry. You did so much for me." I reach for his arm. "I wasn't trying to discount that."

"I don't need recognition for taking care of you, Lucy. It was a privilege. But that doesn't mean it didn't kill me to see you like that. Or that I could ever forget what it felt like to watch you struggle just to stand up, while carrying our baby, for God's sake. And don't think I haven't had those same thoughts. I just care about you enough to keep them to myself."

I swallow down the lump in my throat. "Sam—"

"You and the baby are the *only* thing that's consumed me since the moment I heard you were in an accident." He slams his hands down on the counter, making me jump. "The only thing!"

"Not the only thing."

He looks at me and sighs. "What do you want me to say, Lucy? That I'm devastated because Joe died? I am, okay?"

"I know you are."

"And you can say it's not my fault all you want, but I will always feel responsible. *Always.* And not just for Joe."

"Sam." I reach for him again, but he doesn't look up.

"Do you know what it was like to think you were dead, to think that the baby was dead? Because when I walked into that hospital, I was preparing myself for the worst." He swallows down the emotion he can't hide. "When I found out you were okay, as overjoyed as I was, I prepared myself to tell you the baby was gone, because I didn't think I was lucky enough to get to keep you both. And I saw your heart shatter in my hands—I played it in my head again and again," he says, smacking his fist into his other hand. "It was so fucking real that when they said she was okay, it took me to my knees. I still don't believe it."

"Sam."

"I watch your belly getting bigger and I know she's alive, growing inside you. *That's* why I want to win this match. Because I want to take care of her. And every penny I earn ensures that I'll be able to do that. She's the reason I've been working so hard. I want to win for her, okay?"

"Okay." I wipe the tears from my cheeks and wrap my arms around him, and he lets me. "I'm sorry."

"I almost lost you, Lamb," he says hoarsely.

"Shhh…" I look up at his stormy eyes, watching the waves settle. "You didn't lose me. I'm right here." I reach for his scruffy face and pull his mouth to mine, letting his soft lips heal the cracks in my heart and consume the sadness that's cleaved to the broken pieces for the last couple of months.

He winds his arms around me and holds me close as he pushes and pulls my lips with his. I savor the way his tongue moves over mine, moaning desperately into his mouth, but he pulls away. "We shouldn't."

"We should," I say, pulling his mouth back to mine.

"You're still healing," he mumbles against my lips.

"It's been eight weeks, I'm all better. The doctor cleared me." I pull his shirt up and rub my hands over his chest, then I drop them to his pants.

"What about the baby?"

"The baby doesn't know."

"I haven't showered."

"I don't care," I groan, needing so badly to be close to him.

"What about dinner?"

I reach for the knob on the stove and turn the heat off. "It can wait."

He grabs my bottom through my leggings and squeezes it in his strong hands. "It's been so long," he groans against my neck, kissing me up to my jaw.

"Too long."

He takes my hand and practically runs to the bedroom, dragging me behind him.

"Sam!" I laugh as we fall onto the bed and the duvet fluffs around us.

He pulls his shirt off and climbs over me and I gaze up at him. *Has he put on more muscle?* I don't have long to ponder it. He pushes my shirt up over my stomach, kissing it softly as he makes his way up to my breasts. He releases them from my shirt, which lands somewhere on the floor, and kisses them softly, gently squeezing them in his hands. "Does that hurt?" he asks, unnecessarily concerned. They haven't been sore since my first trimester.

"No." I shake my head and he drops his mouth to them again, giving them the utmost attention.

He rubs his hand over my stomach and the baby kicks beneath it. He pauses and looks up at me.

"We missed you," I whisper.

He brings his face back to mine and I gaze into a calm sea of blue and brown. "I missed you too," he says, kissing me softly, "so much."

I melt beneath him, savoring the weight of his body, which he carefully holds on top of me as his lips move down my neck. He reaches for my pants, pushing them down a little, then he sits up and slowly tugs them over my hips, exposing the six-inch scar that runs along the side of my bottom. He leans down and kisses it softly, then he tosses my pants—and his, which he removed with lightning speed—onto the floor.

He smiles as he crawls over me again, and I reach for his face, pulling his dimples and full lips back to me. "Make love to me, Sam," I plead against his lips, desperate to feel him inside me, desperate to feel the connection I've missed so terribly the last two months, desperate for him to soothe the aching spot inside my heart, and desperate to heal his.

He moves his hand down my body, navigating around the small bump between us, and rubs the burning place between my thighs, which aches almost painfully for him. He exhales a heavy breath and groans against my neck. I pull his face back to mine and watch his lips part as he rubs himself against me and slowly pushes inside.

So slowly.

I try to rock my hips up, but it's impossible with my belly pressing against his marble stomach. I reach for his bottom and urge him deeper. "It's okay, Sam, you're not going to hurt me," I whisper.

He stares into my eyes as he pushes all the way inside me, then he squeezes his eyes shut and grumbles against my neck, "Oh, God, Luc." He stills for a moment, throbbing inside me, and I savor the familiar feeling of him, and the way our hips are pressed together. He pants softly against my neck as he begins to move, slowly rocking in and out of me, extinguishing the flames and igniting new fires inside me.

"You sure you're okay?" he asks huskily.

"More than okay," I pant up at him, and he smiles softly.

He runs his hand up my body and reaches for my hand. He laces our fingers together and holds my hand tightly, pressing it against the bed as he takes me to a place I've missed for so long. The fire sears beneath my skin, flames licking places inside me that have been asleep since the accident, and I feel Sam bringing me back to life.

He rolls onto his back, pulling me on top of him, and I moan at the feeling of him reaching and filling me as he rocks his hips up and I sink down on him.

"Is this okay?" he pants, putting his hand on my hip again.

I grab his hand and lace our fingers together again. Then I reach for his other hand. "Stop asking me if I'm okay," I whisper, smiling as I slowly move up and down on him.

He drops his head back and closes his eyes. But after a few seconds, he opens them and watches me move, consuming me with the look in his eyes. He raises his painted arm and rubs his palm between my breasts. "You're so beautiful."

I exhale a quiet breath and lean forward to kiss him, holding his scruffy face in my hands, and with our mouths pressed firmly together, he sits up and wraps his arms around me. He reaches for my hair tie and gently slides it down my ponytail, letting my hair fall loosely over my shoulders and around my face. He runs his fingers through it, holding it off my face as he kisses me, tugging my lips between his the way that I love.

We move up and down together, rediscovering the connection that's been patiently waiting in a shadow of sadness. "I love you," I whisper, inhaling the breath he exhales against my lips, and it swirls through my lungs, making me dizzy. He kisses me and our tongues move together, coaxing the flames higher. They wrap around me, searing up my thighs and racing to the tips of my fingers and toes. He holds me tighter, and I tense under his strong hands as I surrender to the flames, letting them consume me until all that's left is a smoldering husk. I cry out as Sam pulls me down against him and shudders beneath me, groaning against my neck.

He stills and looks at me with satiated eyes. "I love you, Lamb."

I smile and exhale a satisfied breath. "I know."

He falls back against the pillows, and I lie down next to him and put my hand over the lion that covers his heart. "We're going to get through this, Sam. Together."

He pulls my shoulders onto his chest, my tummy pressed against his side, and wraps me in his strong arms.

"Everything's going to be okay," I whisper, and for the first time since the accident, I have hope that it's true.

CHAPTER 15

LUCY

I wake to the smell of coffee and bacon, and it puts a smile on my face. I stretch my arms and legs out in the middle of the bed and look outside at the bright blue sky. May is my favorite month in Atlanta. The mornings are cool, the afternoons are warm, and all of the trees are full and green again. I exhale a contented breath, throw the duvet back, and look at my growing bump, which has worked its way out of my pajama top. "Good morning," I say softly, and she rolls under my belly button, making me smile. "Can you hear me?" I ask louder, patting the spot, but she doesn't move. "Baby," I sing, gently pushing on either side of my stomach, but she stays still.

Sam walks into the room, looking freshly showered, carrying a tray of pancakes, bacon, and coffee. "What are you doing?" he asks, watching me with a concerned look on his face.

"Trying to get her move"—I sit up—"but she's not cooperating."

He puts the tray down on the nightstand and sits on the bed beside me.

"You made me breakfast?" I ask with adoring eyes.

"Well"—he leans over and kisses me softly—"I decided to take the day off. I was thinking that maybe you could too."

I smile and nod. "Okay," I say without an ounce of hesitation.

He puts his hand on my tummy and rubs it softly, and the baby bumps it twice. He smiles with wide eyes and rubs it again.

"Maybe she was waiting for you." I glance up at him. "Tell her good morning. She knows your voice now."

He gives me a wary look, but leans down and says softly, "Good morning, baby."

I smile and lie down again. "A little louder."

He puts both of his hands on my protruding stomach, hiding the entire bump behind them, and says again louder, "Good morning, baby."

She rolls and kicks hard against his hand.

"See," I say over the tight feeling in my chest, and he laughs. "She knows you."

He rubs his hands back and forth and leans down again. "I have a surprise for your mom today. But I think you're going to like it too." She kicks again and he looks up at me. "We're going to go see a house."

I sit up and pull my shirt down over my stomach. "We are?"

"The realtor called this morning. She has one she wants to show us. She said it has potential…" He narrows his eyes.

"Potential is good."

"It has to be great. This is the house we're going to raise our kids in." I smile at him and he hands me a cup of coffee. "This one's decaf."

"Thank you." I can't stop smiling. For the first time since the accident, everything feels *right* again. I take a sip and look up at his freshly shaved face. "Hey."

He looks up at me from his coffee.

"I love you."

He smiles and puts his coffee down on the nightstand. "I love you too."

"It's been a while since we had pancakes," I say, eyeing the tray.

He reaches for a plate and hands it to me. "It's been a while since we did a lot of things. But I want to change that."

My heart bubbles with hope.

He scoots back against the pillows beside me and stretches his legs out. "I want to make a deal with you."

I narrow my eyes. "What kind of deal?" I ask, smiling over my mouthful of pancakes.

He laughs and wipes the corner of my mouth with the back of his finger. "I've been doing a lot of thinking this morning and…" He inhales a deep breath and exhales it slowly. "I'm going to retire."

I choke a little on my pancakes.

"You okay?" he asks, patting my back.

I swallow and clear my throat. "You what? Sam, have you really thought this through?"

"Actually, I've given it a lot of thought over the last couple of months," he admits. "I'm going to be twenty-eight soon. I've been fighting for over a decade. I've had a great career, and that's how I want to be remembered. As a champion. Not as some guy who didn't know when to quit."

I reach for his hand and hold it in my lap, feeling a strange ache in my heart. "Are you sure?"

"Boxing was all I had for a really long time. But now I've got you. And you," he says to my tummy. "It's time."

"Sam, I don't know what to say."

"Don't say anything yet, because there's a but…and I still haven't told you your side of the deal."

"Okay," I say tentatively.

"I want to finish out my contract. Joe worked too hard to get me this far to stop now. And if I break it, I walk away from seven figures for each fight, I'll lose my endorsements, and I'd pretty much be handing my title over to Carey Valentine."

"Why do you say that?" I ask, trying to keep my voice light.

"Because he's the new me." He looks at me and sighs. "That's what everybody's been saying." He drops his head back against the headboard. "He has almost as many knockout wins as I do, except that he's five years younger and in the prime of his career. People love him. He's practically forcing me into retirement, whether I want to go or not."

"People love *you*. I see it every time you're in the ring. They go crazy for you, not the other guy."

"That's because the other guy hasn't been Carey Valentine. Wait until I go up against him, you'll see who they love more." He laughs softly, but I can't find the humor. If this guy is as good as Sam says he is, I don't want him anywhere near Sam.

"Go up against him?" I ask, suddenly fraught with concern. "When?"

"August. Fight three in my contract is against the one and only Carey Valentine."

"Right before the baby's born," I say softly.

He laces his fingers with mine, and I see a storm brewing behind his beautiful eyes. "I don't want you to worry, Lamb. I know how good he is, which is why I'm working so hard to be even better."

I press my lips together and nod over the lump in my throat. "And then you're done? No more fighting?"

"What better way to go out than beating the *second* best fighter in the WBA?" He gives me a sideways glance and winks.

I ignore the fear that's slithering through my mind and whispering quietly in my ear, *He'll get hurt right before the baby's born.* "Okay."

"Now for your part of the deal," he says, narrowing his eyes, and I look at him expectantly. "Sell the studio. Or give it back." He reaches for my hair and tucks it behind my ear. "I don't like that he gave it to you, Lucy." He shrugs unapologetically.

I inhale a slow, quiet breath and consider it payment for Sam. I can get another studio. I can't replace him. "Okay, I'll sign the deed back over to him this week," I agree, surprised by the relief it gives me to finally make a decision about it. If I wait to find another studio, it could be months before I do it.

He smiles softly and rubs his thumb over my cheekbone. "Whatever house we pick will have room for a home studio. You can paint all hours of the night, if you want."

"That'd be good."

"And there are plenty of available spaces downtown for a new storefront. You and Sebastian can pick whichever one you want. You could even buy one in New York, if that's what you really want." He brushes his thumb across my chin. "Whatever you want. Wherever you want."

I shake my head. "I want to be wherever you are. And I'm still not letting you buy me a new studio."

He grins and nods in agreement.

"I think between all the paintings I've sold and what I'll make off my contract with Molly, I should be able to buy something soon."

He smiles softly. "I know it's hard to give it up, Lamb," he says, staring into my soul. "When something's been a part of you for so long, it's just..." He closes his eyes and exhales. "If you can give it up and start over"—he looks at me again—"I know I can too."

I look into his vulnerable eyes and say with certainty, "You've got yourself a deal, champ."

He smiles and pulls me into a hug. "I couldn't do this without you."

I close my eyes and relish the feeling of unity between us, knowing that no matter what the uncertain future holds, we'll face it together.

"Think you could tell Miles for me?" he asks.

I sit up and give him a sympathetic grin. "You're on your own there."

"Maybe he can go work for Carey Valentine," he says, reaching for his coffee.

I grab my plate of pancakes and give him a dubious look.

"Miles always says, if it makes money, it makes sense."

I smirk. "Did he get that from a movie?"

"Probably."

"What about Tristan?"

"I figure he'll start working with some of the up-and-comers. But what I'd really like to do is open a gym with him in the Park. Maybe find some kids who need a chance."

"Like Joe did with you?"

"Yeah, something like that."

I pull my eyebrows together and chew the corner of my mouth. "Won't that be kind of dangerous?"

He gives me a small smirk. "I survived eighteen years there. I think I can handle it."

"You didn't have money back then. Have you forgotten what happened with Molly?"

He shakes his head. "Do you remember that story Joe used to tell us about what the Park used to be like a long time ago? Back when his dad lived there?"

Images of *Leave It to Beaver* pop into my head. "Yeah."

"Well, what if we could make it like that again?"

I give him a reluctant smile, because I think I know where he's going with this. "Sam, I don't know if that's possible."

"Not all at once. I mean, it might take years, decades even. But what if we started with a community center? A safe place for families to go, where I can teach kids how to box and you can teach them how to paint. We could hire good people from the community and give them a safe place to work."

I smile and nod. "I think that would be pretty incredible."

"I want to give our daughter the world," he says, putting his hand on my stomach. "But I also want her know where we came from."

I put my hand over his. "Me too."

* * *

I hold Sam's hand as we walk across the shiny marble floor in the lobby, catching a glimpse of my reflection in a mirrored wall. Sam convinced me to show off the bump, something I've yet to do, so I put on a white tank top and my stretchiest pair of black skinny jeans, which are riding low on my hips, under my tummy. I tied a flannel shirt around my hips for reinforcement, pulled my hair up into a ponytail, and threw on my comfiest pair of Chuck Taylors, because the realtor called with a few more houses she wants to show us.

Sam looks effortlessly stylish in a pair of worn in gray jeans, a black V-neck T-shirt, and a black Atlanta Falcons hat.

"Well, look at you," Terrance says, eyeing my stomach. "Baby's getting bigger, huh?"

"Hey, Terrance." I smile and nod. "She's definitely growing."

"Won't be long before she's keeping you up all night, like mine." He gives an exhausted smile.

Sam laughs and shakes his hand. "How are you doing today, Terrance?"

"Not as good as you." He smiles and puts his hand on Sam's shoulder. "I see you got a little extra pep in your step I haven't seen in a while. What are you up to?" he asks, eyeing us suspiciously.

Sam laughs and tells him, "We're looking to buy a house."

Terrance drops his head and grabs his chest. "Don't tell me that, Sam. Don't tell me the champ's leaving the building."

"Not for a while probably. We just want to get a head start before the baby gets here."

"Well, I sure will be sorry to see you go."

"Thanks, Terrance."

"You need me to get the car for you?"

"No, we're going to take a walk and get some lunch first."

"Okay. Well, let me get the door." He pulls the heavy glass door open and we walk outside.

"See you later, Terrance," I say as we step out of the shade of the building into the sunshine.

I throw on my Ray-Bans and Sam does the same. He takes my hand and I lean in and whisper, "We totally look like a celebrity couple."

"Lucy, we are a celebrity couple."

I laugh quietly and say, "You are a celebrity. I'm not. Let's get that straight."

"Well, technically, I'm not either. I'm an athlete. It's not quite the same thing."

"Close enough," I say, letting him lead me down the sidewalk.

I look up at the bright sun that's shining in the blue sky, warming my exposed shoulders, and reflecting off the mirrored buildings that line the street.

Sam tugs my hand and pulls me close, and I see a homeless man approaching us. His shirt is tattered and dirty, and his pants, which are hanging off his hips, are torn at the knees. He mumbles something and scratches his long wiry beard.

Sam stops and stands in front of me. "How ya doing?" he asks the man, reaching for his wallet. He pulls a few bills out of it and hands them to him. "Make sure you get a good dinner tonight, okay?"

"God bless you," the man mumbles, taking the money in his blackened hand. "God bless you."

Sam pulls me beside him again and we continue down the sidewalk.

"Sam, that was really sweet. How much money did you give him?"

"I don't know, eighty bucks."

I scrunch up my face. "Eighty bucks?"

"Now he can eat for the rest of the week."

I wrap my hand around his arm and look up at him. "You're a good man, Sam Cole."

"Hey!" Someone calls from behind us. "Champ! Hey, champ!"

Sam turns around and a man reaches for his hand with a big smile on his face. "What's up?" Sam says, shaking his hand.

"I was at the fight at the Garden last year. I saw you knock out Mario Sanchez."

I have to remind myself that I wasn't the only one there that night.

"I had shit seats, but that was one of best fights I've ever been to. You're a fucking beast."

Sam takes my hand again. "Thanks, man."

We turn around and start walking again, but the guy reaches for Sam's shoulder.

"Hey," Sam says, shrugging him off. He lets go of my hand and stands in front of me. "You don't need to put your hands on me, man."

"Sorry. I'm sorry." He holds his hands up and looks at me. "That's your girl?"

Sam's shoulders tense and my lungs begin to work a little harder. "Yeah, that's my girl."

"That's your kid in there?" he asks, looking at my stomach, and I move closer to Sam.

"Yeah, that's my kid, so how about you back up a little, all right?"

"Oh, yeah, yeah. I didn't mean any disrespect. I was just wondering if I could get a picture with you, that's all. I'm a huge fan."

Sam's shoulders relax and so do mine. "Yeah, all right." Sam nods and watches him pull his phone out of his pocket.

"I'll take it," I offer, but Sam gives me a firm look. "It's fine," I say, taking the phone from him. Sam stands next to him and holds his fist up and the guy does the same. "Smile," I say, but neither of them do. I take the picture. "Okay." I hand the phone back to him.

"How about one more of the two of you?" he says, holding his phone up to take a picture.

"Nah, man." Sam pushes his phone down. "You got your picture."

"Damn. Take it easy," he says, looking at his phone.

"Your phone's fine, I just don't want you taking pictures of my girl."

I reach for Sam's hand. "Come on, let's go." I pull him away and we start to walk down the sidewalk again.

"It's not like I asked her to take her top off," the guy says under his breath, and I close my eyes.

I squeeze Sam's hand, but it does little to stop him. He turns around and closes the space between them. "What the fuck did you just say?"

"Sam, stop it," I say, pulling on his shirt. "Let's just go."

He ignores me and asks again, "What did you say?"

The man stares at Sam, seemingly regretting his words. "Nothing, man. I didn't say anything."

"Why don't you go ahead and delete that picture."

"Oh, come on, champ. Don't be like that."

"You want me to do it for you?"

"No," I say, reaching for Sam's arm. "He doesn't." I give Sam a pleading look. "Let him keep his picture. I'm sure he's very sorry. Right?" I give the guy a sharp look.

"Yeah," he says, nodding. "Yeah, I'm sorry."

"Come on." I pull Sam away and take his hand again. "Let's go, I'm hungry."

I glance over my shoulder as we walk away, and I see the man tapping away on his phone. I'd love to know what he's writing, but I'm sure I'll hear about it soon enough. I'm just glad Sam is retiring soon. Hopefully then, the attention from the media *and* rude fans will die down.

*   *   *

"So, what do you think?" our realtor, Kaitlyn, asks in her bubbly southern accent as we exit the second *mansion* she's shown us this afternoon.

"Honestly, I think it's too big," I say to Sam. "I don't know if I could be comfortable in that much space. How would we even keep it clean?"

"You would hire a maid, of course," Kaitlyn says, looking at her phone. "One sec." She holds up a pink acrylic fingernail and answers a call.

"Sam, could we maybe try to find something a little smaller? And a little less, I don't know…shiny?" I glance up at the fancy glass doors and bronze fixtures.

"Lucy, this house is beautiful. It's got everything we need.

Room for a gym, a studio for you. And look at this view." He puts his hands on my shoulders and we look out over the rolling green lawn that's speckled with tall, leafy green trees that cast shadows on the driveway that winds through them all the way to the front gate. "I know it's big, but isn't that what we want? Something we can grow into?"

I turn around and hold my head back. "How many kids do you think we're going to have?"

The corners of his mouth turn up and he crinkles his eyes. "At least five."

"Ha!" I laugh and shake my head. "You must have me confused with someone else. Two is my quota. *Maybe* three, if you're lucky."

"Y'all are never going to believe this," Kaitlyn says, hurrying back over to us on her skinny high heels. "A house just went on the market a few blocks from here. It's much smaller than this, at around nine thousand square feet, but still has everything you're looking for...a gym, a music studio that can be converted to your art room, a pool, a four-car garage, and a nursery built right off the master suite," she says, touching my arm. "What do you say? Do you want to head over and take a peek?"

I look at Sam and shrug. "Okay."

We follow behind her silver Range Rover as she leads us down a tree-lined street to the other house. The dappled sunlight shining through the branches throws shadows on the windshield and reminds me how much I miss suburban life. I've been in the city so long, I forgot how comforting it is. "I miss this," I say, looking out of the window at the manicured lawns and houses we pass.

"What?"

"Trees. Grass." I look over at him. "I like this neighborhood."

"Me too."

"I still think this house is going to be too big, but maybe it could work."

Kaitlyn turns down a driveway and stops in front of a closed wrought iron gate that's flanked by jasmine-covered white brick walls. She lowers her window and enters a code on the keypad, and the gate slowly opens. Sam winds the steering wheel and his engine purrs as he turns into the driveway and follows behind her.

We drive up the paver driveway and park in front of a cozy two-story white brick home that's adorned with modern black carriage lights and dark wooden garage doors. Green jasmine is climbing up a few of the walls. A set of arched, walnut-colored double front doors are situated in the middle of a wide front porch that's covered in varying shades and shapes of gray slate tile. Two oversized, cushioned white wooden swings are hanging in front of the windows behind the tall white columns, adding to its charm.

"I like this house," I say, getting out of the car.

Sam smiles at me over the roof of the car and shuts his door.

"Okay, y'all, what do you think?" Kaitlyn asks, walking up the steps to the front door.

"I think it has tons of character," I say, walking up the steps behind her. I squat down and touch the half-inch grout between the stone tiles. "This is beautiful. Sam, look at this craftsmanship." I stand up and look at the glass inserts in the front doors, appreciating the straight, clean lines.

"These doors were custom made," she says, unlocking them. "Aren't they gorgeous?" She smiles and waves us inside behind her. "Well, come on, y'all."

I walk in before Sam and I'm enveloped in clean white walls, textured wooden floors, and vaulted ceilings that are adorned with weathered wooden beams and large glowing light fixtures that warm the entire space.

"The seller is calling this farmhouse chic," Kaitlyn says, walking through the house. "Everything you see was designed by one of Atlanta's top interior designers."

"What kind of farmhouse looks like this?" Sam asks, shaking his head.

"Come on, let's go check out the kitchen."

We follow her into the open kitchen, which is nestled in the back of the house and surrounded by windows that overlook a sparkling blue pool and large green lawn that's bordered by thick trees.

"Look," I say to Sam, pointing to the far corner of the yard. "A playground." I turn around and see him smiling, leaning against the white marble counter that cascades down the side of the island, and I know...*we're home.*

"I like it," he says to me.

"Me too."

"You've got white uppers," Kaitlyn says, looking at the tall cabinets that encase the kitchen. "But these dark lower cabinets will be great for hiding little fingerprints."

"I love the contrast." I look around the open space and touch the shiny white backsplash. "Especially these tiles."

"So, you don't think it's too big?" she asks, raising her eyebrows over a small smile.

"No." I shake my head and look at Sam. "It actually feels really cozy. I like it." I bite my smiling lip. "A lot."

He turns his hat around backward and looks at Kaitlyn. "We'll take it."

"Sam!" I laugh.

"Don't you want to see the rest of the house first?" She looks at him like he's crazy. "At least let me show you the gym. And the nursery!"

"Yes," I answer for him, wrapping my arm around his waist. "We'd like to see the rest of it."

CHAPTER 16

LUCY, ONE MONTH LATER

I love this town," Sebastian says, standing in front of the floor-to-ceiling windows in my and Sam's suite looking down at the Las Vegas strip that's glittering below.

"Too bad Paul is missing it," he says, shaking his head. "But duty calls."

"Well, I'm just glad he'll be your plus-one for the Aurelia Snow exhibit later this month. It's been a while since we all hung out...Ahh"—I shake my hands out in front of me—"every time I mention it, I get butterflies now. It's like the closer it gets, the more nervous I get."

"That's because it's everything you've been working for since I met you. New York is your endgame."

I put my hands on my growing stomach and shake my head. "I've got a new endgame now."

"Just don't forget that as soon as she's out, you've got five other exhibits to start preparing for."

"I know," I say confidently, even though I have no clue how I'm going to balance the baby with my growing career.

Sebastian notices my uncertainty. "Hey, do you know how many working moms are out there kicking ass right now? You've got this. And, lucky for you, you can bring your baby to work."

"To where? I still have to find us a new studio, remember?"

"Yes, I'm aware. But let's just worry about getting you and Sam moved into your new house first, okay? Still the end of the month, right?"

"Yeah, right after we get back from New York. And after we get settled in the new house, I'm not doing *anything* until the after the baby's born," I declare, though it's not likely. I've still got to get everything in my studio moved out and into storage.

"Don't forget that you need to actually give the deed you signed back to Drew *to Drew*," he reminds me.

"I know. It's been in my bag for weeks. I'm just, not ready to see him...like this," I say, looking down at my tummy.

"Lucy, it's been months. I'm sure he's moved on. And it's not like you have a cold that's going to go away anytime soon. You need to get it over with."

"I know. I'm going to do it when we get back." I look up at the crystal chandelier hanging from the ceiling in the two-story living room and say, "I love this room."

"This"—he glances around the open space, which is encased in glass, clean lines and rich colors—"is not a room, it's an apartment. For like, famous people."

I laugh. "Like Sam?"

"Yeah, and I hear he has this really cool, really fun, really pretty fiancée who's staying here too." He taps his finger against his chin. "Lucy something."

"Want some help with your tie?" I ask, ignoring him.

"What's wrong with my tie?"

I reach up and start tugging it into place. "It's crooked."

"Oh." He stands still while I adjust it.

"I'm surprised no one's come up with a couples name for you and Sam yet."

"A couples name?"

"You know, like Bennifer or Brangelina."

I scrunch up my face. "That's because we're not famous. At least, I'm not. And also because that's stupid."

He looks up to one side and I can see the wheels turning in his head. "What about Sucy?"

I roll my eyes, refusing to entertain him.

"Samucy? No, that sounds too much like Shamu," he says to himself. "Lusam...Lum...Lam!" he says with excited eyes. "Lam," he repeats.

"Absolutely not."

"Lam, the new it couple."

I ignore him and smooth his lapel. "I think all the Vegas glitz and glam has gone to your head."

"But it's perfect. Isn't that what Sam calls you anyway?"

"He calls me Lamb," I say quietly, as if someone besides Sebastian—the only other person in the room—might hear. "With a B. And you cannot call me"—I shake my head—"or us that. Like, ever. Okay? It's weird."

"Okay, okay." He holds his hands up. "I'll come up with something else."

"No you won't." I point at him.

He grins and narrows his eyes. "I think this pregnancy is making you feisty. I like it."

I sigh and put my hands on my stomach. "It's not the pregnancy. It's this fight. I've been on edge since the moment we arrived here."

"Yes, I'm aware," he whispers.

"Really? Is it that obvious?"

"Well, maybe not to everyone else, but I know you. And I know when something's wrong." He gives me an expectant look. "So are we going to talk about it?"

I look up at him and admit, "I just have a bad feeling, Bas. I don't know why, maybe it's some kind of weird pregnancy intuition, but I can feel it in my bones, like a loud warning vibrating through me."

"Warning you about what?"

"Tonight. The fight." I close my eyes and exhale an anxious breath. "I know I sound crazy."

"You think Sam's going to lose?"

I shrug. "I don't know. I just don't feel good about it."

"Lucy, Brody Crawford is good, but Sam is better. Far better. He's not going to lose tonight," he says confidently.

"I'm not worried about him losing. I'm worried about him getting hurt."

He gives me an empathetic look and puts his hands on my arms. "You've always worried about that, Luc. But that's why he's been training so hard. He'll be fine."

"He was upset this morning, Bas. He barely spoke on the flight here. I think going into the ring under the lights for the first time without Joe is dredging everything back up. I could see it in his eyes, festering away inside him. I just don't know what to expect tonight."

"You think he'll lose his edge?"

"No. I think it'll be ten times sharper."

"Is that a bad thing?"

"Sebastian, before Joe, Sam used to get into fights all the time, usually over me. I know what happens when he fights with his heart instead of his head. He's careless."

Someone knocks on the door.

Bas hesitates, then crosses the room to answer it. "Hey, Miles."

"You guys ready?" Miles asks, walking inside. His eyes light up when he sees me, but concern quickly takes over. "Sweetheart, what's wrong?"

"Nothing," I lie. "I'm ready." I give him a small smile and grab my clutch off the couch.

He stares at me for a second. "You sure?"

"Yeah."

"You look great. That's a hell of a dress."

"She looks like a pregnancy goddess," Bas gushes, taking my hand. He spins me around to show Miles the back of my simple, backless black dress. It wraps over one shoulder and hugs my belly, which is no longer concealable, and falls all the way to my strappy stiletto-clad feet.

Miles raises one of his dark eyebrows and gives a subtle nod, but seems far more interested in the time. "Come on, we've gotta go."

"You make seven months pregnant look hot," Bas whispers to me, and I smile over my apprehension. He wraps my hand around his arm and we follow Miles out of the room.

* * *

The crowd is alive tonight at the legendary MGM Grand in Las Vegas... The younger, quicker fighter, Brody Crawford, vying for a belt he's yet to claim... He's got a hard fight ahead of him tonight... Sam Cole, the more seasoned boxer, is not ready to relinquish his title just yet...

He's not ready to retire yet either, the other announcer says, and I give Sebastian a knowing look.

The arena rumbles with cheers. and my chest vibrates from the music echoing off the walls. I mindlessly rub my stomach, wondering if the music's vibrating her too.

His pregnant fiancée, Lucy, is looking anxious for the fight to begin.

"Camera's on you," Bas says to me, and I smile reflexively.

Sam has said that he can't wait to be a father... I sure hope it's not a girl. One of the announcers laughs. *God help the boy she brings home.*

I try not to smile at the thought I've had a hundred times, but the corners of my mouth turn up defiantly.

The lights dim and the spotlights cascade across the crowd like rays of sunlight filtering through the dark. They move from one corner of the arena to the other, lighting each section to the beat of the music, which grows louder. My heart grows louder too, pounding away inside my chest against my will. I take slow, deep breaths and try to relax. *He's going to be fine*, I repeat like a mantra, again and again.

Sebastian reads me and says, "He's going to be fine."

I nod and fight back the fear that retaliates when Sam begins to make his way toward the ring. My pulse races and pounds behind my ears when I see his new coach leading him through the crowd, and suddenly I'm caught in unexpected storm of grief and anxiety. I work hard to keep it off my face, but it's so strong I could drown in it. "This isn't right," I say to Sebastian, who gives me a worried look. "He's never fought without Joe."

"He'll be fine," he says, but it does little to reassure me.

Sam Cole is being led by his new coach, Chris Torino, following the death of his lifelong coach and mentor, Joe Maloney, in March... Our hearts go out to him and his fiancée, Lucy, who was also involved in the tragic car accident... She was lucky to come out of it with only minor injuries.

"Minor injuries?" Bas scoffs.

Tonight will be the first time Sam has entered the ring without him.

Or Tristan Kelley, the other announcer adds, *his longtime trainer and friend... He has his work cut out for him tonight. We'll see how he does without them.*

"I don't feel good about him," I say to Miles, eyeing Sam's new coach as he climbs up into the ring after him.

"You don't like him because he's not Joe. You'd feel that way about anybody right now."

"He doesn't care about Sam, he barely even knows him."

"He's a good coach, one of the best. And he cares about winning. He's good for Sam."

"Is that what you care about?" I ask, clapping numbly with the crowd. "Winning?"

"Hell yeah, I care about winning. How do you think he got this far?" He gives me an incredulous look.

"It's not just about winning, Miles." I look up at Sam, whose face is frighteningly calm. His whole body is calm, a stark contrast to the energy that usually exudes from him before a match. He's not cheering or enticing the crowd, he's not bouncing from foot to foot. He's saving every last ounce of it for the fight, like an animal before it attacks its prey.

"You think you'd be moving into that beautiful house if he didn't win? You think you'd be staying in that suite or wearing that dress?"

"You know I don't care about any of that," I shout over the noisy crowd.

"Easy to say now."

"God, Miles, do you even care about Sam?" I yell at him over the announcers, who are talking about Brody Crawford as he approaches the ring.

"Do I care about Sam?" He raises his eyebrows and gives me an exasperated smile. "Are you fucking kidding me?"

"It's a simple question."

"Lucy, that's enough," Bas says. "Now's not the time. Cameras, remember?"

But I don't care about the cameras. Sam is about to go into battle without his brothers, and Miles looks happy about it.

"Lucy, you know I love you," Miles says, swinging his arm around my neck. He kisses my cheek. "I love Sam too." When I don't respond, he looks at me and says earnestly, "Yes, I care about Sam."

"And when he loses…will you care about him then?"

He pulls his arm away and claps with the crowd. "I thought you knew me better than that."

"I do."

"No." His face is a mix of disappointment and hurt. "If you knew me, you wouldn't be asking me that."

"You're right, I'm sorry." I reach for his arm. "Hey…" I tug on it until he looks at me. "I'm sorry."

"Yeah"—he gives me a halfhearted nod—"okay."

"Half of his family is missing right now, Miles. I'm just a little protective. And worried."

"I'm worried too, but it won't do him any good if he knows. So put a smile on your face, please." He glances up at the ring and I see Sam looking at us.

I smile at him over the anxiety that's now cemented around my heart and see the animal inside him subside for a fleeting moment. But when Brody Crawford takes his stance in front of him, I watch it return.

I hold my breath as the fight commences.

Crawford throws the first punch, but Sam blocks it and returns a jab and a fast left hook.

We might be seeing something new from Sam tonight…He isn't wasting any time…Ohhh!!

Sam takes a punch to the face that happened so fast I barely saw it.

Brody Crawford is making sure we remember just how fast he is…I don't think anyone saw that coming, including Sam.

The referee steps between them for a moment, then they begin again, returning punches back and forth, until they're dripping with sweat. Neither one of them is letting up, and neither is the crowd.

"There you go, baby!" Miles shouts when Sam throws a left hook that leaves Brody stumbling backward.

But seconds later Sam takes a hard blow to the jaw, and I watch the light leave his eyes for a moment. When it returns, he inhales a deep breath and explodes at Crawford, giving him everything he's got, but Crawford gives it right back.

I proceed to watch the next several rounds between my hands, praying that each one is the last.

By the eighth round, they both look as horrible as I feel. Brody is bleeding from his mouth, and Sam's left eye is completely swollen shut. He's taken too many hits to count.

"Get your gloves up! Protect that eye, Sam!" Miles screams at him.

When the bell rings, I drop my face to my hands and exhale.

"Are you kidding me?" Bas screams when the ref gives the round to Crawford.

Sam Cole is looking the worse for wear…

Brody Crawford wins the round, but he doesn't look much better, the other announcer says. *I don't know if anyone expected Crawford to last this long, especially not Sam… This is not the Sam Cole we're used to seeing… You can't help but wonder if the loss of Joe Maloney is taking its toll on him tonight.*

When the ninth round begins, the baby starts rolling around inside my stomach, reminding me of everything that's at stake. I close my eyes and pray, *Please God, don't let him take another hit.*

By the looks of it, Crawford has won most of the rounds tonight… And that's another hit to the head for Cole!

The air rushes out of my lungs on an emotional wave that rushes up to my eyes. I pull hands up to my face and hold my breath until it goes away.

Miles leans over and says, "He's all right. He can take it."

"Well, I can't." I turn to Sebastian, but Miles grabs my hand. "You gotta be stronger than that, Luc. He can't see you upset right now. You gotta be strong for him, okay? You hear me?" he shouts over the crowd.

"Yeah, I hear you," I shout back. I inhale a shaky breath, sit up straight in my chair, and force myself to watch. "Come on, Sam!"

And that's the end of round nine, going to Sam Cole this time...By the looks of them, I can't believe either one of them is still standing.

Sam falls into his corner and slouches on a stool while they tend to his eye and give him water. When he spits it out, it's full of blood.

Sebastian takes my hand and squeezes it in his. "He's okay."

"Sam," I call, and he looks up at me with his good eye. *I love you*, I mouth.

He stares at me for a long, silent second and then gets to his feet again. He stands across from Crawford on tired legs, his overworked blood vessels stretching across his exhausted muscles like roads on a map. He turns his head to the side and spits blood out of his mouth.

"I can't watch this," I say, looking at Sebastian.

"Yes!" Bas shouts when Sam blocks a jab.

Sam Cole might be getting his second wind...I didn't see that coming, but he sure did.

Sam throws a left hook, a right hook, and another left hook that leaves Crawford hanging off him. Sam pushes him back against the ropes.

"There you go, Sam, there you go!" Miles screams. "Show him who the fucking champ is!"

Crawford pushes off the ropes and throws two punches at Sam's ribs, but Sam lowers his elbow and protects himself.

"That's right, baby," I whisper beneath my hands. But Crawford punches low, connecting with Sam's hip near his groin.

That was a low blow for Crawford!

Sam stumbles back and Crawford takes the opportunity to hit him again before the referee intervenes. The ref grabs Brody's arm and pulls him over to the side of the ring, giving Sam space and a minute to catch his breath. "That's one point. Low blow. One point," he says, holding up his gloved finger.

One point for that low blow. Crawford is losing a point.

The ref puts his hand on Sam's shoulder and asks, "You all right, you ready?"

Sam nods and puts his gloves up in front of him again.

"Okay. Time in, let's go."

Sam stands across from Crawford and the energy in the arena swells. But the cheers and jeers of the crowd turns to white noise in my head when they start throwing punches at each other again. After a few seconds, they bear-hug each other, waiting for their energy to return, until the ref breaks them apart. Then suddenly, like two sharks attacking each other, they explode with wild energy, throwing punches back and forth so fast, I can't tell who's punching who, until Crawford connects with Sam's face so hard it sends him flying backward onto the bloodstained mat.

Everything falls silent as I watch the referee stand over Sam and start counting. I see his mouth moving, but I can't hear him. Sebastian squeezes my hand and I glance up at his horrified face. I look to my left and see Miles screaming, the blood vessels in his red neck bulging with every word I can't hear.

The baby kicks hard and the sound of the electrified arena rushes back into my ears, forcing the air out of my lungs.

Sam Cole is not getting up. I don't believe it. Cole is not getting up, ladies and gentlemen... This might be it.

The referee keeps counting, *Seven... eight...*

This is a sad moment if you're a Sam Cole fan... And a scary moment for his fiancée, watching from beside the ring... He is out cold.

"Ten!" the referee shouts, and it rings through my ears like a gun firing. The accompanying cries from the crowd pierce through me like the bullet it released.

And that is it. The belt goes to Brody Crawford, the new light-heavyweight champion.

The doctor rushes over to Sam and puts his hands on his shoulders, but Sam doesn't move. He puts one of his gloved fingers inside Sam's mouth and removes his mouth guard.

Miles rushes to the ring and climbs up between the ropes. "Get her back to the dressing room," he shouts at Grady, who promptly takes my arm.

"No!" I shout, watching them hold smelling salts under Sam's nose and pat his cheeks before Sebastian drags me away.

* * *

I pace around the dressing room in my bare feet, practically drowning myself in a bottle of water. "I told you I had a bad feeling, Bas. I knew it was too soon for him to be fighting again after losing Joe."

"It was the way he fought," Bas says, shaking his head. "He put everything into those first few rounds."

"Why would he do that? He never does that."

"That wasn't him. That was the coach. Joe would have never

let him do that. He would have tired Crawford out first and then finished him in the last few rounds." He drops his head back against the wall he's leaning against.

"Lucy," Miles calls, walking into the room, and I rush over to him.

"How is he?"

"Doc's finished with him. He says he's all right."

"As in, he has another concussion, all right?"

"No, no concussion this time. The doctor said he was lucky. He likened it to hitting your funny bone. Said it was temporary nerve trauma near the base of his skull, but it's fairly common with knockouts and relatively benign."

Tears fill the rims of my tired eyes. "He's really okay?"

He shakes his head. "This one really messed him up, Luc," he says disheartened, and the disappointment is reflected in Sebastian's eyes. "The only person he wants to see right now is you."

I hurry to the adjoining room, leaving Bas and Miles behind me.

"Grady will wait outside until you're ready to go back to the suite."

"Okay," I say over my shoulder, closing the door behind me.

I walk into the messy room and find Sam slouched in a chair with his head hanging. "Sam?" I walk over to him and he slowly lifts his head, but barely enough to look at me. He mumbles something, but I don't understand him. "What?" I bend down and put my hand on his face, and he groans softly. "I'm sorry," I whisper, and he mumbles something again, but I can't make out what he's saying. "Sam, hey, look at me," I say, squatting down in front of him, and he looks at me with one eye. The other is swollen shut and purple all the way to his temple.

"I'm sorry," he mumbles.

I grab a nearby towel and lift it to his mouth and wipe the blood and saliva dripping from it. "You don't have anything to be sorry about, Sam. I'm so proud of you."

He tries to take the towel from me, but he can barely lift his arm.

"What is it, baby? What do you need?"

"I need to take a shower," he mumbles, trying to stand up.

"Okay." I hold his arms. "Careful," I say, praying he can stand up, because there's no way I can lift him. "Want me to get Grady?"

"No...no." He gets to his feet and I wrap my arm around his waist. I walk with him to the shower and turn the water on.

"Want me to help you get your shorts off?"

He drops his hands on the counter, but doesn't answer.

"I'm going to take your shorts off, okay?"

He stands still while I pull his bloodstained shorts down, noticing every bruise and red mark on his body.

He lifts his head and looks at himself in the mirror. "Fucking disgrace," he says quietly.

"Come on, baby." I help him into the large, clean shower and he sits down on the tile floor. "Sam."

He leans back against the tile wall and slowly shakes his head. "Just wait out there for me," he says, closing his eyes.

"No, I'm not leaving you."

"You don't need to see me like this." He pulls his knees up and his head hangs down to his chest.

"Want me to wash you?" I ask, ignoring him, but he doesn't

answer. He just sits in the streaming water with his head hanging.

"I'm sorry," he says again, and his shoulders rise up and down. He holds his hand up and I quickly wrap mine around it. "I didn't mean to let you down."

"Sam, you didn't let me down." I fight back tears that are battling their way to my eyes and sit down in the shower next to him, ignoring the water that's pelting me and soaking my dress. "You didn't let Joe down either," I say, dropping my head to his shoulder.

He lifts his head and drops it back against the wall and I watch a silent tear roll down his flushed cheek.

I reach for his tortured face and hold it in my wet hand. "You are the most important person in the world to me." I put my hand on the slippery, wet material covering my stomach. "To us. Tonight *we* won, because we still get you. That's all that matters. And we'll take you any way we can get you. Without titles, without belts, without the fame or money that comes with it. Because none of that matters if we don't have you."

He looks at me, but doesn't say anything.

I wrap my arm around his stomach and put my head on his shoulder, and we sit together in the dressing room shower until the water washes away the blood and sweat and tears of the night.

CHAPTER 17

LUCY

I wake to the Nevada sun shining through the windows that encase our suite. It glows pink over the dark outline of the mountains on the horizon under a clear blue morning sky. I sit up and stretch my hands over my head, nearly forgetting about last night, until I look over at Sam and see him lying in a small pool of blood, which has stained the pillowcase under his mouth. He's snoring softly, so I don't bother to wake him while I do an inspection of his injuries.

His eye isn't as swollen, but it's still purple, and blood bruises have appeared on his back that look like rug burns. His hands are red around his knuckles and the short stubble around his mouth is stained red with dried blood.

I get up and go downstairs to the living room and dial the concierge. "Good morning, I'd like to order room service... Um, just one of everything... Okay, thanks... Oh, and some coffee please. Regular and decaf... Okay, thank you." I hang up the phone and head back upstairs when I hear the TV on in our room.

I mean, look, the guy is at the end of his career. If you don't want to admit that...I'm not arguing with you. I'm just saying that last night shouldn't define his entire career. Sam Cole is still one of the greatest boxers of our time...No one's saying he isn't. The guy has twenty-six wins and twelve knockouts. He's had a longer run than any of the boxers he started out with. But now he's going up against guys who are younger and quicker. He can't keep up!...Well, Carey Valentine's banking on that. He said recently that he's ready to show the world who the new champion is...Carey might get the chance when he goes up against Brody Crawford next month. But I'll tell you, Sam Cole won't lose a match at the Garden. It's where he got his first belt and, if rumors are true, it's where he'll get his last...So your money's on Sam, whether Valentine takes the title from Crawford or not. Is that what you're saying?...That's what I'm saying...Can I get you to say it to the camera?...Hey, I'm a Sam Cole fan through and through. My money's on Sam. He'll beat Carey Valentine...You heard him, ladies and gentlemen. If you want to lose your hard-earned money, place your bets on Sam Cole in August when he goes toe to toe with Carey Valentine at the Garden.

Sam is sitting up in bed, holding the remote, staring at the TV.

"Hi." I walk over to the bed and sit down next to him. "Why are you watching that?"

"I wanted to retire on my terms. Not theirs."

"You are." I scoot over to him.

"No." He turns the TV off and puts the remote down. "I'm a fucking joke now."

I look at his beautiful eyes through the bruises. "Sam, you are not a joke." I push his hair off his forehead. "You lost. And that's okay. Because it shows that you're human, despite what some people think." I smile softly. "You're flesh and blood, like everyone else, and you can fall like everyone else. It's how you get up that defines you."

"I have to beat Carey Valentine," he says resolutely, and my skin pricks with quiet fear.

I take the pillow from behind him, and start shimmying off the bloodstained pillowcase. "You don't have to prove anything to anyone, Sam."

"Yes I do." He gives me a disconcerted look and gets up, groaning quietly as he stands.

I grab a bottle of water and the ibuprofen off the nightstand and shake a couple into my hand. "Here." I hand them to him. "Take these."

He swallows the pills down and gets up to look at himself in the mirror. "Fuck," he says, inspecting his face. The doorbell rings and Sam looks at me in the mirror.

"I thought you'd be hungry, so I ordered room service." I head back downstairs to get the door.

By the time Sam comes down to join me, the dining room table is covered in steaming breakfast plates, from waffles to omelets and everything in between. He looks at the table and then looks at me. "Is the whole crew coming for breakfast?"

"No, I just didn't know what you'd want and I didn't want to wake you. That obviously didn't pan out."

He sits down at the table and reaches for an omelet.

"Want some pancakes?" I ask, holding the plate up.

He shakes his head and grumbles quietly, "Not in the mood."

Okay.

I sit down across from him and pick up a piece of bacon, but I can barely swallow it by the time I'm done chewing. Sam is staring at his plate, silently eating his omelet without looking up.

"The baby was cheering for you last night," I say, forcing a smile when he looks up at me. "She was kicking a lot." I shrug. "I think she liked the music. Or maybe she hated it, I don't know." I laugh softly.

He puts his fork down on his clean plate. "Probably isn't good for her," he says impassively and stands up. "I'm going to go take a shower."

"Okay."

I finish my coffee alone with my thoughts, then I grab another piece of bacon and take my phone out onto the terrace that overlooks the mountains and the quiet strip below. I inhale the cool morning air and walk over to the edge of the glass balcony wall. I gaze out at the orange sun climbing over the mountains in the distance, ignoring the city below me, and listen to the occasional call of a bird.

My phone buzzes in my hand and before I even look at it, I know that it's Sebastian, the only person who would call me this early.

"Hey," I answer, holding my phone to my ear. "I was just going to call you."

"How's he doing?"

"Um..." I press my lips together and shake my head. "He's not good. Last night was rough. And judging by this morning, I'm not sure today is going to be any easier."

"Well, whatever you do, don't let him turn on the TV."

"Too late."

"Is he watching right now?"

"No, he's in the shower. Why, what are they saying?"

"That they think it's time for Sam to retire. They said he should have beaten Brody Crawford hands down."

I drop my face into my hand and groan softly. "Bas, if he couldn't beat Crawford, how is he going to beat Carey Valentine?"

"Thanks for the encouragement," Sam says, surprising me, and a small part of me considers flinging myself over the glass.

"I have to go," I say, hanging up on Bas. "Sam, that's not what I meant." I follow him back inside, dragging my heart behind me.

"Don't worry about it," he says, sitting down on the couch.

"Sam, please, you know that's not what I meant."

"It's fine, it doesn't matter." He folds his hands together and pulls them up to his mouth.

"Yes, it does matter." I sit down next to him. "I'm sorry." I reach for his arm. "I know that's the last thing you needed to hear right now."

"If that's how you feel, it's how you feel. I said don't worry about it." He stares blankly across the room.

"Don't worry about it?" I huff. "All I can do is worry about it. All I can do is think about you fighting Carey Valentine in *two* months." I drop my head to the side and look at his bruised face. "Look at you," I cry, shaking my head.

"So, what, you don't like the way I look now?"

"It's not funny, Sam. Do you even know how many hits you took last night? Because I couldn't keep count."

He closes his eyes and drops his head back against the couch.

"Two months," I say again. "That's all we have left. Then everything changes, everything's different. It's not just about us anymore."

"You think I don't know that?" He looks at me and stands up. "You think I don't know that?" he asks again, louder.

"I know you're going through something right now, but—"

"What?" he shakes his head.

"You don't have to admit it, because I know it." I get up and stand in front of him. "I know you, Sam. Even if you wish I didn't right now, I do. And I know you're still dealing with Joe's death. I know you haven't been able to get past it. And I know that last night, it was all you could think about, because he wasn't there. That's why you fought the way you did."

"The way I fought? The way I fought was to win. The way I fought was for everything I've worked for my whole fucking life. The way I fought was *for* Joe!"

"No…Joe wouldn't have let you fight like that."

"Let me fight like what?"

"Like you had nothing to lose," I cry.

He pulls his hands to his head and runs his fingers through his wet hair. "I had everything to lose last night. Everything! My whole fucking career in one night!" he shouts, slapping his hands together.

"Your career," I whisper, watching him drift further and further away from me.

"Do you know what it feels like to have everything you've worked for stripped away in a single moment? A moment that will be played for the world to see over and over and over again. A moment that will overshadow every accomplishment, every record, every title I've ever held. One moment"—he holds his finger up—"that destroyed everything. Do you know what that's like?"

I blink back tears that sting my guarded eyes. "No, I don't know what that's like. But I know that it's not everything."

He puts his hands on his hips and drops his chin. "I don't expect you to understand."

I exhale a shocked breath. "Enlighten me."

"Last night was what, the fifth fight you've been to? You haven't been a part of this long enough to understand the magnitude of what losing the way I lost means."

I release an incredulous breath and lock my armor into place. "Thanks for that reminder," I say, blinking up at him. "I almost forgot that while you were out there building your career, I was watching through a microscope. I watched you win, I watched you get famous, I watched you sow your wild oats for the whole world to see." I cross my arms over my round stomach and shake my head. "I'd almost completely forgotten about that."

"That's what you want to do right now? You want to compare lives while we were apart? All right, let's talk about the fact that you almost married someone else. Let's talk about that!" he shouts in his deep voice.

I turn around and stalk up the stairs.

"What, you can give it, but you can't take it?"

I stop halfway up and put my hands on either side of my

stomach. "Is this not enough for you? I'm carrying *your* child," I cry. "Yours! Not Drew's." He stares at me and I stare back, and I wonder how we got here. "Maybe all this would be easier if I wasn't." I regret saying it as soon as the words leave my mouth.

"What did you say?"

The baby rolls inside my stomach and the guilt settles on my shoulders like a lead blanket. "I didn't mean that." I grip the brass railing and close my eyes. *I'm sorry*, I say to her, making a silent vow to never let anything come before her again. Including Sam. I can't protect him from himself, but I can protect her.

"Yeah, well, maybe it would be."

I open my watery eyes and force my heavy feet to carry me the rest of the way up the stairs, silently wincing through a Braxton Hicks contraction that turns my stomach into a tight ball.

Sam climbs up after me. "Lucy."

"I think I'm going to stay with Sebastian for a little while when we get home," I say, wiping my cheeks. "If Paul's okay with it."

"What?" He stares at me, but I can't look at him.

I open my suitcase and start sorting through my clothes. "I think I just need some time to myself...away from everything for a little while."

"Away from me?"

I steel my heart and look up at him.

His face is unreadable, but his chest is heaving up and down.

"Away from the stress. It's not good for the baby," I say honestly, choking back tears. "The house will be ready in a few weeks. Maybe it can be a fresh start."

"A fresh start? You want to stay with Sebastian until we move?"

"It's only a few weeks."

"What about New York? The exhibit?"

"I think you need time too, Sam. I think…maybe I should go alone."

He runs his hand through his hair. "See, that's where you're wrong…I don't need time."

"Yes you do, Sam."

"No I don't," he says firmly, reaching for my arm. "I don't need anything…except for you. Please, Lamb, don't do this," he pleads.

My stomach tightens again, but I ignore it. "I love you, Sam. I just need some time to catch my breath."

He lets out a heavy sigh and his hands fall away. "Yeah," he nods and looks at the floor. "If you think it's best." He looks up at me again with empty eyes. "Whatever's best for the baby."

I swallow hard and nod. "Okay."

* * *

I lift my heavy head and turn my pillow over and cry into the other side. The early morning light that's peeking through the covered window in Paul and Sebastian's guest room tells me that I've cried myself into a new day. I pull the silky sheet up to my face and wipe my tears, but more come.

"Lucy," Sebastian says softly, cracking the door open. I peek up at him and he walks into the room and sits on the bed beside me. "Are you okay?"

I shake my head and squeak, "No."

"Come here." He pulls me up off the pillow and into his arms.

I lay my head on his shoulder and cry into his T-shirt. "What am I doing, Bas?"

"You're taking a break." He rubs my back. "You just needed a break."

"I'm sorry."

"What are you sorry for?"

"I'm a mess." I sit up and wipe my face on my shirt. "A hot pregnant mess."

He pulls a few tissues out of the tissue box on the night-stand and hands them to me. "You're allowed to be a hot mess right now."

"Do you think I did the right thing, Bas? He's so vulnerable right now."

He gives me an earnest look. "I know Sam's going through a lot right now, but so are you. Aside from the ex-hibit coming up and recovering from a car accident, you're growing a tiny human. And she needs you." He smiles softly. "She needs you healthy and strong and ready to be the best mom you can be for her. That's why you're taking a break. For her."

"She needs her father too."

"It's just a break, Lucy, not a breakup."

"It hurt him, Sebastian. What if he doesn't forgive me?"

"For doing what's right for his daughter? Sam Cole loves two things: you and the baby." He closes his eyes and says, "Okay, three things. Boxing is obviously important too."

I close my eyes and the tears come again. "He was so broken after the fight. I've never seen him like that before."

"He's human. He's going to break from time to time." He hands me the box of tissues. "So are you."

"I just want everything to go back to normal."

"Normal?" Bas laughs. "Nothing about you and Sam has ever been normal. You're life has been a whirlwind since the second he came back into it."

"Is it too much to ask for a gentle breeze from time to time?"

"Breezes are boring. Breezes are *Drew*. Sam is a storm, filled with thunder and lightning. But isn't that what you love about him?"

I nod and let go of the idea of a quiet life, because know I'll never have that with Sam. "I'm sorry I woke you up. Did I wake up Paul?"

"No, he's still snoring away." He rolls his eyes and laughs softly. "Hey, I know something that will cheer you up." He gets up and opens the curtains, and soft sunlight fills the room. "Let's go shopping for the new house."

I sniff and smile at him. "Okay."

"Get up, get a shower, brush your teeth." He pulls me up by my hands and I stand in front of him. "You'll feel better, I promise. I'll go make some coffee."

"Okay."

He leaves the room and I gather my clothes off the back of the green tufted armchair in the corner. I choose my stretchy gray Henley dress and a pair of sneakers.

After my shower, I dry my hair and pull it up into a messy bun on the top of my head. I grab my bag and my sunglasses and meet Sebastian in the kitchen.

"Ready?" he asks, handing me a to-go cup of coffee while

looking effortlessly casual in a scoop-neck black and white striped T-shirt, navy blue slacks, and crisp white sneakers.

"Yep."

We drive through the city, going from store to store, and I follow Sebastian around as he picks out furniture and various pieces of décor he thinks would be perfect for my and Sam's new house.

"I like this," I say, rubbing my hand over a faux fur blanket that's draped over the back of a leather chair. It's marbled with beige and brown and gray lines that blend together.

"Looks like wolf fur," Bas says, and I move my hand away.

"Then Sam wouldn't like it."

He pauses and looks at me. "Why?"

"He has a thing with wolves."

Bas gives me a funny look, but I only notice it for a moment. My heart takes off in a sprint when I see who's behind him, and my stomach tightens under my dress.

"Lucy," Drew says, making his way around a large wooden table that's separating us.

Sebastian's eyes widen and he mouths, *Is that Drew?*

I ignore him and keep my eyes on Drew, afraid that if I look away I might not be able to keep my feet from carrying me to the nearest exit.

"Hey," he says, standing in front of me, and something about his familiar voice resonates deep inside me.

"Hi, Drew," I say, sounding as surprised as I am.

Sebastian turns around and looks at him. "Hello, Drew. It's nice to see you," he says cordially, and I give him a quick glance.

"Hi, Sebastian. How have you been?"

"I've been well. Thanks."

"That's good to hear," Drew says, looking at me again, staring for a second too long. "You look...you look great, Luc." He glances down at my stomach and shakes his head. "Wow." He smiles softly and it tugs hard at my heart. "It's a good look on you."

I press my lips together and tuck a stray piece of hair behind my ear. "Thanks," I say quietly.

He eyes the engagement ring on my hand. "So when's the big day?" He smiles over the sadness in his eyes, and I see the life we were supposed to have reflected in them.

"We, um, we haven't set a date yet." I smile uncomfortably. "Maybe after the baby's born."

He puts his hands in his pockets and looks at my stomach again. "I can't believe you're going to be a mom."

"Me neither," I say with wide eyes, trying to pretend that a piece of my heart isn't breaking for him.

"You're going to be really great," he says sincerely, and it squeezes my heart so hard I can barely breathe.

"Lucy, wasn't there something you were meaning to talk to Drew about?" Sebastian says, looking at me expectantly.

"What?" I blink up at him and he gives me a knowing look. "Oh, right," I say, finding my way out of the emotional rabbit hole I fell into. I look at Drew. "Drew, I um, I don't know if you got my letter or not, but—"

"If this is about the studio, Lucy...it's yours. I wanted you to have it. There's nothing to talk about."

"Is that why you didn't call?"

"I got your letter," he says, dropping his chin, "but I just didn't know what else to say."

"Drew, I know you want to give me the studio, and I'm so

grateful, but…" I reach into my purse and pull out the deed that's been burning a hole in it for the better part of a month. "I can't accept it." I hand it to him. "I signed it back over to you."

"Lucy."

"We can be as out soon as you need, but if you could give me a few weeks, that would really help."

He gives me a look that tugs at my heart. "Take as much time as you need."

I open my mouth to thank him, but before I can get any words out, a tall, pretty brunette with a bright white smile walks over to us. "There you are," she sings in a soft southern accent, putting her hand on Drew's back. "I thought I lost you." She looks at us and smiles. "He hates when I drag him around from store to store like this."

Drew looks at me and says, "Lucy, this is Katherine. My girl-friend."

The word catches me off guard and although I have no right whatsoever to feel any kind of jealousy, I do. "Hi," I say over the feeling in my chest, and reach out to shake her hand. "It's nice to meet you." I smile at her.

"Lucy? *The* Lucy?"

I give Drew a curious look. "I guess so."

"I'm sorry, I just never expected to actually meet you. Now that you're famous and all."

"It was bound to happen eventually," Drew says to her.

"I'm not famous," I say quietly, shaking my head.

"Just look at you," she says, eyeing my stomach. "How far along are you?"

"Oh, um, around seven months," I say guardedly, and I feel Sebastian tense beside me.

"Well, you didn't waste any time, did you?" She smiles over the insult disguised by her pleasant voice.

"So, who are you, what do you do?" Bas asks, dropping his head to the side.

"I'm Katherine Campbell." She smiles and reaches out to shake his hand. "Second vice president of the AWC."

He shakes her hand and squints his eyes. "I'm sorry, I don't know that acronym."

"The Atlanta Women's Club."

"Ahhh. Okay." He presses his lips together and bobs his head. He smiles at me, then smiles at her. "Makes sense," he says, crinkling his eyes.

"You must be Sebastian Ford. Lucy's assistant, right?"

"I am, yes."

"Not today. Today, he's just my friend." I wink at him.

"Aren't you lucky to have him to do this sort of thing." She glances around the store. "I bet Sam hates shopping."

"Um…" I shake my head, unsure what to say and annoyed by her presumption.

"We should get going," Drew says, giving me a small smile.

"Yes, we don't want to miss our lunch reservation. I'm starving," she says, putting her hand on her flat stomach.

"Okay," I say, watching her wrap her long, skinny, French-manicured fingers around his arm.

He pulls away and leans in to give me a hug. I reach around him and awkwardly pat his back. But he squeezes me in his arms and says quietly, "It was really good to see you."

"You too," I say to him before he releases me.

"Nice meeting y'all," Katherine says, pulling Drew away.

When they're gone, Sebastian falls into an oversized chair

and pulls me into his lap. "Oh, my God." He puts his hand on my stomach and speaks to the baby, "Don't worry, you never have to see that mean lady ever again."

I laugh softly. "She wasn't that bad."

"She totally insulted you, and what was with that smug look? *I'm president of the AWC*," he says in a high-pitched voice.

"Second vice president. Get it right."

"Oh, pardon me."

"Janice must *love* her," I say, widening my eyes dramatically. "Oh my God, Drew's going to marry his *mother*!"

"What? Who said anything about them getting married?"

"Oh, as if Drew could escape those claws. It's inevitable."

"Yeah." I shrug. "You're probably right. But good for him. He deserves to be happy."

"You're right. He deserves her," he says, smirking.

"Sebastian. You just never liked Drew—Ow!" I put my hand on my stomach, which is promptly followed by Sebastian's.

"What is it?" he asks, alarmed.

I inhale a deep breath and put my hand over his. "Do you feel that?"

"Yeah, your stomach is like a rock."

"It's a contraction."

His eyes get big and he sits up straight, moving me with him. "It's too early for contractions," he says, panicked.

"It's just a Braxton Hicks, not the real thing. I've been getting them a lot lately. The doctor said stress can bring them on." I raise my eyebrows at him.

"Oh. Well, I thought shopping would decrease your stress

level, but clearly I've steered you awry. Let me make it up with lunch?"

I smile at him. "Lunch sounds good. But nowhere that takes reservations, okay?"

"Made-to-order tacos it is."

CHAPTER 18

SAM

Tristan leans over and puts his hands on his knees for a few seconds to catch his breath.

I stop walking and put my hand on his shoulder. "You okay, you need to take a break?"

He shakes his head and stands back up. "No." He starts walking again. "Doctor said I have to push myself."

"Okay." I walk beside him.

He smiles wide and laughs. "Who would have ever thought a walk around Piedmont Park would be pushing myself."

"It's been a couple of miles. Don't be too hard on yourself."

He puts his hand over his heart and says, "Come on, Joe, we can go a little farther."

I look over at him. "It's weird, isn't it? It's like he's still here or something."

"Tell me about it. I love the guy, but when Molly wants to take my clothes off, I feel like he's in the room with us."

"Ahh, she probably wouldn't mind." I smirk.

"Hey, now, don't talk about my girl like that."

I hold my hands up. "Sorry, sorry."

"Speaking of girls, what's going on with you and Lucy? You guys work everything out yet?"

"No. She's still staying at Sebastian's."

"It's been a few days now, hasn't it? You're okay with that?"

"No, I'm not okay with it. But what am I going to do about it? She wants some time to herself, so that's what I'm giving her. She says stress isn't good for the baby, and that we can start fresh when we move at the end of the month."

"The end of the month? What about New York?"

"She said she wants to go alone." I shrug over the disappointment digging into my heart.

"But you're still going to go, right?"

"Not if she doesn't want me to."

"Sam, you have to go. She wants you to, believe me."

I exhale a heavy breath and shake my head. "I've already messed things up enough with Lucy. I don't want to overshadow her big moment in New York by making my first public appearance since the fight. Any media attention she gets should be about her, not about me losing to Crawford, especially when all anyone wants to do is give me crap about it. She doesn't need that kind of negativity right now."

Tristan stops walking and stands in front of me. "That sounds like an excuse to me."

"What?"

"You lost a fight, Sam. Get over it already. Everybody else has. Including the media." He gives me an unapologetic look and shrugs. "Shit happens. But it's over now. You know why you lost that fight. You didn't have Joe, you didn't have me, you let that Torino guy get inside your head, and it fucked you up.

But he's gone now. Now you've got me," he says confidently.

I look at him and ask, "You sure you're going to be ready? You've been away from the ring a while."

He waves me off and starts walking again. "You don't worry about me, all right? It's what's in here," he says, pointing to his head. "And here." He points to his heart. "Me and Joe got your back. You're going to beat Carey Valentine. And you're going to retire like a fucking champ." He holds his fist up and I hit it with mine.

"Lucy's not going to like it."

"She agreed that you would finish out your contract, right?"

"Yeah, before Las Vegas. Now she thinks I'm going to be punch-drunk before the baby even gets here."

"Well," he says, "after that fight, can you blame her?"

"No. I guess not."

"Look, I just got a new heart. I plan on being around a long time, and I plan on my best friend being around with me. I don't want to see you punch-drunk either." He looks over at me and holds his hand up to his chin. "Drool all coming out of your mouth, rambling on about the weather." He laughs and so do I. "I'm not going to let that happen. You tell Lucy that. You're going to be ready for Carey Valentine. You're going to beat him, and you're going to do it the right way, the way Joe would've wanted you to. Without getting punched in the head too much, understand?"

"Yeah."

"You'll start training tomorrow."

"Okay."

We walk a little farther, until we get to a bench where Tristan can sit down, and I sit down next to him.

"It's fucking beautiful, isn't it?" he says, looking at the lake and the green trees reflecting on its surface like a mirror. The tall buildings in the distance frame the view.

"Yeah. A lot different than where we grew up."

"Now look at us." He grins at me. "Kings."

I huff and ask, "Of what castle?"

"Dude, you need something to cheer you up. You want to go get a tattoo or something?"

"Today?"

"Yeah, why not?"

I look at my blank forearm, a stark contrast to the sleeve on my other arm. "I've been thinking about getting a new one, but I haven't made an appointment with Pete yet."

"You're Sam Cole, you don't need an appointment."

"I'm glad you think so, but Pete Masters is the best tattoo artist in the city. He's always booked solid."

"You're Sam Cole," he says again. "One of the best boxers of all time. I think he'll fit you in."

* * *

I lie back in the black leather chair in Pete's studio with my eyes closed, listening to the buzz of the tattoo gun as he carefully paints Lucy's face on my forearm.

"Holy shit," Tristan says, and I open my eyes. "That's incredible."

Pete stays focused on his work, oblivious to Tristan standing over him as he layers shades of gray ink on my arm, replicating a picture of Lucy that I showed him. I took it one morning when she wasn't looking. Her face is turned to the side and her blue eyes are lit by the morning sun coming in our bedroom. Her blond hair is falling around her face in loose waves, and her full lips are parted slightly. It's my favorite picture of her.

"I thought Lucy was the best artist I knew, but"—he shakes his head—"Pete's giving her a run for her money."

"So how does it look?" I ask, pointing at Tristan's chest.

He pulls up his shirt and shows me the initials he had tattooed over his heart, next to the long scar that now runs down the middle of his chest. *JPM*.

"Joseph Patrick Maloney."

"The one and only," he says, lowering his shirt. "Hope he's smiling about it, wherever he is."

"It's Joe we're talking about. You know where he is."

He pulls up a chair, sits down beside me, and watches Pete work. "You think he's with his parents?"

I nod, ignoring the sting of the tattoo needle scraping across my skin. "Yeah, I do. I think he's in a good place."

"Me too."

CHAPTER 19

LUCY

I watch the familiar New York City skyline come into view as we descend through the clouds and approach JFK airport. I recall the last trip I made to the city to watch Sam fight Mario Sanchez at Madison Square Garden. I put my hand on my stomach and gaze out at the buildings and skyscrapers that fill the horizon, reflecting on how much my life has changed since then.

"Ladies and gentlemen, we're beginning our decent into John F. Kennedy International Airport," the pilot says over the speaker. "We should be on the ground in just a few minutes, but until then, please stay seated with your seat belt on. Thank you."

"It's weird, isn't it?" Sebastian says, leaning over my shoulder to look out of the window.

"What?"

"Everything that's happened since the last time we were in New York."

I give him a suspicious look. *How is he always inside my head?*

"Who knew that the Cole-Sanchez fight would change my life," he muses, and I laugh. "I don't think anyone in the world could have convinced me that less than a year later, you'd be pregnant with Sam Cole's baby." He sighs and rests his chin in his hand.

"Me neither." I shake my head and frown. "Or that we'd also be fighting."

"You're not fighting. You're taking a mutual break."

"That's what people do before they get divorced. And we're not even married yet."

"People get divorced because they don't know when to take a break. It was the right thing to do. You'll see."

"Bas and I took a break before we got married," Paul says, joining the conversation.

"What? You did? You never told me that," I say to Bas.

"It was a long time ago. Paul wanted to move to Florida, and I wanted to stay in Atlanta."

"So what happened?"

"I went to Florida," Paul says. "For a little bit anyway. And then I realized that no matter how much I missed my family and wanted to be near them, it wasn't worth losing the most important person in my life." He wraps his hand around Sebastian's, and it tugs at my heart.

"He also realized that the music scene was bigger in Atlanta than Orlando," Bas adds with a smirk.

"I should have asked Sam to come. It feels wrong going to the Aurelia Snow exhibit without him."

"It's probably for the best, Lucy." Paul shrugs. "He's taken a lot of crap from the media since the Crawford fight. Being in New York would only exacerbate it."

"Hey, Lucy?" Sebastian says with wide eyes. "Guess what!"

I give him an apprehensive look. "What?"

"We're going to an Aurelia Snow exhibit." He grabs my hand and bites his lip. "Which is featuring your painting!"

I laugh. "I know." I squeal quietly and pull my hand to my mouth, which Sebastian promptly pulls away from my face.

"Do you know how many germs are in this petri dish?" He glances around at the other passengers on the plane. "Don't put your hands near your mouth, sweetie."

Paul rolls his eyes. "You are a germaphobe."

Sebastian looks at him and says, "Yes, and?"

I laugh and rest my head back against the seat as we approach the airport, racing over the water below. I close my eyes as the wheels of the plane skid along the runway, keeping them shut until we eventually come to a stop on the tarmac.

"Luc, I'm going to need my hand this weekend," Bas says, and I release my grip on it. He shakes it out in front of him and mouths, *Ow.*

"Sorry." I give him apologetic eyes. "You know how much I love landing."

"Or taking off, or turbulence of any kind," he teases.

I nod once. "Correct."

When the pilot gives the okay to exit the plane, Paul stands up, but Grady gets up from his seat directly in front of us and holds his hand out. "Wait a minute," he says to Paul, who sits back down. Grady says something to the steward, who then stands at the back of the first class seats while we gather our bags from the overhead bin, and I'm reminded of the biggest change since we were here last.

I fumble through my purse for my sunglasses and throw them on, keeping my eyes on the back of Grady's shoulders as we exit the plane and walk into the busy airport. I doubt anyone would recognize me without Sam, but the thought is still unnerving. I put my hand on my stomach and the baby moves beneath it, kicking and rolling a knee or a shoulder, and she bumps my hand up and down.

When we get to the baggage claim, someone shouts at us from nearby, startling me, and I curse under my breath. A camera-toting man approaches us, but I do my best to ignore him. A few passersby glance up at him, but most are too busy to care why he would want a picture.

"Come on," Grady says to us. "Let's go to the car. I'll come back in and get your bags."

"When's the baby due, Lucy?" the man asks, like he knows me.

"None of your business," Sebastian snaps, and Paul quietly scolds him as we hurry toward the exit.

When we get outside, Grady leads us to a waiting SUV with tinted windows, and I quickly climb into the back seat, eager to disappear behind them. Sebastian and Paul climb in after me.

"Can you please turn up the air?" I ask the driver.

"You okay?" Bas asks, gauging me.

"Yeah." I rest my hands on my tummy and look over at him. "If you say I'm out of shape, I'm going to hit you."

"I wouldn't dare say that to a pregnant woman. Especially not one evading the paparazzi."

"Honestly, Lucy, you can't even tell you're pregnant from the back," Paul says, winking at me.

I lay my head back against the seat rest and pat Sebastian's knee. "Please don't tell me you're taking us on another tour of Manhattan, because I don't think I can keep up this time."

"Unfortunately, no. The only thing we have time for this trip is work." He checks his phone. "I need to call the studio and confirm our arrival time."

"What time does it start?" Paul asks.

"Six. But I want to get there earlier."

* * *

Sebastian walks into my hotel room and smiles at me. "Just like an angel."

"Can you help me?" I ask, handing him my necklace.

"Sure." He takes it from me and clasps it behind my neck. "You look beautiful."

"Thanks," I say, staring at myself in the mirror, grateful that my dress still fits almost as well as it did six weeks ago when Sebastian picked it out. There's just a little less room in the middle, but otherwise it's still just as comfortable. I straighten my gold bar necklace over the V neckline and adjust the soft white material that flows over my growing stomach all the way down to my strappy blush-colored stilettos. "Is my hair okay?" I ask, looking at Sebastian, who's standing behind me.

"It looks gorgeous," he says, spinning me around by my shoulders to see the layers of loose waves that are cascading down my exposed back.

I reach for the delicate gold bracelet on my wrist that Sam gave me when I was seventeen and sigh.

"What's the matter?" he asks, dropping his head to the side. "You look serene and beautiful. You're ready for this."

"I don't feel ready. Not without Sam. He should be here. I should have asked him to come. I know he would have."

"Yes, he would have. But I'm here," he offers. "And I know I'm not Sam, but I'll support you any way that I can today."

"I know you will." I smile softly at him in his snug black suit. "You look very handsome."

"Thank you." He smiles and holds his elbow out for me. "Shall we?"

I wrap my hand around his arm and he escorts me to the waiting car downstairs.

I check my phone for the umpteenth time while we sit in unmoving traffic between towering buildings that block what's left of the afternoon sun, hoping for a missed call or text from Sam.

"Still nothing?" Bas asks.

I shake my head and call him…again. But it just rings and rings, until it goes to his voicemail.

Hey, this is Sam. Leave a message.

"Hey, it's me. We're headed to the show. I just wanted to talk to you. I love you, Sam…I miss you. Bye."

"Lucy, maybe when we go home you should go see him. I think it's been long enough, don't you?"

"I guess I'll know when I talk to him," I say, fidgeting with the sparkly engagement ring on my left hand.

Sebastian looks at his watch. "Is there any faster way than this?" he asks the driver, who shakes his head.

"Relax, Bas. It's only four thirty," Paul says to him. "The show doesn't start for an hour and a half."

"Which at this rate is what time we'll show up. That's unacceptable," he says with wide eyes. He looks at the traffic map on his phone and starts suggesting alternate routes to the driver, who I'm pretty sure is ignoring him now.

Bas exhales an exasperated breath through his nostrils, and it makes me laugh.

"I'm so glad I provide you so much amusement," he says, narrowing his eyes at me.

"Bas, I love you. Have I told you that lately?"

"No, actually, you haven't. But it's nice to hear," he says, shrugging a shoulder. "Finally!" he shouts, when we start moving again.

Nearly an hour later, we arrive at our location, and Sebastian practically leaps from the car. I wait for Grady to open my door and he holds my hand while I get out. "You look great, Lucy. You sure you don't need me to come in?" he asks, leading me around the SUV.

I pause and look at his kind face above his thick muscular neck. "Thanks, but that's okay. I think it would just cause unnecessary attention."

"Okay, well I'll be right outside."

"Oh, Grady, you don't have to wait. Really, I'm fine."

"Sam hired me to keep you safe, Lucy, which makes you my top priority. I'll be right outside," he reiterates.

"Okay." I look up at the inconspicuous storefront situated between two large sliding garage doors on the first floor of a four-story red-brick building.

"Lucy," Sebastian says impatiently. He grabs my hand and

pulls me across the sidewalk, but there's a line of people waiting to get in.

"Bas, let's just get in line."

He gives me an impossible look.

"It's fine," I say, noticing the glances we're getting. "We can wait like everyone else."

He gives me an exasperated look and says, "Absolutely not."

"Sebastian"—Paul gives him a stern look—"you are crazy if you think we're cutting in front of that line. Lucy's right."

Bas presses his lips together and pivots on the heel of his shiny black shoe. "Fine," he says under his breath.

We get in line and Sebastian crosses his arms over his chest. But after a few minutes, he looks at me and says, "No. It's too hot, you're pregnant, and you're a featured artist in the show." He pulls out his phone and makes a call. "Hi, this is Sebastian Ford." He turns around and speaks quietly into the phone. "Yes…Mm-hmm…Okay, great. Thank you." He hangs up and steps out of the line. "Are you guys coming or what?"

"Sebastian."

He leads us up the sidewalk to the door, where we're promptly greeted by a suited man with a clipboard. "Sebastian Ford?"

"Yes, and this is Lucy Bennett. An artist in tonight's show," he says loud enough for others to hear, and I close my eyes.

"Well, welcome. It's wonderful to have you. If you'll step right this way"—he gestures us inside the air-conditioned studio—"Aurelia will be out to meet you in a moment. In the meantime, feel free to look around."

"Thank you," I say, following Sebastian inside.

"Oh, my God, look at this place," he whispers.

The two-story room is surrounded by white walls that are adorned with colorful paintings and a floating staircase that stretches across the space, twisting as it curves up to the second floor. There are paintings beneath it that follow its curve, some you have to look up to see.

"Wow," I say, staring up at it. I look at the paintings, letting each one pull me in a little further.

"Lucy!" someone calls, and I turn around. A thin woman with short black hair and straight-cut bangs smiles at me. Her lips are painted red, contrasting with her fair skin, and she's wearing matching red suspender pants over a sheer black button-down shirt.

"Aurelia," I say, smiling at her.

She opens her arms and puts her hands on my shoulders, bringing me in to kiss my cheek. "It's so wonderful to finally meet you. Such a talent."

"The pleasure's all mine. It's honestly a dream to meet you. Your gallery is incredible," I say.

"Thank you. It didn't happen overnight, that's for sure. But I'm quite proud of it." She looks at Paul and raises her eyebrows. "You must be Sebastian."

"Oh, no, actually, I'm his husband, Paul." He glances at Sebastian, who's waiting patiently to say hello.

"It's a pleasure to meet you," Bas says, reaching for her small hand.

She gives it to him and smiles. "Nice to finally meet you, Sebastian."

"I am so impressed by everything you've done. You truly are an inspiration."

"Thank you. I aspire to be." She smiles at me and says, "We're going to open the doors in just a few minutes. I want everyone to have some time to look around, get a drink, relax, and then I was hoping to have you and the other artists take a few minutes to talk about your work. Okay? It really helps people connect to the painting when they understand the meaning behind it and what the artist was going through when they painted it."

"Oh, um—" My skin suddenly feels clammy.

"Of course that would be okay," Sebastian says for me.

I smile over the unexpected wave of anxiety I'm now riding. "Yeah. Sure."

"Great. I'll come find you when it's your turn." She winks at me and spins around. "No, no, Michael, that doesn't go there."

"Sebastian," I say through my teeth. "I can't give a speech. I don't have anything prepared."

"It's not a speech. It's just talking about your painting. You do it with me all the time."

"That's different. Talking about my *private* feelings with you isn't quite the same as discussing them with a room full of strangers." I glance at Paul, whose worried look is plastered onto his face. "You might as well ask me to take my clothes off in front of them. As a matter of fact, that would probably be easier."

Sebastian takes my hand and holds it between his. "Lucy, just breathe. Just take a deep breath."

I squint over the contraction that's taken over my abdomen and inhale a slow, deep breath.

"Just relax."

I exhale as the contraction passes and look up at him. "What am I supposed to say?"

"Don't worry about that. When it's your turn to speak, you're going to look at me and tell me about the painting. Like you've done a hundred times before. Can you do that?"

I nod reluctantly. "Yes."

"Okay." He smiles at me, but it does little to ease my nerves. "You've got this."

I close my eyes and think of Sam. *I need you.*

As the next hour passes, Paul and I follow Sebastian around the gallery, watching him schmooze his way through the crowd, eliciting smiles and laughter wherever he goes. I lean in to Paul and say quietly, "He has his own gravity."

Paul smiles. "Don't I know."

"Lucy...Lucy," Aurelia calls my name, waving me over to the staircase.

Sebastian turns to me and gives me a gentle push. "Go, go."

We follow Aurelia up the stairs to the second floor, which we haven't explored yet. When I reach the top, I pause and gasp. My painting is floating in the middle of the dimly lit room, suspended from the ceiling by nearly invisible wire, lit by several small spotlights. But it's not the painting of Sam I was expecting. It's the painting of *me*. I look at Sebastian, who pulls his mouth to the side and shrugs. "I thought it was your turn to be in the spotlight."

"Sebastian." I shake my head and begin to say that he shouldn't have offered up my painting without asking me, but as I look at it and think of everything I've been through to get to this moment—the struggles and the successes—I realize it's the perfect painting to commemorate this milestone in my career.

Paul walks toward it, stepping in front of the people standing around it. "Sorry, excuse me." He stares at it for several seconds, then he looks over his shoulder at me with watery eyes. "It's beautiful."

Sebastian looks down at me with a small, apologetic smile.

"Lucy, come on," Aurelia says, waving me over. She stands next to the painting, while everyone gathers around her.

"Knock 'em dead," Sebastian whispers.

I look up at him and nod, then I make my way over to Aurelia and stand next to my painting.

"Okay, everybody." She presses her hands together in front of her. "I'm so excited to introduce you to this next artist. She's one of the most talented contemporary realist artists I've ever had the pleasure to know, and lucky for us, she chose to unveil her latest piece, *Stronger*, here tonight." She looks at me and smiles. "Lucy Bennett."

I smile at the crowd, full of unfamiliar faces. Some are smiling back and others are staring at me blankly. "Um..." I glance up at my painting and then back at the people in front of me. "As Aurelia said, the painting is called *Stronger*." I smile nervously, wishing Sam were here, and search for Sebastian. When I find him I keep my eyes on him as I say, "I, um, I've never done a self-portrait before, and I certainly never thought I'd do one like this. It wasn't my best moment." I laugh softly and so does the crowd. "But it was real." I look at the painting again. "There are storms we have to weather in life." I smile tentatively at the crowd, thinking of Sam and everything we've been through this year. "This was one of those times. But I had a dear friend help me through it," I say, finding Sebastian again. "Sebastian Ford, you are the reason I painted this. And your friendship has made *me* stronger." Everyone looks at Sebastian and he beams at me. *Thank you*, I mouth to him.

Everyone claps as Aurelia steps beside me again. "Thank you for sharing that, Lucy. I know everyone here feels the emotion you felt that day. It truly is a breathtaking piece."

"Thank you, Aurelia."

She gives me a warm smile and then disappears into the crowd, and I'm enveloped in Sebastian's arms. "You did so good."

I look up at him, relieved that it's over. "I meant what I said."

"I know, and I'm sucking up every ounce of emotion right now, so please don't say anything else." He kisses my forehead and releases me.

"Lamb."

My breath catches in my throat and my heart races.

I look up and see Sam surrounded by several surprised faces, who whisper to each other as he passes them. But they might as well be invisible. All I see is him, dressed in a navy blue suit that's tailor-made, staring at me with beautiful, sad eyes. His hair is impeccably styled and his flushed cheeks are freshly shaven.

I fight back tears that rush to my eyes. "Sam? What are you doing here?"

He pulls his eyebrows together and says quietly, "I know you didn't want me to come tonight, but I had to. I'm sorry, I just—"

"Stop." A worried look falls over his face, but it disappears when I reach for his hand. "I'm so happy you came."

"You are?"

I nod and a tear rolls down my cheek. "I'm really happy."

He pulls me into his arms and his words come out in a quiet rush. "I'm so sorry, Lamb, for everything. I was messed up after the Crawford fight. But that wasn't me."

The warmth of his strong embrace reaches places inside me that only he can get to. Places that have been cold since I left him in Las Vegas. "I know it wasn't."

"I want you to come home, Luc. Please. I was wrecked after Joe died, but without *you*...I don't know what to do. You and the baby are my entire world, my whole future. I'm lost with you."

I nod, but can't say anything over the emotion I'm trying to contain.

"I promise I'll never lash out at you like that again. I know you were only trying to help."

I shake my head and say quietly, "I shouldn't have underestimated how hard the loss was for you. I'm sorry. And I'm sorry that I left." I press my lips together and shrug. "After being on my own, that flight-or-fight mode is really hard to overcome."

He holds me tight and says, "I just want you to come home, Lucy. Please...I need you."

"Okay."

He gives me an uncertain smile. "Okay?"

"Yeah." I smile softly. "I need you too, Sam."

He exhales a relieved breath and reaches for my face. "I missed you so much," he says, looking into my vulnerable eyes. Then he kisses me softly and rights all the wrongs in the world. He looks down at my round stomach and drops his hands to either side of it. "I missed my girls."

"We missed you too."

"How is she?"

"She's good." I laugh and wipe a stray tear from my eye.

"She's gotten bigger."

"It's only been two weeks."

"I know, but I can tell."

I scrunch up my face and laugh. "Are you trying to say that I look bigger?"

He shakes his head and gives me a sexy smile. "No. You look…" He pulls his hand to his mouth and rubs it over his chin. "Sexy as hell."

"Sam," I say, glancing around at the people around us.

"Seriously." He holds my hand up and drops his eyes over me. "You're so beautiful," he says softly, showing me a glimpse of his dimples.

I press my hands to his chest and whisper, "You're not so bad yourself."

He grins, putting his dimples on full display for everyone to see, and I could swear I hear a few hearts dropping. He reaches for my hand, holds it against his chest, and says, "Come dance with me."

"Oh, I don't think there's dancing here, Sam," I say, glancing around as he pulls me over to a dimly lit area of the room, wondering where Sebastian and Paul disappeared to.

"Says who?" He pulls me close and wraps his arm around my back. "I like this song." He begins to rock me back and forth to the slow rhythm of Dua Lipa's "Homesick," and the lyrics settle over me like a warm blanket when Sam whispers them in my ear. "You give me a reason, something to believe in, I know, I know, I know… You give me a meaning, something I can breathe in, I know, I know, I know."

I look up at him, and he's the only other person in the room.

"Do you know how much I love you?" he asks.

"As much as I love you."

"It's not always going to be easy, Lamb. I won't promise that. But I can promise it will be easier together. You and the baby are the most important thing to me. Even when I'm feeling sorry for myself and acting like a jerk. Okay?"

I inhale a shaky breath. "Okay."

"The painting, your painting...why didn't you tell me about it?"

"I didn't know Sebastian volunteered it for the show tonight."

He nods softly and asks again, "Why didn't you tell me about it?"

"I don't know."

"Lucy, I want *all* of you. The good parts and the bad."

"I know."

"Tonight I listened to you tell a bunch of strangers about a storm you were weathering that I didn't even know about. Was I the storm?"

"No, it wasn't you. I mean, it was, but it wasn't *you*. It was everything. It was you getting hurt, it was Tristan and Joe, it was the baby, even though I didn't know about her yet. I was just caught up in it all and Sebastian happened to be there. I guess you could say he was my life raft that day."

"Well, I'm happy he was there for you." He rocks me slowly to the music. "But I wish you'd shown me the painting." He stops dancing and looks at me. "It's really amazing."

"Thank you."

"You better not let anyone buy it."

I laugh softly. "I won't."

"Lucy, I love you. Whether you're mad or happy or scared or sad. I know it's not always going to be perfect between us, and we're probably going to have to weather a lot of storms over the years. But I want to be your life raft. And want you to be mine."

I look at his handsome face and admit, "Sometimes it's hard for me to tell you when I'm feeling scared or insecure, especially about us. You've been dealing with so much lately. But I promise I'll be up front with you from now on. I won't ask for your heart without giving you mine in return, completely and honestly."

He pulls me close again. "That's all I want."

"What is this, a dance party?" Bas asks, making his way over to us as the music changes to another Dua Lipa track. He snaps his fingers to the up-tempo beat of "Be the One" and slowly rocks his shoulders from side to side as he closes the space between us. "Hey, Sam." He grins. "When did you get here?"

I look at Sam, then I look at Bas. "Wait. Did you know he was coming?"

He sways from side to side and turns his palms up. "Guilty."

My mouth pops open and I give him wide eyes. "You let me mope for the last two days!" I smack his arm and he laughs.

"Well, I couldn't ruin the surprise."

"You were moping?" Sam asks, smiling softly.

"Of course I was. I hated the idea of being here without you."

He wraps his arms around me and pulls me close. "I wasn't

sure, but I didn't want to miss something this important to you."

I look up at his sincere eyes and kiss him softly. "Thank you for surprising me." I look over at Sebastian. "Is that why you were such a freak on the way over?"

"Well, he was supposed to surprise you before the show, but his flight was delayed."

I shake my head and laugh. "Did you know?" I ask Paul.

"Nope. This was one of the many Lucy secrets I wasn't privy to." He narrows his eyes at Sebastian playfully.

Sebastian waves him off and keeps swaying to the music. "He's still mad that I didn't tell him about you and Sam when you first got back together."

"Or that you were pregnant," Paul says to me.

I wrap my arm around Bas's waist and press my cheek to his shoulder. "That's because he's the best friend anyone could ask for." I give Paul an apologetic look.

Sebastian smiles and takes my hands, and swings my arms back and forth as he sings, "Oh, baby, come on, let me get to know you, just another chance so that I can show that I won't let you down, oh no…No, I won't let you down, oh no."

I laugh and sway back and forth with him to the music, un-til he gives my hand to Sam, and he takes Paul's. I smile at them dancing between paintings and people who are watching and smiling too. Sam lifts my hand and I spin under his arm, but I quickly yank it down when I see an unfamiliar shadow of ink inside his sleeve.

"Did you get a new tattoo?" I ask, pushing his jacket up his arm.

He unbuttons his sleeve and shows me the tattoo on his

forearm, and I gasp when I see *my face* taking up a rather large section of his skin.

My mouth falls open, but all I can say is, "Sam."

He smiles softly. "Do you like it?"

I bob my head and put my hand over my mouth. "I can't believe you had my face tattooed on your arm," I say, blinking back tears.

He looks at me and says, "I didn't want to go another day without seeing it."

I release a quiet breath and say softly, "You don't have to."

He wraps his arms around me, and I hug him tightly.

"Hey, what do you say we stay in the city for a couple of days?" he asks, putting a wide smile on my face.

"Really?"

"Yeah. You can show me around like you wanted to. We can see the sights."

I press my lips together over an amused smile. "You want to go sightseeing?"

"I mean, it might be cool to see the city from the top of the Empire State Building."

I nod softly. "I'd love to do that with you, Sam."

"And maybe you could show me that art museum you like so much."

"The Met?"

"Yeah."

My excitement quickly wanes when I think about what Paul said. The paparazzi will be worse here. "Do you think it's a good idea? I mean, with how the media's been lately."

He holds his head back and grins. "You worried about me?"

"Always."

He shrugs. "People can say whatever they want about the Crawford fight. They're going to do it anyway, whether I'm here or in Atlanta. But this might be our last chance to get away for a while."

I inhale a slow breath and gaze up at him, relishing the moment and the promise of the next couple of days alone in the city with Sam. "Okay."

CHAPTER 20

LUCY

I love the Met for five reasons. One: it's old. Nearly 150 years old. Two: it's massive. You can spend an entire day in it and not see it all. Three: it sits on the edge of Central Park. Sometimes when you're inside, you forget that you're in the city, because all you see from the windows is green. Four: the art. From Georgia O'Keeffe to Claude Monet, the Met is home to some of the most extraordinary art in the entire world. Five: afternoon tea.

The midafternoon sunlight filters into the café through the floor-to-ceiling windows that overlook Central Park, reflecting off our teacups. I dunk my peppermint tea bag in the hot water a few times while it steeps and Sam does the same. He holds his teacup between his strong hands and I giggle softly. "You're so cute."

He studies the sandwiches and scones on the three-tiered silver plate stand and grabs one of the egg salad sandwich wedges. "How am I supposed to fill up on these?" he asks, popping the whole thing in his mouth.

I grab one of the cucumber wedges. "You're not. It's afternoon tea. It's just a snack."

He picks up a lemon raspberry tart and flicks the raspberry off onto his plate. "Is this supposed to be dessert?"

"Yes." I laugh.

He leans across the table and says, "Tonight, we're going somewhere good." He winks and leans back in his chair.

"Where?" I ask curiously.

"It's a surprise."

I purse my lips over a smile. "Okay. But first, I want to show you one more painting."

He grabs another sandwich wedge. "Okay."

We finish our afternoon tea and meander through the sprawling galleries for another hour, until we reach *Woman with a Parrot*. I stare at the painting, recalling the last time I was here with Sebastian and Paul, laughing quietly to myself at Sebastian's interpretation.

"You wanted to show me a naked woman?" Sam asks, giving me a sideways glance.

"No. Well, yes. But not because she's naked. Because I love this painting. I love how uncontrived it is. It was very provocative for its time."

"Because she's naked?"

"Because of her *ungainly* pose and *disheveled* hair," I say, quoting an article I read about its early reviews. I shrug. "It was the eighteen hundreds. But what I really love are the shadows and light. So realistic."

He crosses his arms over his chest and studies the painting. "Like on her hair." He points and drops his head to the side. "The way the light reflects off her curls."

"Yeah." I smile up at him. "Exactly like that."

"I see why you like it." He wraps his hand around mine and pulls me closer to him. "Thanks for showing it to me."

"You're welcome," I say, yawning.

He gives me a small smile. "You ready for a nap?"

"Yep."

*　*　*

I stand in front of the bathroom mirror in our suite with my arms above my head, trying to pin my hair up in an intentionally messy yet somewhat dressy updo, which is no easy task.

Sam walks up behind me in a fitted black suit with a cream button-down shirt that's open at the collar, and it takes everything in me not to turn around. But I've *almost* got it.

"Can I help?" he asks, taking the bobby pin out of my hand and assessing the situation.

"Sure." I drop my tired arms and lean on the marble counter while he pushes the pin in place. I hand him another one. "Can you put one on the other side too?"

He studies the back of my head for a few seconds and then, with a very serious face, slowly pushes the bobby pin in. "Okay…" He holds his hands out a few inches from my head and assesses his work. "Done."

"Yeah?" I tilt my head from side to side to make sure it feels secure, then I grab my mirror off the counter and turn around to inspect his work. "It looks good," I say, smiling at him. "Thank you." When I lower the mirror, he's staring at me.

He drops his eyes over my tummy-hugging short-sleeve scoop-neck dress, which I purchased today out of necessity—

my suitcase ran dry a few days ago. It's a dusty pale blue color, accented with a delicate floral design that cascades over one shoulder all the way down to the opposite corner where the hem hits my knees. I paired it with strappy silver high heels that wrap around my ankles.

Sam puts his hands on the silky material over my stomach, then he looks at me and says, "You are stunning pregnant. Have I told you that?"

I shake my head and gaze up at him.

He pulls his eyebrows together and says, "I used to imagine us having a family one day, and I'd have these visions of you being pregnant, but they didn't compare to this." He rubs his hand over my stomach, and I feel a familiar heat begin to smolder beneath my skin.

"Maybe we should skip dinner tonight," I say, biting my smiling lip.

He wraps his arms around me and pushes me back against the counter, enveloping me in his warm, clean scent as he presses his full lips to mine. He kisses me softly and says, "As tempting as that is, we're not skipping dinner." He laughs softly and releases me. "Come on." He laces his fingers with mine and pulls me behind him.

"That wasn't nice," I say, pouting at him as he leads me out of our suite.

"You should have fed me a real lunch."

I stop in front of the foyer mirror and straighten the dress over my bump, turning from side to side.

Sam watches me with an amused smirk on his face and his dimples go straight to my heart...and other parts of my body I'm trying to ignore. He drops his head and puts his hands in his pockets, then he looks up at me with a grin that sends my heart sprinting. "You ready now?"

My eyes follow his handsome face down to his tailored black suit and shiny tobacco-colored dress shoes, and I begin to second-guess my outfit. "Are you sure this dress is okay?"

"It's perfect for where we're going."

"And where is that again?"

He laughs and takes my hand, then pulls me out of the suite and down the hall to the elevator, where Grady is waiting for us.

"You two look great," Grady says when we reach him.

"Thanks, so do you." I wink at him.

He tugs on his suit jacket. "What, this old thing?" he says in his deep voice before he presses the button for the elevator.

"I appreciate you sticking around for the last couple of days," Sam says to him.

"Anything you need, champ."

When the elevator doors slide open, Grady ushers us inside. He presses the button for the first floor and we drop forty-eight floors to the lavish lobby below.

Sam holds my hand as we walk through the freezing lobby, ignoring the subtle glances and whispers that follow us wherever we go. Once we're outside, the warm summer air erases the goose bumps from my arms, and we climb into the back of a waiting SUV, disappearing behind the tinted windows.

I look up at the glittering skyscrapers that tower over the street we're driving down, admiring the way the lights shine on the city below like a moon, even on a cloudy night. Each time we come to a stop, I listen to the sounds outside—people talking, some shouting, music playing, horns honking.

"I love New York," I muse.

Sam grabs my hand and pulls it into his lap. "I like it a lot more now," he says, smiling at me.

We come to a stop in front of Central Park, which is lit by the orange glow of the streetlamps that line its paths. The driver gets out and I give Sam a curious look. "Are we here?"

"Yeah." He opens the door and reaches for my hand. "Come on."

I take his hands and step down onto the pavement, glancing up at him curiously as he leads me around the SUV. When I see a waiting horse-drawn carriage, I pull my hand to my mouth and laugh nervously. "Is that for us?"

"What better way to look like a tourist than with a carriage ride through Central Park?" He laughs and pulls me over to it. He climbs up after me and we sit down.

Grady takes the seat next to the driver and the horse begins to slowly trot in front of us, carrying us into the dimly lit park.

Soon, the faint sounds of the city are drowned out by the click-clacking of the horse's feet against the pavement, and a warm breeze blows through the trees above us, rustling the leaves that glow in the warm, ambient light of the streetlamps, contrasting with the twinkling skyscrapers that tower in the distance. I hold Sam's hand and snuggle up next to him. "I've actually never seen the park at night. It's really pretty."

After a few quiet seconds, the horse passes gas, and we both start laughing.

"Super romantic, right?" Sam says, shaking his head.

"So romantic."

He drops his head and looks over at me with a crooked smile. "Sorry."

I put my chin on his shoulder and kiss him softly. "This was actually a really great surprise."

"This isn't the surprise."

"What?"

"Well, it was part of it, but there's more." He looks through the trees and points to the glowing lights in the distance. "That's where we're going."

I give him a curious look, but he doesn't offer any more clues, until we arrive at Tavern on the Green, where we're promptly greeted and escorted to a private table outside under a ceiling of twinkle lights.

I squeeze his hand across the table and whisper quietly, "Now this is romantic."

* * *

Sam traces his fingers over my arm, waking me from a light sleep.

I roll over and look at him lying beside me in the early morning light that's pouring into our suite. "Hi."

"Good morning."

"Why are you always up so early?"

He laughs softly. "We have a flight to catch."

I groan and roll over and clutch my pillow. "But this bed is so comfortable."

He reaches around me and rubs my stomach, and I love the feeling of him holding me, holding *us*, close to him. He drapes his heavy arm over mine and reaches for my hand. "You have to get up," he says, rolling me onto my back.

"But I'm so tired. I'm pregnant. I need sleep."

He puts his mouth on my neck and groans softly. "I know a way to get you up." He pushes my shirt up and rubs his hands over my round stomach, and the baby kicks hard. He leans over and says, "Good morning to you too." He kisses the spot gently and then works his way up to my breasts, pushing my shirt off them and massaging them in his hands.

I close my eyes and run my fingers through his thick hair, moaning softly.

"I see you're awake now." He sits up and grins.

I grab his hand and pull him back to me. "Where do you think you're going?"

"We have a flight to catch." He laughs.

I sit up and tug my shirt off over my head and climb onto his lap. "Don't we have just a few minutes?" I rub my hands over his round shoulders and down his chest. He smiles, but he doesn't move, so I put my mouth by his ear and kiss the sensitive skin beneath his earlobe. "Please?" I take his hand and put it on my breast. "Pretty please?"

He squeezes it softly and grumbles, "How can I say no?" He looks at me with eager eyes and a big, bright smile that makes me giggle. "You asked for it," he says, laying me back against the bed and making me squeal at the quickness with which he kisses me. He tugs my bottom lip between his teeth and sits up, pushing the covers out of the way and tossing the pillows off the bed. He yanks his pajama pants off and kneels next to me naked, and the sunlight shines on his painted body.

"Stop," I say, sitting up to appreciate the work of art before me. He freezes and I watch his chest rise and fall. I reach for his hand and turn it over and look at the new tattoo on his forearm. "I still can't believe you had my face tattooed on your arm," I say, rubbing my thumb across it and appreciating the work of his tattoo artist.

"It's not just any face. It's the most beautiful face in the entire world." He brings his lips to mine again. "One I plan on seeing every day for the rest of my life."

I smile softly and say, "I like that plan."

"Since we're in agreement," he mumbles against my lips, "where were we?" He kisses me deeply, massaging my tongue with his until my fingers are digging into his arms. He lays me back against the bed and drags my panties down my legs, kissing my thighs and tummy as he makes his way back to my mouth.

He kisses me for another long second, before he falls back on his heels and kneels between my legs. He wraps his wide hands around my thighs and pulls my bottom onto his lap, leaving my back on the bed as he carefully pushes into me, leaning forward slightly until his sculpted stomach is pressed against my tummy. He lets out a small groan and then reaches under the small of my back to support me as he begins to move. He slowly rocks in and out of me, and I grip the sheets in my fisted hands, moaning softly at the heavy, full sensation that travels all the way down to my toes.

I look up at his scruffy face, full of intensity, and watch the muscles in his torso flex each time he moves, accentuating the V that points to the source of pleasure between my legs, sending flames racing to every single part of my body each time he falls back on his heels, stroking me in just the right spot. I close my eyes and feel Sam's hand move over my swollen breasts. He rubs them softly, then he leans over me and drops his mouth to my sensitive nipples, taking turns with them as he pushes deeper inside me, and I feel myself beginning to unravel.

I hold my breath as the flames blissfully incinerate every fiber in my body, then I gasp for a breath that resonates through me and fans the smoldering embers, half aware that Sam has wrapped his arms around my back. He holds me up off the bed a little as he moves, squeezing me and groaning as he pushes into me one last time.

After a few silent moments, he lifts his head from beside mine and pants, "We're going to be late for our flight."

I give him a satiated smile and exhale a labored breath. "It's not my fault that you don't have any willpower."

"Only when it comes to you." He kisses me softly and climbs off me. "Tristan will kill me if I'm not back in time to train this afternoon."

I drop my worried eyes and nod.

"Hey," he says, lifting my chin. "It won't be like last time. I promise."

I push down thoughts of Las Vegas and try to convince myself that he's right. *It's his last fight. And he has Tristan this time.* I swallow down my worry and say, "Okay."

CHAPTER 21

LUCY

"Well, that's all of them," Bas says, wiping his hands together as the movers carry what's left of my paintings to a waiting truck outside my studio. "Your paintings are on their way to a dark, desolate storage unit." He puts his hands on his hips and sighs.

"Well, I hoped that my home studio would be ready by now, but the contractor said two more weeks for the renovations." I swivel from side to side in the chair behind the front desk. "I'm just happy Sam and I got everything unpacked so we can start getting ready for the baby."

He raises his eyebrows and smirks. "That's got to be some kind of record for you. It's only been, what…a month and a half since you and Sam moved in?"

"Yeah." I laugh. "I think I'm nesting now or something."

"Speaking of which, did you and Sam pick out furniture for the nursery yet?"

"Actually, we're going to later today."

"What about *Lionheart*? Did you hang it yet? I'm dying to see how the painting looks on the wall in Sam's gym."

"Not without you. I need you there to supervise."

"Probably best," he says seriously. He opens his calendar on his phone and asks, "So how long should I plan I keeping the rest of your paintings in storage?"

"I don't know. Maybe three months?"

He presses is lips together and gives me a disapproving look.

"I promise that after the baby's born, we'll find a new gallery and they'll see the light of day again."

"And what am I supposed to do until then?"

"Hello." I get up and walk around the desk. "Find us a new gallery. And try to sell the rest of my paintings to help pay for it." I laugh and his eyes light up.

"You'd really trust me to do that? Find a new location, I mean."

"I'd *only* trust you to do that. I actually think it would be the perfect assignment for you while I'm on maternity leave. In addition to coordinating everything for the remaining *five* exhibits I agreed to participate in before I knew I was going to have a baby."

"You know, it's not required that you attend them all in person to participate. Your name alone should get the paintings a lot of attention now that you have Molly branding you and splashing your artwork on T-shirts across America."

"It's kind of full circle isn't it? Molly was the reason people started talking about me when Sam and I got back together, after our run-in on the elevator. And she's the reason people are talking about me now."

"Except now they're talking about your talent, *not* Sam."

I give him a dubious look.

"Okay, they're talking about your talent *and* Sam. But mostly your talent."

"Well, soon they'll have something else to talk about," I say, putting my hands on either side of my belly. "Honestly, I may never leave my house again after she's born."

He gives me a worried look.

"I'm serious, Sebastian. I don't want anyone taking pictures of my baby."

"Well, you'll have to come out of hiding eventually if you plan to attend any of the exhibits. But you can leave the baby safely at home."

The thought of leaving my baby, who isn't even here yet, fills me with unexpected anxiety. I rub my stomach and say, "I think maybe you're right—we should pick the top three and only attend those. And by top three I mean whichever ones are the furthest out on the calendar."

"Don't worry about the exhibits, Luc. I'll get everything lined up while you're maternity leave, just like you said."

I nod and let go of the unnecessary worry.

"How long do you think that will be exactly?"

"I don't know. How long does it take to return to one's previous state after pushing a tiny human out of their body?"

He gives me a pained look. "I can't believe you're actually going to have to do that in a few weeks."

I chew the corner of my mouth. "Me neither."

"Are you nervous?"

"Yep."

"Well, you shouldn't be. Women have done it since the

beginning of time, and you have something they didn't. An epidural."

"I don't want an epidural." I ignore the way he's looking at me. "I'm not worried about how much it's going to hurt, Bas. I'm worried about Sam *seeing* everything."

He narrows his eyes and nods slowly. "Okay, well, have you mentioned this irrational concern to Sam?"

"It's not irrational. And, no."

"Why not?"

"What am I supposed to say? *Hey, Sam, I'm really worried that after I push the baby out, you'll never be able to look at my vagina the same way.*"

He shakes his head. "Yeah, you probably shouldn't lead with that."

I drop my chin and say seriously, "I don't think I want him to see it."

"You don't want him to see the birth of his child?" He gives me an incredulous look.

"Not really."

"Okay, now you're being irrational. You can't really mean that."

"Yes, I do! Look at me, Sebastian," I whine, putting my hands on either side of my giant belly, which has consumed the middle part of my body. "I look like an alien." I scrunch up my face and ask, "Do you even know what happens during the delivery? It's humiliating."

He pulls his dark eyebrows together and says, "Unfortunately, yes. Paul and I watched a birth video when we were researching surrogacy. Which we immediately regretted," he says quietly. "Some things you can't unsee."

I pull my hands to my face and groan loudly.

"Oh, come on, it's the miracle of giving birth," he says, pulling my hands away.

"That's what people say to make women feel better about losing their dignity."

He laughs and pulls me into a hug. "Lucy, Sam loves you. Just like all the men around the world who've watched their wives give birth. He's not going to care."

"I'm not his wife."

"*Yet*. And that's not the point. The point is, he loves you."

"But it's *Sam*. I'd rather you watch than him."

He shakes his head and releases me. "Well, that won't be happening."

I open my mouth and shove his arm.

"What?" He laughs. "I love you, but that's Sam's department."

I groan. "Maybe he won't want to watch either."

"Lucy, you are *crazy* if you think Sam isn't going to want to see his daughter come into this world."

I close my eyes because I know he's right. "He just better stay up by my head."

"I don't think you're going to care where he is, as long as he's there to hold your hand during contractions. And if I know you, which I do, he's the *only* one you're going to want doing that."

"You're probably right."

"Of course I am." He grabs my hand and pulls me to the middle of the empty studio. "So…" He glances around the open space. "Are you ready to say goodbye?"

I look at the bare walls, remembering everything it took

to get here and all the hard work that went into my exhibit. Most of the memories involve Drew in some way, which only adds to the distance between them. It feels like a lifetime ago, yet I can still remember the feeling of walking inside for the first time—trepidation mixed with pride and determination.

"So strange," I muse.

"What?"

"How different everything is now. How different I am. How much my life has changed since opening this studio." I look at him and smile. "I didn't even know you yet."

"That is strange."

"I thought I'd be sad about letting it go, especially today, but I'm not. I actually feel really…hopeful."

"Hopeful?" He smiles.

"Yeah. I mean, if anything, this last year has taught me that life is full of surprises. You just never know what's around the next corner."

"Like maybe…a fabulous two-story loft gallery that rivals Aurelia Snow's?"

I laugh and drop my chin. "Maybe."

He smiles and takes my hands in his. "To hope."

I swallow down the emotion that moves through me, not because I'm sad, but because I'm overcome with gratitude and faith. The future used to be this giant question mark. And in many ways it still is. But one thing is certain now. A future with Sam. "To hope."

* * *

I sit on the paper that's covering the examination table in my doctor's office with an equally uncomfortable paper blanket draped over my naked lap, kicking my slightly swollen feet together.

Sam smiles up at me from the chair he's sitting in. "I'm going miss these appointments after the baby's born."

I arch an eyebrow. "Why?"

"It's kind of fun watching you squirm around on the table and get paper stuck to your butt."

I narrow my eyes. "Funny."

"Very, actually." He stands up and walks over to me with a grin. "You sure you're going to be okay while I'm gone?"

"Hmm…" I look up to one side. "Will I still be pregnant when you return?" I look at him and nod. "Most likely. Will I be okay watching you fight Carey Valentine from eight hundred miles away?" I shake my head and look down at my bare feet. "Probably not."

He stands between my knees at the end of the examination table and puts his hands on my thighs. "I'm ready this time, Luc. It won't be like the Crawford fight." He lifts my chin and looks into my eyes. "I promise."

There's a knock on the door. "How's my favorite patient?" Dr. Fletcher asks, walking into the room with a smile. He pauses when he sees us. "Everything okay?"

Sam reaches out to shake his hand. "Just giving Lucy a little reassurance about my match tomorrow night."

"Ahh, that's right."

"Now, I just need you to give *me* a little reassurance about the baby. Still three weeks, right?"

"Well, let's take a look and see. Lucy, why don't you go ahead and lie back?"

I'd rather no one be poking around my lady parts, but I've come to realize it's a necessary part of having a baby. And I've also come to love Dr. Fletcher. He has five children of his own and the patience to prove it. He always takes his time with me and never makes me feel like I have absolutely no idea what I'm doing. Which I don't.

"How have you been feeling, Lucy? Any contractions?"

"Just Braxton Hicks," I say, trying to get comfortable on the crinkly paper that covers the padded table. "Same as the past few months." I pull my shirt up over my stomach, which is now the size of a beach ball, and Sam reaches for my hand.

Dr. Fletcher puts his hands on either side of my stomach and pushes gently, but it feels like he's rearranging my organs. "She's head down now," he says, pressing down hard.

"That's good, right?"

"Very good. Breech babies don't come out very easy," he says.

"Breech. What's that?" Sam asks.

"Bottom first. That's not what we want. But not to worry, your baby's bottom is right here," he says, pushing on the top of my stomach again. "Feel right here," he says to Sam.

Sam puts his hand on my stomach and pushes his fingers against the spot. "That's it? That's her bottom?" he asks fascinated, and I smile. I don't think I've ever heard Sam use the word *bottom* before.

"Yep." Dr. Fletcher reaches for Sam's wrist. "Push a little harder," he says, pulling his fingers down the side of my stomach. "Feel her back?"

"Yeah."

"And that?" He pushes Sam's hand against my lower stomach. "That's her head."

"Wow," Sam says. "That's incredible."

Dr. Fletcher grins. "Cool, huh?"

"She's so big now," Sam says, smiling at me.

"I'd say she's about six pounds," Dr. Fletcher says, pulling out his measuring tape. He stretches it from my pubic bone all the way up to my breastbone. "Right on track for thirty-seven weeks."

Sam squeezes my hand and I smile at him, until Dr. Fletcher raises the dreaded stirrups and locks them into place. "Okay, let's see what's going on inside and then—since you are my favorite patient—I'll do an ultrasound just to be sure," he says, redeeming himself.

"Okay." I scoot my bottom down toward the edge of the table and prop my feet up in the stirrups. "Sam," I say, tugging him back a little.

He stands by my shoulder and waits patiently for the verdict.

"Well, Lucy, you're not dilated at all," Dr. Fletcher says, pulling his gloves off. "As far as I can tell, you're still two to three weeks out."

I exhale a relieved breath and so does Sam.

"It's your first baby, they usually take their time. In fact, I don't want you to be discouraged if you're still pregnant on your due date." He grabs a pamphlet and hands it to me. "I want you to read this. It's explains the stages of labor, so you'll know when it's the real thing."

"Okay," I say, taking it from him.

"Now, are you ready to take a look at your baby?"

I bob my head and smile. "Yes."

Sam smiles at me while Dr. Fletcher turns on the ultrasound machine and squeezes warm jelly on my stomach. "How does that feel? Okay?"

"Mm-hmm, it's fine."

He presses the wand to my stomach and the fast swooshing sound of the baby's heartbeat echoes through the room. "That's a great sound, isn't it?" he says, smiling at us.

"The best," Sam answers, and I squeeze his hand.

"There she is," he says, pointing to the black-and-white monitor. "See her face?"

"I see it." I gasp, watching her open and close her mouth.

"Is she sucking her thumb?" Sam asks, astonished.

"Yeah. Look, you can see her whole hand." He freezes the frame. "Five perfect fingers."

I stare at the screen with awe. "She's perfect."

He moves the wand around some more and takes a few measurements. "Everything looks really good."

"Could you maybe just check her heart?" Sam asks, and I glance up at him, because I know he's thinking about Tristan.

"Sure let's take a look," Dr. Fletcher says, clicking something on the computer that lights up the screen with red and blue. "This shows her blood movement. See it in the umbilical cord?"

"Yes," I say, feeling Sam tense beside me.

"You can see it moving through her heart," he says, pushing the wand around on my stomach. "And it's doing exactly what it's supposed to. Her heart looks great." He smiles at Sam. "Nice and strong."

I look up Sam. "Just like her dad."

Dr. Fletcher prints a few pictures for us and turns off the ultrasound machine. "Everything looks great, guys. A few more weeks and you'll get to meet your baby girl."

"Thanks, Dr. Fletcher," Sam says, shaking his hand.

"My pleasure."

"Dr. Fletcher, you'll definitely be the one delivering the baby, right?" I ask, sitting up.

"I only have one other patient due this month, and she's being induced tomorrow. After that, I'm all yours, Lucy."

"Okay," I say, smiling. "Just making sure."

"I'll see you next week, okay?"

"Okay."

"Oh, and champ?" He holds his fist out in front of Sam. "Knock his ass out tomorrow."

Sam smiles and hits Dr. Fletcher's fist with his. "You got it, Dr. Fletcher."

* * *

"What do you think about this one?" I ask Sam, who reaches for the tag on the cream-colored crib and begins reading about its safety features.

He puts his hand on the side rail and gives it a tug to test its durability. "Looks good."

"It's really beautiful, isn't it?" I ask, touching the floral applique on the front of the crib that matches the one on the back.

"It's all hand-sculpted," a salesperson says, joining us. She smiles and asks, "When are you due?"

"Oh, um—"

"A couple of months," Sam answers, and I smile along with the lie. Even though people know I'm due soon, he doesn't want the media catching wind of my exact due date.

"Well, this particular piece would have to be ordered, but it should arrive well before your little one. And it's on sale," she says exuberantly, gesturing to the four-thousand-dollar price tag that I didn't see before.

I look at Sam and suggest, "Maybe we should look at a few more before we decide."

"Okay, well, let me know if you have any questions," the salesperson says, before leaving us.

"Sam, this crib is four thousand dollars," I say, shaking my head. "It's too much."

"Not for our only daughter. If this is the crib you like, let's get it."

"Let's just look at a few more, okay? We don't even know if this crib would arrive in time."

"Well, what about that one?" he asks, pointing across the showroom to an antique white crib that has tufted upholstery on the back with arched molding that resembles a beautiful headboard standing about a foot higher than the slats in the front. It's the perfect mix of vintage and modern.

"Oh, Sam, I love that one," I say, crossing the showroom to go look at it. I'm delightfully surprised when I see that's it's priced much lower than the last one we looked at.

I wait for Sam to inspect the safety features.

"What do you think? Should we get this one?" I ask, hoping he likes it as much as I do.

He smiles and puts his hand on the mattress, rubbing it over the pink sheet that's covered in tiny white flowers. "Yeah, I can see her in this."

I beam at him, feeling like my heart my explode. "So can I."

"Let's get this whole set," he says, gesturing at the coordinating dresser and changing table, which together costs a small fortune.

I nod over the sticker shock, like I have a hundred times since we started buying furniture for our new house, and ask, "Are you sure?"

"Lucy, stop worrying about the price tag. This furniture's going in our baby girl's room. I want for the very best for her."

I smile softly over my reluctance. "Violet is one lucky little girl."

"No, no, no. Her name is Caroline."

I laugh and shake my head. "I thought you like Ava."

"I don't know, I think Caroline has a nice ring to it."

"Well, we'll just have to see what sticks when we see her."

"Okay." He laughs. "I'll go get the saleslady."

"Okay."

I look at the crib again, admiring it, and spot a plush white glider in the corner of the display with a matching ottoman. I walk over to it and sit down, and I'm instantly enveloped in its comfort. I put my feet up and start rocking backward and forward, and my eyes close automatically. *Oh, yeah. That's the stuff.*

"We'll take that too," Sam says, and I peek my eyes open at him. He's got a big smile on his face that's accompanied by my favorite pair of dimples.

I smile at him and say softly, "Thank you."

CHAPTER 22

LUCY

"Good morning," Sam says, joining me in the baby's nursery. "What are you doing up so early?"

"I couldn't sleep," I say, folding a small white onesie and putting it away in the dresser, which Sam had delivered yesterday, just hours after we bought it. He wanted everything to be done before he left for New York today.

He pulls the folded onesie out of the drawer and holds it up between us. "I can't believe she'll be this small." He lays it on my stomach and it stays in place.

I fold it again and put it back in the drawer. "If she's so little, why am I so big?" I groan, bending over to get another onesie out of the laundry basket.

He laughs and wraps his arms around me. "You aren't that big."

"I feel like a whale."

"Well, you don't look like one," he says, kissing the top of my head. He releases me and I pick up another onesie to fold.

"Luc, I have to leave soon. My flight's in a couple of hours. Tristan and Miles are on their way over."

"Okay," I say, glancing up at him.

"Hey." He reaches for my hand. "It's *not* going to be like last time."

"You don't know that."

"You were right." He pulls me close. "I shouldn't have fought Brody Crawford. I wasn't ready. But I'm ready now, Lucy. I've never been more ready."

I swallow the lump in my throat and nod. "Okay."

"Lucy, if you don't want me to do it, I won't do it. Okay? I won't go…if that's what you really want. Because as much as I want to win tonight, it's not more important than you."

I close my eyes and put my head on his chest, ignoring the contraction that's slowly moving across my stomach. "No, Sam, that's not what I want."

"Do you mean that?"

I rest my chin on his chest and look up at him. "I want you to win too. I want it *so* badly for you. And I know how much you need it. Especially since it's your last match. I'm just worried. I can't pretend that I'm not."

"You don't have to worry this time, Lamb."

"That's what you always say."

"I know. But I'm asking you to trust me. It's going to be different this time."

"Just promise me you'll fight smart. Promise me you won't get hit in the head a lot."

"I'll do my best." He laughs softly.

"It isn't funny, Sam."

He closes his eyes and falls into the glider in front of the window. "I know."

"No, you don't. You don't know what it was like to see you after the last fight. You could barely speak," I say, recalling how frightening it was to see him like that. "You could hardly lift your head up."

"I know, Lucy."

"Please stop saying that, because you *don't* know. You don't know what it was like for me."

"Come here," he says, holding his hand out. I take it and he pulls me down into his lap. "Come here," he says again softly, wrapping his arms around me. He rocks back and forth. "I don't know what that was like for you. But it must have been pretty scary."

"Yes...it was."

"My number one job is to protect you. From anything that might hurt you, including moments like that. I'm sorry I didn't do my job that night."

"Your number one job should be to protect yourself. I need you here with me, okay? Our baby needs you here. In one piece. Promise me you'll fight smart tonight."

"I promise. I've learned my lesson, Lucy. I wouldn't be going into this match if I wasn't sure I could beat Valentine."

"How are you so sure?"

"I don't know how to explain it, I just feel it inside. I think maybe...maybe its Joe. I think that maybe he's watching out for me."

I swallow down the emotion that's suddenly choking me. "I'm sure he is."

"And I've got Tristan this time. He was pretty upset after the Crawford fight. He was pissed, actually."

"Yeah?"

"Yeah. He said he plans on being around a long time and doesn't want to see me punch-drunk either. He wants me to fight smarter."

I smile softly. "Because he loves you too."

"Yeah, he does. So I'm pretty damn lucky to have him in my corner tonight."

I nod against his chest and sigh. "I'm sorry I can't be there."

"What are you talking about? You know you'll be there." He presses my hand to his chest over his heart. "You're in there deep. Where I go, you go."

I smile over the fear that's pulsing through my veins. "I love you, Sam Cole."

"I love you too, Lucy Cole."

I laugh and shake my head. "Not yet."

"See, I've been thinking about that, and I'm not sure I'm okay with it anymore."

"Sam, if you think I'm putting on a wedding dress before this baby is born, you have another thing coming."

"I'm not asking for a wedding."

"Well what are you asking for?"

"Lucy, I don't want our baby's last name to be Cole if yours isn't."

I smile softly. "The baby won't know the difference."

"I want us to be a family." He rubs his hand over my tight stomach. "The Cole family."

"You want me to change my name?"

"I want to get married, Lamb. We don't need a wedding. I don't care about that."

"Me neither," I say, wrapping my hand behind his neck. "I never even wanted a wedding."

"Well, it's settled then." He holds my face and rubs his thumb across my cheek. "We're getting married."

I smile and drop my forehead to his. "Nothing would make me happier."

"Sam, you up there?" Miles calls from downstairs.

"You know, I really thought we'd take the keys away when we moved," I say, shaking my head.

Sam kisses me and stands up, bringing me to my feet with him. "We're getting married!" He swats my bottom and it makes me laugh. "Miles," he calls down the hall, "we're getting married!"

I follow him downstairs, but not nearly as fast. By the time I get there, he's already outside talking to Tristan. "Hey, Miles."

Miles holds his hands out and looks at me. "Luc, you're getting bigger every time I see you."

"Gee, thanks, Miles."

"I meant the baby," he says, pulling me into a hug. "Come on."

"Did I hear somebody say they're getting married?" Tristan asks, walking through the front door with Sam.

"Hey, Tris." I laugh. "I guess so."

"When exactly is this happening?" Miles asks.

"Tomorrow. As soon as we're back," Sam says excitedly.

"How about next weekend? We need to find somebody to do it."

"Okay. Next weekend it is."

"Now that we've got that worked out, you want to go get your bag?" Miles asks, looking at his watch. "We gotta go."

Sam gives me a firm kiss, then he bends down and kisses my belly. "I've got to go, baby."

I laugh and watch him run up the stairs to get his bag. But as soon as he's gone, the fear returns, weighting my shoulders. I look at Tristan and Miles and plead, "Please don't let this be a repeat of last time."

"Lucy, you don't have anything to worry about," Miles says unconvincingly.

"Are you kidding me right now, Miles?"

"Lucy, I've known you and Sam most of my life," Tristan says, putting his hands on my shoulders. "I love you both. I am not going to let that happen, okay?"

I duck my head and blink back tears that I've been holding in all morning.

"Come here," he says, wrapping his strong arms around me, and I'm comforted to know that he's in good health again.

"Are you sure *you're* ready?" I ask him.

"I'm more than ready. Tonight's our night, Luc." He holds up his fist. "This one's for Joe."

* * *

My phone rings on the kitchen table a few a feet away from me, but I'm too busy gripping the kitchen counter to care. I inhale a slow, deep breath as a contraction passes, and turn off the faucet over the sink, which I abandoned when the contraction snuck up on me. I turn around and lean against the counter and close my eyes, but my phone rings again, demanding my attention. I go grab it and answer it. "Hey, Bas."

"Are you going to come answer the door? I've been standing here knocking."

"Yeah," I say, making my way across the house.

I hang up and open the front door. Sebastian is standing on my front porch in the dark, lit by the glow of the carriage lights. "Sorry, I didn't hear you knocking."

He bats away a bug and grips the takeout in his hands. "Well I suppose it's hard to hear all the way across your giant house."

"Ha. Ha." I step aside and he walks into the foyer.

"You okay?" he asks, giving me a concerned look. "You look flushed."

"Yeah, I'm fine." I close the door behind him and lock it.

"Well, I hope you're hungry." He holds up the bag in his hand. "I brought Indian."

"Hunger is sort of a constant state with me these days," I say, following him to the kitchen. "So...yeah."

He laughs and puts the bag down on the kitchen island. "Have you talked to Sam?" he asks excitedly.

"Yeah, just a few minutes ago. But the commissioner was coming in so he had to go."

"Oh, my God," he groans, squeezing his eyes shut. "This could be the last fight of his career. I can't believe we're not there."

"This *is* the last fight of his career," I confirm. "And please don't rub it in. I've been stressed about it all afternoon."

"Sorry." He gives me a small shrug, "I won't mention it again. This is a stress-free zone," he says, waving his hands over the counter and food. "It's not good for the baby, remember?"

I inhale a deep breath and blow it out slowly. "I know."

"He's going to be fine."

"Yeah," I say, trying to convince myself.

"How did he sound when you talked to him?

"Good. Ready."

"Tonight's going to be different. I can feel it."

"I hope you're right," I say, trying to let go of my worry.

"I usually am." He winks. "Come on, let's take our plates to the living room so we can watch the preshow before the fight starts." He rubs his hands together excitedly.

"Okay. You want something to drink?" I ask, on my way over to the fridge.

"Water's fine."

I open the fridge to get him a bottle of water and another Braxton Hicks contraction squeezes my stomach. I pause and close my eyes and wait for it to pass, but my eyes pop open when it squeezes me harder, forcing the air from my lungs with a quiet breath.

"You okay?" Bas asks, waiting for me to turn around.

"Mm-hmm," I say. "Just looking for some water."

He pulls the other refrigerator door open. "It's right there," he says, reaching over my shoulder to grab it.

"Oh…" I release my grip on the door handle as the contraction passes. "I guess I didn't see it."

"Hey," he says, putting his hand on my arm. "Sam's going to be fine."

I inhale a deep breath and exhale it quietly. "You really think so?"

"Yeah, I really do. Now, come on, let's go watch."

"Okay."

We take our food to the living room and sit on the couch in front of the ridiculously large TV Sam had mounted above the white brick fireplace between the built-ins that go up the wall on either side.

"This is incredible. It's like we're there," Bas says, staring up at the giant screen.

We welcome you to our live coverage at Madison Square Garden, where tonight we'll see current titleholder Carey Valentine and former champion Sam Cole battle it out in the light-heavyweight title showdown... I'm not sure I've ever seen a crowd quite this excited. Carey Valentine fans are ready to see him prove that he deserves the title he's defending tonight, which he took from Brody Crawford just last month... Which, of course, many say is a title Crawford himself didn't actually earn—a title Sam Cole carried for a few years, not months... Look, we all know you're a Sam Cole fan, but some small part of you has to think he's met his match. Heck, some would argue that he met his match in Las Vegas when he lost his title to Brody Crawford... Brody Crawford? No way. Crawford's a great fighter, but he's not Sam's match. That loss had more to do with Sam and less to do with Brody... You're saying Sam beat himself that night... That's exactly what I'm saying. I've talked to Sam and I believe wholeheartedly he wasn't in a good place that night... Mentally, you mean?... That's exactly what I mean. The loss of Joe Maloney took its toll on him, and he wasn't ready to be back in the ring... Do you think he's ready tonight?... I talked to Sam about twenty minutes ago. The Sam Cole we're going to see tonight isn't the same fighter we saw in Las Vegas... I sure hope you're right. That would mean one heck of a show for this New York crowd.

I put my plate down and squeeze Sebastian's hand as the commentator introduces Sam, articulating every syllable as he says slowly, *Ladies and gentlemen... Sam... Cole!*

"Lucy...Lucy! Ow!" Sebastian says, pulling his hand away.

I ball my empty hands into tight fists and squeeze my eyes shut through another contraction.

"Lucy, what are you doing? Sam's getting into the ring." He wraps his hand around my arm and shakes me. "Hello? Earth to Lucy."

I exhale loudly and open my eyes as it leaves me, sucking in another breath. "Sorry," I pant.

"What is happening?"

"It was just a contraction. I'm fine."

"You don't look fine."

"I've been getting them for months. I'm fine," I say, turning my attention back to the TV. I watch Sam bounce from foot to foot inside the ring, cheering on the excited crowd as "Phenomenal" blares through the arena speakers. I smile softly as my anxiety begins to subside. "He looks like himself tonight."

"Yeah, he does," Bas says, bringing a forkful of rice to his mouth as he watches intently.

The camera zooms in on Sam's face, and he looks into it and says, "You watching, baby?"

"Oh, my God," Bas says over his mouthful, bumping my arm with his.

I smile and nod. "We're watching," I say quietly.

For those who don't know, Sam is going to be a father soon...Very soon. In fact, his fiancée, Lucy, wasn't able to make it tonight because she's too far along to leave their home in Atlanta...No doubt, she's watching this on TV and routing for Sam...We wish them both the best.

"Ahhh," I groan, leaning over.

"What is it? What's wrong?" Bas asks, but I can't answer.

"Another contraction," I grit through my teeth.

"Lucy, are you sure these are Braxton whatevers?"

I nod and breathe through it, until it goes away. "Yeah, the doctor just checked me yesterday. He said I had at least two more weeks. I wasn't dilated at all. I think I just need to get some water. I probably didn't drink enough today. I'll be right back." I get up and go to the kitchen to pour myself another glass of water.

"Hurry up," Bas calls from the living room. "They're about to start."

"Be right there," I say as another contraction grips me. I lean over the sink and suck in a lungful of air, but it's forced out with a loud, "Ow."

"Lucy?" Sebastian walks into the kitchen and sees me hugging the kitchen sink. "Are you having another contraction?" I nod, but don't answer. "What can I do?"

"Nothing," I say. "I'm fine. I just need to sit down." I take my glass of water back to the living room and Sebastian follows me.

I sit back down on the couch and stare at the TV as Sam and Carey circle each other inside the ring. Sam waits for Carey to throw the first punch, but he dodges it and follows with a fast right hook. At the same time, my stomach tightens under my shirt again.

"I have to pee." I get up again.

"You can't hold it?" Sebastian asks, glancing up at me quickly before turning his eyes back to the TV.

I shake my head and walk down the hall, slowly pacing up and down it, until the contraction passes. But before I reach the living room, another one wraps around me, squeezing tight. "Ahh," I cry, squeezing my eyes shut.

"Oh, my God," Sebastian says, finding me holding on to the wall. "I'm calling the doctor." He pulls his phone out of the pocket of his joggers. "What's his name?"

"No." I shake my head. "You don't need to do that. It's just Braxton Hicks. I'm not in labor." I catch my breath and walk back into the living room.

"Are you self-diagnosing right now?"

"Look at the stupid brochure," I say, pointing to the *Stages of Labor* pamphlet on the coffee table. "Women think they're in labor all the time. It's normal to have contractions like this at the end."

He picks it up and quickly skims over it. "Yeah, when they're in labor!"

"Sebastian, I am not in labor. Do you hear me? Sam is eight hundred miles away right now, fighting Carey Valentine," I say through my teeth, looking up at the TV. "I am *not* in labor."

He puts the pamphlet down and presses his lips together. "Yeah. Okay." He pushes a button on his watch and sits back down on the couch.

"What are you doing?"

"Timing your contractions."

"Why?"

"The brochure says that when you have contractions five minutes apart for an hour, you're having a baby." He holds his wrist up. "Time's started."

"I'm *not* having a baby," I say, leaning against the arm of the couch.

"I sure hope not," he says, glancing over at me, unable to hide the concern in his voice.

I put my hand on my stomach and take a slow, calming breath before sitting back down. *I am not having you tonight, do you hear me?*

"Yes!" Bas shouts when Sam knocks Carey back against the ropes.

This is definitely not the same Sam Cole we saw in Las Vegas, I'll give you that… Carey Valentine fans did not like that hit, but Sam seems pretty happy about it.

Sam dodges several punches that Carey returns and then he throws a left hook at his face.

"Hell yeah! Show him who the fucking champ is!" Bas shouts, and I give him a surprised look.

"You've been hanging around Miles too much."

Sam throws another left hook that leaves Carey with a bloody nose.

"Wooo! Yeah!" I shout, sitting up and clapping, but another contraction soon takes control of my body, making every muscle tighten. *No, no, no, no, no!* I lean back against the couch again and close my eyes.

And this is why Sam Cole is such a dangerous boxer. There aren't many southpaws in history that can hit as hard as he can.

"Lucy, what are you doing?"

I shake my head back and forth. "Mmm-mmm."

"Mmm-mmm, what?"

"Shhhh. Don't talk."

"Are you having another contraction?"

I don't answer.

"How long have you been having it?"

I still can't answer him.

"Lucy Marie Bennett."

After a few more seconds, I open my eyes and he resets his watch. "Tell me when the next one happens."

I inhale a deep breath and sit up. "Okay."

Sam Cole wins the second round.

"Yes!" Sebastian makes a fist and I smile. "He's going to win tonight, Luc," he says excitedly, and I can't help but feel the way I used to feel when Sam fought, before the Crawford fight. *Hopeful.*

Carey Valentine looks unfazed by the first two rounds as they make their way back to the center of the ring. Sam has done a great job protecting himself tonight, especially after the beating he took in Las Vegas.

I tap Sebastian's arm and he looks at me. "What?"

I nod and close my eyes.

"Another one? Already? Shit, Lucy."

I ball my fists up and press them against my thighs as my stomach turns into a tight ball that seems to be squeezing my organs and uterus together.

"Thirty seconds," Bas says, and I grab his hand. "Forty seconds," he says, and I squeeze it harder, trying to will the contraction away. "A minute."

"Shit!" I say, keeping my grip on Bas's hand. I huff loudly and fall back against the couch when it finally passes.

"A minute and ten seconds. Lucy—"

"I'm not in labor," I pant, shaking my head back and forth.

And Sam Cole has won another round.

I open my eyes and see him sitting in the corner of the ring, covered in sweat, but there's no blood that I can see. "He's winning, Bas," I say, smiling.

He glances at the TV and nods, then he looks at me again. "Lucy, if you have another contraction in the next two minutes, I'm calling the doctor."

"I won't." I give him a weak smile. "I promise."

He gives me a doubtful look.

"I promissssss," I say through my teeth as another contraction pulls me up off the couch.

He huffs. "You promised!"

"I'm *not*... in labor," I grit through my teeth.

He stands up and pulls his phone out of his pocket. "Oh, my God. We have to tell Sam. I have to call Miles."

I hit his hand with my balled-up fist and knock his phone to the floor. "Don't you dare."

He picks up his phone and puts his hand on his hip. "Lucy, if you're in labor, he needs to know."

I look at him like he's grown a second head. "Are you kidding?" I ask, looking up at the TV. "He's in the middle a fight. A career-defining fight. And I am *not* in labor," I say for the hundredth time. "It hasn't even been an hour. They're going to go away." As soon as I say it, another contraction grips me.

Sebastian helps me back to the couch and he sits beside me quietly, until it passes.

"I'm not in labor," I cry, accepting that I might actually be. "I *can't* be in labor. Dr. Fletcher said that we still had time. He told Sam to go to New York."

Bas nods and takes a deep breath. "Honey..." He wraps his hand around mine and says softly, "I know what your doctor told you, but I think you're in labor. And it's going to be okay." He smiles softly. "We're not going to panic and we're not going to freak out, because everything's going to be fine. We just need to breathe." He blows out a slow breath. "We both just need to breathe."

I nod and swallow down the fear that's racing through my veins. "Okay."

"I need the number to your doctor's office. Where's your phone?" he asks calmly.

"It's in the kitchen."

"Okay, I'll go get it." He gets up slowly and smiles softly. "Just stay calm and try to relax."

As soon as he's gone, another contraction wraps around me all the way to my back.

I don't hear Sebastian return, but I feel his hand wrap around mine. "You're doing great," he says, holding my hand until it's over.

I open my eyes and look at him. "They really hurt."

"I know. You have to breathe through them, okay?"

"I'm trying."

"Okay," he says, handing me my phone. "Let's call your doctor."

I scroll through my contacts searching for the number.

Sam Cole takes a hard hit to the face.

My head snaps up.

"He's fine, Lucy. It's the fourth round and he's blocked almost every hit. I need you to focus and find your doctor's number."

"Okay," I say, pulling it up.

Sebastian takes my phone and holds it to his ear. "Hi, this

is Sebastian Ford. I'm calling for Lucy Bennett, who's a patient of Dr...."

"Fletcher."

"Dr. Fletcher...She seems to be in labor...Yes, we've been timing them...They're less than five minutes apart, actually... Okay, thank you."

"What did they say?"

"They're paging him. She said they'd call back if he wants you to go to the hospital."

"If," I say, sighing with relief. "See? This is normal. It could just be a false alarm." I stare at him, no longer able to breathe or blink because another contraction is twisting my torso.

"Lucy?" He waves his hand in front of my face. "Lucy, are you having another contraction?"

"Mm-hmm," I squeak.

And the bell marks the end of the fifth round. By the looks of things, I'd say Sam Cole has won this round too.

"I think I need to stand up," I say, getting to my feet.

"Are you sure that's a good idea?"

"Yeah," I say, waddling to the kitchen.

I put my hands on the cool marble counter and walk laps around the island, while Sebastian watches me. "This is better," I say, ignoring the way my cami has rolled up over my belly. It feels better not binding me. "I think maybe a bath would feel good."

"A bath? Right now?"

"Yeah." I make my way over to the stairs.

"Okay," he says hesitantly. He follows behind me as I slowly climb the stairs.

I pause halfway up and grip the banister. "Ahh," I cry quietly as a contraction squeezes me.

"Maybe a bath isn't a good idea, Luc."

"I want a bath. It'll relax me."

"Okay." He follows me to my room and turns the TV on while I undress in the bathroom.

I dim the lights and pour some bubble bath into tub, then I light the candles that surround it. When it's full, I step in and sink beneath the water, just in time for another contraction to strike. I sit up and put my hands on the sides of the tub, wincing through the pain. When it subsides, I lean back in the water and sink beneath the bubbles.

After ten minutes and several more contractions, Sebastian shouts from my room, "Sam just knocked Carey Valentine to the mat!"

I close my eyes and smile.

"He's getting back up, but Sam looks great. He's still got a lot of energy."

I press my lips together and nod over tears that suddenly sting my eyes. "Please don't come yet," I whisper, putting my hands on my stomach. "You have to wait for your daddy to get back. I can't do this without him." Tears run down my cheeks as another contraction wraps around me.

"Lucy," Sebastian says softly through the cracked door, "can I come in?"

"Yeah," I squeak over the contraction.

"Are you okay?"

"No," I cry.

He kneels on the floor next to the tub. "I know you're scared right now. It's okay."

I pull my sudsy hand to my eyes and cry into it. "I can't do this without him, Bas. I need Sam."

"I know you do."

"Wait until the fight's over, then call Miles, okay? Maybe he can get a flight home tonight."

He bobs his head. "Of course. I'm sure he'll be able to. Don't worry."

"If he doesn't, will you promise you'll stay with me? Because I don't have anyone else," I say, looking up at him.

"Oh, Lucy. You don't even have to ask." He reaches for my hand. "I would never leave you. We're in this together, whether we want to be or not." He smiles and I nod over the tears rolling down my cheeks.

Another contraction grips me, squeezing me beneath the water, and I squeeze Sebastian's hand.

"Okay, just try to breathe, you're doing great." He inhales a deep breath and blows it out slowly, and I do my best to copy him. "See, you're doing it."

I nod and squeeze his hand harder.

"It won't last too much longer, just keep breathing."

When it passes, I open my eyes and let go of Sebastian's hand. "I'm sorry."

"You don't have to be sorry."

"I think maybe I should get dressed now. Has anyone from Dr. Fletcher's office called back?"

"No, not yet. Want me to get you a change of clothes?"

"Maybe a pair of yoga pants and a tank top?"

"Okay, I'll be right back."

I step out of the tub and grab a towel, hurrying to dry myself off before another contraction renders me useless...and naked. I wrap it around me and stare at myself in the mirror. *You can do this.*

Sebastian walks back into the bathroom, unfazed that I'm wearing nothing more than a towel that barely wraps around my stomach.

"Oh, *SHIT*," I say with wide eyes.

Sebastian's face falls. "What, what is it?"

"I think my water just broke," I say, afraid to look down at my wet feet, which I just dried off.

Sebastian looks down and gasps. "Either that or you just peed on the floor."

I look down and see a puddle around my feet, but I don't have long to fret over it. A contraction stronger than I've felt before moves from my front to my back, practically squeezing me in half. "Shit," I cry, putting my hands on the counter and leaning over it.

"Screw the doctor, I'm taking you to the hospital."

CHAPTER 23

SAM

Carey Valentine is bleeding from the right eye as he retreats to his corner following a brutal tenth round… That eye looks pretty bad, but the doctor is looking at it now… If he sees a problem, he'll stop the fight… It looks like he's okay.

"Listen to me," Tristan shouts, crouching down in front of me, while I sprawl my tired arms and legs in the corner of the ring. "You've got to make him miss. He can't get a straight left hook on you. Don't let him hit right. Keep making him use that left hand, okay?"

"I'm trying. He's fucking fast."

"So are you." He wipes my forehead with a towel. "Slow him down, he's getting tired."

"I am too."

"Just watch his right, that's where his strength is. Keep on him, tire him out, stay on his right side. Okay?"

"Yeah, okay." I shrug off Mikey, who's trying to give me water. "I'm good," I say to him, barely able to hear myself over the crowd.

"Look at me, Sam," Tristan shouts, grabbing my attention again. "This is your night. He's not going to take it from you. We're not going to let him. *We* got you," he says, patting his heart. "It's your night. Now go take it."

He jumps down out of the ring and I stand up on my tired legs, forcing my heavy feet to carry me to the center of the mat.

Both fighters looking tired as we enter the eleventh round...While Sam appears to have won most of the earlier rounds, it looks like the last few went to Carey...It's going to be a close fight to the finish.

Carey stands across from me, holding his gloves up, but I see his arms swaying a little. *I'm not that tired.* I drop my head from side to side and wait for the bell. When it rings, I throw a left hook without hesitating that takes him by surprise.

"Use your speed, Sam, use your speed!" Tristan shouts from beside the ring.

I throw another left hook and a right hook that connects with Carey's face, but he swings his arm around me to keep from stumbling back. "Get off me!" I growl over my mouth guard, punching his shoulder with my right glove, but he pushes me across the mat into the corner.

"That's holding!" Tristan and Miles shout in unison. "He's holding!" Tris yells again.

Carey punches me several times, hitting my shoulder and neck and jaw, so I go to body shots, hitting his ribs a few times, before the referee pulls us apart.

"Get off, get off." The ref pushes Carey across the mat and I follow him back to the center of the ring. "You good?" he asks me, and I nod.

I take my stance in front of Carey and square my tense shoulders.

"He's no champ!" Miles shouts, and Carey smiles over his mouth guard. He takes a swing, but I dodge it.

"There you go," Tris says, circling the outside of the ring with me. "Keep moving those feet, keep moving, Sam! Move your head." Carey punches left and I miss it. "Good!"

He dodges my right hook, but I inch closer and throw a hard left hook that smacks the side of his face and resonates through my arm all the way up to my shoulder. Carey stumbles back, but I stay on him.

"Apply that pressure, Sam! Apply the pressure," Tris shouts at me, and I feel the energy from the crowd behind him buzzing through the arena. But Carey comes back with a fast right hook that connects with my face, and it pauses the world around me for a second. I blink as the arena comes rushing back into my ears, but Carey's glove connects with my face again.

"Come on, Sam! Watch his right!"

I move my feet and watch him circle me.

"You can't beat me!" he screams through the blood and sweat pouring down his face.

The bell rings in my ears over my pounding heart.

I don't believe it! I don't think anyone thought we'd see twelve rounds tonight…Both fighters look tired…Carey Valentine definitely looks worse off with that cut over his eye, but I don't think he's ready to give up yet…Can you blame him? He's got a lot to prove…So does Sam. A whole career and a much talked about retirement. He is not going to go quietly into the night…Maybe Carey was a little too confident agreeing to this match.

Tristan climbs into my corner and crouches in front of me while Mikey gives me water. "You've got to punch and get out of the way, Sam. Just keep moving."

"What do you think I've been trying to do all night?"

"Yeah, well, just keep doing it. Stay focused. This is the last one, okay? This is it. This is your moment. Now you get back up and you take it. Don't let him steal it from you, you take it! Take it for me and Lucy and your baby. Take it for Joe."

SAM, EIGHT MONTHS EARLIER

"Sam, what's eatin' ya?" Joe asks, watching me hit the speed bag.

"Nothing. I'm fine."

"You've said three words all morning. You're not fine." He sips his coffee from a paper cup. "Did I do something?"

I stop hitting the bag and look at him. "No, Joe, you didn't do anything. I'm sorry. I just have a lot on my mind."

"So I noticed." He raises his thick eyebrows and asks, "Are you going to tell me what it is?"

I drop my head and catch my breath for a few seconds. "Lucy's pregnant."

His eyes widen a little, but he does his best to hide his shock. "She's pregnant?"

I bring my gloves up and begin hitting the speed bag again. "Yeah. She found out last week."

He nods and sips his coffee again. "Well, that's…a surprise."

"Yep." I keep hitting the bag.

"Is it a good surprise?" he asks carefully, and I drop my gloves again.

"Yeah…it is."

The corners of his mouth turn down and he gives me a concerned look. "But you're worried."

"Well, yeah. I mean, I'm happy about it, I really am," I say, smiling over the worry that's consumed my every thought I've had since I found out. "I've always wanted kids with her. But now that it's happening, I'm just, freaking out a little. I don't know anything about being a father. I guess I'm just worried that I'll mess it up somehow."

He walks over to a chair and sits down. "You remember your first match?"

"My first amateur match?" I ask, sitting next to him.

"Yeah, what was his name? Pritchett something?"

"Danny Pritchett." I nod over a small frown. "I hated that kid."

"You were scared of that kid," he clarifies.

"Yeah." I laugh. "I was."

"You were scared of him because he was good. He was really good."

"Yeah, way to take it easy on me for my first match."

"I put you up against him, because I knew you were better than he was. You just didn't know it yet."

"I won that match."

"Yeah, and almost every other one after it." He holds his head back and turns his palms up. "Now look at you."

"So what are you saying? I was scared for no reason?"

"No, you had good reason. Everyone was scared of that kid."

He laughs. "Just like every parent is afraid of screwing up. It's normal to have doubts about becoming a father, Sam, but...I think this kid is pretty damn lucky."

"You do?"

He puts his hand on my shoulder and says, "You're going to be a great father, Sam."

I smile and hold my glove out. "Well, I've had a pretty great role model."

He smiles and hits my glove with his fist. "Come on, Rocky, we've got work to do."

* * *

"Protect yourself, Sam! Keep those hands up," Tristan shouts from beside the ring.

I bring my shoulder up to my ear and block a punch that Carey throws at me.

Look at that defense. I'll tell you, this is the work of Sam's long-time trainer—and coach tonight—Tristan Kelley, who worked alongside Joe Maloney for years.

"Good! Good!" Tristan shouts.

Carey punches me again and I fire back with a strong right hook.

"Protect yourself!"

"Finish him, Sam, finish him!" Miles screams.

I throw a left hook and uppercut to his ribs, pushing Carey back against the ropes, but he pivots and gets around me, pushing me against them instead.

"Get off the rope! Get off the rope!"

He punches me hard and the arena goes quiet again.

Come on, Sam, Joe growls in my ear, *show him the lion inside you.*

I push off the ropes with a loud roar. "Ahhhh," I yell, hitting Carey hard.

It's a fight to the finish... Sam Cole is firing away.

"Yeah, baby," Miles screams. "Show him who the real champ is!"

"Southpaw, Sam, southpaw!" Tristan screams, and I pull my left arm back, releasing it with all the power I've got left.

Southpaw uppercut and Valentine goes down!

The mat shakes under my feet and the ref runs over and begins counting over Carey. *One... two... three... four...*

He is not getting up. This might be it, ladies and gentlemen. Carey Valentine is not getting up.

Carey pulls his knees under him and falls over again.

Seven... eight...

"He's done, he's done!" Miles shouts, charging the ring.

Ten! the referee shouts, and the arena goes crazy, flooding my ears with screams and cheers.

The fight is over and Sam Cole has regained his title as the light-heavyweight champion of the world!

I close my eyes and drop my head, feeling Miles and Tristan's arms around me. "You did it, baby! You did it!"

I lift my heavy arms and hug Tristan. "This was you, it was all you."

Ladies and gentlemen, the announcer says over the arena speakers, *from Madison Square Garden in New York City, at three minutes and two seconds into the final round, your winner by knockout, the light-heavyweight champion of the world... Sam.... Cole!*

Everyone shouts and crowds into the ring around me. Miles holds my arm up, and I put my gloves in the air as Mikey and Leon wrap the heavy belt around my waist. The cameras move in, getting close-ups of me, and I can only think of one thing. *Lucy.*

"Call Lucy," I say to Miles over the noisy crowd and the pounding inside my chest. "Call Lucy!"

He pulls his phone out of his pocket and makes a concerned face when he looks at it. He looks up at me and Tristan. "Come on, let's get to the dressing room. Move," he shouts to the people around us. "Sam, come on," he says, leading me and the rest of the team down out of the ring.

I hold my gloves up and smile for the cameras that follow us through the arena, until we're alone in the dressing room.

Miles closes the door behind us.

"What is it, Miles?"

"Hold on," he says, holding his phone to his ear. "I couldn't hear out there. I got a message from Sebastian." He listens with the same concerned look on his face.

Tristan grabs my sore shoulder and squeezes it. "They probably couldn't wait to congratulate you."

Miles lowers the phone and gives me a panicked look. "Lucy's in labor."

I blink at him a few times and shake my pounding head. "What? No, that's not right. She can't be."

He puts the phone on speaker and plays the message again.

Miles, it's Sebastian. When the fight's over, I need you to have Sam call me. Lucy's in labor. We're on our way to the hospital now...

Not until the fight's over, Lucy says in the background, and my drained heart races inside my aching chest.

After the fight, have him call me, Sebastian reiterates.

"Get these fucking gloves off me now," I shout to anyone within reaching distance. "Come on!" I shout, holding my gloves out. Tristan quickly begins to unlace them. "Call him back now," I say to Miles. "Put it on speaker."

Miles calls him and holds the phone out in front of me while it rings. "Miles?" Sebastian answers.

"Sebastian, its Sam. What's happening? Where's Lucy?"

"Sam, thank God. You need to come home. Get a flight as soon as you can. I think she's going to have this baby tonight."

"How long has she been in labor?" I ask, shocked.

"Since before the fight. Her water broke during the fourth or fifth round. I can't remember, it's all running together."

"Her water broke?" I ask, panicked.

"Yes! We're on our way to the hospital now. She's been having really strong contractions."

"Put her on the phone."

"Hold on."

"Sam?" Lucy cries into the phone.

"Hi, baby. Are you okay?"

"Yeah," she says unconvincingly.

"I'm so sorry. I shouldn't have left. If I had known—"

"You won." I hear the smile in her voice, which resonates deep inside my aching chest. "You did it, Sam. I'm so proud of you."

I close my eyes over the conflicting feelings of joy and angst. "I'm coming home, Luc, just try to hold on for me. I want to be there so bad."

"I know. I want you here too." Her voiced trembles.

Tristan tugs my gloves off, and I take the phone in my wrapped hand and hold it up to my ear. "I'll get there as fast as I can."

"Just try to hurry." She stifles a cry. "I need you."

I swallow the guilt that's choking me. "I will. I love you, Lamb."

There's silence.

"Lucy?"

Ahhhh, I hear her cry away from the phone.

"Lucy?"

"She's having another contraction," Sebastian says, and my heart pounds inside my chest.

"Sebastian…"

"I know. Just…hurry, okay?"

"Okay."

I hang up the phone and hand it back to Miles. "You have to find us a flight now. We have to leave."

"Yeah, okay." He makes another call.

I look at Tristan, who's as shocked as everyone else in the room. "We have to go now, where's my bag?"

Miles holds his phone away from his mouth and says, "This is going to take a few minutes, go get a shower."

"I don't care about a shower!"

"Go take a shower." He nods toward the bathroom. "You can't meet your baby girl looking like that."

I exhale a frustrated breath and hold my hands up in front of Tristan. "Cut the tape off."

He pulls me over to a chair and sits me down, then he works to get the tape off. "You've got to get checked by the doctor before we go. It's regulation."

"Well, where the hell is he?"

"I'll go get him." He finishes cutting the tape off my hands and then goes to get him.

I open and close my sore fingers a few times, eyeing my red knuckles.

Leon grabs my face and turns it from side to side. "Your cheeks are a little red, but your face looks okay. I don't see any swelling."

Tristan returns with the doctor, who steps beside Leon and says, "Why don't you let me take a look?"

"Hey, doc, I feel fine," I say, eager to get in the shower, but he takes his time with the examination. He looks in my eyes and ears, he checks my reflexes, he feels my ribs. Finally he looks at Tristan, who's watching intently, and says, "All clear, he looks good."

"Thanks, doc," Tristan says, shaking his hand.

"Much better than last time," he says to me, giving me a slanted look.

"You should have seen the other guy," I groan, getting up.

"I did."

I roll my eyes and head for the shower.

"You need any help?" Tristan asks.

"No, I'm good. I'm tired, but I feel okay." Besides the sudden burst of adrenaline and anxiety that's still pulsing through my veins.

"All right, I'll get you some ibuprofen and some water. I'll put it on the counter. Take it when you get out."

"Okay." I take off my shorts and look at myself in the mirror. My hair is wet with sweat and there are red marks on my face and chest, but no blood or cuts. I close my eyes and inhale a slow breath. *This is not how I wanted to meet my daughter.* I open my eyes and turn on the water. When it's barely warm, I step in.

I shower in record time, trying to keep my thoughts off Lucy, but it's impossible. I struggle between the guilt of not being there, the fear of something going wrong, and the sadness I'll never be able to erase if I miss our daughter's first breath. I get out and dry off, eyeing the bag that's hanging on the back of the door, which is holding my suit for the press conference.

"Miles," I shout, and he comes into the bathroom. "You're crazy if you think I'm doing the conference."

He shakes his head. "Obviously you're not doing the conference. Relax. But what the hell else are you going to wear?"

"I've got his bags," Mikey shouts, carrying my duffle bag into the bathroom. "I called the hotel and had them bring everything over." He smiles. "You're lucky the hotel is only a few blocks away."

"Thanks, Mikey." I open it and search for my joggers and a T-shirt. When I find them I get dressed and find my sneakers.

Miles walks back into the bathroom. "Sam, I couldn't get a flight in the next hour."

"Then keep looking."

"So I chartered a private jet."

"Oh…you did?"

"Yeah, it's ready to go when we are. We just have to get to Teterboro." He looks at his watch. "Traffic shouldn't be too bad at this hour. Get your shoes on."

"How long is the flight?"

"About two hours."

I close my eyes and exhale a worried breath. "What am I going to do if I miss it, Miles?"

"You're not gonna miss it. I'm not gonna let that happen, okay?"

"Okay," I say, knowing he has no more control over the situation than I do.

"But hurry your ass up. You ready?"

"Yeah, I'm ready."

"Let's go!"

CHAPTER 24

LUCY

I lay my head back against the seat rest in Sebastian's car and close my watery eyes, but tears roll down my cheeks.

"He'll make it, Lucy, don't worry," Sebastian says, driving much too fast.

I grip the door handle nervously. "Please slow down."

He gives me a worried look that's mixed with empathy and takes his foot off the gas a little. "Sorry."

"We have time. I'm probably not even dilated yet."

Ow! Shit! I grip the door handle again as another contraction squeezes my stomach. My fingers curl around it tightly as it pulls harder and harder. "Shit!"

"Just hold on, we're almost there. It's not too much farther."

The contraction releases its grip on me and I rejoice for the minute it allows me to catch my breath before another one hits. I reach for the door handle again and grit through my teeth, "I had no idea it would feel like this. It burns."

"I'm sorry, sweetie. We're almost there. Just a couple more streets." I look up at the downtown buildings that glitter in the night sky and tower over the one-way streets that lead to the hospital. I stare at them, thinking fondly of our apartment, surprised that I actually miss it a little. When I see the hospital, I inhale a deep breath, feeling only slightly better.

"Okay," Sebastian says, pulling through the circular drive in front of the main entrance. "We're here." He gets out and runs around the car to open my door, which I practically fall out of into his arms, because as soon as my feet hit the pavement, another contraction strikes. I hold on to him and cry against his chest, squeezing his arms tightly, until it's over. When I loosen my grip on him, he looks down at me and says, "Okay, I now have a totally different opinion about those moaning pregnant ladies you see in the hospital on TV."

I give him a worried look. "Was it not quiet?"

He pulls his mouth to the side and shakes his head.

"Sorry." I pout. "It hurts."

"Sweetie, you can cry and moan as loud as you want." He rubs my back and grabs my things. "Come on, they're waiting on you." He pulls me inside to a waiting wheelchair and a man wearing gray scrubs.

"Lucy Bennett?" he asks, greeting us with an enthusiastic smile.

I look up at Sebastian and say softly, "It's supposed to be Cole."

Sebastian gives me a funny look and answers for me. "Yes, she's Lucy Bennett. She's a patient of Dr. Fletcher."

"Okay, Lucy, why don't you go ahead and have a seat." He pushes the wheelchair toward me, which I happily fall into. "How are you guys doing tonight? Are you ready to have a baby?" he asks excitedly.

"Oh, um…" Sebastian smiles and shakes his head. "I'm not the father."

"Oh"—he gives Sebastian a firm nod—"well, good for you."

"No, I, um…" He looks at me and then looks at the man and says simply, "Thank you."

I smile and take his hand as the man begins to push me, squeezing it tightly as another contraction works its way around my stomach.

"Her contractions are getting pretty strong," Sebastian says, wincing with me.

"How's your pain level, Lucy?"

"On what scale?" I grit.

"Let's just go with a solid seven?" Bas offers.

"Okay, well we can help with that. After we get you upstairs, we can have the anesthesiologist come talk to you."

"I don't want an epidural," I say to Sebastian, catching my breath.

"Mm-hmm." He presses his lips together and nods over a concerned smile. "Let's just see how you feel once you get settled in and then you can decide."

The man wheels me into the elevator and we ride up to the maternity floor in uncomfortable silence, until the doors open and I'm greeted by two nurses in blue scrubs. One has short blond hair that's pushed off her face by a stretchy white headband and the other has long curly brown hair that's pulled back into a ponytail.

"Hi, Lucy, I'm Sarah," the blonde says, giving me a welcoming smile.

The brunette brings her hands to her hips. "I'm Meghan. We'll be your nurses tonight."

"Hi," I say, glancing up at them.

"Okay, Lucy, I leave you in their capable hands," my wheelchair driver says, smiling at me. "Good luck."

I reach for Sebastian's hand as another contraction squeezes me, and he looks at the nurses expectantly. "Is her room ready?"

"Yes, right this way," Meghan says, leading us to the far corner of the floor, away from the elevators and the nurses' station. "Here's your suite," she says, walking into the spacious room.

Sebastian pushes me across the hardwood floor to the bed. "Is this where she'll have the baby?"

"Yep," Sarah says, closing the blinds over the large windows that overlook the city. "This is where she'll labor, and when the time comes, we'll give the room a bit of a clinical overhaul so that Dr. Fletcher can deliver her right here."

"Is he here?" I ask hopefully.

"Yes. But he's currently prepping for a C-section."

"Right," I say, remembering that I'm not his only patient. "How long does that take?" I ask selfishly.

Meghan looks up from the various devices she's checking around the room and says, "Don't worry, Lucy, he'll be here."

"Are you expecting anyone else?" Sarah asks, helping me up onto the bed, which is surprisingly soft.

"Yes, my fiancé. He's flying back from New York right now."

"Oh, good," she says. "We were worried he wouldn't make it back in time."

"You know who he is, then," Sebastian says.

"Yes. But don't worry. Your privacy is our *second* highest concern," she says, winking at me.

"What's your first?" Sebastian asks, putting my bag down.

"The baby, of course."

"Oh, right," Sebastian says.

"Speaking of which," I groan, and close my eyes.

"Okay, just take deep breaths," Sarah says calmly as the contraction wraps around me. She puts her hand on my back and says again, "Deep breaths." I try to breathe in and out as she rubs my back through the contraction. When it passes, she smiles and says, "Good job."

"Lucy, why don't you go ahead and get changed," Meghan says, handing me a soft open-back hospital gown, reminiscent of my days after the accident. "We'll be back in a few minutes. Everything off, ties go in the back."

They leave the room and Sebastian gives me an empathetic look, as if he's watching my dignity jump off me, one traitorous piece at a time. "Want me to step out?" he asks, while I gather the gown in my hands.

"No, just turn around. I wouldn't want to scar you for life with my alien body."

"You know I really don't care."

"My dignity is abandoning me by the second. I'd like to hold on to as much of it as possible for as long as I can."

He laughs and turns around and patiently faces the wall while I change into the gown.

"The nurses are young," I say, yanking my yoga pants off my ankles.

"Yeah, but they seem to know what they're doing."

I pull my shirt off over my head and say, "As long as Dr. Fletcher is here, that's all I care about."

"That's *all*?" he asks, turning his head toward his shoulder.

"Well, obviously that's not all I care about." I tie my gown behind me and sit back down on the comfortable bed, feeling slightly better to be out of my binding clothes. "Okay," I say, scooting back against the pillows. "You can turn around."

Sebastian turns around and sits on the edge of the bed. "Reminds me of the last time I saw you in a hospital bed." He pulls the warmed blankets up over my legs and stomach. "How's that?"

"Better." I close my eyes and exhale softly.

"Of course, you weren't smuggling a beach ball under your blankets back then."

I laugh, but another contraction squeezes me, pulling me up off the pillows. "Ow," I cry, gripping the rail on the side of the bed.

"Okay, just breathe," he says calmly.

"I'm trying," I cry.

"He's right, you have to breathe through them, or they'll hurt a lot worse," a new nurse says, walking into the room.

I look up at her stern face and the wiry gray hair that surrounds it.

"Did you take any Lamaze classes?"

"No," I say, grimacing.

She gives me a disapproving look. "The hospital offers them for a reason."

"Actually, many would argue that Lamaze is a dated technique and the rhythmic breathing can worsen the pain," Sebastian says confidently.

I smile at him as the contraction releases its grip on me. *The baby books.*

"Well, they probably haven't delivered as many babies as I have," she says to him.

"Will you be delivering *mine*?" I ask, trying to sort through feelings of concern and confidence.

"No," Meghan says, walking back into the room. "Her shift just ended."

"I just came to get an update for Dr. Fletcher."

"Oh," I say, glancing between them.

"Lucy, I'm going to go ahead and check you now," Meghan says, and Sebastian springs to his feet. "We'll see how far dilated you are." She smiles and pulls on a pair of gloves.

"Okay." I push the blankets off me and scoot down a little, but another contraction burns across my stomach. "Ow!"

"Okay, just breathe," she says calmly, waiting to check me until it's through. "Just tell me when it's over."

When it passes, I gasp, "It's over."

"All right, let's see how far dilated you are." She does a quick examination and I pray that I'm not dilated very far. She looks up at me and pulls her gloves off. "You're about three centimeters."

"That's good right?" Sebastian asks hopefully. "That means we have time?"

"Yes, she has to get to ten centimeters before she can push."

"And how long will that take?" he asks, giving her a serious look.

"Good luck," the older nurse says to Meghan, and then leaves the room, in exchange for Sarah, who returns with a smile.

"Don't worry about her," Meghan says. "She's always cranky at the end of her shift," she whispers.

"But she's delivered a lot of babies?" I ask, wondering how much experience Meghan and Sarah have.

"Yes. But so have we," Sarah says confidently, and I exhale a comforted breath.

She reaches around me. "I'm going to get you hooked up to a fetal monitor now and then we can call the anesthesiologist."

"Oh, but I don't want an epidural."

"Okay," she says, helping me sit up. "Well, you don't have to decide right now. Just let us know if you change your mind."

"Okay." She fastens the monitor around my stomach and it fills the room with the fast swooshing sound of the baby's heartbeat. "I love that sound," I say, falling back against the pillows.

"Is that the baby's heartbeat?" Sebastian asks, and I realize he's never heard it before.

"Yeah." I smile up at him.

"It's so fast," he says, pulling his dark eyebrows together.

Meghan pats his shoulder reassuringly. "That's a good thing."

"Dr. Fletcher said her heart's really strong. Just like Sam," I say quietly to myself.

Sebastian reaches for my hand and sits beside me on the bed again. "He's going to make it, Lucy."

"We'll be back soon. Just let us know if you need anything," Sarah says, following Meghan out of the room.

"Want some of these really yummy-looking ice chips?" Sebastian asks, picking up a small plastic cup.

"Sure."

He hands me the cup and I let a few small pieces of ice fall into my mouth. As they melt, the cool water runs down my throat and it actually makes me feel a little better. "Can I have some more?"

"Yeah." He shakes a few more pieces into the cup and hands it back to me, but I almost crush it in my hand when another contraction wraps around me, squeezing me hard. I feel Sebastian take the cup from me. "Just breathe. Inhale… Exhale."

When it's over, I drop my head back against the pillows and pant, "Maybe I should just get the epidural."

"Okay. If that's what you want."

"I'm just so tired," I say, wondering how I'm going to endure this for hours.

"Do you want me to call the nurse?"

"No, not yet." I close my eyes. "I can keep going. If I can just sleep for a few minutes, I think I can keep going."

"Okay."

I fall into a reprieve of sleep, but minutes, or maybe seconds later, another contraction jerks me awake. "Ow!" I cry, squeezing Sebastian's hand, which is still wrapped around mine. I close my eyes again and take deep breaths, bearing the pain until it passes. Then I fall back asleep for a few minutes.

This goes on for a while.

"Lucy, I need to check you again," I hear Meghan say, and it pulls me out of the light sleep I'd just fallen back into.

I open my eyes and nod reluctantly. "Okay." I scoot down on the bed a little.

"Did you get some sleep?" she asks, pushing my knees apart.

"A little," I say, wincing as another contraction strikes.

"Five centimeters. You're moving quickly."

"What?" I groan with what little air is left in my lungs.

"Already?" Sebastian asks, unable to hide the worry in his voice.

She looks at the paper that's feeding out of the monitor beside the bed. "You're having strong contractions, Lucy. They're moving you along quickly."

I give Sebastian a panicked look. "Call Sam. See how much longer."

He pulls his phone out of his pocket and holds it to his ear. "The call won't go through. Maybe they're in the air."

"Try Miles."

"Don't worry, Lucy. Even though you're progressing quickly now, sometimes labor will stall," Meghan says.

"Same with Miles. I'll try to send a text."

"We don't get great reception in the hospital," Megan adds, giving him an apologetic look.

Sebastian raises his eyebrows and asks, "Why don't they put *that* on the brochure?"

I look at my stomach and say firmly, "Stay. In. There."

Meghan laughs. "Just hang in there, he still has plenty of time. I'll check on you again soon."

"Bas, text him the room number."

"I'm trying, but it won't go through." He picks up the hospital phone. "Maybe I can get through with the landline." After a few seconds he says, "It's going straight to voicemail."

"Leave a message."

"Okay."

A short minute later, another contraction pulls me up off the pillows. I lean over and put my feet on the floor.

"What are you doing?" Sebastian asks.

"I need to walk." I reach for his hand and slowly walk

around the bed, groaning and crying through the pain. "Ow!" I groan, dropping my hands on the bed. "This fucking hurts!"

Sebastian waits for it to pass before saying, "Lucy, I really think you should get the epidural now."

"Mm-hmm," I squeak, climbing back into the bed.

"I'll go get the nurse."

"Mm-*HMMMMM*." The air rushes from of my lungs as another contraction burns through me.

"Another one?" he asks, pausing at the door, but I don't answer. "Nurse! Meghan…Sarah…somebody!" he shouts from the door, and then rushes back over to me.

"I want the epidural. I want the epidural," I cry, gripping the bed sheets in my hands.

"Lucy, what's going on?" Sarah asks, hurrying over to me.

"I need the epidural. I need it now. Please," I cry.

"Okay, I'll call the anesthesiologist. Just hang in there, you're doing great."

I try to focus on the swooshing of the baby's heartbeat, but it slows down when the contraction squeezes me harder. "Did you hear that?" I ask Sebastian. "The baby's heartbeat slowed down."

"I didn't hear it."

"Get the nurse again."

Sebastian calls for Sarah again and she comes back into my room. "The baby's heart rate is slowing down," he says to her.

She checks the paper feeding out of the monitor beside the bed. "Yes, it did drop a little, but it's nothing to worry about. It happens with contractions because they're pushing on the baby too."

"Are they hurting her?"

"No, she just feels the pressure, kind of like a firm squeeze."

"Okay."

"Lucy, I'm Dr. Mooney," an unfamiliar man says, entering the room. "Dr. Fletcher asked me to come check on you. I'm the attending physician."

"Is he still in surgery?" I ask, trying to remember that the other mother needs him more than I do right now.

"Yes." He gives me a warm smile. "But he should be here soon."

I nod and exhale an anxious breath. "Okay," I say quietly. "It's going to be okayyyyyyy!"

"You're having another contraction," I hear him say, but I'm too lost in the pain to look up. "This graph shows her contractions," he says to Sebastian. "You can see how strong they are and how quickly they're coming. She's not getting much of a break in between them."

When the contraction passes, Dr. Mooney asks, "Lucy, would it be okay if I checked your progress now? I want to see how these contractions are moving you along."

I nod and drop my knees to the side and tug Sebastian back by my head.

Dr. Mooney looks up at Sarah and asks, "What was she at last?"

"Five centimeters, about thirty minutes ago."

"She's at seven now." He pulls his gloves off. "You're progressing quickly, Lucy."

"But I don't want to progress quickly. I'm waiting on my fiancé. He's flying in from New York. Is there something you can do to slow it down?"

"Sometimes the epidural slows it down a bit," Sarah says.

Meghan walks back into the room, followed by a man in green scrubs, who I pray is the anesthesiologist.

He smiles at me. "Lucy, are you ready for your epidural now?"

I nod over the contraction that's burning across my stomach. "Yes," I say through my teeth, balling my hands into tight fists.

"Lucy, it was a pleasure to meet you," Dr. Mooney says, before leaving the room. "Please tell Sam congratulations for me. We were all rooting for him."

I nod and give a strained thumbs-up.

"Okay, Lucy, I need you to sit up and let your legs hang over the side of the bed."

I inhale a deep breath and blow it out slowly, then I sit up and scoot to the edge of the bed. "Like this?" I ask, dangling my feet over the side.

"Yes, but…" He looks at Sebastian and asks, "Do you get light-headed easily?"

"Oh, um, no." He shakes his head and gives me a curious look.

"Okay, I need you to come stand in front of her," he says, positioning Sebastian in front of me. "Lucy, I'm going to move you to get you in the right position, but then I don't want you to move. Okay?"

"Okay."

He puts his hands on my back and bends me over my knees, squishing my stomach against my legs. "Keep your head down" he says, running his latex-covered finger down my spine, and I do as I'm told. "Keep her in this position," he says to Sebastian. "No matter what. Do not let her move."

"Okay," Sebastian says, and I hear the concern in his voice.

"Lucy, you cannot try to sit up. Understand?"

"What happens if she sits up?" Bas asks.

"She's not going to. Right, Lucy?"

"Right." I hold my breath through the sharp pinch I feel in my back. "I'm having another contraction," I groan, unable to breathe in this position.

"I know," he says calmly. "But it should be the last one you feel. Just don't move." A rush of cool burns beneath my skin. "Almost done."

"You're doing great," Sebastian says, smiling at me, but his face is a shade lighter than normal.

"Okay, you can sit up."

"You're done?" I ask, lifting my head tentatively.

"Yep. You should feel better in a few minutes."

"Thank God," Sebastian says quietly, letting go of me. He turns around and inhales a deep breath.

"You okay?" I ask him.

He turns back around and pulls his fist to his mouth. "Mm-hmm." He nods. "I'm great," he whispers.

"Okay, well, can you come back?" I ask, noticing that my legs suddenly feel like there are cement blocks tied to them.

He raises his eyebrows and approaches me with caution.

"I can't move my legs," I tell him.

"That's the idea," the anesthesiologist says. "You won't feel anything from about your chest down."

"Really?"

"Look," he says, pointing to the monitor beside the bed. "You're having a contraction right now."

"I can't feel it."

"At all?" Bas asks.

"No, not at all." A huge smile spreads across my face.

"Oh, thank God," he says, sitting on the bed beside me. He falls back against it dramatically. "I don't know how much more I could have taken."

I laugh and try unsuccessfully to move back on the bed. "Could you help me?"

He sits up and helps me scoot back against the pillows. "Seriously, I'm going to kill Sam."

"Sebastian."

"Actually, I'm going to kill your doctor for telling him it was okay to leave. And then I'm going to kill Sam."

"It's not Dr. Fletcher's fault." I watch the contraction on the monitor and exhale a joyful breath. "It's nobody's fault," I say, momentarily blissed out.

"Okay, Lucy, why don't you try to get some rest now," the anesthesiologist says. "It won't be long before you have to push."

Push? I can't push until Sam gets here.

Sebastian tries to hide the worried look on his face. "He's right. You should just try to get some sleep."

* * *

I wake to a dimly lit room and Sebastian, whose face is glowing in the light of his phone. "Any word from Sam?" I ask him, trying to sit up.

He gets up from the couch across the room and pulls a chair up next to the bed. "No, not yet."

"What time is it?"

"It's late. You've been asleep for an hour."

"Really?" I ask, thankful that more time has passed.

"Nurse Meghan was in here a few minutes ago, but she didn't want to wake you. She said you'll need your strength to push."

"Well…" I exhale a determined breath. "I'm not doing that without Sam."

He presses his lips together and says, "Just try to get some more sleep."

"I'm not tired now. I just wish Sam would get here."

"I know." He puts his hand on mine and gives it a small squeeze. "Me too."

"Did you sleep at all?" I ask him.

"Yes. No. Not really," he admits. "I was updating Paul in the waiting room."

"Paul's here?"

"Of course. He came as soon as he got my message."

I exhale a heavy breath and drop my head back against the pillows. "I'm sorry you had to fill in for Sam tonight. But I'm really glad you're here."

He gives me a tired smile and sighs. "This isn't exactly how I saw your birth story going, but I'm glad I'm here too." He glances up at the screen that's monitoring my contractions. "Woah, that one's off the charts. You can't feel it?"

"Nope," I say, shaking my head. "I just feel the pressure." I look down at my contracting stomach and take a deep breath. "A *lot* of pressure."

"You thirsty? I can offer you ice chips or"—he shakes the cup—"ice chips."

I laugh and reach for the cup, but when he hands it to me, I freeze. "I have to get up," I say, giving it back to him.

"What?"

"I have to go to the bathroom," I say again, unable to ignore the overwhelming urge. I put my hand on Sebastian's arm and try to scoot to the edge of the bed.

"Lucy, you can't get up," he says, reminding me that my legs are no longer connected to my brain.

"I have to. You have to help me."

"Hold on!" He runs to the door and calls down the hall for the nurse.

Oh, God. I can't stop it. I push into the sensation.

"Lucy? What are you doing? Are you pushing?"

"No," I say, trying to stop. But. I. Cant. Stop. Pushing.

"Stop!" he orders. "Don't push. I've got to get the nurse."

"I can't," I grit through my teeth.

"Lucy, what's going on?"

"She's pushing!" Sebastian exclaims.

"Okay, I'll go get Dr. Fletcher."

The sensation leaves me as quickly as it came, and I gasp for air. "You have to stay in there," I cry to the baby. "Please. Just a little longer. Your dad will be here any minute," I say, trying to convince myself.

"Where's my favorite patient?" Dr. Fletcher asks, walking into the room a few seconds later.

I burst into tears as soon as I look at him. "You're here."

He walks over to me and reaches for my hand. "I'm so sorry, Lucy. I never would have encouraged Sam to go to New York if I thought you'd be going into labor so soon."

"I know…it's okay." I smile over the tears and worry. "He won."

"I know." He gives me a small smile and pats the back of my hand. "How are you holding up?"

"Okay," I lie.

"Well, let's take a look and see what's happening."

"I don't want to push until Sam gets here." I groan as the urge comes back with no way for me to ignore it. "How. Do. I. Stop?"

"You can't, Lucy. You have to do what your body's telling you to do."

"No." I shake my head and tears run down my cheeks. "She can't come until Sam gets here." I drop my head back against the pillow and try to fight it, but it's a losing battle.

"It's going to be okay," Sebastian says, holding my hand while Dr. Fletcher examines me, but I see the worry in his eyes too.

"Okay, Lucy, push against my hand." I do, but not by choice. "I can see the top of the baby's head," he says. "You're fully dilated."

I exhale as the urge leaves me again. "You can see her?"

"Yep." He smiles. "She's got a head full of hair."

"She does?" I cry, conflicted with feelings of awe and angst. Sebastian pulls his hand to his mouth and his eyes mist over.

Dr. Fletcher looks at me and says, "Lucy, I know you want to wait for Sam to get here. I want him here too. But your baby is ready now. She's not going to wait. I need you to help me deliver her, okay? I can't do it on my own, unless it's in the OR, and I know you don't want that."

"No," I say, shaking my head.

"Okay then. Every time you have a contraction, you're going to feel the urge to push. I need you to listen to your body and push into that feeling."

"Okay," I cry, nodding over the tears that keep rolling down my cheeks.

"You can do this, Lucy," Sebastian says, squeezing my hand.

* * *

"Lucy, here comes another contraction, it's time to push again," Meghan says, but I can barely lift my head.

"I can't, I'm too tired." I shake my head and cry, "I can't push anymore."

"Yes you can," Sebastian says, putting his hand behind my neck. "Come on." He lifts my head and helps me curl my shoulders forward.

"You can do it, Lucy, just a little more," Sarah encourages.

I close my eyes, squeeze every muscle in my body, and push as hard as I can.

"Push, Lucy, push!" Sebastian and Meghan say in unison.

"I'm pushing!"

"You have to push harder, Lucy," Dr. Fletcher says, looking up at me. "I need your help, remember?"

"I can't," I cry, falling back against the pillows. "I can't do it anymore." Tears leak from my eyes, dampening the strands of hair that are sticking to my sweat-sheened face. "I need Sam. I can't do this without him. I don't want to do this without him," I say to Sebastian.

"Lucy, listen to me," Dr. Fletcher says, sounding unusually firm. "You're having very strong contractions and you've been pushing for over an hour. If the baby's heart rate keeps dropping, I'm going to have to do an emergency C-section. I don't know how much more she can take."

"What? No." I cry harder.

"I know that's not what you want, but if you don't deliver soon, I won't have a choice."

"Look at me," Sebastian says, squeezing my hand tight. "I know you need Sam right now. I know you don't want to do this without him. I don't want that either. But what we want doesn't matter right now. The only thing that matters is getting the baby out safely."

"I need you to give me just a few more pushes, Lucy," Dr. Fletcher says. "But they have to be strong."

Sebastian looks at me and says, "Be strong for her, Lucy. You can do this."

I nod my tired head and close my eyes, anticipating the next contraction. *I can do this.* I inhale a deep breath and blow it out slowly.

"Lucy!"

I open my eyes and see Sam rushing over to me. "Sam!" I cry, feeling my overworked heart beat faster inside my chest. I look up at his weary face through my watery eyes. "You made it."

He reaches for my face and kisses me. "I'm sorry," he kisses me again, "I'm so sorry. I tried to call when we landed."

"Poor cell service," Sebastian says, with a look of exasperation and relief.

"It's okay." I laugh through the tears that are running down my cheeks.

"I love you," Sam says, kissing me again.

"I love you too," I cry with relief as the cloud of worry and sorrow vanishes.

"I thought I was going to miss it."

"You almost did," Dr. Fletcher says, giving him a tentative smile. "I just need Lucy to give me a couple of strong pushes."

Sam quickly assesses me. "Are you okay? Are you in a lot of pain?"

"She got an epidural," Sebastian answers. "But she's been pushing for over an hour. She's exhausted."

"Okay, Lucy, it's time to push again," Meghan says from the other side of the bed.

"Make this one count," Dr. Fletcher says.

"Okay." I lift my head and push into the contraction that's squeezing me—and the baby, I'm reminded.

"Hold her shoulders," Sebastian says to Sam.

"Like this?" The feeling of Sam's familiar hands on my back gives me a renewed energy, and I push harder.

"Good," Dr. Fletcher encourages. "Keep pushing."

"I'll be right outside," I hear Bas say through the pulsing in my ears.

"No," I grit through my teeth.

"Lucy, focus," Dr. Fletcher says.

"Keep pushing, baby," Sam says softly, and I push harder.

"Good," Dr. Fletcher says again. "Just like that."

I exhale and fall back against the pillow. "I need a break," I pant, feeling the pressure of the contraction leave me.

"Okay, but I want another push like that with the next contraction."

I nod at Dr. Fletcher. "Okay."

"You're doing so good," Sam says, pushing my hair off my face.

I look over at Sebastian, who's standing near the door. "Hey," I call to him, stretching my arm out.

He walks back over to me and takes my hand, and I give him a conflicted look. He smiles softly and says, "This is your time...for you and Sam." He squeezes my hand. "I won't be far."

"Thank you," I say, giving him a weak smile.

"Anytime."

Sam puts his hand on Bas's shoulder. "Thank you, Sebastian. For everything. I don't know what we...what I would have done if you weren't here."

"My pleasure," he says, giving me a sincere look. "Oh, and Sam?" he says, before leaving. "Congratulations on the win."

"Thanks." Sam smiles, but gives me a remorseful look.

"I'm so proud of you," I say, squeezing his hand, but another contraction forces me to start pushing again. I lean forward and Sam puts his hands behind my shoulders again, pushing me forward. I squeeze every muscle in my body, groaning through my clenched teeth.

"Okay, Lucy, the baby's crowning," Dr. Fletcher says, and my heart beats faster.

I feel Sam leaning over me to look, and as much as I want to yank him back and tell him *no*, I can't. Especially not when I hear him say, "Oh, my God, she has hair." The awe and emotion in his voice dissolves every trivial concern I had.

"Keep pushing," Dr. Fletcher says. "Don't stop."

Sam drops his head to mine. "We're about to be a family."

"Push, Lucy, keep pushing!" Meghan shouts, and I curl my shoulders into the contraction.

"Okay, Lucy, here she comes."

"Keep pushing, baby, keep pushing," Sam says, squeezing my hand, and I search for the last ounce of strength inside me.

I push as hard as I can…and then everything slows to a quiet still around me.

My heart pounds inside my chest, echoing in my ears as I watch Dr. Fletcher work in slow motion. I look up at Sam, whose eyes fill with tears that spill down his cheeks, and the world disappears.

I look at the tiny pink baby in Dr. Fletcher's hands, holding my breath, afraid that if I exhale, I may never be able to inhale again. My head spins and I close my eyes, but when I open them again, the world rushes back to me with the most beautiful sound I've ever heard.

My baby crying.

I let out a joyful sob and Sam drops his forehead to mine. "She's okay?" I ask Dr. Fletcher, who lays her on my chest.

"Yes, you have a healthy baby girl," he says, smiling. "She just needed a little help getting the fluid out of her lungs."

I look down at the tiny pink screaming creature on my chest and put my hands on her warm back. "I love her already," I say to Sam, awed by the quickness in which my heart has grown to make room for her.

He puts his hand over mine and kisses her forehead. "Because she's perfect."

"Shhh…" I say against her head, kissing it softly. "Don't cry, baby." I rub her back and her puffy eyes peek open at Sam. She goes quiet and gazes at him, blinking a few times.

He smiles and cups her tiny head in his hand. "Hi, little lamb," he says to her, and new tears fill my eyes.

"I need to take her for just a minute," Sarah says, scooping her off my chest too soon.

Sam follows her to the warming table and watches her take

the baby's measurements. "Six pounds, seven ounces," she reports, and I smile at Sam. He puts his finger in her little hand and my heart swells when she curls her tiny fingers around it. Sarah cleans her up and wraps her up like a burrito before handing her to Sam, and for a moment everyone else in the room disappears. All I see is Sam, holding our baby in his arms, gazing at her with a look of love and wonderment. He kisses her forehead and bounces her softly as he carries her over to me.

He places her in my arms and sits on the bed beside me.

"What are you going to name her?" Meghan asks, adjusting the pillows behind me.

I look at the little burrito in my arms and smile softly. "Josephine," I say to Sam, who gives me a small, surprised smile. "After her grandpa Joe."

He rubs his hand over his mouth and nods, but doesn't say anything.

"I like that," Meghan says. "She looks like a Joey."

I reach for Sam's hand and he says huskily, "He would have really loved her."

I blink back new tears. "Yeah." I touch her velvety cheek and run my hand over her soft caramel brown hair. "Joey," I say softly.

CHAPTER 25

LUCY

I open my eyes to the afternoon light that fills my hospital room and carefully roll over in my bed, thankful that I can feel my legs again. I look at Joey's bassinet, but it's empty.

"Hey," Sam says quietly, smiling at me from the chair across the room. His feet are propped up, and the baby is curled up on his chest, asleep.

I smile and try to sit up a little. "You look comfortable."

"Yeah, she's been keeping me company," he says, rubbing his hand over her back. He drops his chin and kisses the top of her head. "She was fussing a little bit, but I wanted to let you sleep."

I exhale an emotional breath. "Thanks."

She lets out a little cry and he pats her back. "I think maybe she's hungry." He gets up and walks over to me and I adjust my pillows, pulling one into my lap to prop my arms on. He hands her to me and she nuzzles my chest, opening her tiny mouth and mewling softly as she searches for my breast.

"I guess so." I laugh, pulling her close so she can find it.

Sam sits on the edge of the bed beside me and rubs her tiny head. After a few seconds, he looks at me and says, "You're amazing."

I stare at her tiny face and watch her nurse. "She's doing all the work."

He reaches for my face and I look up at him. "*You* are amazing. I'm so sorry I wasn't here," he says, unable to hide the guilt in his eyes.

"You were here for the most important part." I look down at her and smile softly. "That's all that matters."

"If I had known,"—he shakes his head—"I wouldn't have gone. I would have forfeited the fight to be with you."

"I know. But I'm so glad you didn't have to," I say, smiling at him.

"Really?"

"You won," I say, unable to hide my pride and belated excitement. I reach for his face with my free hand and repeat, "You won, Sam!"

He smiles. "Yeah, I did."

"Let me look at you," I say, inspecting his face.

He touches his forehead. "I think I got a bruise here," he says, rubbing the spot.

When he moves his hand, I look at it. "It's just a little red." I turn his chin from one side to the other. "Your eyes look good."

He gives me an heartfelt look and says, "I tried really hard not to get hit."

"You did a good job." I pull his mouth to mine and give him a soft kiss.

"It was hard. Carey Valentine is as good as everyone says he is."

"He's not as good as you."

He drops his head and gives me a small smirk. "Did you get to see any of it?"

"The first few rounds. Between contractions." I close my eyes and shake my head, recalling last night's events. "Thank God Sebastian was there."

He wraps his hand around mine. "You have no idea how bad I wanted to be here. When Miles told me you were in labor…" He pulls my hand to his mouth and exhales a heavy breath. "It was torture." He rubs Joey's soft little cheek with the back of his finger. "If I had missed it, I would have never forgiven myself."

"But you didn't," I say, crinkling my eyes at him.

He smiles and says, "Thanks to Miles."

"Why, what did he do?" I ask, giving him a slanted look.

"There weren't any commercial flights available, so he chartered a private jet."

"He did?"

"Yeah. He said he wasn't going to let me miss the second biggest moment of my life."

I give him a curious look. "Second? What was the first?"

He reaches into his pocket and pulls out my engagement ring. "When you said that you'd marry me."

I open my mouth and widen my eyes. "When did you get that?"

"I had Miles go get some of my things from the house. He said it was laying on the bathroom counter."

I give him apologetic eyes. "I took it off to take a bath, but then my water broke, and, well…"

"I know. Sebastian told me." He slides it back onto my finger. "Speaking of getting married."

"I know how important it was to you to get married before she came."

"Actually"—he laces his fingers with mine—"it's not too late."

I look down at the baby asleep on my breast. "Um, if you haven't noticed."

"It's not too late for the birth certificate," he says, smiling.

"Oh...what?" I ask, covering myself back up.

Someone knocks on the door and cracks it open. "Lucy?" Sebastian calls from the other side of it, and my heart swells.

"Come in," I say, eager to see him.

"Hey," he says softly, walking into the room with Paul. His eyes bounce between me and Sam and the baby, but ultimately land on the baby. "Oh, my God." He leans over her and gasps. "I just can't get over how precious she is. Can I hold her?" he asks tentatively.

"Of course."

Sam carefully scoops her out of my arms and hands her to Sebastian. "Careful," he says, cupping her head as Sebastian takes her. "You have to hold her head up."

Sebastian cradles her in his arms and stares at her with awe. "She's perfection," he says, putting his finger in her tiny hand. "I'm your uncle Sebastian." Paul looks over his shoulder and touches her little cheek. "We are so having a baby," Bas says to him, and Paul smiles adoringly. Bas looks at Joey again and says softly to her, "You nearly gave me a heart attack last night."

"I'm sorry." I laugh, shaking my head.

"You were worth it," he says to me. "And so were you," he

whispers to the baby, carefully laying her in the bassinet beside my bed.

"Sebastian." Sam reaches for him and pulls him into a hug. "I can't thank you enough for what you did last night."

"Oh." Sebastian pats his back. "It was an honor." Sam releases him, and Sebastian goes on to say, "But if you ever do that to me again, I may never forgive you."

Sam laughs. "Fair enough."

"Don't worry, if I ever get pregnant again, he's going to be chained to me the whole time," I tease.

"If?" Sam pulls his head back and smirks. "More like when."

I smile and shake my head, but someone else knocks on the open door. "Can we come in?" Tristan asks, poking his head into the room.

"Yeah, come in," Sam says to him.

Tristan walks in, followed by Molly, whose eyes fill with tears as soon as she sees the baby.

"Hey guys." I smile at them as they walk over to me.

Tristan leans down and gives me a hug. "Congratulations."

"Thanks. And, thanks for looking out for Sam last night," I say quietly.

"I told you I would." He winks at me and stands up.

He glances over at the baby and smiles. "You sure picked one hell of a night to go into labor."

"Tell me about it," Sebastian says.

"It's definitely one that none of us will ever forget," Sam says, folding his arms over his chest.

"Yeah, because we were on the flight from hell," Tris says, rolling his eyes dramatically.

"Why? What happened?" I ask glancing between them.

"Nothing happened. I was just a little anxious about getting back here."

"Anxious? Is that what you call it?" Tristan shakes his head.

Molly leans down and squeezes me in her arms. "Congratulations."

"Thanks, Molly."

She releases me and makes her way around the bed, giving Sam a quick hug before turning all of her attention to Joey. "Oh, my gosh, she's so precious," she gushes, touching Joey's cheek with the back of her finger.

Tristan walks over to Sam and looks at the baby asleep in the bassinet. "I guess I would've been freaking out too."

Tristan puts his hand on Sam's shoulder. "So, this is Joey?"

Sam smiles and nods. "Want to hold her?"

Tristan squares his shoulders and pulls his hand to his chest. "Oh, no, I don't think I should," he says, shaking his head.

Sam rolls his eyes. "Sit down." He pushes Tristan down into a chair. "Now hold your arms out, like this," he says, showing him. He leans over and picks the baby up out of the bassinet and hands her to Tristan.

"Careful," Molly says, hovering over Tristan's shoulder.

"What if I drop her?"

"Don't," Sam says seriously, and I tense with concern. "Hold her head," he says, putting Tristan's hand under her head.

Tristan holds her against his chest and covers her back with his wide hand. "She's so little and warm." He smiles and drops his cheek to the top of her head. "Look at her snuggling up to me."

"You look good with a baby in your arms," I say, smiling at him.

"You really do," Molly adds.

"Oh, no." He shakes his head. "This is the closest I want to come, right here." He kisses the top of her head and smiles again. "You're never going to be allowed to go on a date, you know that, right?" he says softly to her.

There's another knock at the door. "Hey," Miles says, walking into the room with a giant smile on his face.

I look up at Sam. "He really doesn't understand the concept of knocking, does he?" I laugh and Sam shakes his head.

"Is the little princess ready to meet her uncle Miles?"

"Hey, Miles."

He bends down to give me a hug. "Hey, sweetheart. You doing okay?"

"Yeah." I squeeze him and say softly, "Thanks for getting Sam back here in time."

"I wouldn't have let him miss it for anything in the world." He kisses my cheek and stands up. "Okay, let me take a look at her," he says, crossing the room. He leans over Tristan and stares at her. "Wow," he says with a big smile on his face. "Now that's a good-looking kid." He stands up and pulls Sam into a hug.

"She's beautiful, isn't she?" Sam smiles proudly.

"Yeah, just like her mom. Thank goodness she didn't get your ugly mug."

I shake my head and Sam laughs.

"You can hold her," I say to Miles, just to watch him squirm like Tristan did.

"Yeah?"

"Yeah," Sam says, and Miles reaches down and scoops her up from Tristan without pause.

I tense for a moment, but he cups her head and holds her carefully as he brings her to his chest. "Hey, pretty girl," he coos, bouncing her up and down gently, and she peeks her eyes open at him. "Well, hello." He smiles at her.

After a few seconds, he notices the surprised looks on our faces. "What?"

"Nothing," I say, stifling a confused laugh.

"Sorry to break up the party," Meghan says, walking into the room. She hands me a clipboard with a piece of paper and a pen attached to it. "I just need you to fill this out for the birth certificate."

"Wait," Sam says, taking it from me. "Not yet." He narrows his eyes at me. "We have to do something first."

* * *

"Sebastian, is this really necessary?" I ask, sitting on my hospital bed in front of him, while he blow-dries my freshly washed hair. "You're going to wake up the baby." I look over at her asleep in the basinet beside the bed.

"She's fine, she's in a milk coma." He continues tugging my hair with a round brush.

"I guess you can add hairstylist to your resume now," I tease.

"I'm not sure I've quite got the hang of it," he says, blowing my hair all over my face. "But you only get married once. And call me crazy, but I think you'll want a picture to commemorate the occasion. And I don't want you looking back at it one day, wishing you'd washed your hair."

"Okay, okay." I laugh. "You've made your point."

He grabs my makeup bag off the side table and plops it in my lap. "Or wishing that you'd put on a little makeup."

I laugh again. "It's killing you, isn't it?"

"What?"

"That we're not having a real wedding."

He pauses and clears his throat. "I've come to terms with it."

I reach over my shoulder and put my hand on his. "Have I told you lately how much I love you?"

"It does help ease the pain a little."

I laugh and pull out my mirror. "I could use a little concealer."

"And maybe some gloss. And a little mascara."

"Bas, I just had a baby, let's not call a dandelion a rose."

"And let's not call a rose a dandelion. *Rose*."

I smile and put on some makeup while he finishes my hair. By the time we're both done, you'd never know I've only had a few hours of sleep in the last forty-eight hours.

"Okay, here are your options," Bas says, pulling things out of my bag. "Stretchy black yoga pants or…loose gray yoga pants."

I lean across the bed and reach for the loose gray pants.

"White shirt, no arguments." He throws it at me. "Go change."

"Okay, watch the baby." I get up and walk to the bathroom, taking much too long to change. When I return, I find Sebastian sitting in the rocking chair in front of the window, rocking the baby. "She was crying," he says, patting her back.

"She seems pretty happy now."

"Yeah." He smiles at me. "You look great. Ready to get married in your hospital room."

I laugh and sit back down on the bed. "Thanks."

"Hey." Sam walks in and I drink him in. He's showered and shaved and his caramel-colored hair is perfectly styled. He's wearing dark gray jeans, his brown leather utility boots, and a fitted white T-shirt that shows off the tattoos on *both* arms now. I wonder how long it will be before Joey takes up a spot on his skin.

"Hi," I say, smiling up at him.

He leans over and kisses me. "You look beautiful."

"You're sweet."

Miles, Tristan, and Molly follow him in, each carrying a large vase that's overflowing with white lilies, hydrangeas, and orchids.

"What is this?" I ask, happily surprised, as they place them around the room.

Sam sits on the edge of the bed and reaches for my hand. "It might not be a big wedding, but you should still have flowers."

I smile at him and squeeze his hand. "They're beautiful. Thank you."

"One more," Paul says, carrying in a beautiful arrangement of pink hydrangeas and white roses. He hands me the small card attached to them, which simply says, *Congratulations. All my love, Janice.*

I smile and let go of the last thread of guilt that held me to my past. I tuck the card away and look up at Sam. All I can see now is my future.

A large man walks into the room with a warm smile on his face.

Sam stands up. "Lucy, this is the chaplain."

"Hi Lucy, I'm Pastor O'Brien." He reaches out to shake my hand.

"Hi." I shake his hand. "It's nice to meet you."

"And is this the little one?" he asks, making his way over to Sebastian. "Miss Josephine?"

"Yes." Sebastian smiles and stands up.

The chaplain puts his hand on Joey's back and says something softly that I can't hear. But it makes Sebastian smile. He turns around and looks at me and Sam. "Are we ready?"

Sam looks at me and I nod. "I should stand," I say, putting my feet on the floor.

"No need," the chaplain says, putting his hand up. "It works just as well sitting down."

I give Sam a conflicted look, but he sits down next to me and says, "You just had a baby. Don't get up." He reaches for my hands and holds them in his.

"Okay."

"Are there rings to exchange?" the chaplain asks.

I shake my head, but Sam smiles at me and says, "Yes, there are." He looks at Miles, who reaches into his pocket and pulls out two shiny white gold rings.

"What?" I ask, smiling as he hands me one of the bands.

Sam looks at me and says, "I hope they're okay. I know they're simple."

I nod and put my hand on his face, and he kisses me.

"Not yet!" The chaplain laughs, and we sit up straight. "Okay, Lucy, put the ring on Sam's left hand and then repeat after me."

"Okay." I smile at Sam and slide the thick, shiny band onto his left ring finger, careful of his knuckles, which are still red from the fight. Then I repeat the words that the chaplain says. "I, Lucy Bennett, take you, Sam Cole, to be my husband." He smiles at me and my heart swells inside my tight chest. "To have and to hold from this day forward...for better or for worse...for richer or poorer...in sickness and in health...to love and to cherish, until we are parted by death." I swallow down the lump in my throat as our entire life flashes before me.

I'm Sam, by the way. Sam Cole...Kids like us have to stick together, Lucy...We're going to get out of here one day, Luc. I promise...Marry me, Lamb. Be with me for the rest of our lives.

Sam reaches up and wipes a tear from my cheek.

"Okay, Sam, put the ring on Lucy's left hand."

He slides the band onto my left ring finger and holds my hands in his. He repeats after the chaplain, "I, Sam Cole, take you, Lucy Bennett, to be my wife." He smiles wide and new tears fill my eyes. "To have and to hold from this day forward...for better or for worse...for richer or poorer...in sickness and in health...to love and to cherish, until we are parted by death." He reaches up and tucks my hair behind my ear. "One more thing," he says, gazing into my soul with his beautiful eyes. "Lucy, I've loved you since I was twelve years old. We didn't have much back then, but I had everything, because I had you."

I nod over my tears, because I felt the exact same way.

"And then I lost you." He shakes his head and wipes my cheek. "I had everything I ever dreamed of, but I still had nothing, because I didn't have you." He shrugs. "The wins, the money...none of it matters without you." He holds my face and I wrap my hand around his wrist. "I give it all to you, Lucy. Everything I was, everything I am, and everything I want to be. It belongs to you...I belong to you. And you belong to me."

I wrap my hand behind his neck, blinking back tears that spill onto my cheeks. "I want it all. The good parts and the bad. I want you, Sam, forever."

He pulls my face to his and kisses me hard.

"By the power vested in me, I pronounce you husband and wife," the chaplain says exuberantly, and everyone cheers and claps loudly.

The baby cries and I look up at Sebastian, who's sniffing and wiping his face. Sam gets up and takes her from him, then Sam sits back down on the bed beside me. He holds her against his chest and she quiets down. "We're a family now," he says softly to her, and I bite my smiling lip.

I reach for his face and kiss him again. Then I drop my forehead to his and whisper, "The Cole family."

He puts Joey in my arms and holds her tiny hand in his. "I have two lambs to protect now."

I rub her soft cheek. "She's the luckiest little girl in the world."

He exhales an emotional breath and whispers, "Thank you."

"For what?"

"For taking a risk on me."

"Oh, Sam, you were never the risk. You were the reward."

He smiles softly over the emotion he can't hide and shows me the dimples in his flushed cheeks. "I love you, Lamb."

"I love you too. Now and always."

EPILOGUE

Lucy, Four Years Later

Can I have four?" Joey asks, standing beside me in the kitchen, holding her plate up.

"Four?" I laugh. "You can't eat four pancakes."

"But I'm four," she says, smiling up at me with her caramel-colored curls hanging around her face. Her light blue eyes crinkle as she smiles, and her dimples go straight to my heart.

"Okay," I say, scooping the pancakes out of the pan and sliding them onto her plate.

"Thank you," she says, carrying her plate over to the table.

"Don't forget the bacon," I say, taking her a piece.

"Mommy?" she asks, lowering her milk, leaving behind a milk mustache.

I wipe it with a napkin. "What, baby?"

"Do I have a grandma?"

"Um." I pull the chair out next to her and sit down.

"Because Maddie said that everyone has a grandma."

"Well, no, not everyone. You don't have a grandma or a grandpa."

"But why?"

"Well,"—I tuck her soft curls behind her ear—"because my mommy, who would have been your grandma, died a long time ago."

"She did?"

"Yeah." I sigh. "She would have loved you though."

"Well, what about your daddy? Did he die too?"

"No, but I didn't really know my daddy."

She gives me a concerned look. "That's sad."

I nod. "Yeah."

"Who took care of you?"

"Well, when I was little, like you, I had foster parents that took care of me. But when I got older, I met your daddy and then he took care of me."

She smiles over a mouthful of pancakes. "Just like he takes care of me?"

"Yep," I say, touching the end of her nose.

"There are my girls," Sam says, walking into the kitchen. He makes his way around the table and kisses the top of Joey's head. Then he leans over my shoulder and kisses my cheek.

"Mmm, you smell good," I say, letting him pull me up out of the chair and into his arms. I run my hands over the lapel of his dark suit jacket. "You look good too."

"Big day today." He widens his excited eyes and leans down to kiss my round belly. "Morning, baby." He gives my stomach a little rub and I follow him over to the coffee.

"Daddy?" Joey calls across the kitchen.

"What, baby?"

"Did you live with your mommy and daddy?"

He gives me a curious look and I quietly explain, "She's very curious about her grandparents. Or lack thereof."

"Oh." He makes a cup of coffee and carries it over to the table, and sits down beside her. "Well, baby girl, no. I didn't live with my parents."

She gives him a worried look. "Am I going to get to stay with you?"

"Of course." He puts his hand on her cheek and smiles softly. "We're a family. Families stay together. And when your little brother gets here, he'll be part of our family too."

She smiles and puts her hand on his face. "Good. I love you, Daddy."

"I love you too, little lamb."

"I just wish I had a grandma, like Maddie."

He sips his coffee and sits back in his chair. "Did I ever tell you about your grandpa Joe?" he asks her, and she widens her blue eyes.

"That's my name."

He smiles. "Yeah, that's who you're named after."

"But Josephine's a girl's name," she says, shaking her head.

"Yeah, but Joseph was your grandpa's name. Joseph Patrick Maloney. We called him Joe. He was kind of like my daddy."

"Did you live with him?"

"No, but he took care of me for a really long time."

"He did?"

"Yeah. He's the one who taught me how to box." He makes two fists and holds them up in front of Joey, and she hits them with hers.

"When you wear the funny red gloves on your hands?" She giggles.

"They're called boxing gloves," he says seriously, and I laugh. "He really wanted to meet you," he says, leaning in close to her. "But he's not here anymore."

"Where did he go?" she asks innocently, and it tugs at my heart.

"He went to heaven, baby," Sam says, and I swallow the unexpected lump in my throat.

"Oh." She looks down at her plate and nods, but when the doorbell rings, she looks up and says excitedly, "Uncle Miles is here!"

I look at Sam. "It's about time you took his key away," I say, smiling over the sadness that quietly echoes inside me.

"I didn't," he says, getting up from the table. "That's probably Tristan."

"Joey, you might not have a grandma, but you have way too many uncles," I say to her. She follows Sam to the front door, and I clean up her plate.

"Something smells good in here," Tristan says, following Sam back into the kitchen.

"Hey, Tris." I give him a hug. "I made pancakes and bacon. Make a plate." I smile over his shoulder at Molly. "Oh, my gosh," I say to her when he releases me. "Look at you!"

She gives me a quick hug and a peck on the cheek. "Six months today." She puts her hand on her stomach. "Just a couple of months behind you."

"You weren't showing the last time I saw you."

She shakes her head and laughs. "I know, he's definitely getting bigger now. He's been kicking like crazy too."

"That's because he's going to be a fighter, like his dad," Tristan says, swinging his arm around her neck. He kisses her cheek, and she bats him off.

"Sorry"—she widens her eyes—"you'll have to excuse my husband."

Sam stands behind me and puts his hands on either side of my stomach. "We all know who the fighter's going to be."

"Um…" I pull my head to the side and look up at him. "You better think again, champ."

He laughs and gives Tristan a knowing look.

"Jo-Jo," Miles calls across the house, letting himself in.

"Uncle Miles!" she squeals and runs to greet him.

He walks into the kitchen a few seconds later with Joey on his shoulders. "You guys ready to go or what?"

"Just waiting on Sebastian and Paul. Sebastian was meeting with a buyer at the gallery this morning."

Miles looks at his watch. "Okay, but we've gotta go in a few minutes. We can't be late for the grand opening."

"What's a grand opening?" Joey asks, holding on to his forehead.

He reaches up and flips her down off his shoulders, making her laugh. "What's a grand opening?" he asks, giving her wide eyes.

She smiles and shows him her dimples.

"A grand opening is when you open something for the very first time."

"Like a present?"

"Kind of like a present, yeah. Except that it's a building."

"A building?" she says with wide eyes.

"Yep. And today we're opening a very special building. A community center that your daddy helped build for kids just like you," he says, poking her stomach.

"What's a community center?" she asks, stumbling over the word.

"It's a place where kids and their families can go to play and have fun, where they feel safe."

"Like a home?"

"Kinda like a home, but for lots of families, not just one."

Sam kneels down next to Miles and asks Joey, "Do you know what we named it?"

She shakes her head and her little curls bounce around her face.

"The Joseph P. Maloney Community Center."

"Oh," she says seriously. "Is that where heaven is?"

I laugh over the tears that prick my eyes.

"No, baby. We just wanted to remember Grandpa Joe, so we named it after him."

"Oh. That was nice of you, Daddy."

He pulls her into his arms. "Come here," he says, standing up with her.

"Sorry we're late!" Sebastian shouts across the house. "Sorry we didn't knock. It was open." He walks into the kitchen with Paul on his heels. "Oh, well I see Miles is here, so no need to knock." He laughs and so do I.

"Hey, Bas." I reach for his neck and give him a hug. "How did it go this morning?"

"Well, the buyer couldn't decide on a painting."

"Oh," I say, disappointed.

"So he decided to buy three."

I gasp with excitement. "Three? Good job!"

He closes his eyes and bows. "You're welcome."

"Girl, you are on fire," Molly says with excited eyes. "Between your gallery and the new baby line for Rock Love Threads, I think it's safe to say you've made it."

I laugh and shake my head. "I'm not sure I'll ever feel like I've made it."

"That's what makes you great," Paul says, winking at me.

"Thanks for hurrying over," I say to him and Sebastian. "I know it isn't easy with a baby in tow."

"Are you kidding?" Paul says, swinging the car seat hanging on his arm. "We wouldn't have missed this for the world."

I lean down and look at baby Liam asleep and snug in his seat. "Well, when you have the best baby in the entire world," I say softly.

"Ha!" Bas throws his chin up. "You wouldn't say that if you spent a night at our house."

"He's got a point," Paul says.

Sebastian steps around him and looks at my dress. "I love this dress."

"You should, you picked it out."

"Huh, I thought it looked familiar."

"Uncle Bas," Joey says, and Sam puts her down. She runs over to Sebastian and he kneels down to give her a hug. When she releases him, he holds his head back and gasps. "You've gotten bigger since last week."

Her smile lights up her face. "Do you like my dress?"

He presses his lips together and nods. "I do. You look so pretty."

"Mommy said I can only wear it on special occasions."

"That's right," I say, wrapping my hand around Sam's. "And today is definitely a special occasion."

Sam gives me an excited smile and says, "Let's go."

I look around the room at my chosen family, the one that I dreamed of as a child, and see Sam at the center of it all. His dimples light up my heart, which is so full, I sometimes wonder how much more joy it can hold. But then my baby rolls inside my tummy, reminding me that this is just the beginning of a lifetime of memories and moments like this, with a family that I love.

I reach for Joey's hand and look up at Sam, feeling my heart swell inside my chest when he looks at me with his beautiful eyes. "Okay," I say to him, "let's go."

Acknowledgments

Thank you to my incredible family, who never complained while I locked myself away in my office to finish this book. To my husband, Kevin, for your unwavering support and pride in my writing. I wouldn't be able to do this without you. Thank you, my love! Especially for picking up dinner when I was too busy to cook. To my kids, Chris, Josh, and Lyla, you are my heart. Hopefully one day, when you're old enough, you'll understand why I love to write so much.

Thank you to my mom, Kathie, for all the morning chats about Sam and Lucy. You always get me (and my characters). Your enthusiasm and encouragement means the world to me. To my sister, Karen, for always telling me that I can do it when I don't think I can. Thank you! You are more than a sister, you're a best friend, and I'm so grateful for you.

Shannon Baum, you know I love you more than my luggage. Thank you for believing in me. Thank you for always pushing me. Thank you for twenty-seven years of memories! You're more than a best friend, you're a sister.

To everyone else who has supported me along this journey, your words of encouragement gave me the confidence to keep going! Especially Angie King, Anne Rae, Katey Reneau, Brooke Hoisington, Nikki Morley, Amy Huber, Jennifer Kopf, Julie McNally, Lori Scarborough (who yanked me out of the writing closet and exposed me for what I really am—a writer brimming with stories), and the rest of my work family who wholeheartedly embraced my side hustle. Thank you!

A special thank-you to my agent, Joanna Mackenzie. I am so grateful for everything you've done to get this story out into the world. Thank you for championing my work, for advocating for me, and for always giving me the best advice!

Thank you to the staff at Forever, who believed in this book, especially my editor, Lexi Smail. I have loved collaborating with you and talking all things Sam and Lucy. You've taught me so much, and I will always be so thankful for your guidance.

Last, but not least, to all my readers, I hope you enjoyed Sam and Lucy's story! It's hard to say goodbye to these characters, but I have many more that are waiting to be written.

About the Author

Robin Huber is a lifelong daydreamer, a lover of music, and an avid cook with a knack for plotting emotionally charged love stories on her way to work. It keeps her from losing it in traffic. She's admittedly an introverted extrovert and a proud Aries with a somewhat unhealthy dependency on her horoscope. She's a director by day, a writer by night, a wife to her high school sweetheart, and most important, a mom to her three crazy kids (she means beautiful children). When she's not writing, you can find this Florida native with her toes in the sand, holding her Kindle and probably a Corona too.

Learn more at:
robinhuberbooks.com
Twitter @RobinHuber80
Facebook.com/RobinHuberWrites